The Gathering

THE GATHERING

BY K.E. GANSHERT

Edited by: Lora Doncea
Cover Design by: Okay Creations
Interior Design and Formatting by: BB eBooks

For Amy.

Three years ago, we talked about this crazy book idea I had over chips and salsa in Colorado Springs. Wish we were having the same while celebrating the final installment! You are a genius brainstorming buddy and an amazing friend. Sinceriously.

CHAPTER ONE

NOBODY'S LISTENING

I thought I knew what insanity felt like. When I saw things nobody else could see. When my nightmares started unfolding in real life. When a much-too-popular, achingly handsome boy started watching my every move. When I was locked up in a mental hospital against my will and told everything I knew to be true was a figment of my imagination.

I thought I knew.

But all of that was nothing compared to this.

The hub has erupted into pandemonium. All the lights are on, and since windows do not exist down here—deep in the bowels of a ruined warehouse—it might as well be day instead of the dead of night. Everyone is awake and focused on the defector. The one who betrayed me. The one who betrayed him. Everyone is panicked over what this means—Claire out there, knowing all she knows about our location, our names, who we really are.

How could she do it?

That is the question of the hour. But I don't care about her. I don't care about why she defected or the ramifications of her decision. All I care about is *him*—the boy across the hall, unable to wake up. And yet very, very much alive.

Despite what everyone thinks, Luka's soul has not been destroyed.

I saw him. I heard him. He's being held hostage, tortured by the white-eyed men. His screams echo inside my head. They won't stop. Nor will the way he arched up in agony as black mist lacerated his body. Every second that ticks past is one more second closer to losing him forever. And that is something I cannot let happen. Because if Luka dies, then so will everything else.

I scratch the inside of my wrist and begin to rock like the patients in straitjackets at Shady Wood. Link sits beside me on the couch, mindlessly twisting his Rubik's Cube. Nobody will listen—not Gabe, not Cap, not Sticks or Non. They think I'm in shock. They think I'm in denial. They keep talking about Clive DeVant—our new Cloak—who's supposed to arrive with Dr. Carlyle in the afternoon, and Fray—one of our old Cloaks—who's supposed to leave with Dr. Carlyle to a hospital in Northern Michigan, but if we stick around until tomorrow, we might all end up in jail.

"What are we going to do?" someone asks.

"What if Claire's already gone to the authorities?"

"She has all of our names. She knows all of our faces."

"Are we safe?"

Something feral claws up my throat. A wild beast of a thing, but before it can escape, Cap raises his hand. It's a simple gesture, and yet, coming from him—our leader—the hub goes quiet.

"I'll figure out what to do about Fray and Clive. In the meantime, everybody needs to return to their room and pack a bag."

The wild beast of a thing claws free. "We can't leave!"

"Claire has left us no choice," Cap says.

"We're not leaving Luka here." The hot words bring me to

my feet. "Y-you'd be murdering him!"

Everybody stares.

Nothing can be heard but the steady tick-tick of a clock on the far wall of the common room.

"If you are underage," Cap's silver eyes do not leave mine, "return to your room immediately and wait for my instruction."

Slowly, the room begins to clear. Ellen and Declan obey first. A tearful Rosie, then Bass, Jose, Ashley, and Danielle. Jillian lingers, shooting several glances my way, before she, too, obeys orders. Link stays.

"It's time to return to your room," Cap says.

"He's alive. We can still save him."

He paws his face, the palm of his hand scratching against the stubble on his cheeks. I can tell he doesn't know what to do with me anymore.

"Luka is gone." The lifeless words belong to Gabe.

"Why?" I practically spit the question. "Because you couldn't get your sister back?"

"Tess." Cap says my name like a low warning.

I don't care. I don't care if I hurt Gabe. I don't care that I'm disobeying orders once again. I don't care about anything but the boy down the hall. Luka isn't gone. At least he wasn't an hour ago. I have no idea how much longer my declaration will hold true. And therein lies the crux of my insanity. I'm standing here trying to convince these people that he's alive while every breath I take draws him closer to death.

Link gently takes my arm. "Come on. Let me take you to your room."

I jerk my elbow away. "I'm not leaving him."

Cap pushes out a terse breath. "We have more pressing

matters at hand."

"*More pressing matters?* He's being tortured. Right now, at this very moment. And we're standing here letting it happen." What can be more pressing than that? Before the question can fully form, I know Cap's answer. As captain of this ship, he has to make decisions for the collective whole. It's what he's always doing. He has to think strategically, and if that means sacrificing one for the sake of the rest, then that is what he will do.

I absolutely hate him for it.

Link pulls me away.

"He's going to die!" I try wrenching my arm free, but his grip is surprisingly strong. "Do you hear me? If we don't get to him right now, he will die!"

Link pulls me further away.

"Gabe!" I turn wild eyes on him—my last hope. If anybody knows this kind of agony, he does. "Please. Help me. Luka is alive. I swear to you, he's alive. We can't leave him here!"

Gabe does nothing but look away from my manic pleas.

And Link drags me out of the room. He circles his arm around my waist and pulls me away while I scream and flail, not strong enough to resist, tears running like scalding heat down my cheeks. Rosie stares out from the crack in her bedroom door, her eyes big and wide in her face. Link murmurs words of comfort I do not hear. He holds me until I've stopped thrashing. Until the wild thing has crawled back inside and curled into a whimpering ball.

"Listen."

All I can do is shake my head. I should have listened a long time ago, but not to Link. I should have listened to Luka, who never wanted to go on our mission in the first place. And yet, I insisted. I ignored his reservations. I never considered that it might be *his* life in danger. "It's my fault. He's there because of me. He knew something would go wrong, but I wouldn't listen. I went and because I went, he had to go, too. And now he's being tortured." The memory of his scream grows so loud and sharp in my mind that I wince. "You have to believe me. Please believe me."

"Xena, look at me." Link takes hold of my face and tips up my chin so that I have no choice. His caramel eyes are steady and familiar. "Listen to me. If Luka is still alive and the other side is holding him hostage, it's because they want *you*."

"I know that." And I will gladly trade places.

"So you know what that means."

Another hot tear tumbles down my cheek.

Link catches it on the pad of his thumb. "They aren't going to kill him. If they kill him, they lose their leverage."

"I know that, too. But I also know what I saw. If it continues for much longer, he won't be Luka anymore." My chin trembles. "Please, Link. We can't leave him."

Link's steady resolve solidifies. "We won't."

Those two definitive words calm me more than anything else he could have said or done.

"I have an idea. Let me run it by Cap."

CHAPTER TWO

MOLTEN LAVA

"Twenty minutes," Cap says.

I slide onto one of six chairs in the training center and fidget with the hemp bracelet around my wrist. It belonged to Luka. He insisted I wear it in case it offered even a hint of protection. "What if Claire's not sleeping?"

"Then we will have no choice but to leave this place and disband." The look Cap gives me is clear. This is as far as he's willing to take this. If Link and I cannot locate Claire, if we cannot find out whether she truly defected or simply left out of shame, then he will have to make decisions I will not like. "Do you understand?"

I swallow and look away, my head incapable of nodding.

If not for Fray's fragile health, if not for Clive scheduled to arrive tomorrow, I'm positive Cap never would have agreed to Link's plan. Thankfully, Cap doesn't want to leave. Disbanding in the dead of night isn't his style.

"Twenty minutes will be enough to learn what we need to learn." Link attaches a probe to my left temple. Usually, he attaches two. One that sends electrodes to the part of my brain that is most active during sleep. Another that brings me to the dojo—a shared dream space Link created for training purposes. But we're not going to the dojo tonight. We're going to find Claire and we can't wait around for sleep to take us in our beds.

Time is of the essence.

I rest my head against the chair and squeeze my eyes tight, praying with every ounce of faith I have that Claire will be asleep. Finding her now, figuring out what she's up to, is the first step to saving Luka.

"All right, we're both attached." Link has taken the chair next to me. He grabs my ice-cold hand and gives it a confident squeeze. "You can push the button in ten ... nine ..."

I close my eyes tight and focus on Claire, the betrayer. I imagine her the first time I saw her, when Luka and I arrived at the hub. Her white-blond hair loosely braided down her back. Her regal beauty. The way her nose turned up in the air without trying. The shock of seeing her down here, in the hub, after having studied her file for days.

"Six ... five ..."

The grating way she flirted with Luka. The victorious feeling of taking her down in the dojo. The hateful look in her eyes when Cap announced he would be training me.

"Three ... two ..."

Her foot reaching out to trip me as we battled inside the walls of Shady Wood. Her look of triumph when I fell.

"One ..."

Wind whips hair around my face. I'm no longer laying in the training center; I'm standing beside Link outside a home I've been to before—with Luka, when we were searching for Claire, who at the time was nothing more than a patient file Dr. Roth left behind.

Now she stands on the front stoop, pounding on the door, while trees bend beneath the force of the wind.

My hands curl into tight fists. The blood in my veins turns

to molten lava.

Link sets his hand on my shoulder. "We'll learn more if she doesn't know you're here."

He's right, of course. As much as I want to shove my fist in her face, now's not the time. I duck behind a row of emaciated bushes and strain to hear above the wind.

"Please Mom! It's me." Claire glances up at the ominous, swirling sky and pounds harder. "Please open up."

Link approaches behind her. "Claire?"

She whirls around, her icy blue eyes wide with panic, her face streaked with tears. "Link?"

"What are you doing?" he asks.

"I-I'm trying to get to my parents, but they won't let me in." She wipes at her cheeks. "How did you get here?"

"How do you think?"

The wind loses some of its strength.

Claire looks up at the clouds. They no longer swirl as threateningly as they did seconds ago. She peels a strand of hair from her lips. "This is a dream. You're spying on me."

"I'm not spying. I'm checking." He holds up his hands, as if to show her he means no harm. "You left without telling anybody. We're all worried."

I grit my teeth. Not one part of me is worried about her. She's been bad news from the beginning. I should have realized the danger I was putting Luka in—the danger I was putting everybody in—by going on such a high-stakes mission with Claire on the team.

Her chin trembles. "I never meant for Luka to get hurt."

"But Tess—you wanted *her* to get hurt?" Link's question is gentle. Non-accusatory. Everything opposite from what I feel.

"I just wanted things to go back to the way they were before she came. I-I wasn't thinking. I made a mistake. I shouldn't have done it. All I want is my mom and dad, but I don't think they want to see me."

Liar. Lies. I don't believe a single note of her remorse.

"Have you told anyone about our location?" Link asks.

"No. I would never do that. But I couldn't stay. Nobody wanted me there. Not even you."

Link shifts his weight. His back is to me, so I can't see his face. I have no idea if he's falling for the act or not.

"I would never put you in danger, Link, never. I just want to go home to my parents. That's all I want." She turns around and beats the door with her fists, begging the wood to let her inside.

"She didn't defect." Link peels off his probe and swings his legs around, bringing his feet to the floor. "She's not going to give our location away. She just wants to get to her parents."

Cap looks from me to Link, waiting for me to verify.

I don't contradict him, even if I don't believe a word of Claire's sob story.

Cap rubs his forehead.

A glance at the clock tells me it's four in the morning. Two hours have passed since I saw Luka, bound and tortured. I'm so desperate to get to him, it feels as though a hole is burning a wide path through my heart.

Cap looks at Non and Sticks, who stand inside the small room. "What do you think?"

"It buys us some time," Sticks says. "At least until Clive arrives and Fray is gone."

"And Luka's back," I add.

Nobody listens.

"Non?" Cap asks.

She slides her hands down her head, flattening her bushy hair to the sides of her face. "Gabe's standing guard above ground. If danger arrives, he'll be able to alert us in time to carry out emergency protocol."

Emergency protocol? I don't know about any emergency protocol. We've certainly never practiced an emergency drill during my time at the hub. But of course there would be something in place. Cap would have thought of that.

He rubs his knuckle along his bottom lip, then pushes out a breath. "You two can return to your rooms," he says to me and Link. "We'll stay for now."

Link's plan worked.

Cap doesn't think Claire will betray us.

He believes we're safe.

I don't. Not for one second.

But I'm willing to risk the safety of everyone at the hub if it means getting Luka back.

CHAPTER THREE

UNSTABLE

His hands slide up my back, his lips feverish on mine as I curl my fingers into his hair and pull him closer. He wraps his arms all the way around my waist and pulls me closer too. Only there's nowhere to go. Our bodies are pressed tight, with his slightly bent over mine. I wrap my arms around his neck and he stands up straight, lifting my feet off the sand. It's a hungry kiss. A desperate kiss. A euphoric, blissful kiss. Because it's Luka. He's here. He's alive. And I can't get enough of him.

A wave rolls up onto the beach, hitting our legs, pushing us sideways.

Luka pulls away, his green eyes hungry and bright. "I love you, Tess."

"I love you, too." Saying the words out loud makes my heart soar straight up to the sky. I don't think it'll ever come down.

A throat clears, extra loud.

I turn around in Luka's arms. Link stands a few yards away, toeing the ground. I slide down Luka's body and plant my feet in the rocky sand. This is the first time anybody has showed up on our beach. "What are you doing here?"

"I thought we'd find Luka."

"I have found Luka. He's right—" I turn around, but Luka's arms no longer hold me. Luka is no longer near me. He has disappeared. "Where did he go?"

"He was never here."

"What do you mean?"

Link scratches the back of his head, his cheeks pink. His cheeks are never pink. "Come on, Xena. You know how this works."

My soaring heart crashes hard. "I was constructing him?"

He nods.

All the ache and panic I've felt since waking up from our rescue mission returns, so fast and so completely it knocks my breath away. The Luka I was just kissing was a projection—a figment of my imagination. "But I went to bed thinking about him. He's all I thought about." After we found Claire, Cap ordered Link and I both to bed. I went willingly, eager to find Luka. To make sure he's still alive. "Why aren't I with him? What went wrong?"

"I don't know. You could try thinking of him now."

Right. I can hop to Luka from here. I found him once, which means I can find him again. And if he can be found, then he also can be rescued.

Link offers me his hand. Incredibly grateful for his help, I take it and close my eyes. I picture Luka's dark hair in a constant state of disarray. Smooth, olive skin. Grass green eyes. The subtle smell of wintergreen and fabric softener, even down here in this basement. I picture the heady way he looks at me— like I, Teresa Eckhart, am his entire world.

Nothing happens.

My feet remain on the sand, my fingers laced with Link's.

I close my eyes again, squishing them so tight my nose wrinkles. I think about the confident cadence of Luka's voice.

The way he commands attention whenever he walks into a room. I think about the shield he threw inside Shady Wood's staircase, so powerful it obliterated one of our enemies. His strength, his confidence, his passion, the way he stands up for things that aren't popular.

I remember the day I first saw him in Current Events with Mr. Lotsam. The shock of recognition that flickered in his eyes. I recall the first time we met in a dream, on a beach like this one. I relive our first kiss in the locker bay of Thornsdale High School, being carried in his arms as he rescued me from the Edward Brooks Facility. Sleeping beside him on a squeaky mattress in Motel California.

Still. Nothing.

Panic balloons inside my chest, morphing into this un- wieldy thing. This happened once before, a couple days ago, when I tried jumping to my grandmother's dream. I couldn't find her either, and when we finally arrived at Shady Wood to save her, she was already gone. It was too late.

I turn to Link. "What's happening? Why can't I find him?"

He waves. Not his hand, but his entire body. It crimps in a way that isn't physically possible. And then slowly, he fades away.

"Link?"

The beach flickers, like a blip on a television screen before it loses reception. Everything goes black, then comes back into focus. Another blink. Another, and then …

I sit up in bed, my breath coming in quick rasps. What happened? Why couldn't I get to Luka? Why did Link leave me? I tear the covers off my legs. Maybe if I'm nearer to Luka, I'll be able to reach him. That's how I got to him before. I fell asleep beside his warm body and woke up in the place he was being held prisoner.

I pull open my bedroom door.

Jillian tumbles inside, her hand on the door knob. She quickly regains her balance and takes a few steadying breaths. "Holy smokes, you scared me."

I'd apologize if the what-ifs weren't pelting my thoughts like an onslaught of sharp hail.

Indistinct chatter filters down the hallway.

Jillian looks over her shoulder toward the sound, then back at me. "Link sent me. He's waiting in the training center."

I follow Jillian past our makeshift classrooms; both are dark and empty. There will be no classes today. There will be no classes ever again. Not down here. Dream spying on Claire may have bought us some time, but we will never be able to go back to the way things were. Life as we know it in the hub is over.

Inside the training center, Link stands behind the computer, punching keys on the keyboard.

"Why did you leave last night?" I ask.

"I didn't leave. You booted me out."

I join him by the computer. A string of numbers scroll down the screen. I have no idea how Link makes sense of them. "What do you mean?"

"Your dream wasn't stable."

"Why not?"

"Because you aren't sleeping well."

A pocket of hope opens up in my chest. "Is that why I couldn't get to him?"

"If I had to take a guess, I'd say it's a combination of that," he punches some more keys, "and the fact that he's probably resisting you."

"Resisting me? Why would he resist me?"

Link stops and looks at me. Usually, he's an open book. Usually, he's all devil-may-care and adventuresome—a combination that infuriates Luka to no end, since most of Link's adventures include me. Last night, Link was my serious-as-a-heart-attack ally. Today he's something else. Something I can't read.

"If you showed up before, he knows you'll come back. And if you come back, you could get hurt. Call me ridiculous, but he seems like the kind of guy who'd rather be tortured to death than put you in any sort of danger."

Of course. It's exactly the kind of thing Luka would do.

Jillian sighs, like it's romantic.

"How am I supposed to get to him, then?"

"The same way we got to Claire." He holds up the probes we attached to our temples a few hours ago. "This will put you in a deep sleep. You won't have to fight against an unstable dream. You'll only have to fight against Luka's resistance. If he's being tortured as badly as you say, then it shouldn't be too difficult."

I throw my arms around Link's neck and hug him tight. The gesture must catch him off guard. It takes a second before he wraps his arms around my waist and hugs me back.

Jillian peeks out into the hallway, then closes the door and clicks the lock. "Cap will murder all three of us if he finds out what we're doing."

"He won't. He's too busy getting Fray ready to leave with Dr. Carlyle." Link untangles another set of probes and connects it to the computer. "All right, Jilly-Bean. I want to make sure you know what you're doing."

She joins him, paying careful attention as he points out important number strings.

Confusion prickles my thoughts. "Are you leaving?"

"Of course not." He attaches a set of probes beneath his collar and hands me a set of my own. They monitor our vitals. A precaution to avoid things like cardiac arrest. "I'm going with you."

I shake my head. He isn't a Fighter. He isn't even a Shield. He's a Linker. Hence, his nickname. There's no reason for him to come along and put his life in jeopardy.

"Someone has to make sure you aren't constructing."

"I would know if I was constructing."

"You didn't last night."

A slow burn works its way into my cheeks.

Last night, if Link hadn't interrupted my make-out session with imaginary Luka, who knows how long it would have continued, or where things would have led. "That was a little different than watching Luka being lacerated by crazy white-eyed demon men. I would never construct a torture scene."

Link brushes a strand of hair from my face and gently attaches a probe to my left temple. "Show me, then."

"You're putting yourself in danger."

"It's about time, don't you think?"

"Link ..."

He rolls his eyes. "I'll be fine. Don't worry about me. Worry about you. I'm a little concerned you won't be able to control yourself."

"What do you mean?"

"This isn't a rescue mission."

"But I thought—"

"If Luka's really being held hostage, we're going to need

backup. I won't be any help to you in there. All we're doing is going in, learning as much as we can, then reporting to Cap. He can't ignore us both. Think you can handle that?"

Go to Luka—watch him being tortured—and do *nothing*? I'm not sure it's possible. But Link's waiting for an answer, so I give him a nod and attach the probes beneath my clavicle. The monitor picks up the erratic thumping of my heart as I take a seat in one of the chairs.

"Okay, Jilly-Bean. If either of our heart rates exceeds 200 BPMs, wake us up."

Mine is already more than halfway there.

As if reading my mind, Link takes my clammy hand and gives it a short squeeze. "Come on, Xena, take some deep breaths or we'll be done before we start."

I inhale deeply through my nose. Exhale completely through my lips. Then I close my eyes and focus all my energy on Luka.

CHAPTER FOUR

GALLONS AND GALLONS

I stand in a cold, dark chamber with my hand tucked inside Link's. The hairs on my arms rise to attention. Something is off. Something is different. It's like we're not in the right place. Link pulls me behind a stack of wooden crates. We squat low, our eyes adjusting to the dark, and I realize what it is.

Silence fills the chamber.

There are no blood-curdling screams.

I peek over the crates and my knees almost buckle. Thirty or forty yards ahead, in the same spot as before, Luka sits on the ground, his back propped against a metal beam. His body does not twist in agony. His hands do not clench into fists. His shirt does not stretch against his taut muscles as he arches up in torment. This time, he's deathly still. And he's no longer surrounded. Only one white-eyed man stands guard.

My muscles coil. I can take on one. One's nothing. I shift forward, but Link grabs my shoulder and pulls me back just as the *tap-tap-tap-tap* of shoes against cement echoes through the chamber.

"Any sign of her?"

An icy chill hugs the back of my legs. I would recognize that voice anywhere. It's him—Scarface. The man who's been hunting me ever since I fought him in the ICU to protect my brother. If not for the two jagged scars running the length of his cheeks, his face would be completely ordinary. Altogether forgettable. Luka and I gave him the scar on the right. I have no idea how he got the one on the left.

"Not yet," the guard answers.

"I was certain she'd return before now." Scarface clucks his tongue and folds his hands behind his back. "Such a pity. Our guest is looking rather peaked, don't you think?"

The guard laughs.

Scarface crouches down, like a parent bending low to look a small child in the eyes, and grabs Luka's chin. "Tell me, Mr. Williams, where is the girl? Are you keeping her from us?"

Luka glares at him.

"So brave. So noble. So *romantic*. And such a waste of energy." He lets go.

Luka's head flops forward, like he's too weak to lift it on his own.

"You know, Mr. Williams, there's more than one way to skin a rabbit." Scarface studies the nails on his hand. "In fact, I have another plan in the works as we speak. Make no mistake, I will have your sweet Tess."

Luka lunges, but it's no use. A ribbon of black mist curls from the guard's fingers and binds Luka tighter.

"Temper, temper." Scarface straightens and faces his skeletal crony. "If he has enough energy to keep our Little Rabbit away, we must be going too easy on him."

The guard's lips stretch into a twisted smile. The black mist wraps itself around Luka's skull and pulls tighter around his chest.

Luka's body twists. His scream rents the air. Before I can move, before I can call out, Link grabs me around the waist and startles us both awake.

Jillian and Link follow me up and down the hallways without saying a word. I must look certifiable. I can tell by the way everyone stares as I pass them. Like maybe I really do need the medicine I pushed down the grate my first night here. It's hard to care with Luka's scream ringing in my ears.

I find Gabe in the kitchen. "Where is he?"

He hands Rosie a box of Cheerios. "Who?"

"Cap. He's not with Fray, so where is he?"

"I saw him with Non." It's Rosie who answers, her voice small. It's the first time I've heard it match her size. "They were in Luka's room."

"He's alive, Gabe. If you don't believe me, ask Link." I don't wait for a response. I leave for Luka's room. When I arrive, I throw the door open. It crashes against the wall.

Non turns around with a stethoscope in her ears. My attention slides to Luka, lying impossibly still in the bed. His eyes are closed, his face relaxed. But all I can see is him writhing in pain on the cold, cement floor. All I can hear is his scream.

I grit my teeth. "He's alive."

Cap sits in his wheelchair in the corner. "Non has confirmed that for us."

"I mean his soul is alive. His soul is alive and you're doing nothing."

"I'm doing what leaders do."

"Which is what? Letting one of your men die when you could save him?"

Cap rolls himself closer, his eyes flashing. "Ensuring that more of my men don't end up like him."

"He doesn't have to end up like this at all!" I want to pull out my hair. I want to tear my clothes. I want to bang my fists on the ground. Anything to get him to listen. "Luka's soul is alive. Link can verify it."

"It would be a suicide mission."

I blink. The words stun me into stillness. So does the faint hint of shame pulsing beneath them. All of it spins around me, making the room tilt. Cap believes me. Cap believes me and he's still not going to do anything. I feel sick.

He drags his hand down his face. "They're after *you*. Luka is the bait."

"You're a coward."

"I'm not going to march you to your death. You're too important."

"Why? Because of some stupid prophecy that we know next to nothing about? One you didn't even believe until recently?" I run my hands back through my hair and curl them into fists. I've embraced the fact that my gifting is extraordinary, but that doesn't mean I have to embrace a prophecy that puts me in charge of saving humanity. Cap's stacking the weight of the world on my shoulders when I can't even hold myself up. "This thing I have? It means *nothing* without him. It's useless without him!"

Cap's lips flatline.

Non stands by the bed, watching.

Luka sleeps.

And screams.

He's doing that even if we can't hear it.

My breath grows ragged. "Do what you want. I'm going after him."

"I'll go with you." The voice comes from behind me.

I spin around.

Gabe stands in the doorway, his dark eyes every bit as emotionless as always. Once upon a time, I thought he was born without a personality. Later I learned that Gabe was a Keeper like Luka. But he lost his *anima*, his breath of life. Her soul was snuffed out by the enemy, and her body slowly followed. "Link told me what he saw."

The tension digging into my shoulders releases its talon-like grip, followed by a flood of relief. Gallons upon gallons upon gallons of it. Gabe believes me. Gabe will help.

His dark stare slides to Cap in his wheelchair. "Our guests have arrived."

CHAPTER FIVE

RAMIFICATIONS

Gabe stops, blocking my entrance to the common room as Cap rolls ahead of us. "There's a distinct limit to how far he will be pushed."

My brow puckers.

"If you want Cap's help, I recommend a little self-control." He raises his eyebrows at me, then walks inside, where several people have already gathered with Dr. Carlyle and the hub's newest member—Clive DeVant. He's slightly older and thinner than his dream self, but he stands at attention in the exact same way, as though waiting for someone—*anyone*—to say *at ease*. His stare slides from Gabe to me as I approach. It has to be weird, seeing so many people you've only ever met in a dream.

Cap rolls forward and shakes Dr. Carlyle's hand. "Non's waiting for you in Fray's room."

Never one for small talk, Dr. Carlyle disappears into the hallway.

All that remains is the vigilant soldier.

"At ease," Cap says. "You're safe down here."

Clive's shoulders relax a tiny fraction.

I'm not so sure they should, in light of Claire.

Cap motions to the hodgepodge of shabby furniture be-hind us. We all sit. So does Clive, his posture stiff as he takes in the entirety of the common room—the ramshackle furniture, a wired television, a foosball table, a few scattered desks. I remember seeing it for the first time, when Luka and I were the ones being gawked at. It's hard to believe we've been here for three-and-a-half months.

"You have quite the operation down here."

"We'd give you a tour," Cap says, "but there's no point. I'm afraid we've brought you into a precarious situation."

"I'm sure it's better than the one I came from."

This is true. I was never in Shady Wood, but I know what it's like to be locked up and drugged against my will.

"The night we rescued you, one of our members betrayed us. She has since left. We're fairly confident she hasn't defected, but even so, our location has been compromised. We'll be leaving as soon as we find new lodging."

"And rescue Luka."

Cap daggers me with a sharp look.

I mash my lips together and swallow my escalating sense of urgency, Gabe's advice fresh in my mind. He's right. Cap has his limits. And too often, I don't just toe the line, I stomp right over it.

Cap sets his hands on top of his wheels, reverting his attention back to Clive. He peppers him with questions. Did he run into any problems? Is his strength fully intact? Does he know of any other groups like ours?

My knee begins to bounce. "Did you know a patient at Shady Wood named Elaine Eckhart?"

Clive shakes his head. "I was isolated from the other patients."

"She was the other person we were trying to rescue. When we got to her room, she wasn't there." A cold finger runs up my spine at the memory of all those empty beds—of my grandmother's empty room. "Do you know where she might have gone?"

"If her room was empty, then she's dead. They're killing patients off in droves."

His words come like a sucker punch to the gut. I don't know why. Non led me to the same conclusion the night before. It hadn't come as a sucker punch then. But then, I'd been a zombie, incapable of processing anything. And until now, it was just a theory. I think I've been secretly hoping that once we rescued Luka, we could go find her.

"It's happening," Sticks says.

"What is?" Jillian asks.

"The prophecy."

"What prophecy?"

My madness grows. I'm two seconds away from clamping my hands over my ears and screaming. Keeping the panic inside takes every ounce of effort. "Cap." His name escapes on a desperate plea. "Please. We're wasting time."

He exhales a long, resigned breath, and turns his attention to Gabe.

"I have to go with her," he says. "You know why."

"It's a trap," Cap replies.

I come to the edge of my seat. "Then we have the advantage. We know it's a trap. And we aren't walking in blind. Link and I know the layout. Plus, we have a Cloak to hide us."

"Anna will be in no state to go on another rescue mission."

"I don't mean Anna." I look at the man sitting across from me—square jaw, hair cut to army regulation. Did they give haircuts in Shady Wood, or did he stop somewhere along the way and get it done? "I mean Clive."

"He just arrived."

Clive doesn't pay attention to Cap's concern. My invitation has ignited a spark in his eye. It's one I recognize. Equal parts eagerness and retribution. The enemy has stolen from him, too. Two years of his life, and—if his file has anything to say about it—a wife and two sons. The fire in his eyes meets the madness in mine. "Just tell me what to do."

I could kiss him. I could grab his cheeks and kiss Clive DeVant square on the forehead.

Cap runs his hands down his emaciated thighs. After years in his wheelchair with no physical therapist to keep his legs active, his muscles have atrophied. "All right. Tell me what we're up against."

"The first time, he was surrounded by guards. The second, there was only one. The man with the scars was there, too."

"Was Luka bound?" Gabe asks.

"Yes."

"We'll need to release him from the restraints."

"And then what? He can startle?"

"If they've been torturing him, he might not be strong enough."

A vision of Luka, unable to lift his own head, flashes in my mind. "He's not strong enough."

"Then someone will need to startle for him."

It doesn't sound overly difficult, especially if there's only one guard on duty. So why the unease? It oozes inside of me like pus from an infected sore. "That's it? If we can do that, Luka will come back?"

Gabe doesn't answer. Because Gabe doesn't know. How long can a body and a soul be separated before the damage is irrevocable? I'd ask Dr. Carlyle, but something tells me he didn't learn that one in medical school.

"Tess." Cap's grim voice draws my attention. "If he's being held hostage and tortured by the enemy, then you need to prepare yourself."

The muscles in my throat tie into a knot.

"We may be able to rescue him, but I wouldn't count on Luka being the same if we do. There are bound to be ramifications."

CHAPTER SIX

THE TRUTH ABOUT BAIT

There are bound to be ramifications.

The words gnaw at me.

I should probably examine them. Brace myself. I saw the lacerations with my own eyes. I heard his screams. I watched his body twist in anguish. How will there not be ramifications? But if I dwell on that possibility—that we might rescue Luka, and yet he might not be the Luka I know—my cracked mind will break completely. So instead, I shove his words into the same box I've shoved my dad's incarceration and focus all my energy on the mission.

There are only six chairs in the training center, six sets of probes, so Cap has rounded up a team of six. Four Fighters— me, Sticks, Jose, and Cap. One Keeper, Gabe. And our new Cloak, Clive.

Rosie objects. Vehemently. She wants to go. It's a ridiculous thought, one Cap doesn't even consider. The quickness with which he dismisses her suggestion has her slinking out of the cafeteria in the middle of our plotting. It's the first time I've ever seen her not finish a meal.

When the last of the plans are finalized, I go search for her. She and Bass are the hub's two Runners, which means Rosie's used to being needed. She's used to being useful. Since our partially-failed mission at Shady Wood, Cap hasn't allowed her or Bass above ground. The inactivity seems to be taking its toll. I want to check on her, make sure she's okay.

She sits on her knees in her room, playing a game on the floor. I watch as she bounces a small ball and swipes up a handful of silver jacks. She's quick, but not as quick as Bass. Nobody can ever beat him.

I cross my arms and lean against the doorframe. "You want to talk?"

"Cap called it a suicide mission." She bounces the ball again and swipes up the rest.

Rosie wasn't there for that conversation, which means she's been eavesdropping.

She uncurls her fingers and stares down at the jacks in her palm. "What will happen if none of you come back?"

I picture the scene—our bodies lying in the training center with no Fighters left to come after us. What will happen to Rosie and Link and Jillian? Will they stay until our hearts stop? And if they do, will they be caught because of Claire? Will they be locked away and drugged like Clive and my grandmother? I shake the image away. I have no idea if we'll make it out alive. But I do know there's a time for honesty. This isn't it. "We'll be back. Luka will, too. Everything's going to be okay."

Before she can call my bluff, I give her a tight smile and leave her sitting on the floor. Link's waiting for me out in the hallway. Judging by the look on his face, Rosie's not the only eavesdropper in the hub.

I scratch the inside of my wrist. My eczema burns so hot it's like I'm pressing hot coal against my skin. But I can't stop. It's turning into this compulsion, this habit I can't control. "Will you promise me something?"

He sticks his hands in his pockets.

"If I don't come back, if something goes wrong, don't wait around. Take Rosie and Jillian and get out of here. Go somewhere safe."

"So you'll let us risk our lives for Luka, but not you?"

"Please Link, promise you won't try to save me." I scratch my wrist harder, wishing the fire would go numb. I want the past seventy-two hours to be one giant nightmare. I want to wake up inside a hub where Luka is okay and my grandmother's still alive.

"Hey." Link reaches out and gently stills my scratching fingers. "You're Xena Warrior Princess, remember? You can save yourself."

A throat clears loudly behind us.

Clive stands at the end of the hallway. "The captain sent me to find you. He says we're ready."

My heart speeds up as I follow him through the antechamber toward the training center. I focus on Link's steady presence beside me and stare hard at the back of Clive's shoulder, grateful he's here. On the cusp of his freedom, he could very well be marching to his death. "Thank you for helping us."

Clive doesn't stop. He doesn't slow or turn around. Our shoes echo in the silent hallway, and then, just when I think he won't say anything at all, his low voice fills the quiet. "I know what it's like to be separated from someone you love."

By the time we arrive, the training center is crowded. Only a few are missing: Non, who stands guard above ground; Declan, who's taken Gabe's place at the door; Anna, repotting plants in the greenhouse while casting a cloak around the hub like always; Fray, who left two hours ago with Dr. Carlyle because his heart is on the verge of ruin. And Luka, asleep inside his dark room. Rosie slips quietly inside behind me and stands next to Jillian, who places her hand reassuringly on Rosie's shoulder.

Gabe lifts Cap from his wheelchair and sets him in one of the chairs. Once Cap is settled, he addresses the team, though his attention locks on me. "We do not, under any circumstances, leave Clive's cloak until I give the command."

I nod.

"As soon as Luka is free, Gabe will get to him and startle. Once they've startled, all of us will follow. If you are in danger, you will startle before we complete our mission."

I want to object. I want to shake my head in protest. Instead, I force myself to sit in the last remaining seat. Link gives us each probes to attach beneath our collarbones, then quickly hooks another probe to our left temples.

He saves me for last.

"Come back to me, Xena." He sets his hand over mine. I was scratching my wrist again. *"All* the way back."

I think I know what he means, so I nod.

He nods at Jillian, who stands behind the computer with her finger poised over the keyboard, then turns back to me. "Go time in three … two … one."

One second I'm looking into Link's eyes. The next I'm not.

I start linking. First Cap, then Gabe. Things are fine until I search for Sticks. It takes longer than it should, and when I finally manage, a stab of pain pierces my temple. Wincing, I blink rapidly and pull in Jose. The pressure in my ears mounts. It's like my brain is being squeezed.

"You okay?" Cap's voice sounds far away. As if I'm at the

bottom of a well, and he's yelling down from the top.

"I'm fine." But my voice sounds far away, too.

This usually doesn't happen until I've linked at least eight people. My max is nine. I'm only at four, with one more to go. Breathing heavily, I use every last drop of mental energy I have to find Clive.

It's not easy. The pain is sharp and intense. But I finally manage.

The six of us stand in a circle. I wait for the pressure to stabilize. This is what happens when I'm done linking. The pressure ebbs a little, but not nearly enough. I'm still breathing like a woman in labor.

"Are you sure you're okay?" Cap asks again.

I wipe the prickles of sweat from my forehead and nod. The six of us hold hands as I squish up my face and think about Luka.

Nothing happens.

There's no tug of a doorway. No shift in gravity. We remain standing in this nebulous dream space. I force my rising panic down and squeeze Cap and Clive's hands harder.

Luka ... Luka ... Luka ...

Nothing.

I blink a few times—an attempt to chase away the blurriness encroaching from the periphery of my vision—and try again.

Still nothing.

This happened in my dream with Link on the beach, but my dream wasn't stable because I wasn't sleeping well. I don't have that excuse here. The probe hooked to my left temple ensures that I am in a deep sleep.

I try again, and again, and again. Until beads of sweat roll down my temples and my chest heaves.

"Tess," Cap says.

I don't stay to hear what he has to say. I startle awake and tear the probes away.

Link places his hand on my arm. "Whoa, whoa. What's going on? Why are you awake?"

"I can't get to him. I can't get to him!" We must be too late. Just like we were too late with my grandmother. I tear the last probe off my chest and hurry out of the room. Away from all the stares.

If only I could get away from my panic.

It follows me. Hounds me. All the way to Luka's room. I stand for a moment on the threshold. Then I go to his bedside and drop to my knees. I tear the hemp bracelet off my wrist and tie it onto his.

"Please, Luka. I need you to be okay. I need you to come back." I bury my face in his sheets and clutch his warm, lifeless hand. Tears leak from my eyes, soaking into the thin cotton. "All of this is my fault. You didn't want to go. You said you had a horrible feeling. You begged me to listen, but I didn't. I went anyway."

And because I went, so too, did he.

The truth of it—that he was captured and tortured, all because I wouldn't listen—crushes me. I cry until the tears run dry. I cry until my entire body aches. I'm supposed to be his breath of life, and yet I feel like I've lost mine.

"Tess?"

I twist around, my kneecaps smarting against the hard floor. Cap sits in his wheelchair in Luka's doorway. I sniff and wipe my cheeks. "We waited too long."

"I don't think so."

"But I couldn't get to him. He's—"

"*Bait.* You don't get rid of the bait before you catch the fish."

"Then why couldn't I find him?"

"You were having a hard time linking." Cap rolls inside. "You never have a hard time linking."

I lean back on my heels.

"Link seems to think that you're too distraught, and because of that, you're not performing like you're normally able to perform. You used all your energy linking everyone. You didn't have any left to reach Luka."

"So how are we supposed to get to him?" My question comes out breathless. Hopeful. Terrified.

"We know Luka's captor is somewhere in Detroit, well within Link's territory."

"But he can't link all six of us. The most he's done is four."

"He doesn't have to. You can get there on your own. As far as the rest of us, Link will do what he did when we rescued Anna. He'll link one of us at a time. As soon as we're through the doorway, he can sever the link, and link someone else. He'll take Jose's place in the chair, which means we'll be down a Fighter."

I wipe at my face again. "You really think he's still alive?"

Cap jerks his head toward the door. "Let's go find out."

CHAPTER SEVEN

DEATH MARCH

Water drips somewhere. A slow *plink-plink* that echoes into the silence. Clive and Gabe are already here, crouched to my left. In front, the same wooden crates Link and I hid behind earlier. I peek over them and there he is. Luka. Relief comes like a seismic wave. It tears through my body, making everything—muscle and ligament, bone and marrow—quake. Luka's still here. He's not gone. He lies unmoving on the floor, bound by one guard. Just like last time.

Cap puts his hand on my arm.

He's arrived and crouches beside me with his finger held up to his lips. Sticks has arrived too. All of us squat beneath Clive's cloak.

I motion toward Luka. I want to shout, "Now!" I want to race ahead, fight off the solitary guard, grab Luka, and startle awake so all of this can be over. But Cap's grip tightens on my arm, his attention sliding from one corner of the chamber to the other. When he's finished with his inspection, he waves for us to follow him around the crates, out into the open. Clive's cloak is strong and bright. There are no holes or thin spots like Anna's.

Luka stirs on the floor.

Clive's cloak broadens and spreads, allowing us to move apart, to surround Luka and the guard on all sides.

Luka stirs again.

The guard shifts.

All of us stop.

And suddenly, out of nowhere, Scarface appears. He stands in front of Luka, his hands clasped behind his back, his head slightly cocked, as though listening for a pin to drop. "Is that you, Little Rabbit?"

I hold my breath. He can't see me. There's no way. Not inside Clive's cloak. But my heart thunders so loudly it drowns out the *plink-plink* of dripping water. So loudly that maybe he can hear me.

Luka sets his hands on the ground and tries to push himself up.

A Grinch-like smile pulls up the corners of the man's lips, turning his white scars into the shape of crescent moons. "I *knew* you would come. Didn't I know she would come, Mr. Williams? Isn't love so ridiculously irrational?"

"Please, Tess," Luka begs. "Startle."

"Oh no, Tess! Please, don't startle. Come closer instead and give Mr. Williams the kiss he's been fancying. The kiss he can't stop thinking about." Scarface claps his hands together and laughs. A cackle so delighted and amused it raises every hair on my body. "Your dear lover is a parched man and your lips are like water. Won't you come closer and let him drink?"

Luka's shoulder muscles tremble as he pushes himself a little higher. "No, Tess."

"*Yes, Tess.* Now is your chance. There's only two of us." Scarface lifts his hand to himself and the guard. "Surely a powerful Fighter like you can handle the two of us."

Blood pounds in my ears. I move to take a step, but Cap raises his hand in a sharp, attention-getting motion. His steely eyes command me to wait. To be smarter.

"No kiss for Mr. Williams? Pity. And here I was hoping to watch the romantic reunion." He shrugs, like it's my loss. "Tell me, how *is* everyone? Good? Are you sure? It's hard to know who to trust these days, don't you think?"

He's baiting me with Claire, but it won't work. I never trusted her to begin with.

The four of us begin moving forward again. Clive stays behind, his cloak extending along with us as we close in.

"Lucky for me, you're not the only one trying to reunite with a dear loved one." Scarface's eyes glitter, and then narrow into calculated slits. "You know the deal."

The words have me stutter stepping.

What deal?

"I'm sorry. I don't have a choice."

The hollow voice comes from behind me. I turn around and watch in horror as Clive takes a step back and drops his cloak. The darkened chamber fills with white-eyed guards. Twenty at least. And we are completely visible. One hundred percent exposed.

With his eyes never leaving mine, black mist curls from Scarface's fingertips. He aims it at Luka, but it doesn't wrap around him this time. It seeps inside of him. He arches up violently, almost completely off the ground, and screams. His body bends like I've never seen a body bend. Like his spine has snapped in two.

No! I run toward him, anger and hatred morphing into pure adrenaline. It courses through my veins as I take four guards out at once. In the periphery of my vision, Cap and Sticks fight off three at a time. Gabe throws a shield that scatters five. Luka continues to twist and scream as more guards appear. Like Shady Wood, they come out of nowhere, filling the entire chamber.

Sticks falls and black mist binds him.

No.

I do a running kick that throws two against the wall.

Six surround Cap and take him down.

No!

Fury propels me forward as Scarface drops back like a coward, flashes me a sickening smile, and disappears. Luka falls to the ground. I punch and kick and strike. But there are too many. We're going to lose. There's no way we can win. No hope of victory. All I want now is to reach Luka one last time. Touch him one last time. I strike one of the guards with the heel of my palm. Sweep the legs of another.

"Tess!" Gabe yells.

Our attention collides and holds through the chaos. His lips pull into a thin, resolved line. And then he throws another shield, bright and blinding. Only he doesn't throw it at our enemy. He throws it at me. It barrels forward like a rolling wave of billowing heat.

I don't have time to understand. I don't have time to process. All I can do is brace for the impact. But no amount of bracing can prepare me for what happens next.

The shield does not slam against me. It slams inside of me. Like an atomic bomb of explosive power, so hot and so big I will rupture into a million fragmented pieces if it remains. On instinct, my body convulses and I hurl the power out.

There's a brilliant flash of light. So piercing, so overwhelming, there's nothing but white. It charges through the chamber with a sonic boom, engulfing everything in its path. And when it's gone, so is the enemy. None remain. Cap and Sticks are no longer bound.

I don't wait around to see what will happen next.

I sprint forward and dive at Luka's crumpled body. I grab onto his neck and scream at everyone to startle.

CHAPTER EIGHT

AN ETERNITY

I sit up straight in the chair. I don't wait for anyone else to come to consciousness. I rip the probes off my chest and my temple. I fling open the door and tear down the hallway. I don't stop until I reach the antechamber that leads to the boys' corridor.

There's nothing but dark and silence.

My heart booms great giant beats that throb against my eardrums. I have a whole new understanding of the phrase— *frozen in fear*. Because that's me. I want to sprint ahead, and I want to sprint away. But I can't do either. I can do nothing but stand with trembling knees, wondering why the hallway is still dark. Why isn't Luka coming out of his room? Fear terrorizes me. So does Cap's warning.

There are bound to be ramifications.

I can see it—the black mist oozing inside of him. Luka's body snapping. Were we too late? Scarface thought he had me. So why wouldn't he destroy him? The bait had served its purpose. My booming heart booms harder.

And then …

A latch clicks.

The door to Luka's room slowly opens. He steps into the hallway. Luka, his dark hair sticking up in every direction. Luka, awake. Luka, alive.

His eyes meet mine.

I stand there, unable to move. Unable to breathe.

He takes a step toward me, then sets his hand against the wall, as if he needs the support. The invisible chains of fear holding me in place fall away. I run and throw myself into his arms. He lets out a soft *oomph* as I collide against his chest. His arms slide around my waist. Mine wrap around his neck. He's okay. Luka's okay. I hold on tight, repeating the two words over and over and over again. *Luka's okay. Luka's okay.* I can't get over them. I will never get over them.

"You could have been killed." His lips are hot against my ear. A few days worth of scruff scratch against my skin. "If I were a better Keeper, I'd be livid."

My entire body thrums to life.

His hands span the width of my ribcage, and in a moment of total relief and passion, he pushes me against the wall and crushes my lips with his. I'm pinned in the best possible way. I can't get enough of him. I will never, ever be able to get enough of him.

"I thought I lost you," I murmur between kisses.

"Only for awhile."

"It felt like an eternity."

Luka slides his fingers into my hair and presses his forehead against mine—his eyes as intense as the raging sea. He kisses me again, so achingly soft I melt against him. I want to stay here forever, kissing Luka. I don't want to move forward, into the unknown. I definitely don't want to move back, into the hell that was yesterday. But fragmented bits of information intrude on my euphoria, sneaking into the crevices of my mind like pesky rodents.

Clive, apologizing.

Clive, dropping the cloak.

We risked everything to rescue him from Shady Wood. He was inside Leela's car. We invited him into the hub. He acted like he was on our side. I *trusted* him. I *thanked* him. And then he handed us over to the enemy on a silver platter.

Heat licks up my chest. Because of him, Non almost became a widow. The hub almost lost its leader. Jillian and Link and Rosie and all the rest would have been left to deal with the fallout. All of it would have happened, too, if not for Gabe and the mysterious shield he threw at me. What *was* that? And why are Luka and I still alone? Doesn't anyone care that we succeeded? That Luka's back and well with no ramifications that I can see?

"I don't understand what happened," I say.

"Neither do I."

Footsteps approach.

Luka and I step apart.

Jillian walks toward us, her mousy brown hair pulled back in a ponytail, her clothes as worn and faded as everyone else's. She gives Luka a wobbly smile. "It's good to see you up."

He pushes his fingers through his hair. "It's good to be up."

She bites her lip.

A cold feeling slinks between my shoulder blades. "What's wrong?"

"It's Gabe." Tears pool in her eyes. "He's dead."

CHAPTER NINE

THE DEVOURING

I'm no stranger to death.

I saw it claim a doctor and a nurse outside a fetal modification clinic in a fiery explosion. I watched it persuade a desperate man to stick the barrel of a gun inside his mouth and pull the trigger. I couldn't stop it from claiming a catatonic woman behind a steering wheel as fumes of exhaust gathered in her garage. I witnessed its merciless appetite as it threw up a carnage of bodies on a stretch of California highway.

But in the light of day, with my skin burning beneath scratching fingers, death is an entirely different beast. In the light of day, I've only stared it in the face twice. First with Dr. Roth, hanging from a noose at the end of his hallway. Now Gabe, lying in a chair inside the training room. His eyes are closed. His frozen lips slightly upturned, as if he welcomed death like an old friend. Link told me once that when Gabe's *anima* died, Gabe died in a way, too. Now he's dead in every way. I don't understand how.

Jillian sniffs. "I was watching the monitors when his vitals flatlined. There was no warning or anything. One second he was fine, and the next ..."

With glazed-over eyes, Luka stares down at Gabe's still form.

"What's going to happen to him?" My question escapes

43

without inflection. Today has encompassed too many emotions. The effect has left me wrung dry. I know I should feel sad about this loss, *responsible* for this loss, but all I feel apart from numbness is relief that the one lying dead in the hub is not Luka.

"I don't know." Jillian's lip trembles. "Maybe if Link had been in charge instead of me, he would have noticed something. Maybe Gabe wouldn't be dead."

I squeeze Jillian's hand. "This is not your fault."

She wipes her eyes. "After you left, Cap yelled at Sticks and Jose to grab Clive and then he ordered all of us out."

A slow-rising anger works its way through the numbness. After everything we did for him, after everything we risked for him—*how could he?* "Do you know where they took him?"

"The conference room."

I march into the hallway, leaving Jillian and Luka behind. I pass the greenhouse, where Anna hums softly to herself. I don't stop until I reach the end of the adult dormitory corridor. A thin strip of light shines beneath the closed door of the makeshift conference room. Before I can knock, the door flies open and Cap rolls out, his gray stubble scruffier than I've ever seen. Deep lines bracket his eyes as he looks past me. "Where's Luka?"

"With Gabe." Who's dead somehow. "What happened to him? Why did he die?"

"*Kataphagon.*"

"What?"

Cap rubs his scraggly cheeks, then pulls his face long with a sigh. "*Kataphagon.* It's a Hebrew word that means *the devouring.* The contemporary name for it is transurgence."

I shift my weight from one leg to the other, ready for him

to finish his mini lesson in etymology and move on to the information I want—why did *Kataphagon* kill Gabe? And why does the strange word make my skin prickle with foreboding?

"That wasn't a shield Gabe threw. It was his life. It's something only Keepers can do."

My foreboding turns to dread. It sinks like an icy rock into the pit of my stomach.

"Once the Fighter absorbs it, their power is magnified. How much depends on the strength of the Keeper."

As if remembering the sensation, the tendons in my fingers flex. It was like a thousand suns had entered my body. As soon as I threw it out, it devoured the guards. It devoured Gabe, too. "Did Gabe know he would die?"

"Yes."

My mouth turns acidic. "So he basically committed suicide."

"*Mori est Vivire.* To die is to live. He didn't take his life, Tess. He gave it. And because of that, you're here. Because of that, Luka is here. To a Keeper, it's the most honorable way to go."

I press my lips together to keep my rolling stomach from staging a revolt. Did Gabe teach Luka about transurgence? I push the question away, scrambling about for something else to focus on. I just got Luka back. I can't think about losing him again. "The man with the scars said there were other ways of getting to me. I thought he was talking about Claire. But He was talking about Clive, wasn't he?"

"It would appear so."

"Do you think he got to anyone else?"

"I don't know." Cap sets his hands over the wheels of his chair and pushes himself forward. "But I have the immense pleasure of finding out."

"What are you going to do?"

"What I should have done after Claire tripped you." He rolls down the hallway. "Interrogate every member of my team."

Clive sits in a chair inside the small room, his wrists and ankles bound by rope. He doesn't fight against his restraints. He doesn't even lift his head to see who walks inside the makeshift jail cell. The sight of him obliterates the numbness I felt while staring at Gabe.

I picture Clive, the way he was the first time Link and I jumped into his medicated dream—standing at attention, alert and ready. A soldier prepared for battle. Turns out, he was preparing to battle for them. I led us on a mission to rescue the enemy. And because of that, Luka was tortured, I brought a betrayer into our midst, and Gabe is dead.

Contempt digs into my shoulders. "We risked everything for you, and you stabbed us in the back."

I wait for a response. Something—*anything*. But he doesn't react at all, and the longer the silence stretches, the deeper the contempt digs. I want to tear him apart. I want to make him bleed with regret over what he's done. I want Gabe's death to be his fault, not mine. "If not for us, you'd be locked up in Shady Wood. Or maybe you'd be dead like my grandmother."

He lifts his chin. His expression isn't indifferent, or resentful, or calculating. It's filled with desperation, an emotion I mistook for eagerness. After all the enemy had stolen from him, I assumed he was ready to fight back. "You know what it's like," he says.

I narrow my eyes. "What *what's* like?"

"Being separated from someone you love."

The sparse details of his file wiggle into place. I studied it enough to have it memorized. Divorced with two kids and no visitation rights. "You mean your sons?"

"My children. My *wife*. She put a restraining order on me. All because of my *gifting*." He spits the word like it's something foul. "It's not a gift. It's a curse. It took everything from me."

"And handing us over would get it all back?"

"We made a deal, and he made me a promise."

"*Who*—the man with the scars? He doesn't make promises. He spins lies. He's incapable of telling the truth." I shake my head, disgust blistering beneath my skin. "You're not a soldier. You're a coward. You're a traitor."

"You would do the same thing."

The accusation burns. "I would never do what you did."

Clive lifts his chin higher and looks me directly in the eye. "You can make me into a villain if it makes you feel better. Go right ahead. Think what you want to think. But at the end of the day, I know who I am."

"And who's that?"

"A husband and a father, willing to do whatever it takes to get my family back."

"That's the difference. I wouldn't do whatever it takes."

He raises his eyebrows, as if calling my bluff.

I hate how one simple gesture can infuse me with such doubt. I convinced Cap to let us stay here, in a compromised location, even though I didn't believe a word Claire spoke in her dream. I had no problem putting everyone in jeopardy to rescue Luka. My conscience never tinged. There wasn't even a prick.

CHAPTER TEN

WEAPON OF CHOICE

Jillian moves her bishop three diagonal spaces left.

I study the board haphazardly, my mind spinning in too many directions. Luka alive. Gabe and my grandmother dead. Clive's betrayal. His accusation. Claire out there, knowing our names and location. Scarface torturing Luka to get to me. *Transurgence.*

Off in the corner, Declan and Jose play foosball. Bass and Rosie kick a Hacky Sack. Ashley and Danielle sit together on one of the couches, whispering behind their hands, and Ellen reads *A Midsummer Night's Dream* in her favorite armchair.

By all accounts, it looks like a normal evening. Everyone hanging out after dinner, happy that classes and training are done for the day. Someone would have to look closer to notice the current of tension pulsating through the room. It manifests itself in the tense set of Declan and Jose's shoulders, Rosie's restlessness, the way Ellen keeps peeking over the pages of her book toward the spot by the door where Gabe usually stands.

On the television, a news anchor drones on about a new immigration law and its implications for the country. Jillian watches with her bottom lip tucked between her teeth. I move a pawn forward. She pushes her knuckles against the floor and sits up on her knees. "Don't you think it's odd?"

"What?"

"This." She motions to the TV. "One second Cormack's talking about cleaning up the streets and the next she's talking about taking more people in. She's speaking out of both sides of her mouth, but nobody ever calls her on it. I mean, she's the president. If there's one thing our country's any good at, it's nitpicking our leader."

I try to drum up some interest in the conversation, but my brain has reached capacity. I glance toward the hallway, eager for Luka to appear. He's currently being interrogated by Cap, which makes about as much sense as Cap interrogating me. Luka would have an easier time turning himself into a piece of lint than he would have turning me over to the enemy. And yet Cap summoned him, Luka didn't object, and so far, he's been gone for forty-five minutes. It's driving me nuts, all this waiting. We should be packing up and leaving, not hanging around. "Hey Jillian?"

"Oh, sorry." She quickly moves—taking my knight with her castle.

"It's not that." I could care less about the game, evidenced by my sparse army. She's taken seven of my pieces. I've taken two of hers and both are pawns. I scratch the inside of my wrist, then quickly pull my sleeve over my hand. If I don't stop, I'm going to give myself scars. "What did Cap ask you in there?"

"If I've ever been in contact with anyone on the other side."

"Have you?"

"No." Her cheeks turn pink, like the idea horrifies her. "Never."

"Did he say when we're going to leave? Or where we're going to go?" Now that Luka's safe, I'm eager to make sure everyone else is safe, too.

"No. Just that Link's working on it."

Link.

He's been so busy helping Cap, I haven't seen him since we rescued Luka. I glance again at the entryway. This time, it's not empty. Luka strides inside the common room with a confidence that's as much a part of him as his green eyes and messy hair. My muscles go weak. I still can't believe he's okay. Apart from being moderately dehydrated, there haven't even been any of those ramifications Cap warned me about.

He nods at the board. "Who's winning?"

"Who do you think?"

"You aren't doing so bad," Jillian says.

I look up at Luka. "She's being nice."

He smiles and gives my knee a gentle nudge with his shoe. "You're up."

"*I'm up?*" Why would Cap need to interrogate me?

Before I can voice anymore of my confusion, Luka pulls me up off the floor, threads his fingers with mine, and kisses my temple. "Just go with it," he whispers.

And so I do.

Luka tells Jillian he'll finish the chess game for me in a little bit and everyone stares as we walk out of the room, Danielle and Ashley most intensely. As soon as we reach the empty hallway, Luka pulls us to a stop. With the subtlest turn of his wrist, my entire body moves. Somehow, I'm leaning against the wall with his lips on mine and for one heady moment, my frantic thoughts disappear. All that exists—all that matters—is this.

He stops much too soon and presses his forehead against mine. "When I was in that chamber, only one thing kept me sane."

"What was that?"

"Replaying our last kiss on the beach."

Warmth swirls in my chest. I relived it, too. A hundred times. Once, in front of Link.

"I promised myself if I ever saw you again, I wouldn't stop kissing you like that."

"Why'd you stop then?"

The corner of his mouth quirks into a delectable half-grin. "Because Cap is waiting. And purpling is against the rules."

Purpling. Cap-lingo for boys and girls getting too close. "I think Cap has more pressing matters to worry about than purpling."

"And there's the silver lining." He places his hand against the wall, right above my left shoulder, leans in and kisses me again, slower. Like we have all the time in the world. His lips travel across my jaw and find my neck.

It feels so good, my toes curl. "Hey, um, Luka?"

"Hmm?"

"W-why is Cap interrogating you and me?"

He pulls away, his face turning serious. He glances over his shoulder, takes my hand, and gets us moving again. "Very few people are aware the other side is after *you*, specifically. There's no reason to make it public knowledge."

"So Cap didn't actually question you?"

"Not about my allegiance, no."

"What did he question you about, then?"

Luka's eyes flicker. Become guarded. "If I learned any-thing."

"You mean, while you were ..."

"Away?"

Away. It's way too tame for what really happened. I tug at my shirtsleeves. "Did you?"

"I was too preoccupied to pay much attention. The only thing I could think about was making sure you were safe."

I shake my head. Luka was being tortured and yet all he could think about was *my* safety? I can't tell if that's a Keeper thing or a Luka thing. "Do you trust everyone here?"

"I don't *know* everyone here. Not well, anyway. I don't think it hurts to be extra cautious. I'm glad Cap's doing the interrogations." Luka stops in front of the classroom door and presses a kiss against my temple. "I'm gonna go perform some triage on your chess game. See you when you're done."

Inside the classroom, amidst antiquated textbooks, Cap sits in his wheelchair at one of the tables. He's looking old and worn. In need of a haircut and a shave and a really good night of sleep. I take a seat across from him. "How're the interrogations going?"

"Largely uninformative."

"And our game plan?"

"Still being solidified."

"When are we leaving?"

Cap massages the bridge of his nose. "Tomorrow, most likely."

"*Tomorrow*? Isn't that a little risky?"

"You said Claire wasn't an immediate threat."

I try not to squirm, or think too hard about DeVant's accusation. *You would do the same thing.* "What about Clive? He knows our location. He had a Greyhound ticket to Detroit."

"According to you, the enemy was already aware of our location in Detroit. It's a big city. Anna has her cloak up and Non is standing guard." Cap sets his hand over a walkie-talkie on the table. "She'll send an alert at the first sign of danger."

"Non's fallen asleep before."

"I know what I'm doing, Tess. I need you to trust in my leadership."

The words sting. Luka's reservations weren't the only ones I ignored. Cap had them, too. He didn't want to rush into a rescue mission. He wanted more time to research and plan. But Clive was a Cloak. What more was there to research? I never stopped to consider the fact that he might be a backstabbing Cloak. I didn't care to consider it. Not when I'd been so focused on freeing my grandmother. Shame creeps into my cheeks. "I really messed things up, didn't I?"

He shrugs. "We learn and we move on. That's what leaders do."

"I'm not a leader."

"Yes, you are."

I shake my head.

His eyes hold steady on mine. Over the past few months, I've gotten to know him fairly well. He took me under his wing. Pushed me to be stronger than I thought possible. In return, I'm certain there's nobody in the hub who gives him more pride, or more fits of exasperation, than me. Somehow, this man who I first knew as a file marked Josiah Aaronson has become as close to a father figure as I'm going to get apart from my own. And right now, that father figure looks like he's about to impart some wisdom.

"I believe in you." Cap doesn't do flattery. Doling out compliments is not part of his DNA. If he says it, he means it. I just don't understand how he can speak those words. He folds his hands on the table. "But I also know how the enemy works. Fear is his weapon of choice. He uses it to sow seeds of division, doubt, mistrust. We can't let him get a foothold."

"I thought that's what these interrogations were for."

"I don't mean among us. I mean within us." Cap leans forward. His silver eyes don't just look, they penetrate. They dissect. They eviscerate. It's like he's examining the very depths of my soul, where the enemy's weapon runs rampant. "Fear only has power when we let it make our choices."

My fingers start scratching again.

"I believe in the prophecy. I believe you're The One."

I pull at my sleeves. He's talking crazy. The One is supposed to save lives, not put them in danger. That's all I can seem to do.

"But hear me on this. What I believe? It means very little unless you believe it, too."

CHAPTER ELEVEN

A NEW HOME

Cap told everyone to meet in the common room after dinner, but he's with Link and people have started without him. I sit on one of the couches next to Luka as heated conversation floats around us.

"What are we going to do with Clive?"

"We can't bring him with us."

"We can't let him go. He knows too much."

"What if we lock him up and leave him here?"

"He'll starve to death."

"Maybe that's not such a bad idea."

"That's an awful thing to say."

"He's the enemy, isn't he?"

He's just a dad who wanted his family back.

The thought comes out of nowhere—an intrusive, uninvited guest I want nothing to do with. I don't want to sympathize with Clive. I don't want to understand his motives. I don't want to understand him, period. All I want is to make sure the people I care about are safe. I glance at Rosie and Jillian and the knot in my stomach pulls tighter.

Voices rise.

Accusations are thrown.

Fear is his weapon of choice. He uses it to sow seeds of division, doubt, mistrust. We can't let him get a foothold.

Whoever *he* is, I think he already has.

Nobody agrees on anything. Not on Clive or what to do with Gabe's body or who to trust or where we'll go or what we'll do once we get there. It's all arguments and scowls and passionate objections. Hurt feelings and panic escalate. By the time Cap finally rolls into the room, poor Rosie's face has turned the color of chalk and judging by his expression, he's heard the gist of the conversation—probably from all the way down the hall.

"This is not how wars are won."

Everyone goes silent.

"Emotions cannot steer our decisions. We make them based on fact."

"Here's a fact," Danielle says. While everyone else wears the signs of stress, her eyes have taken on an odd glow. She's the kind of girl who thrives off of drama. "We're sleeping with the enemy down here. For all we know Clive could be communicating with the other side right now."

Declan rolls his eyes. "He's not a Linker."

"It doesn't matter. If he's opening his mind, they can get to him."

"They can get to all of us," Ashley adds.

Declan mutters an exasperated curse under his breath. He seems to be taking Danielle and Ashley's fear mongering personally. "Only if you're inviting them in."

"So you think Claire actively invited them in? She was one of the first people down here. If she wasn't trustworthy, then who is?"

Cap raises his hand sharply.

Declan—who had opened his mouth to respond—presses his lips together.

"Clive is under control. Right now, we have bigger issues at hand."

"Like the genocide," Luka says. It's the first he's spoken since the heated conversation began.

Bass narrows his beady eyes. "What genocide?"

Cap pushes out a heavy breath. "Patients in mental rehab facilities are being killed off. Link's confirmed it. Whole databases are disappearing around the country."

"What does that mean?" Jillian asks, rubbing Rosie's shoulder reassuringly.

I glance at Non. She sits in one of the worn-out chairs we've pulled into a slapdash circle, squinting at Cap and rubbing her chin. So far, she's been as quiet as me. "If it's fact you're after, you'll find it in the journals."

"What journals?" Declan asks.

Jillian scrunches her nose. "You mean those composition notebooks Tess is always looking at?"

Everyone's attention turns my way.

Yes, those. Non had me study them. She wanted me to find the connections. Genocide was the common theme. They also referenced a prophecy. One I never would have thought had anything to do with me until I overhead Cap and Luka's early-morning conversation in the cafeteria last week. Those journals are currently tucked beneath my bed.

"The ones in Tess's possession are only a small subset of the whole collection. The rest are with a Scribe named Cressida Rivard." Non winds a loose thread from the hem of her shirt around her finger and gives it a yank. When she looks up, she seems surprised that we're all still staring. "The Rivard family became a safe haven for me many years ago. Cressida's grandfather was the Scribe before her. Once he fell ill, Cressida was chosen."

"Chosen for *what?*" Jillian asks.

And by who? I want to add.

"Preserving the history of The Gifting. The Scribe is charged with studying, recording, and transcribing the accounts of those who came before. These accounts also contain several prophecies."

Luka shifts beside me, his jaw tightening. If he doesn't want anyone to know the enemy is after me, specifically, then I'm sure he really doesn't want anyone to know about a prophecy that may or may not be about me and the demise of our kind.

"Where does Cressida live?" Cap asks.

"In New Orleans, in the family mansion."

He looks at me like he's waiting for me to jump up from the couch and insist on going. Like I should want nothing more than to hightail it south so I can learn more about these journals and the prophecy that is no doubt contained within. The prophecy he believes is about me. "You should go," he finally says.

A week ago, I would have been chomping at the bit to learn more. But now? I'm done taking the lead. I'm done making the decisions. It only seems to put people in danger. "If you think it's a good idea."

His eyelids flutter, like my response catches him off guard. He's not used to me being so docile. "I do think it's a good idea. I also think you'll need a team. Luka will obviously be a part of it."

"So will I." The eager words belong to Jillian—a Shield with no exceptional strength or power. But she's my friend and I trust her, which makes her worth more than five hundred

Cloaks.

Cap nods, like it's a good idea. "Anybody else?"

I want to hold up my hands and tell him to stop looking at me. This isn't my team. I'm not leading it. But I can't help picturing the boy with the caramel eyes and the shaggy hair and the mischievous dimples. The boy who makes me feel brave and confident. Right now, I could use some of both. "What about Link?"

A muscle in Luka's leg twitches. He's never been Link's biggest fan, mostly because he thinks Link treats my life too casually.

"It's a good idea. The four of you will go to New Orleans to see what the journals have to say." Cap looks from me to everyone else. "The rest of us will go to Newport."

A collective gasp tumbles through the room.

"*Newport?*" The glow in Danielle's eyes goes dark. Her face turns the color of the oatmeal we eat most mornings.

I can understand why. There's nothing left of Newport. It ceased to exist fifteen years ago, after a group of terrorists targeted the naval base and decimated the entire city along with it. The survivors were evacuated and nobody returned. From all accounts, it's a wasteland.

"What could possibly be in *Newport?*" Ashley asks.

"Headquarters for The Gifting. It's where everyone is gathering." Cap spins his chair around and starts rolling away, as though the meeting is adjourned.

I set my bag of toiletries beside the journals stacked on my dresser. After the meeting, I pulled them from beneath my mattress and flipped through the pages. I rub my thumb over the strange swirly symbol on the cover of the one on top. It's on all five of them, in the same place—upper right corner. I don't know what it means.

There's a soft *knock-knock* behind me.

I turn around.

Luka stands in the doorway, leaning against the frame. He wears a pair of sweatpants and a white undershirt, his hair damp from a shower, his face clean-shaven. "Can I come in?"

I lift my arm in invitation.

He walks to my bed, snagging my hand and pulling me with him as he goes. My heart accelerates as we sit facing each other on the mattress.

"You were quiet during the meeting," he says, rubbing his thumb across my knuckles. "I wanted to come check on you. Make sure you're okay."

His feather-light touch has goose bumps racing up my arms. "I should be asking *you* that question."

When he looks up, there are traces of shadow beneath his eyes. "As long as you're okay, I'm okay."

"I think that goes both ways."

Luka smiles a little, then holds up his fist, showing off the hemp bracelet I tied to his wrist earlier. "How'd this get here?"

"I thought you could use it more than me."

He starts to untie it, but I place my hand over his. My fingers are shaking. My eyes start to sting. And the knot of fear in my chest tightens. "I want you to keep it."

"Hey." Luka dips his chin, his face filled with compassion. With calm. "You know it's just a bracelet, right?"

The stinging in my eyes turns to burning. No amount of blinking will chase away the embarrassing tears. I look down, twisting each of the beads inside the hemp. "I can't lose you again."

"You won't."

Why then, can I not stop thinking about *transurgence?* The harder I try to push it away, bury it deep, the more it demands my attention. I want to make Luka promise that he will never—under any circumstances—do what Gabe did in that chamber. But I'm afraid of bringing it up, because there's a chance Luka doesn't know about it.

He rubs his thumb along my jaw and draws me closer. As soon as his lips touch mine, I ignite. All my fear, all my anxiety, all my relief—it gathers like the perfect storm. I curl my fingers into Luka's damp hair and pull him closer. Only this time, we're not out in the hallway. We're in my room.

On my bed.

My back slowly lowers onto the mattress. Luka leans his body over mine. I press a kiss against his neck. But suddenly, he stops. He puts his hand on the mattress, his smoldering eyes moving from me to the opened door. Cap would skin us alive if we closed it. I can almost see the same thought running through Luka's mind. He moves to the edge of my bed and pushes his fingers through his hair, giving us space so we can catch our breath.

"I, uh, should probably go," he says.

I don't want him to go, so I take his hand.

He glances at the door again. Cap made the rules clear. No purpling allowed. Luka is nothing if not respectful. But I also know he lives to make me happy.

Call me manipulative, I hold his hand tighter. "Stay."

"Tess, you're driving me crazy."

"Please. Just stay."

It works.

With a sigh, he runs his hand down his face and shuts off the light. Leaving my door wide open, he climbs into my bed and opens his arms. I lay my head on his chest, listening to the sound of his heartbeat while he plays with my hair.

"I'm sorry we didn't get to your grandma in time," he finally says.

"She probably thought I abandoned her."

"You didn't, though."

"She lived such a tragic life." Tormented for years. Committed to a mental institute by her own son. Locked up since I was two. The hope of rescue dangled in her face only to have her life snatched away. I wanted to give her something better. I wanted to take her away from that place, get to know her, and maybe find out why she tried kidnapping me all those years ago. In her journal, she wrote that I had the power to save her. Was she talking about the prophecy? And if so, what did she know about it?

My gut tightens into a cold fist. "I'm scared."

"I know."

"What if something bad happens to my mom and Pete? Or my dad? Or what about *your* parents? You never talk about them."

"That's because I don't think about them."

I lift my head off his chest. "They're your parents. Of course you do."

Luka shakes his head and tucks a strand of hair behind my ear. "I stopped thinking about them the second two government officials dragged you out of Lotsam's class."

I bite my lip, unsure how to respond to that one.

"Tess, I know you're scared. I know your mind is going in a million different directions. There are a lot of people you care about. It's one of the things that makes you so strong. And amazing. And beautiful."

Heat creeps into my cheeks. I'm hardly beautiful.

"But I also know that the what-if game will drive you crazy. All we can do is focus on one step at a time. Right now, that step is figuring out what's going on. And the only way we can do that is by getting to New Orleans."

"And if someone recognizes us on our way to the Rivards?"

"Let me worry about that, okay?"

I let out a long breath. I don't want to be on the run again. I don't want to leave this place that has become an odd sort of home. I don't want to deal with prophecies and genocides and whatever evil lurks up above. It's all too much.

Exhaustion drags at my eyelids. I've barely slept in the last seventy-two hours. And Luka's fingers are playing with my hair again. My mind wanders to my best friend, Leela. She's probably waiting to hear from me. Last we talked, I told her about the plan and she followed through with Clive. I hate that he was in her car. I hate that he knows her face and her name. My thoughts grow fuzzier. Less cognizant as I tiptoe to the edge of sleep.

"It's time for you to go to your room." It's Cap's voice. Disapproving. Far away.

There's a brush of lips against my temple. My weight is gently shifted. The mattress springs squeak. I'm alone, and I let sleep take me.

CHAPTER TWELVE

A FAMILIAR SOUND

I wake up inside a mass of hot, sweaty bodies. There's smoke and lights and screaming—not the frightened kind that arises out of terror, but the frenzied kind born of adoration. Through the mob, up on the stage, stands B-Trix, a pop star from London who has people fainting by the truckload.

She begins playing a familiar song and the crowd goes wild.

Beside me, Leela throws her hands up in the air and sings along. I scratch the inside of my wrist. The spot is completely numb. A few lines in, Leela turns to me, her brown eyes bright with excitement. "I can't believe we got tickets to a Trix concert!"

I lean toward her ear and yell back, "I can't believe it either!"

It takes a bit. A few seconds, maybe, before it happens. Leela's eyelids flutter. She looks around the mass of bodies, as if realizing that yes, it really isn't believable. Me and her here together? She brings her arms down to her sides.

The stage and the lights and the crowd disappears.

Her dream world turns into a generic holding place. I expect disappointment, because B-Trix has gone away. Instead, Leela wraps her arms around my neck and squeezes so tight, I can't breathe. "Oh my gosh, Tess! I've been so worried!"

The generic holding space morphs into my old bedroom in

Thornsdale, complete with the breathtaking view of ocean and cliffs and towering redwoods. I want to fling open the window and inhale the briny air. Or better yet, fling open the door and run downstairs to my mom and Pete. If only it would really be them instead of Leela's projections of them.

Leela lets go. "What happened? Why wasn't your grandma there? Oh my gosh, the drive with that man was the most awkward thing in the world. I was so nervous and he wasn't talking and you know how I get when I'm nervous. I kept chattering away. About really stupid things, too. Like how Matt cheated on Bobbi with Summer." Leela mimics gagging herself. "And how Bobbi's been crying in the bathroom and how Summer won't stop talking about it. I kept going on and on like he cared."

I smile at my friend. Man, I've missed her.

"So what happened? Tell me before I go crazy."

"My grandmother is dead."

Leela's eyes go round. She slowly sinks onto my bed. "What do you mean?"

"Her room was empty. So many of the rooms were empty."

"Empty? Tess, what are you talking about?"

"They're killing patients." I sit beside her. "In the mental rehab facilities. Innocent people are being murdered."

Leela blanches. "Why?"

"You've heard President Cormack's speeches. They're a burden to society." But even as I say it, I know that's not the real reason. Whether our government realizes it or not, they are pawns in a master plan. This isn't about eradicating weakness. It's about eradicating The Gifting. And all-too-often, The Gifting are mistaken as crazy. How couldn't they be? In a world where nothing supernatural exists, where that fact has been ingrained into our minds since birth, the only logical explanation for seeing the supernatural is mental illness.

If I hadn't had Luka and Dr. Roth to explain what was really happening, I would have assumed I was crazy like the rest of them. I wonder how many people like me assume they're crazy, check into a "rehab" facility, and never come out again.

"I can't believe she's dead." Leela reaches into my lap and takes my hand. "I'm so sorry."

A lump rises in my throat. I didn't know my grandmother, but that doesn't mean I didn't imagine what it might be like getting to know her, having her with me at the hub. An actual family member. I swallow before the lump can grow any larger. "The guy you drove to the Greyhound station—Clive? He betrayed us."

Leela's mouth drops open.

"You have to promise me you'll be careful. That you'll be on the lookout."

"For what?"

"Danger. Everything's changing, Leela. We have to leave where we are. I'm not sure when I'll be able to visit like this again."

She picks at the nail polish on her thumb. "You'll come back, though, right? When this is all over? This mess will get straightened out with you and your dad and you'll come back and you and I can start senior year together."

The lump returns like a ball of hot emotion. She has no idea how much I want it to be true. I nod down at my lap, even though I'm not sure a world like that can exist again. I don't think going back is ever really an option. And yet, that's exactly what I want to do—go back to the way things were, when strange dreams and flashes of unexplainable light were my worst problems, before I knew anything about prophecies and transurgence. Maybe that's another one of the enemy's weapons. Making us so fixated on what *was* that we aren't able to step forward into what *is*.

Leela catches my eye and gives me a smile so reminiscent of the one she wore that first day in school that it pulls me out of my melancholy. "Can you stay for awhile?"

I smile back. Yes, I can. We have all night, in fact. For now, that's enough.

She grabs a small bin of nail polish from under my bed and removes her favorite color. "Wanna hear a funny story about Beamer and a bottle of ketchup?"

"Yes, please."

Leela twists off the cap and applies the pink shade to my pinkie nail. "It has to do with Summer."

"Even better." The two of us grin at one another.

Leela gets six fingernails into her story when I hear the faint, but unmistakable sound of screaming. Like the concert is coming back. Only no. This screaming is different. It's not thousands of raised voices. It's one.

"He found out how to get into her locker and—"

"What is that?"

Leela stops. "What is *what?*"

"That screaming."

She cocks her head.

The sound grows louder, more defined, and it turns my bones absolutely cold. Because I've heard it before.

"Tess, are you okay?"

"I'm sorry. I have to go." Without explaining anything more than that, I startle.

My eyes pop open in bed.

The screaming continues.

I tear off my covers and sprint toward the noise. Lights come on. Doors open. I sprint faster, then skid to a stop in front of Luka's room. Declan kneels over him as he thrashes in bed and for one illogical moment I think Declan's hurting him. He's hurting Luka in the same way Scarface hurt Luka, because the way he screams and twists is the same, too.

"Wake up, man!" Declan rattles Luka's shoulders.

Luka arches up, his scream splitting the air.

I dig my fingers into my hair. My nails bite into my scalp. *Stop. Make it stop!*

"You're having a nightmare!" Declan yells.

Luka's eyes fly open. He sits up, his sweat-slicked undershirt plastered to his heaving chest. He looks at Declan, looming over his bed. Then he looks at me, huddled in his doorway with my hands smashed over my ears.

CHAPTER THIRTEEN

OFF, OFF, AND AWAY

" **E**verybody back to bed," Cap orders, wheeling down the hallway.

Declan slips past me in the doorway.

Lights turn off. Doors close.

I force my shaky legs to stand, to go to Luka. But he holds up his hand, like he doesn't want me to come any closer.

Cap rolls into the room. "Back to bed, Tess."

"But—"

"You heard me."

Luka sits with his feet on the floor, his head cradled between his hands. "I'm fine," he says. "You can go back to sleep."

Cap nods reassuringly, like everything will be okay.

I stare at Luka. His fingers, which so calmly played with my hair hours ago, are now threaded through his own. I should go to him, comfort him, but it's obvious he doesn't want my comfort. Heaviness drapes across my shoulders as I obey orders and walk away.

Down the hallway, Link's bedroom door is open. I peek inside. Trinkets are scattered about the room—a collection of computers and remotes in varying degrees of assembly. The clock on his bedside table reads 4:32. Going back to sleep isn't going to happen, not when Luka's screams echo inside my skull. So I head to the tech lab instead.

Link is there, sitting in the dark, the computer screen casting his profile in a bluish glow. Did he hear Luka's screaming? I'm not sure how he couldn't have. I'd be surprised if Non or Sticks or whoever's standing guard up above didn't hear it, too.

"Have you been working all night?" I ask.

"I hit a second wind somewhere around two." He stops typing, leans back in his chair, and clasps his hands behind his head.

I scratch the inside of my wrist. "Did Cap tell you that I recruited you to come with me and Jillian and Luka to New Orleans?"

"I've always wanted to see Bourbon Street."

I step inside, sit in the rolling chair beside him, and pick up a stack of identification cards near his elbow. "Did you make these?"

He nods.

"Impressive."

"Yeah, well. Your superpower is battling monsters in the night. Mine is forgery." He picks up his Rubik's Cube and begins twisting. "Just call me your friendly neighborhood identity thief."

Link's always underestimating himself, just because he can't fight. And yet if I had to nominate an MVP down in the hub, it'd probably be him. I swap the cards for a small, orange container. Familiar white pills rattle inside. I've taken them before, against Dr. Roth's cryptic warning. When I was on them, I no longer saw unexplainable things. I no longer had disturbing dreams. Everything supernatural disappeared. "What're these for?"

"Our group of spring breakers."

He means Ellen, Declan, Jose, Ashley, and Danielle, who will be traveling together under the guise of college friends looking to have some fun in the Big Apple. "They're going blind?"

"Just Jose. Cap thinks it's a necessity."

Cap is probably right. Jose is a Fighter and when it comes to Fighters, we draw the enemy's attention all too easily. Guardians have a much easier time slipping under the radar.

"Is Cap going to take them, too?"

"It won't be necessary. Anna can cloak him."

Right. The two are traveling together with Rosie and Bass, a happy family of four. I don't need the pills either. Since Luka is my Keeper, he can cloak me himself.

Link gives the Rubik's Cube another twist, turning three faces to solid color.

I set the bottle of pills beside the IDs. Two cards are missing from the pile—numbers one and two on the FBI's Most Wanted list. I guess when you're on the world news every night, a convincing ID doesn't matter much. "How are Sticks and Non gonna get to Newport?"

"There's a system of believers around the country. I've managed to locate and contact a few so they'll have safe places to hide while they make their way east." Link tosses the cube on the desk. "Want to see my new invention?"

"A new invention, huh? That's good. I was beginning to wonder what you were doing with your time. You know, other than making fifteen fake IDs and organizing a modern day Underground Railroad."

He rolls himself over to a table and holds up three iPods.

"Um, I think Steve Jobs beat you to that one."

"They're not iPods. They're dream phones. At least that's

what I'm calling them."

"Is there something wrong with regular phones?"

"Other than being easy to track and tap, no. Not at all." He plugs a set of earbuds into one of the iPods and sets the device in my palm. "These are like the probes I use in the training center. The left one will put you to sleep instantaneously. This right one will take you to a shared dream space. Basically, any of us will be able to communicate with Cap, no matter how far away we are. Our territories won't matter and no crazy linking skills are required."

I turn the iPod over in my hand. "How in the world do you know how to do this stuff?"

"Computers are my friends."

"Aw, poor guy. Didn't you have any real ones growing up?"

"Make fun all you want, Sassy Pants, but computers are good friends to have. No unpredictable emotions, no confusing motivations. No manipulative behavior to muddy the water." His dimples slowly disappear as he talks. His expression turns serious, cloudy. Far away. Like he's lost in a world I know nothing about.

I suddenly realize how very little I know about his past. Or anyone's here, for that matter. We don't talk about life *before*. It's sort of this unspoken rule. The strange look on his face has me wanting to distract him from whatever unpleasant memories my teasing brought to the surface. "So let's say I want to deliver a message to Cap. How would I do that?"

The distraction works. His posture perks.

"You would push this button." He presses a button on the iPod in his hand. A light on the iPod in mine turns red. "As soon as Cap sees it, he would push his button ..." Link reaches over and pushes the button on the iPod in my hand. Both of the lights turn green. His touch, however, remains. "Once you see the green light, you put on your ear buds and *voila*. You can communicate safely and securely in the shared dream space. No monsters allowed."

I glance up from our hands, suddenly very aware of the fact that we're alone together in the dark. His eyes search mine. For what, I'm not sure. I just know that I'm being hit by a strange bout of self-consciousness and I'm never self-conscious in front of Link. Confused, I pull my hand away and set the device next to the bottle of pills.

The hub feels strange with so many gone. Almost everyone left before breakfast. All that remains is our four-person team, along with Sticks, Non, and Clive. When I asked Cap what would happen to him, he said Sticks and Non would "take care of it". There was no need to elaborate. I picture Clive now, tied up in the training center with a probe attached to his right temple, awaiting his fate. Anytime he falls asleep, he's transported to the dream dojo, isolated from the enemy. Another one of Link's genius ideas.

I follow Jillian down the hallway, wondering if Gabe's body is still in the training center, too. Shuddering, I step inside the common room. Luka stands in the entryway next to Link. Both of them look up and spot me across the room. A few butterflies take flight in my stomach. Luka and I haven't talked about his nightmare. And I was such a weirdo earlier this morning with Link. He was just showing me how to use the dream phones.

With flushed cheeks, I take in my surroundings one last time, wondering if the foosball table will ever be used again. Or the books in the library. Will they remain closed forever? How long before the plants in the greenhouse wither and die? Will anybody besides us know that life existed down here at all? That below the ground in the city of Detroit, a group of people slept and ate and learned and fought?

Jillian and I join the boys by the steel door—the very one Luka and I knocked on a lifetime ago, when we had no idea what waited for us on the other side. Now here I am, wondering the same thing.

"You ready?" Sticks asks.

I swallow and nod.

Sticks unlocks the bolts and opens the door. The hinges release a groan that echoes down the dark corridor. So do Cap's final words to me before he left.

Whatever happens, stay off the radar.

Luka steps out into the hallway. Jillian, Link, and I follow.

"Good luck," Sticks says.

And just like that, the door closes with deafening finality and the world goes black.

Base is gone.

Luka turns on the miniature flashlight attachment on his Swiss Army knife and shines a path to the stairwell. A mouse scampers along the wall. Jillian's breaths are short and quick behind me. We reach the steps and begin our ascent, the darkness fading the higher we climb. Finally, we reach the main level. Shafts of sunlight slash through bits of crumbling wall. Real-live, actual sunlight. It's been three-and-a-half months since I've seen it.

Squinting, I hurry around piles of debris and step outside into the sun. The glorious sun. It shines overhead against a backdrop of hazy blue. My eyes can't handle the brightness. So I close them and tilt my face up and spread my arms wide. The warmth soaks into my skin. Fresh air ruffles wisps of hair against my cheeks. Not even the Detroit smog can dim the euphoria of this moment.

I turn around. Jillian stands beneath the cover of the warehouse, her hand at her forehead like a visor. She looks uncertain, a little afraid. For her, it's been nearly two years.

"Come on," I say, waving her forward.

She takes a tentative step, and then another, until she's standing beside me with a large grin. I'm not sure how long we stay that way—the four of us, like hungry flowers leaning forward. I only know that after finally getting the sun back, I'm more than a little reluctant to put on my hat and sunglasses.

We don't encounter any signs of life—not even a homeless man or woman—until we reach the seedy tattoo parlor called The Dragon Den. Its neon sign buzzes with electricity. Through the grimy window with a dragon painted on the glass, a tattoo artist moves around inside. The corner, usually home to at least one or two ladies of the night, is completely empty. We wait there for five minutes before the cab arrives.

I don't miss the strange look the cabbie gives us as we climb inside. No matter how hard we've tried, we're a conspicuous group. While Luka and I wear the clothes we arrived in at the hub, Link and Jillian are dressed in faded hand-me-downs that don't fit them quite right. Combine that with our pasty skin and our bulging, tattered backpacks, and we're a motley crew.

Caps' warning—*stay off the radar*—replays in my mind.

As we ride to the Greyhound station, I gaze out the window, careful to avoid eye contact with the cab driver.

Detroit is a different city. It's still run-down, with bars over the windows and police cars on most street corners, but all the commotion is gone. No street vendors hawking illegal paraphernalia. No homeless men digging through trash. No scantily-dressed women flashing too much leg to passersby. No sirens. No gunshots. No fights. The chaos that left me feeling safely invisible when Luka and I first came to Detroit has been snuffed out.

"Where is everyone?" I ask.

Luka presses his leg against mine, but it's too late. The cabbie's eyes narrow at me in the rearview mirror. "Where have you been, girl—living in a cave?"

I drop my gaze.

"Governor's taking a page out of Cormack's book. Cleaning up the streets. Getting rid of the riffraff."

The four of us exchange ominous looks. How exactly are they getting rid of them?

"I say good riddance. And about time." The cabbie flicks on his blinker and moves into the left lane. "This city is finally turning itself around."

CHAPTER FOURTEEN

A NASTY SHOCK

I don't take a proper breath until we're on the bus. Luka gives me the seat by the window. Link and Jillian sit in the seats facing ours. After all the passengers have boarded, the bus finds the highway. I don't speak. It's like I'm afraid speaking will draw attention. So I remain silent while the miles accumulate behind us.

Across from me, Link sleeps with his head resting against the window. Each one of his breaths sends a fresh layer of fog across the glass. He's stretched his left leg out so his foot is right next to mine. Beside him, Jillian walks a quarter up and down the knuckles of her right hand.

Luka sets his hand on my knee. "Breathe."

"Aren't I?"

"It's kind of hard to tell, to be honest." His calm demeanor reminds me of our break-in at Shady Wood—the first time around when our physical bodies were actually there. I'd been on the verge of hyperventilation and he was all confident and collected. Like a legit doctor. "Care to tell me what you're thinking?"

"I'm thinking that I'd like you to knock me out and wake me up when we get there."

"That might draw some attention. Would it help if we talked about something instead?"

For a moment, I almost ask him about last night's night-mare, but I kill the question before it has a chance to live. That isn't a conversation for a greyhound bus. "Like?"

He looks up at the bus's ceiling, as if considering. "How about this. What are you most looking forward to when this is all over?"

I force my lungs to expand and contract. "Learning how to surf?"

He leans his head back against the seat. "You'll love it."

"Except there's a good chance I'll be terrible at it. And I'm slightly terrified of sharks."

One side of his mouth quirks into that crooked grin. It doesn't really help with the breathing situation. "Don't worry. I'm a good teacher. And if a shark comes anywhere near you, I'll throw a shield at it."

I laugh. Some of the tension in my shoulders lets go. "Hey Luka?"

"Yeah?"

"Do you really think this will be over someday?"

His eyes meet mine. They're as serious as a heart attack. "Of course."

I relax against the seat, so immensely grateful that Luka's here. That he's okay. Before I get a chance to reciprocate his question, the temperature plummets.

Jillian stops her quarter walking.

Luka's grip tightens on my knee.

And my stomach turns to rock.

At the front of the bus, right next to the driver, darkness materializes out of thin air. I force my lungs to do as Luka said—breathe. I remind myself that this thing—whatever it is—cannot see me. Luka has me cloaked. I'm safe.

So why then, does the darkness creep closer?

I look at Luka. His brow is furrowed in concentration.

Cold sweat prickles beneath my arms. I don't understand what's happening? Why does this thing keep coming closer? Why isn't Luka throwing his shield?

The dark shadow lunges at me.

I rear back in my seat with a sharp intake of breath.

A blast of light bursts in front of my eyes. It doesn't come from Luka. It comes from Jillian. Her shield slams into the shadowed form. The thing hurls through a woman in a business suit, then disappears.

My attention darts around the bus. I'm positive we've caused a scene. We had to. But the people to our left continue their conversation. A man behind us turns the page of a magazine. Link keeps on sleeping. The bus driver keeps on driving. The woman in the business suit, however, has looked up from her newspaper. She looked up the second the shadow flew through her, and now she's peering at me.

I look down, but not quickly enough. Her stare heats the crown of my head. A few seconds tick by before I'm brave enough to peek. Her narrowed eyes are pinned on Luka, whose face has gone pasty white. I bump his leg with mine. He looks at me, a whole army of questions gathering in his dilated pupils. I have them, too. I just can't focus on them right now. Not when the woman is typing something into her phone. She glances up from her screen, looks from me to Luka, then resumes her typing with fast thumbs.

My mouth goes dry.

She recognizes us. I'm sure of it. She recognizes us from the news, she's notifying the authorities, and there's absolutely nothing we can do. We're stuck on this bus until we reach Fort

Wayne, which isn't for another hour and thirty-five minutes.

The time passes in agony. All I can do is exchange worried glances with Jillian and Luka while the lady keeps on staring. When we finally reach our first destination, our worst fear is confirmed. Two police officers stand on either side of a crooked-nosed man dressed in a navy blue windbreaker with the letters FBI stitched in yellow on his sleeve.

My heartbeat crashes against my eardrums.

The memory of two burly men dragging me out of Mr. Lotsam's Current Events class flashes like lightning, making my heart crash faster. I kick the bottom of Link's shoe. When he doesn't wake up, Jillian gives him a sharp jab in the ribs. He jerks awake and wipes at the corner of his mouth.

A few wordless gestures from Jillian and he's caught up to speed.

The driver parks. The staring businesswoman departs faster than everyone else. My escalating panic is about to hurl me off the bus after her. Maybe we can make a run for it. But Luka's hand returns to my knee and holds me in place, whatever confusion he felt earlier gone. Outside the window, the businesswoman approaches the three men. She points to the bus. The guy in the FBI jacket nods.

My panic shifts into fifth gear. I remember the feeling of being restrained. Of the saccharinely sweet nurse jabbing a needle into my neck. The utter helplessness and confusion of not being able to escape, not knowing what was real. It's going to happen again. Only this time, it will happen to Luka, too. And Jillian. And Link. We'll end up as dead as my grandmother.

Passengers begin filing off, oblivious to the tornado of chaos spinning inside of me. Jillian rummages through her backpack. She pulls out a T-shirt and a small bottle of antiseptic from our first aid kit. As discreetly as possible, she douses the T-shirt in rubbing alcohol.

"Link, take my seat," Luka whispers.

Link does so without arguing.

Jillian shares a nod with Luka, like the two hatched some sort of plan while I wasn't looking. She slides her backpack over her shoulders and joins the passengers exiting the bus. With her thumbs tucked beneath the straps, she steps outside and slips past the police officers undetected. Confusion spins the tornado of chaos faster. Is that it, then? Is Jillian leaving us?

"Put your hood up," Luka says, putting his own hood up, too.

Link and I obey.

Luka slips into an unoccupied seat across the aisle.

Outside the window, the FBI agent leaves the two police officers behind and steps onto the bus.

I grab Link's hand.

He doesn't object.

Footsteps slowly approach, like the man's taking a Sunday stroll. I close my eyes, willing him to walk past us. Praying that this is some kind of freak coincidence and there are other wanted fugitives a few rows behind us. It's no use. The footsteps stop beside Link.

"Excuse me, sir," the man says. "I'm going to need to see some identification."

My pulse taps a violent SOS against my wrists. I want to scratch them. I want this to be an awful nightmare. I want to wake up and see Jillian walking the quarter up and down her knuckles again.

Link doesn't move.

"Sir, I'm going to need to see—"

A deafening explosion rattles the windows.

My head snaps up just in time to see Luka sweep the FBI agent's legs out from under him. Luka grabs the holster of his gun and knocks him out cold over the head. The remaining passengers scream and grapple over one another for freedom, as though the next thing to explode will be this bus. Luka pulls me up and I'm running with him and Link to the back exit. Luka rams it open with his shoulder and we jump out into the madness. Jillian runs toward us, waving us on. Luka pushes me forward.

We sprint as far and as fast away as possible. I glance over my shoulder, but nobody pursues us. The explosion and the ensuing pandemonium must have distracted the other police officers. And thanks to Luka, that FBI agent's unconscious on the bus floor. We keep running, turning up and down side streets at random. We run until my lungs burn, until they might explode. Until Luka grabs my waist and we skid to a halt at the end of an alley.

Link bends over his knees. Jillian clutches her side. Luka leans against the brick wall. For a few seconds, there's nothing at all but the sound of panting and my crashing heartbeat.

"What was that explosion?" I finally ask.

"We needed a distraction." Jillian winces like she has an awful stitch in her side. "So I stuffed the T-shirt into a gas tank and lit it on fire with my lighter."

My mouth drops open.

There's a pause, and then Link starts laughing, still bent over his knees from the long-distance sprint.

"That just popped into your head?" I ask.

She shrugs, then nods toward the gun Luka's holding in his hand. A real-life, loaded gun. I've never seen one up close before, at least not while awake. They were prohibited a long time ago, after we removed the second amendment from the constitution. The only people with guns anymore are the police, the military, and—according to my dad—the bad guys.

"Have you ever used one?" Jillian asks him.

Luka shakes his head.

Jillian holds out her hand. He places the weapon in her upturned palm.

"Have *you*?" I ask.

She turns the weapon over in her hands a few times. "It's a Glock 19. Semi-automatic."

My eyes go buggy. Completely, certifiably buggy.

Jillian sits cross-legged on the ground. She clicks something on the gun and a thin, rectangular box falls from the bottom. She sets it in her lap, holds the weapon out to the side, and gives it a cock. A bullet pings onto the ground and bounces to rest by my shoe. Jillian examines the thin box in her lap, pushes it back into place with the heel of her palm, and pulls the top of the gun back. When she lets go, it zips forward with a sharp latching sound.

"This button right here is the safety. You want to make sure to leave that on. Unless it's pointed at someone you want to shoot. Then you can turn it off."

I think my jaw has unhinged. Who is this girl beside me?

She holds the weapon out to Luka, but Luka doesn't take it. So Jillian tucks the gun into the waist of her jeans.

Somewhere in the distance, a siren wails.

Luka presses his back against the brick wall and peeks out

from the alley. "We have to get out of here before every corner of this town is crawling with police."

"How are we going to do that?" Jillian asks.

He points across the street, toward a run-down gas station. There's a Walmart semi parked in the lot.

CHAPTER FIFTEEN

LOST

The driver must be inside the station, buying a donut or using the restroom. Luka unlatches the back, waves the three of us inside, then climbs in after us and quickly closes the door.

The only light comes from the sinking sun shining through the slats. It's just enough to see our surroundings—crates of bread, fruit, canned goods, juice boxes and bottled water. We make our way to the front and crouch behind boxes of Lay's Potato Chips, safely hidden should the driver decide to check on his inventory.

I stay quiet and still for so long that a cramp seizes my calf. Sitting on a bus, followed by full-throttle sprinting, followed by awkward squatting isn't good for any of our muscles. Just as I'm convinced the truck has been abandoned and we're going nowhere, a door opens and shuts and the engine rumbles to life.

We lurch forward.

I let out a deep breath and stretch my legs.

Link opens up a case of bottled water and tosses one to each of us. I guzzle mine with greedy gulps that suck in the plastic, then move on to a meal of bananas and potato chips.

"Where do you think we're headed?" Jillian asks.

Link peels himself a second banana. "Let's hope it's not the local Walmart."

I glance at Luka, who eats in broody silence.

"Hey, look." Jillian points to the dream phone attached to the waist of my jeans.

The red light is on.

I unclip the device. "It's Cap."

"Do you think they reached Newport?" Jillian asks.

"We're about to find out." I hit the button so the light turns green, remove a pair of ear buds from the front pocket of my backpack, and stick them into place. When I open my eyes, I'm inside the dream dojo. Cap is already there, standing on strong, sturdy legs. His face is like a thundercloud.

"What part of *stay off the radar* did you not understand?"

I pull my chin back. He already knows about the explosion and our narrow escape? I know news travels fast, but this is a little extreme.

"You're not supposed to play the hero right now, Tess. Your job is to keep your head down and get to New Orleans."

My brow furrows. *Play the hero?*

He puts his hands on his hips, his lips pulling so tight and thin I think he might spit. "You just left the hub and you're already off fighting?"

"*Fighting?* I haven't been fighting. We've been too busy running."

His brow furrows back at me. My obvious confusion seems to have punctured his steam.

"Somebody recognized us on the bus. By the time we got to Fort Wayne, an FBI agent was waiting. Jillian had to blow something up to cause a diversion and—"

He holds up his hands. "*Whoa, whoa, whoa.* What are you talking about?"

"A woman recognized me and Luka. She called the police. Jillian blew up a car. Luka knocked out the FBI agent, stole his *gun*, and we hightailed it out of there." Judging by the way Cap's standing there blinking at me, it's a safe bet we're not on the same page. "What fighting are you talking about?"

"Did you say Jillian *blew up a car*?"

"Yes. As a diversion. Now we're in the back of a Walmart semitrailer, headed who knows where." And I'm sure at any minute, the entire event will hit the news. I'm equally sure my face and Luka's face will be everywhere. The only silver lining? Jillian and Link should be fine. The woman never glanced twice at them.

"You really haven't been fighting?"

"No. Jillian threw a shield, but that was it."

Cap rubs his chin.

"Why did you think I was fighting?"

"We reached headquarters a little while ago. As soon as we arrived, the leader asked if we knew anything about a recent altercation. Word of it reached him here in Newport."

"What kind of altercation?"

"A Fighter took out twenty enemy soldiers at one time."

My eyes go wide. When I took out that many at once, it required Gabe's life. If a Fighter was able to do that completely on his or her own, then he or she must be incredibly powerful. "Do you know where the fight took place?"

"Somewhere in Iowa."

"Do you think the Fighter is trying to get to Newport? Do we know if it's a man or a woman? Are there any other clues?"

A shadow rolls across Cap's face.

"I mean, if this person took out twenty at once—"

"Forget about the Fighter."

"But Cap—"

"The journals, Tess. That's your mission. Get to the Rivards in New Orleans and learn as much as you can about the prophecy."

"And how are we supposed to do that? Luka and I are going to be everywhere on the news and ..." I take a deep breath.

"And *what?*"

"Luka's cloak isn't working."

"*What?*"

"Something showed up on the bus. It came at me. Jillian had to throw a shield. It was like Luka couldn't. I don't get it, Cap. What does this mean? Why would Luka's cloak fail?"

He mutters a curse under his breath and massages the bridge of his nose. "We suspected there might be ramifications."

"Ramifications. You mean ... you're saying ..." My thoughts scramble to make sense of Cap's words. "You think Luka lost his gifting?"

"I don't know." Cap frowns. "But if he can't cloak you, then we're in trouble. The quicker you get to the Rivards, the better."

I open my eyes to a sea of green.

Luka is staring at me. "What did Cap say?"

I pull the ear buds from my ears.

Link sits on a crate of pasta, his iPad out and on while Jillian bends over his shoulder. Both are looking at me, too.

I sit up a little straighter. "They reached headquarters."

Jillian lets out a loud breath.

"I guess there are rumors circulating about a really powerful

Fighter on the move somewhere in Iowa. Cap thought it was me."

"Did you tell him what happened?" Jillian asks.

I nod.

"You told him everything?" Luka's question is soaked with meaning.

I nod again.

"What did he say?"

I sever eye contact. I've always been a lousy liar, and right now I'm positive Cap's speculation would destroy him. "Maybe it was just a fluke."

Luka leans against the side of the trailer and kneads his forehead.

"Whoa!"

Jillian and I turn our attention to Link.

He gapes at his iPad. "We just bumped Non and Sticks to numbers five and six on FBI's Most Wanted list."

I scramble over to his side. "*Five* and *six?*"

Link found a live newsfeed. It's playing security camera footage. I watch as the four of us board the bus. Luka steals the agent's gun. A different angle of Jillian blowing up a car. Our faces appear on the screen, along with our real names and the names we used to purchase our bus tickets. Our fake identities are shot. And Link and Jillian are definitely not in the clear.

The camera pans to a female news anchor. "Teresa Eckhart, you will remember, escaped the Edward Brooks Facility this past January with the assistance of Luka Williams. Both are wanted for the murder of Dr. Charles Roth."

"*Murder?*" The word bursts out of my mouth. "His death was ruled a suicide. They can't just change it like that."

Surely the public will notice the blaring inconsistency.

"Apparently they can." Link clicks out of the newsfeed and opens up the FBI's website. He clicks on the Most Wanted list. Sure enough, the four of us are there, with me taking the lead. I am officially the nation's most wanted criminal. With a quarter of a million bounty on my head.

Four hours as a stowaway with no end in sight has me regretting my second water bottle. According to Link and the compass on his iPad, we're veering more west than south, which means we need to get off this truck as soon as possible. Preferably before my bladder explodes.

Just when I think it might, a box of Lay's Potato Chips slides toward my legs. The truck is finally slowing down. Brakes squeak. A gear shifts. Luka holds up his flashlight. Jillian lifts her head off Link's shoulder and looks around with disoriented eyes.

Everything in the back of the trailer slides left as the semi turns, accelerates a bit, then slows again, this time to a full stop. The engine goes quiet. Luka shuts off the flashlight. All I can see are three pairs of round white eyes blinking in the dark.

A door opens and closes.

We scramble to the very front of the trailer, as far away from the back hatch as possible and crouch out of sight behind the bananas. Seconds tick into a minute, then two, then three. The trailer remains closed.

My fingers dig into the wooden crate. If we wait too long, we'll miss our opportunity. I imagine being stuck back here for another five hours. My bladder won't make it. As if reading my mind, Luka motions for us to follow him.

When we reach the back, he presses his ear to the metal.

We could be anywhere. Another gas station. A busy truck stop. Inside a Walmart warehouse. The only way to find out is to open the door. Luka inches it open the tiniest crack.

Jillian peeks outside. "All I can see is cement."

The engine roars to life.

I grab Luka's arm.

He opens the door wider. I don't give myself time to second guess. I hop out into the night and duck behind a row of bushes. Link, Jillian, and Luka jump out behind me. And the semi drives away.

Crickets chirp in the bushes. The air smells like sulfur. It reminds me of the year we lived in Pennsylvania, two miles north of a paper mill. Pete called the town Fartsville, even though its real name was Pinkerton or Tinkerton or something like that. I lift my head over the shrubs. We landed in a deserted rest stop. There's not another vehicle in sight.

"The Eye of Sauron," Link whispers.

I look at him. "What?"

He points.

I follow its trajectory up and to the left—toward a security camera that swivels slowly back and forth on the corner of the building—and duck further behind the bushes. We wait until the camera points as far away as possible, then sprint around to the back of the building. There's an open field. And roughly a hundred yards past that, a stretch of dense trees.

We make a run for it.

Beneath a star-freckled sky, with my backpack jostling back and forth on my back, I sprint for the trees. I don't stop until I'm safely beneath the canopy. Once I am, I rest my hands on my knees and work on catching my breath, my bladder temporarily forgotten.

Luka sets his backpack against a tree. A shaft of moonlight filters through the leaves above and slashes across his face. He looks absolutely perfect. And absolutely tortured.

"Somebody run at Tess."

I stand up straight. "What?"

He comes to my side, his attention focused on Link and Jillian. "Somebody run at Tess."

Judging by the way they exchange an uncertain look, the two of them are just as confused by the bizarre command as I am. Neither of them move.

"Somebody run at her!"

A flock of sleeping birds take flight overhead.

My confusion flies with them. I know what this is about. Luka wants to see if he can throw a shield. He's been waiting to do this ever since his cloak failed back there on that bus.

Jillian and Link remain in place. I don't blame them. I've seen Luka's shields. Getting hit by one can't be very pleasant.

He grits his teeth. "Please."

It's Jillian who turns sympathetic. She shrugs off her backpack, backs up several paces, screws up her face in the way people do when they're bracing for pain, and begins to run.

"Faster!" Luka shouts.

Her run turns into a sprint, and although she's headed straight for me, I'm not looking at her. I'm too consumed with the boy beside me. His posture is fierce. His face, terrifyingly gorgeous as Jillian closes in. She grows in the periphery of my vision. Any millisecond Luka will throw a shield and the same burst of light that came in the stairwell of Shady Wood will slam into her.

Only nothing happens.

I squeeze my eyes tight.

Luka snags my waist and pulls me out of danger just as Jillian rushes past. He holds me against him for a second, his shoulders rising and falling with quick breaths. When he lets me go, he turns up his palms and stares at his fingers like they hold no power at all.

Chapter Sixteen

Help

We hike through the night, stopping every couple of miles to take a short rest and drink from the water bottles we stuffed in our backpacks. According to Link's iPad, we are in eastern Missouri, heading toward a town called Greeley. It has railroad tracks that run along the Mississippi River, all the way north to Minneapolis, and all the way south to New Orleans. Looks like I'll get to scratch train-hopping off my bucket list.

Luka leads the way. He hasn't said anything since his experiment with Jillian, and I don't know how to pull him free from the dark hole he's fallen into. Honestly? I'm afraid to say anything. I'm afraid if I do, he'll see that deep down, his pain is my relief. Panic has stalked the edges of my mind ever since Cap told me about transurgence. But if Luka lost his powers as my Keeper, then transurgence loses its power, too. The boy I love is safe—a fact that brings a huge sense of release. For Luka? Not so much. Which is why I tuck the emotion away and focus on the path in front of me.

I've always loved hiking. I spent hours exploring the redwoods outside my home in Thornsdale. However, hiking fifteen miles straight with exhaustion dragging at every muscle is an entirely different beast. The best distraction is conversation, and since Luka's not talking and Link has turned into a walking-zombie-of-a-caboose, I'm left with Jillian. I can't stop thinking about the weapon tucked inside the waist of her jeans.

"How do you know so much about guns?" I ask her.

"My dad was in the CIA."

"*The CIA?*" I grab the branch Luka holds for me so it won't fly back and whack me in the face.

"He was a sniper."

My laugh comes before I can stop it. "You're serious?"

"As a heart attack." She takes the branch from me and hands it back to Link.

"Why didn't you ever say anything?"

"It's not something that comes up in casual conversation."

"Wow." I shake my head. "The CIA."

"If he saw that I was on the Most Wanted list, he'd be rolling in his grave."

His grave. The two words chase all my amusement away. Jillian's dad is no longer living. "What happened to him?"

"He was killed on the job."

I step over a jutting root, my mind wandering to my own father. I try not to think about him too much. Currently, he's locked in prison for a crime he didn't commit. A crime I committed, actually. A truth that haunts me. Since I can't do anything to change the situation at the moment, I usually try to push the whole thing away. A mind can only stretch in so many directions before it starts going insane. Still, my father is alive, which means I have hope that I'll be with him again. For Jillian, that hope is gone. "I'm sorry."

She moves through a shaft of moonlight, a sad smile on her face. "He taught me all about guns. I'm pretty sure it gave my mom ulcers."

"Sounds like our moms would be good friends."

"Maybe they will be someday."

I smile at the thought. It's a nice one. "Yeah."

Twigs snap under our feet. I snag a berry off the branch of a tall bush, my stomach growling. Too bad my hiking skills don't extend to berry deciphering. Having no idea if it's safe to eat or not, I let it drop to the ground. "So how'd you end up at the hub?"

"I started experiencing symptoms after my dad died. My mom thought my grief was manifesting itself in bizarre ways, so she brought me to Dr. Carlyle. When I explained my symptoms, he asked to speak with me in private, then he told me what was happening."

"And you just believed him?"

"I didn't have a reason not to. My dad always believed in good and evil. *Jillian*, he'd say. *There are other forces at play in this world. Forces we can't see.* He saw too much darkness with his own eyes to be convinced otherwise, no matter what the government or science had to say about it."

Our moms might be similar. Our dads, on the other hand? Not so much. "So you ran away?"

"He said I was in danger. He told me about the hub. And I left. I haven't seen my family in two years, but I dream about them almost every night."

There's a pang in my chest. A deep ache that rears its head at night, when I'm laying in bed by myself. I'm not the only one missing my family. It must be worse for Jillian. She had to leave her mom in the midst of grieving her dad.

"I keep wondering what they must be thinking, seeing my face on the Most Wanted list." Jillian picks up a stick off the ground and hacks at some weeds. "One thing's for certain. When all of this is over, I'll have a lifetime of crazy stories to tell them."

We share a smile. Not many people would believe the stories we have to tell.

As birds begin to chirp and a soft blush paints the eastern horizon, we reach the outskirts of Greeley. I expect a small, sleepy river town. Maybe a jogger or a dog-walker out before work. I definitely don't expect the sound of men's voices.

All four of us stop abruptly, then duck behind some shrubs. I peek through the leaves. Two police cruisers idle inside a CVS parking lot. A huddle of five men stand nearby. Four of them wear standard police uniform. The fifth wears a navy blue windbreaker that triggers a cold feeling in my gut. When he turns around, a gasp tumbles out of my mouth.

Luka pulls me down, completely out of sight.

My breathing turns jagged. The fifth man is the FBI agent Luka knocked out on the bus. *How is he here?* How could he have possibly tracked us from Fort Wayne, Indiana to the obscure town of Greeley, Missouri? It doesn't make any sense. It's utterly impossible.

Unless …

My attention wanders to Jillian. She volunteered so quickly when Cap said I needed a team. It wouldn't have been hard for her to call the police, not with the emergency phone in Link's backpack and the bathroom breaks we took during our fifteen-mile hike. If our most recent conversation is proof of anything, it's how little I actually know her.

I shake my head. *No.* The exhaustion is talking. I can trust Jillian. She blew up a car to save us. She has a gun tucked into the waistband of her pants, which means she could have taken us hostage if she'd wanted to turn us in. She's number four on the Most Wanted list, for crying out loud. And more important than any of that, she's my friend.

You thought Clive was your ally ...

I squeeze my eyes shut, forcing the dark thought away.

Two car doors open, one after the other.

I squint through the buds of green and watch in horror as a large German shepherd hops out of the back seat. A second— even larger than the first—hops out of the other cruiser. The two dogs sit at attention, their ears perked while every last drop of warmth drains from my face.

The FBI agent pulls a clear plastic bag from the front pocket of his windbreaker. I squint harder, trying to bring whatever's inside into focus. It looks like the same fabric from the Greyhound bus seats. I can hear the dogs' eager *sniff-sniff-sniffs*—like a salt shaker being rattled back and forth—all the way from where I'm laying. The agent closes the bag and slides it back into his pocket.

The dogs lift their heads.

My heart slams into my throat.

I scoot back, away on all fours. The two animals snap their heads in our direction. Luka pulls me up to standing and we take off, crashing through the woods, leaping over rocks and roots. Tree branches and leaves swipe and cut at our hands and faces.

I can hear them behind us. Barking. Running. Closing in. I can practically feel their sharp teeth sinking into my flesh. I can see their jaws locking around Luka's jugular. Panic hurls me forward. I run faster. Faster. And then suddenly, my foot catches. An explosion of pain sears up my ankle. I slam against the ground with a loud *oomph* that knocks out all my wind, and I skid forward, shards of rock and bits of dirt tearing my skin.

Luka pulls me up and somehow, we're tumbling down a steep ravine. We slide to a halt. He drags me back beneath a small cleft and tucks me against his side so I'm pressed between him and a wall of earth.

Everything comes into sharp focus.

I can smell pine and dirt. Wet leaves and moss. The faint scent of fabric softener pressed into Luka's shirt, even now. I swear I can smell dog breath, too. Link and Jillian pant nearby. Luka's heart thuds against my ear. The dogs sniff. They're right over our heads.

And then, a burst of heat so intense, the hairs on my arms curl.

There's a sharp yelp, followed by a high-pitched whine. Footsteps crash to a stop, as though the men have finally caught up with their furry counterparts.

"What's the matter with them?" someone asks.

"Why are they acting like that?" another says between pants.

There's another loud yelp.

The searing heat grows hotter, then slowly diminishes. The barking resumes, only instead of coming closer it fades off to the left.

"They must have doubled back."

"Come on, let's go!"

The men chase after the dogs. And the dogs are running away.

Luka pulls me out of the cleft and up into standing. A strange tail of light—like the dancing spots that come after staring directly into the sun—trails off into the direction the dogs ran.

"What is that?" Jillian asks.

Link stares after the glittering spots as they slowly fade away. "I don't know, but we have to get to the tracks fast."

"Can you make it?" Luka asks me.

The second I bear weight on my foot, pain stabs my ankle like a red-hot fire poker, but I bite back my grimace and nod.

He takes my backpack. "Are you sure?"

A train whistle blows in the distance.

No, I'm not sure. But there's no time for injuries. Gritting my teeth, I break into a jog, doing my best to hide my limp. We skirt around the outer limits of Greeley as the train whistle grows louder. Our jogging turns into a run. The pain in my ankle is nearly blinding. We come out into a clearing, where the freight train rumbles along the tracks.

Link and Jillian's run turns into a sprint. Link tosses his bag into a rail car, grabs onto a handhold, and swings himself in. So does Jillian. I try to catch up, but my legs are shaking so bad I can't go any faster. Tears sting my eyes. I will never make it. But Luka is right beside me. He locks his arm around my waist, pulls me forward, snags a handhold and sweeps us both up into the railcar.

Dark spots swim in my vision. Cold sweat prickles across my skin. My stomach rolls. I cover my face and clench my teeth and try to take even breaths, but the pain is unbearable.

Luka crouches beside me. He rolls up my pant leg, so gently I can barely feel the touch.

"Did she break something?" Jillian asks.

"I don't know."

Their voices grow more muffled, like I'm hearing them underwater.

"It looks broken."

"How is she going to get anywhere?"

"I'll carry her."

It's the last thing I hear before passing out.

CHAPTER SEVENTEEN
ONE FINAL, FADING SNIPPET

"**H**is name is Agent Michael Bledsoe," a familiar voice says. "According to his profile, he's been working for the FBI for ten years. Married for eighteen. He and his wife have two daughters. Their oldest is seventeen."

"Our age."

The floor beneath me rattles.

I open one eye. I'm staring up at a metal ceiling. Sunlight filters inside the strange box, painting everything too bright. My body cries out in pain, the worst of which throbs in my ankle. Memories shift like bits of glass inside a kaleidoscope.

The FBI agent in Greeley.

Being chased by two German shepherds.

Sliding down a ravine.

The blast of mysterious heat.

Hopping on a train. Or rather, Luka hopping me on a train.

I spot him in the corner of the railcar, doing push-ups fast and quick, like he's racing someone. Maybe he's racing himself. Maybe he thinks enough exercise will chase away the things that haunt him. Or get back the things he's lost.

"Hey." Jillian sits up on her knees. "You're awake."

Barely, and I'm not sure I want to be. Never in my life have I wanted a dose of pain medication so badly. My head pounds.

My ankle burns. Every muscle in my body aches. I try to push myself up, but a groan slides past my lips.

Luka pushes all the way up to help me.

Gritting my teeth, I lean back against one of the walls of the railcar. "How long have I been out?"

"A few hours." He hands me a water bottle.

I twist off the cap and take a long drink. When my throat no longer feels like the Sahara Desert, I notice some things. Like how the dirt from the scrapes in my palms has been cleaned away, and ointment rubbed into the cuts. I push up the sleeves of my hoodie. My elbows are bandaged.

"I patched you up with Jillian's first aid kit."

Touched, I look into Luka's eyes. They're as green as clover and as deep as the ocean. Strands of dark hair stick to his forehead. I want to reach out and press away the furrow between his brow. *See*, I want to say, *just because you can't throw a shield doesn't mean you can't protect me.* Somehow, I don't think the words will bring him much comfort. So instead, I say a simple thank you.

Luka shrugs it off.

Across from me, Link peers at his iPad, deep in focus. Jillian sits beside him, clicking her lighter so the flame dances to life and dies, dances to life and dies, over and over and over again. I pull the dream phone off my belt loop. Jillian looks at me over the flame. "The light turned green after you passed out. Luka went in your place."

I pull down my sleeves. "Did Cap have news?"

"Nothing, really," Luka says. "He just wanted to check in."

"Any word from Sticks and Non?"

"They arrived at headquarters."

"Are they okay?"

"They're fine."

Then why is Luka avoiding eye contact? Did Cap tell Luka his theory about the ramifications? "What aren't you telling me?"

"It's nothing."

"It's obviously something."

"Cap doesn't want you obsessing over it."

"Obsessing over *what?*" But as soon as the question escapes, I know. And the knowing has me sitting up straighter. "It's about the Fighter, isn't it? Sticks and Non heard something."

"There's been rumblings of another altercation."

My skin tingles.

Link winks at me over his iPad. "Looks like Xena finally has some competition."

The train rumbles along the tracks, carrying us south. I sit on the edge of the railcar, my feet dangling over the side. Sun shines through the pine trees rolling past, dappling shards of light across the pages of the journal in my lap.

Behind me, one of my sleeping teammates stirs.

I flip another page, skimming the familiar scrawl as if clues about the prophecy might suddenly appear. I search in vain. I've studied these journals extensively. There's nothing but one vague reference.

Link scoots beside me and rubs his eyes. "Couldn't sleep?"

"Not really."

He runs his hand over the crown of his shaggy hair, momentarily flattening a cowlick. "Find anything interesting?"

I close the composition notebook and shake my head, inhaling fresh air deep inside my lungs. "Do you think we'll make it to the Rivards?"

"Of course."

I wish I could have some of his confidence. Honestly, it all feels a little hopeless. Between our faces everywhere on the news and my ruined ankle, I have no idea how we're supposed to get anywhere, especially without Luka's cloak. I can't shake the feeling that this moment—right here—is one final, fading snippet of calm before the end. It doesn't seem like we can climb out of this particular hole. But then I remember the blast of heat and the trail of light that chased the barking dogs away. "Hey Link?"

"Yeah?"

"What do you think happened with those dogs?"

The evening breezes past the open railcar, ruffling his hair. He folds his hands between his knees and gives me a telling smile. "Come on, Xena, you know."

He's right. I do. But sometimes it's nice to hear the things I know verbalized. Sometimes it makes me feel less crazy. Or at least less alone in my craziness.

"We had help," he says simply.

I scratch my wrist. "Why don't you think we have help all the time?"

He gives me a light nudge with his elbow.

"What?"

"Just because we see supernatural things, doesn't mean we see all of it, all the time." I must look confused, because Link sighs and tries again. "Help might not always be as obvious as it was back there in Greeley, but that doesn't mean it's any less present."

"So you think we have help all the time?"

"It's just a theory, but yeah. I guess I do."

His just-a-theory has memories wiggling to the front of my mind, one sharper than the rest. I'm back in Motel California with Luka, before I knew about Shields and Keepers and *anima* and prophecies. We were waiting for Leela, and I had some sort of vision. It wasn't a dream. It couldn't have been. I never fell asleep, and yet for a brief moment in time, I saw them—an army of light surrounding me. As soon as Luka touched my shoulder, the beings disappeared. But that doesn't necessarily mean they went away. How else did we make it to Detroit and find the hub safely?

Someone moves behind us.

I press my hand against the metal floor and twist around.

Luka turns over in his sleep, his eyelids twitching. His head wrenches one way, then the other. He mumbles something incoherent. He jerks and groans.

My hands clamp over my ears. But before his groan can turn into anything louder, Link shakes him awake. The railcar goes quiet. My head does not.

The memory of Luka's scream reverberates inside my skull. I'm not sure it will ever stop.

CHAPTER EIGHTEEN

EXPECTED

I t's time to jump.

The nighttime air is heavy with humidity. And also, the smell of dead fish. We've reached New Orleans. I stand on the edge of the railcar between Jillian and Luka, staring at the dark ground whizzing by. Twenty-five miles per hour has never felt so fast. But there's no other option. If we don't jump now, we'll end up in a coal yard.

Luka takes my hand. My palm is sweaty. I'm too preoccupied with my racing heart and swollen ankle to care. He gives my hand a gentle squeeze. "You ready?"

I nod.

The train lets loose a loud, haunting whistle.

We toss our bags out into the dark, and on the count of three, we jump. I take the full brunt of the impact on my uninjured leg and fall into a roll. Pebble and rock tear through my jeans and bite into my skin.

For a second, all I can hear is the sound of my own heavy breathing.

And then, "Is everyone intact?"

It's Jillian.

There's a glint of black metal an arm-reach away. The gun. It must have fallen out when Jillian tumbled. I should pick it up and give to her. I don't know the first thing about using it.

Instead, I tuck the weapon inside the waist of my jeans as Luka pulls me up into standing.

He has both of our backpacks. "You okay?"

"I think so."

"Link?" Jillian calls.

He hobbles toward us, brushing debris from his clothes. "That looks a lot cooler in the movies."

No kidding.

The last of the train rumbles past. Behind us, the Mississippi River laps at the rocks. In front, another train sits unmoving on a set of parallel tracks, hiding us from view. And a little further ahead, music plays. A jazz band. I limp forward and peek through two of the unmoving railcars. A car-lined street ends in a T, with barricades blocking off the road of what appears to be some sort of festival.

"We should leave our backpacks here. We won't stick out so much that way." Luka shoves our bags beneath the railcar. "Hopefully one of the Rivards can get them for us tomorrow."

Jillian and Link slide theirs beside ours.

I'm not sure the "no backpack" thing will help much. The four of us are a mess. After hiking fifteen miles and running for our lives and sliding down a ravine and jumping out of a train, our clothes are basically wrecked.

"Here, get on my back."

I blink at Luka. "What?"

"It's a party. Nobody's going to notice if a guy has a girl on his back, but they will notice if you're limping around."

As much as I want to say I'm fine, his logic makes sense. And my ankle kills. With Link and Jillian's help, I climb onto Luka's back, trying not to think about my legs wrapped around his waist, or his warm hands on my thighs as we approach the noise.

The music grows louder. The smell of fried chicken and beer gets stronger. Once we reach the crowd, I don't think we look too out of the ordinary. Nobody knows my heart is crashing inside of my chest. Except for Luka. I'm sure he can feel it between his shoulder blades. We weave through the bodies, carving a small path through the partiers. They wear beaded necklaces and funny hats, only it's not Mardi Gras.

A woman with a cartful gives Luka a lewd once-over, calls him honey and hands him two cheaply made glittery top hats. He takes them without looking, puts one on his head and hands one back to me. I put it on eagerly, thankful for the extra cover. And just when I finally convince my heart to settle down—that we're going to be okay—a very inebriated man bumps into Jillian. Hard. The force of the collision has her tumbling into a woman on her left.

I watch it all unfold in slow motion.

The woman's bottle falls and shatters against the cement. Bits of glass and beer splatter her shoes. She shrieks. Takes a step back. Then looks up at Jillian with venom in her eyes, as though she's going to tell her off with a whole lot of four-letter words. But the second she opens her mouth, something in her expression changes. The venom melts away. Her narrow eyes go round as they slide from Jillian to Link, neither of whom have hats.

Luka nudges Jillian forward. Away from the woman. Away from the splattered beer.

I glance over my shoulder. The woman grabs the attention of a nearby police officer and points in our direction.

My heart slams into my throat. I tighten my grip around Luka's shoulders and yell for him to run. His pace quickens.

He cuts through the crowd until we reach a narrow side street. I slide off Luka's back and run for my life, the pain in my ankle a forgotten thing. My hat flies off. I don't stop to get it. We sprint away from the music and the sound of a blowing whistle and I swear, barking dogs. But no. Surely that last one's in my imagination. We run until there's nothing but our heavy breathing and the dark, empty street and our shoes hitting pavement.

I have no idea where we're going or what happened to Jillian and Link. We must have lost them in the crowd. All I can do is hope and pray they are okay as Luka and I keep going, straight ahead toward a crossroad, where a trolley filled with boisterous partygoers rolls past. When the trolley passes, we skid to a stop right in front of the curb.

My eyes go buggy. What I'm seeing can't be possible. This has to be a dream. But when I scratch the inside of my wrist, it burns. Which means Agent Michael Bledsoe is really standing across the street from us, drawing his gun. "Hands in the air! Now!"

Luka shifts in front of me and puts his hands up.

Mine reach into the waist of my jeans and pull out the weapon. The gun. I grip the cold metal between my hands and point it at its original owner. I have no idea what I'm doing. I don't even remember where that safety button is. If I pulled the trigger, I'm pretty sure nothing would happen. Thankfully, Bledsoe doesn't know that.

A block away, a garbage truck turns onto the street and ambles toward us.

"Drop your weapon!" Agent Bledsoe yells.

My hands shake, my attention sliding left, toward the approaching truck.

"Right now. Gun down!"

But it's too late.

The garbage truck passes in front of us. Luka wraps his arm around my waist. Grabs a handhold on the truck's side. And scoops us both off the ground, onto a ledge. The sudden forward momentum gives me whiplash.

Agent Bledsoe shouts.

The oblivious truck driver turns down another street, picks up speed, and turns down another. Luka lets go of the handle and we jump off. I muffle a loud gasp. Fire rages in my ankle. Trying to ignore it, I slink into the shadows and tuck the gun back into the waist of my jeans.

Except for a dingy neon sign across the street advertising a local tavern, the street is abandoned and dark. Any second it will be crawling with cops. We need to get to safety and we need to get there fast.

But where? The tavern?

I glance at the sign. Something on it has me doing a double take. I'm positive I'm seeing things. Except no. I'm not. It's there. Off in the corner, like a hardly-noticeable bit of graffiti. I point at the inky swirls. "Do you see that?"

"What?"

"The symbol on the sign. Upper right corner."

Luka cocks his head and nods.

It's all the verification I need. I grab his hand and pull him across the street.

"Tess, what are you doing?"

"It's safe."

"How do you know?"

"Because that symbol is the same one on all the journals." And the journals belong to the Rivards. And the Rivards are on our side. It can't be a coincidence.

Luka opens the door and we step inside.

Except for a broad-shouldered bartender and a woman wearing a skirt so short it's barely a skirt at all, the tavern is empty. The bartender pours amber liquid into a shot glass. The woman knocks it back and wipes her mouth, smearing a streak of blood-red lipstick across her forearm, then ogles Luka as lewdly as the lady with the hats. "I think some jailbait just stepped inside your tav, Hez."

The bartender refills her glass, not bothering to look in our direction. "We don't serve minors here."

I stay where I'm standing, not nearly as confident on this side of the door as I was on the other. I'd give anything for that hat back. Some measure of cover in case that symbol is a fluke. Luka must have lost his, too, as it's no longer on his head. I swallow. "There's a symbol on your sign out front."

The bartender's attention snaps to me, standing in the doorway beside Luka. He pulls a white rag from his back pocket and begins wiping a beer glass dry, eying us with unmistakable interest.

"What she talking about, Hez? There ain't no symbol on that sign." The lady with the short skirt pours another shot down her throat, then pats the empty stool beside her. "Why don't your tall, dark, and handsome mister come over here? I sure wouldn't mind his company."

Luka's posture stiffens.

The bartender has yet to peel his attention away.

I take a small, hesitant step forward. "Do you know the Rivards?"

He sets the glass on a shelf and studies me for a bit longer. I can't tell if my questions interest him, or if he's recognized our mugs from TV. Finally, he stuffs the rag back into his pocket. "Follow me."

"Where're you goin'?" the woman asks.

The man—*Hez*—doesn't answer her. He doesn't wait to see if we're following either. He walks through a doorway behind the bar. I limp after him—around the bar, through the door, up a set of rickety stairs, into a spacious, sparse room that has a bed, a dresser, a recliner, a TV, and a desk in one corner.

The bartender closes the door behind us. When he turns around, his eyes are bright. Excited. "It's been years since anyone's seen that symbol."

I almost melt into a puddle of relief. "You know the Rivards?"

"Every Believer south of the Mason Dixon line knows the Rivards." He reaches out a meaty paw and shakes our hands. "Name's Hezekiah. Welcome to New Orleans. Cressida has been expecting you."

Chapter Nineteen

Tests

As Hezekiah makes a phone call, I peek out the window of his second floor apartment, my mind buzzing with questions. Namely, how in the world is Agent Bledsoe here in New Orleans when early this morning, he was in Greeley, Missouri? I look at Luka who looks back at me, the same question reflected in his eyes. My suspicion from earlier returns, stronger than before. I hate even thinking it, but what other explanation is there? "It's like somebody's giving the authorities our location," I whisper.

The muscle in his jaw ticks.

"Do you think we can trust Jillian?"

"What about Link?"

"No way. It's absolutely not Link."

My quick response has Luka raising his eyebrows. "He's the one with the phone. It wouldn't have been that hard for him to make a phone call or two."

I shake my head. Vehemently.

"Why not?"

"Because I trust him. One hundred percent. And besides, I volunteered Link to come, remember? Jillian volunteered herself."

"She blew up a car so we could get away."

He's right. She did. I want to trust her. I think I can trust

114

her. But I also thought I could trust Clive. I knead my temples, as if this might loosen the knots in my brain and the worry in my heart. Link is out there. He's out there with a potential betrayer. The thought makes me sick to my stomach.

Hezekiah hangs up the phone and claps his hands. "All right. Time to go."

"Can you help us find our friend? We got split up when we started running."

He starts shaking his head before I can finish. "I'm afraid that's a bad idea."

"But the city is crawling with cops."

"Exactly."

"Link can take care of himself," Luka says.

I shake my head, hating Luka's answer. What if Link had that same attitude when it had been Luka in need of saving? "You owe him."

"I owe him?"

"He helped save you. Nobody at the hub believed that you were still alive. Nobody except him. Without Link, you'd still be—" I stop myself from saying anything more. Luka doesn't need the reminder of where he'd still be. I'm pretty sure he has them every time he falls asleep.

"Link has the address. He knows where to go."

"An address won't do him any good if he's being gunned down in an alleyway!" I turn to Hezekiah. "Please help me find him."

"I will, as soon I get you safely to the Rivards."

A sinking sensation falls through my stomach. What if it's too late by then? But arguing is no use. Luka won't help and Hezekiah won't budge. He ushers us out a back exit, into a navy sedan parked behind the tavern. Luka and I crouch in the back seat while we drive further and further away from the French Quarter, a bluesy sax playing from the speakers.

"Lots of flashing blue and red lights," he says, drumming his thumbs against the steering wheel. "Make sure to stay out of sight back there."

I wrap my arms around my knees, trying to ignore the sharp pain in my ankle and the cool metal of the gun against my back.

"Should we be concerned about your customer in the bar?" Luka asks. "We just left her there. What if someone walks inside and asks her if she's seen us?"

"Stacy'd sooner sober up than talk to a cop."

"And if the police show up at the Rivards?"

The question grabs my attention. If Jillian is the one handing out our location, then of course she'd alert the police that we were headed to the Rivards.

"You don't have to worry about that. The Rivard home is very well guarded."

What's that supposed to mean?

Luka and I exchange a look. His eyes are filled with unspoken words, an entire conversation that saturates the small, dark space between us. He's sorry about Link. He's sorry I'm worried. Just not sorry enough to help me convince Hezekiah to change his mind.

Hezekiah starts humming along with the music.

The scent of jasmine blows in through his opened window. The sweet fragrance makes my dark thoughts feel darker. I picture Claire, reaching out her foot to trip me. Luka, bound and dragged away. Clive, dropping his cloak. Jillian, handing our location to the enemy while pretending to be my friend. Link, somewhere out in the city, cuffed and dragged in for questioning. Or shot in the back by a crooked-nosed FBI agent. The what-ifs expand and swirl into a dense, dark cloud. The pain in my ankle grows worse with each passing mile. Until finally, Hezekiah says it's safe to sit up and a strange glow filters into the car above our heads.

Curious, I rise up onto the seat. A gasp tumbles past my lips.

We've turned down a private lane that leads toward an expansive lawn enclosed by an iron fence. And standing guard on either side of the gate are two sentinel-like beings that light up the night. I gape, the strangest combination of hope and terror joining forces inside my chest, chasing everything else away. For the life of me, I can't decide if I want Hezekiah to slam on the brakes or hit the gas.

"You see 'em, don't you?" Hezekiah watches me in the rear view mirror.

See them? How could anybody *not* see them? I swear, not even my father could miss these things. They are the most magnificent, otherworldly creatures I've ever laid eyes on, with two sets of wings rising up behind them and a golden sword in each of their hands.

Gravel pops beneath our tires as we approach. The creatures are directly outside the window now. I'm a moth. They're the flame. An army of white-eyed men could show up at this very moment, Agent Bledsoe and Scarface leading the way, and I'd be able to do nothing but sit and stare.

The gate groans open.

Hezekiah drives inside the grounds.

And this feeling pours over me. It's one I haven't had in a long, long time. This overwhelming flood of warmth and safety. Like a thousand pounds of dead weight just rolled off my shoulders. I feel light. I feel free. I feel like I could float up to the sky. Hurdle Mt. Everest. Swim across the Atlantic. I look at Luka, an uncontainable smile stretching across my face.

But Luka grimaces, and my smile slides away.

Once we're far enough inside the Rivard property and the creatures are well behind us, I'm able to notice other things. That is, the house. Until the hub, I'd only ever lived in big homes, affluent neighborhoods. A byproduct of my father's occupation. But none of our houses came close to this. The Rivard family lives in a grand antebellum manor of pristine white with soaring columns and large French windows lit against the night.

Hezekiah pulls to a stop in a brick-laid roundabout drive-way that circles a five-tiered fountain. I step out into the balmy night and limp behind Hezekiah toward the front doors. I'm barely more than a few steps before Luka is there, wrapping his arm around my waist to help me along. I catch him hiding another grimace.

Hezekiah rings the doorbell. A long-faced, stiff-shouldered man dressed in a black butler suit answers and welcomes us inside an impressive foyer.

Heels click against polished wood flooring. A regal woman with skin the color of ebony strides into the room, her slim figure clad in a tailored business suit, her smooth dark hair pulled into a tight, low bun that accentuates her high cheek bones. "Thank you, Geoffrey. Zekiah, it's a pleasure to see you." She clasps the tavern owner's hands, kisses both of his cheeks in greeting, then turns to me and Luka. "I'm so glad you made it. Your friends have been worried."

Our friends?

Two familiar faces peek into the foyer—as if making sure

we're not the New Orleans police.

"Link!" I untangle myself from Luka's side and nearly knock him over with a hug. Judging by the tight way he hugs me back, he's as relieved as I am. I bury my face in the crook of his neck, thankful he's okay. Thankful he's alive. I don't let go until the woman with the beautiful skin clears her throat.

I tug at my shirt and glance at Luka, who's carefully avoiding eye contact.

"My name is Vivian Rivard. My daughter, Cressida, is very eager to meet you. Unfortunately, she and her father are away for the evening. Any questions you have regarding the journals will have to wait until morning. I'm afraid I wouldn't be any help to you." Vivian's attention drops to my torn jeans. My scraped palms. The obvious way I favor one leg. "If you wouldn't mind, I'd like to assess your injuries. Please, follow me."

Like Hezekiah before her, she doesn't wait for us to follow.

This time, Luka doesn't wrap his arm around my waist. He scoops me off my feet and walks after her. My entire face catches fire as we enter an open room with cathedral ceilings, a crystal chandelier, and pristine furniture too nice for the likes of me and my filthy self to sit on. But Vivian points to one of the chairs and Luka deposits me on the cushion.

While she props my leg onto a footstool, the ten o'clock news plays on a large screen television. Our faces stare back at me—mine, Luka's, Jillian's, Link's. A reporter stands in front of the festival we just fled and explains that we are still at large and believed to be in the area.

"Don't worry," Vivian says. "You're safe here." She carefully removes my shoe and examines my injury with cool fingers.

"Viv's a doctor," Hezekiah says.

Geoffrey hands her a handheld x-ray machine from a black medical bag like Dr. Carlyle's. I've seen similar machines before—inside the school nurse's office, in the ER when we had to rush Pete to the hospital after he fell off a set of bleachers. As the news changes from four wanted fugitives to the official ceasefire between Egypt and Sudan, Vivian scans the red laser beam down the outside of my ankle, around my foot, and up the inside of my ankle, and studies the small screen in front of her while I study Luka. It's obvious he's having a harder time hiding his grimace.

"It's not broken," Vivian says.

I clasp the armrests of the chair. "Can you check him, please?"

Everyone's attention shifts.

Luka raises his eyebrows. "I'm fine."

"Then why do you keep grimacing?"

"I tweaked a muscle."

Vivian stands. "Where?"

Luka rubs the small of his back. "It's probably from jumping on the garbage truck."

Jillian's eyes go wide. "You jumped on a garbage truck?"

"We ran into Agent Bledsoe."

"What?" Link sounds shocked.

I keep my attention pinned on Jillian's face, watching for any signs of guilt or deception. I see neither, but that doesn't mean I'm in any hurry to give her back the gun.

Vivian lifts Luka's shirt, exposing a slice of toned lower back, and presses her fingers against the spot. "Is the pain sharp or dull?"

"Sharp."

"Hot or cold?"

Luka's brow furrows, as though considering. "Cold."

She presses against the spot some more, then lets his shirt drop. She uncaps a bottle, shakes two peach-colored pills onto her palm, and offers them to me.

I lean away, suspicious, until she assures me it's just ibuprofen.

"After you've had a bath, Geoffrey will wrap your ankle in a poultice. The herbs will help the ligaments heal faster. Once you're cleaned up, you are invited to the dining room for a late dinner." Vivian turns to the butler. "Will you show our guests to their rooms? Luka, if you would come with me, I'd like to run some tests."

I take my foot off the stool. "What kind of tests?"

"Nothing intrusive, I assure you. If all is well, he will join you for dinner."

All must not be well. When I shuffle into the dining room, Link and Jillian sit at the large table, freshly bathed and dressed in clean clothes, courtesy of the Rivards. Luka is nowhere.

I turn to Geoffrey, who helped me navigate the stairs with a pair of crutches after wrapping my ankle. "Where's Luka?"

"Ms. Rivard is running more tests."

"Can I see him?"

"When she's finished with her examination. For now, the lady of the house would like you to eat."

Worry and hunger gnaw at my stomach until it's nothing but a large pit. My last meal consisted of bananas and Lay's Potato Chips. And that was over twenty-four hours ago.

"There's no reason for concern. Ms. Rivard is an excellent doctor." Geoffrey gives me a stately nod and leaves the room.

Link watches him go, then whispers across the table, "I keep calling him Alfred."

"Who?"

"Geoffrey. He's Alfred Pennyworth's doppelganger."

I have no idea what he's talking about.

"Bruce Wayne's butler?"

"Is that Batman?" Jillian asks.

Link shakes his head like he's disappointed in both of us and unwraps his silverware.

Geoffrey returns with three steaming bowls of soup on a silver tray. He places one in front of each of us. "Zuppa Toscana."

I inhale the savory aroma. I've not eaten anything like this since I was dragged out of school and locked in the Edward Brooks Facility. The hub may have kept us fed, but the food was never exactly flavorful.

The first bite has Link groaning. "Rosie would be in heaven."

I dig in, but have a hard time enjoying. My mind's too fixated on Luka and these mysterious tests. Whatever's wrong, it has to be more than a tweaked muscle.

"Did you talk to Cap?" Jillian asks.

I nod. Before I took the most glorious bath in the history of all baths, I contacted Cap via the dream phone to let him know we arrived safely, to update him on the Luka situation, and to inquire about the Fighter. Cap carefully avoided the question and told me to stay focused.

"Does he have any idea how Agent Bledsoe knew we were here?" Her eyes are the perfect combination of round and concerned, which means Jillian's either an excellent actress or Luka's right and she's innocent. I must be looking at her strangely, because her spoon pauses near her lips. "What?"

I look down at my soup, the pit in my stomach growing. I was a fool to trust Clive. I can't afford to be a fool again, no matter how much I don't want my growing suspicion to be true.

Jillian's stare warms the crown of my head. "You don't think *I* had something to do with it, do you?"

"I don't understand how they keep finding us."

She lets her spoon drop into her half-empty bowl with a loud clink.

Link shifts uncomfortably.

Geoffrey returns with fresh salad. Jillian doesn't touch hers. Nor does she touch the main course of blackened salmon on a bed of rice pilaf. We eat in awkward silence. My hunger goes away. But my worry remains. I need to know what's happening with Luka. The waiting is driving me crazy. Thankfully, it's not Geoffrey who brings out the dessert, but Vivian. As soon as I see her, I come forward in my chair. "Is he okay?"

She sets chocolate lava cake in front of Link, Jillian, and then me. "Physically, he's dehydrated and his blood pressure is slightly elevated. Given the circumstances, neither condition is too concerning. His discomfort, however, is growing increasingly worse."

"Why? What's wrong with him?

"I don't believe his ailment is physical."

"What do you mean?"

Vivian sits in one of the dining room chairs. "I sent Hezekiah to the bayou. There is a man there who might be able to help."

"Who is he?" And help with *what*?

"His name is Samson. He's a Healer."

Link forks off a bite of his cake. "What's a Healer?"

"A person who has been gifted with the ability to diagnose and treat non-physical ailments. There are several living out in the swamp. Samson is the best."

Non-physical.

Something tells me she's not talking about emotional, either. I think about Scarface curling his arm around Luka's neck. The black mist seeping inside his body. His inability to throw a shield. His screams in the night. "You think Luka is *spiritually* wounded?"

"I think it's a possibility we ought to examine."

CHAPTER TWENTY

A TUMOR

Vivian calls Samson a swamp-dweller. As soon as he steps inside the Rivard foyer, I can see why. He smells like swamp; the odor is overpowering. Combine that with his wandering left eye, a couple missing teeth, and a severely-stooped back, and I have a feeling he's the kind of guy little kids run away from.

He hobbles inside on Hezekiah's arm, a threadbare knapsack in his other, and starts speaking in a language I don't know. Cajun, maybe? Vivian listens attentively, then leads us up the wide staircase to one of the rooms.

Luka lies inside with his eyes closed, breathing rapidly, locks of dark hair plastered to his sweat-dampened forehead. His jaw is tight. His lips, thin.

Samson sets his bag on the armchair by the bedside.

"It's his lower back." Vivian asks Luka to turn onto his side and exposes the same bit of skin she exposed earlier.

Samson lays his hand over the spot and starts murmuring under his breath. Then he stops suddenly and pulls his gnarled hand away.

I step further into the room. "What is it?"

"This boy has a leech."

His use of English is so surprising at first that I don't process. I have to run his heavily-accented words through my mind a second time. "What's a leech?"

I mean, I know what it is. But Samson can't be talking about the regular kind of leech.

"It's a sort of spiritual parasite used by the other side," Hezekiah answers.

"What does it do?"

"Sucks life away."

My fingers turn to ice.

Samson removes a jar from his bag and pours what looks like oil onto his palm. A stringent odor assaults my nostrils, more overpowering than Samson himself. So strong, in fact, my eyes start to water.

"It also works as a tracker," Hezekiah adds.

"A tracker." The dull words belong to Jillian.

And suddenly, it clicks. That's how Agent Bledsoe knew where we were. It wasn't Jillian. It was this leech. That must be how that dark shadowed thing on the bus found us, too. I come all the way to Luka's bedside and set my crutches aside. "Can you remove it?"

Samson begins to hum. It's a sound that seems to rise up from somewhere deep down in his soul. He rubs the pungent oil on Luka's exposed back and invites the rest of us to place our hands on Luka's body. A ripple of fear crawls up my spine. The whole scene reminds me of the Ouija board, only instead of a planchette, we're putting our hands on Luka.

Samson closes his eyes. His humming turns into a chant.

Luka's skin warms beneath my palm. It grows feverish. Impossibly, dangerously feverish. My mouth goes dry. "What's happening?"

Nobody answers.

And just when I think touching Luka's skin will scald my

palms, his body convulses, and as fast as I can blink, his temperature returns to normal.

Samson's chanting stops. He removes his hands. So does everybody else.

"Is that it?" I ask. "Did you heal him?"

He shakes his head sadly.

"But—"

Samson lifts his gnarled finger and pins me beneath the unwavering stare of his right eye. "*I* did not heal him. But he *is* healed."

"The leech is gone?"

"Yes."

A wave of relief washes over me as Samson gathers his knapsack and speaks with Vivian in more Cajun. I wish he wouldn't. I want to know what he's saying. Especially since they both seem so serious and concerned. Why—if the leech is gone? She nods twice, frowns through most of it, then squeezes Samson's arthritic hands and thanks him for coming.

As soon as Hezekiah escorts him out, I ask what Samson said.

Vivian glances at Luka, now asleep, her frown still in place. "Samson found a ... a tumor on Luka's soul. It happens whenever someone's been touched by evil."

"I thought Samson said he was healed?"

"Of the leech, yes. The tumor remains."

I grip the handle of my crutches tighter. "What does that mean?"

"We're not sure. Symptoms manifest themselves in various ways."

"Is Samson going to come back and remove it?"

"He said there's only one capable of doing that."

"Who?"

"He wasn't clear, which means he either doesn't know or he isn't willing to say."

Vivian offers to show us the library—an odd request this late at night, but since I'm too keyed up to fall asleep, I clunk after her down the stairs and stop in the entryway.

The library is breathtaking, with cathedral ceilings and stone flooring and a series of inlaid arched bookcases and stained glass windows above each one. There's also a fireplace and a proud-looking desk and a table and straight ahead, a dais with an ornate railing and two sets of curved stairs—one on the left, one on the right. I'm so amazed by it all that it takes a few seconds before I realize that while every inch of shelf space is taken, there are no actual books in the room. Every single spine belongs to a composition notebook.

Cap sent us here to find answers and here they are—an ocean's worth.

"You're welcome to browse. Cressida only asks that you handle each volume with care and return them to their rightful location once you are finished. She's very particular about how this room is organized." Vivian's mouth splits into a yawn, which she covers with her fist. "If you'll excuse me, I'm going to turn in."

As soon as her heels *tap-tap* away, Link pivots in a slow circle and lets out a low whistle.

Jillian chooses a notebook at random and begins flipping through the pages. She hasn't said anything since Samson found the leech. A fresh bout of shame washes over me. I bite the inside of my lip, wishing I could take back my accusations from dinner. Why did I have to voice them out loud?

As if realizing our need for some privacy, Link wanders toward the fireplace and examines the ancient-looking relics on the mantle.

I take a step closer to my friend—the one I accused of being a traitor. "Hey, uh, Jillian?"

She slides the notebook back into place and turns around. "It's okay, Tess. You don't have to apologize."

"No, it's not okay. And I do too have to apologize. You've been nothing but loyal, and I threw that loyalty back in your face. I'm really sorry."

"I get it. I really do. Claire and Clive seriously messed with our heads. But we have to be able to trust each other."

"I know. You're right."

"Then let's start with the reason we're here." Jillian runs her finger along several spines. "There's no way Cap wants us to read through all of this. He has to have something specific in mind."

I scratch my wrist. Jillian sacrificed her safety to join me on this journey. She became number four on the Most Wanted list. And I haven't told her anything. I haven't even told Link. "Cap wants us to learn more about a prophecy."

He turns around, a candelabra in hand. "A prophecy about what?"

"A time when The Gifting will face extinction."

He raises his eyebrows.

"Cap thinks the prophecy is coming true."

Jillian's face turns gray. "Is there a way to stop it?"

This would be the part where I tell them all of it. The whole thing—about the One and me and how maybe I'm it. But if I tell them, Cap's beliefs might become *their* beliefs. And

I'm not sure I can handle anybody else placing their hope on my shoulders. If I've proven anything, it's that I can't save one person, let alone an entire race of people. Anytime I've tried, things go wrong. I trust someone I shouldn't and lives are lost. I accuse someone who's innocent and relationships are damaged. "I don't know. I guess that's what we're supposed to find out."

"Well, we're not going to get anywhere tonight. Not without Cressida." Link sets the candelabra back on the mantle. "I think it's time for you and I to pay Agent Bledsoe a visit."

As soon as I fall asleep, I find Link inside a large, dank cave, leaning against a vehicle that can only be the Batmobile. He opens the door and flashes a lopsided grin. "Ready for an adventure?"

"What exactly are we hoping to accomplish by visiting Bledsoe's dream?"

"I think it's time to point out some inconsistencies."

"You think he'll listen?"

"Never know unless we try." He wags his eyebrows and opens the passenger side door wider. "Shall we?"

"If we show up in that thing, he'll never take us seriously." I take Link's hand and pin my mental energy on Agent Bledsoe. Mostly, his crooked nose—like he broke it in a bar fight and never had it reset. And also, the fact that he's prowling around New Orleans trying to find us.

The bottom of the dream drops out from under us. My stomach swoops. Link's grip tightens. And when I open my eyes, we're no longer in the Batcave. We're standing on a stage surrounded by teenagers and the loud boom of rap music. A crowd of faceless onlookers sits elbow-to-elbow in an auditorium. Agent Bledsoe stands at the front of the stage, leading a group of girls through a hip-hop routine, yelling over the music for everyone to keep up.

"This is weird," I mumble as Link pulls me through the dancers and taps our man on the shoulder.

Agent Bledsoe stops.

So does the music.

The second he sees us—*really* sees us—his eyes go crazy wide. They zip from me to Link and back again. Two wanted fugitives standing calmly in front of him. He fumbles inside his coat pocket. I expect him to pull out a gun. Instead, he pulls out a phone, punches a few buttons, and presses the device to his ear. "I found two of them. They're standing right here at my daughter's dance recital."

The audience slowly fades away. The dancers have become very still. Some vanish altogether. Our sudden appearance inside Agent Bledsoe's dream has changed the dream's focus. If we don't tread carefully, the whole thing will disappear and we'll be kicked out.

"No, they aren't running." He seems to realize the oddity of this fact as soon as he says it. He looks at us with a furrowed brow. "Why aren't you running?"

"Because this is a dream," Link says.

The stage is almost completely empty now. All that remains is me and Link and one other girl. Judging by the shape of her eyes and the color of her hair, she's Agent Bledsoe's daughter. Not his real daughter, of course, but his projection of her. She stands like a robot that's been powered off.

Bledsoe scratches his earlobe. "A dream?"

"Unless you usually make a habit of getting on stage at

your daughter's dance recitals." Link waits for his words to sink in before continuing. "Think about it. Why would we come here in real life? We're running from you."

His scratching fingers move from his earlobe to his chin to his chest. It's as though he's having an allergic reaction to the discovery.

"Why are you after us?" I ask.

"You're wanted for murder." He points his accusation at me.

"That's not true. Look at the initial reports. The coroner ruled Dr. Roth's death a suicide. So did the media. So why was it changed?"

Agent Bledsoe's eyes flicker. They are a window to the soul, and I can see a mustard seed of doubt burrowing inside the black depths of his pupils.

"I haven't committed any crimes, unless you count escaping from a mental facility I didn't belong in." Or breaking into the highest security mental rehab facility in the country. I push away the picture of my father sitting inside a prison cell and focus on the man in front of me. "Why should *that* make me FBI's Most Wanted criminal? It's a little strange, isn't it?"

"Y-you set off a bomb."

"It wasn't a bomb. It was a diversion. And nobody was hurt." Jillian made sure the car was empty. She made sure nobody was close by.

The seed in Bledsoe's eye germinates.

Link places his hands on the man's thick-set shoulders. "Do some digging. You'll see the inconsistencies."

Bledsoe's dream blurs at the edges.

Link grips his shoulders tighter, gathering his full attention. "Remember this when you wake up. Don't forget it. We're not dangerous. We've done nothing wrong. Look at the facts."

And just like that, before I can hear another word, I'm pushed like a wave out to sea.

Link is gone.

Agent Bledsoe and his bizarre dream is gone, too.

I float off into nothingness.

Chapter Twenty-One

The Prophecy Revealed

Sunlight streams in through the large windows of my new bedroom. I turn over and spot a familiar backpack sitting on an armchair. Someone must have retrieved them early this morning. I remove the poultice Geoffrey wrapped around my ankle last night. The swelling has gone down significantly, and when I put weight on it, so has the pain.

Ditching the awkward crutches, I make quick work of getting dressed, splashing water on my face, pulling my hair back into a ponytail, and gargling some mouthwash. I grab the five journals from my bag and make a beeline for Luka's room. I want to see how he's doing. But the room is empty, the bed already made.

In the dining room, Jillian and Link eat a plateful of crepes with Vivian and a man dressed in a suit and tie. His skin is more creamed coffee than ebony. Mr. Rivard, I assume.

"Good morning," Vivian says. "Did you sleep well?"

"Yes, I did, thanks. Do you know where Luka is?"

"He ate breakfast earlier this morning with Cressida. She's an early riser. The two are in the library." Vivian introduces me to her husband, Marcus Rivard. I shake his hand, noting the smoothness of his palm as he welcomes me to New Orleans.

Vivian dabs the corners of her mouth with her napkin. "How's your injury?"

"Much better, thanks."

She looks pleased with my quick recovery. "Would you like something to eat?"

I decline and with a polite wave, I backpedal from the room and head to the library. Sunlight shines through the stained glass windows up above, giving the room an entirely different feel from last night. A woman with skin like her mother's sits behind the antique desk. Her hair, however, isn't nearly as tidily pulled back. It's a mess of coiled curls that spring from her head in every direction. Luka stands behind her, looking over her shoulder with his thumbnail wedged between his teeth. He looks healthy and whole and completely engrossed. Cressida wears reading glasses, and is equally focused. So much so that she bites the end of her tongue as she marks something on the page. Luka bends lower and peers at whatever she's writing.

"What are you looking at?" I ask from the entryway.

Luka looks up, his eyes meeting mine. My heart rate picks up speed. I have a million questions. How does he feel? Did he have a nightmare last night? Does he remember what happened? Did he hear what Vivian said about the tumor on his soul? Now that the leech is gone, is his gifting back?

Cressida slips off her readers. "You must be Tess. Come in."

When I reach them, Luka wraps his arm around my waist and kisses my forehead. "How's your ankle?"

I melt against his side. Not a scent of Samson's stringent salve remains. Just soap and wintergreen and … everything Luka. "Mostly healed."

"My father likes to joke that my mother's poultices have magical powers," Cressida says.

"Do they?" I ask.

She smiles. "We were just studying a journal written by a Keeper. We have a few in our collection, but not as many as I'd like. Keepers are quite rare."

So I've been told. "Are you looking for anything in particular?"

"Luka wanted to know whether or not a Keeper has ever lost the ability to protect his or her *anima*."

I glance at him. "And?"

"There's nothing recorded," he says, his green eyes dark.

I guess that answers one of my questions.

"At least that we know of. My grandfather was the Scribe before me. He only died three years ago. I haven't had enough time to read them all." Cressida spots the journals in my hands, a strange glow overtaking her expression. "What are those?"

"A gift from Non."

"Thank you." She takes them from me so carefully, so reverently, that I feel a little guilty for stuffing them haphazardly beneath my mattress these past few months.

"What exactly do you do with them all?" I ask.

"Oh, lots of things. Study them. Add to them. Most importantly, preserve them. Whenever the writing begins to fade, I transcribe the journal into a new notebook. It's very time-consuming work. Every letter has to be meticulously copied and triple checked."

"Wouldn't it be more efficient to digitalize them?" The question comes from behind me. It belongs to Jillian. She and Link must have finished their crepes.

"Efficient, yes. But also dangerous." She sets Non's gift on her desk, then turns around with eyes that are impossibly awake. "Tell me, what are you searching for?"

My heart begins to tap dance inside my chest. I'm not sure I want to learn whatever it is we're about to learn. I lick my bottom lip and take a deep breath. "There was a prophecy given during the fall of Rome, in 476 AD."

Cressida's eyes glow brighter.

"We'd like to know more about it."

She heads to the ladder on the left wall, climbs a few rungs, and skims her pointer finger along the spines. "This particular bookcase is reserved for the prophetic journals. The prophecy you're asking about is one I've studied extensively. I think you'll see why."

She pulls out a notebook and climbs down the ladder. "We don't have the original account. This comes from a secondary source, but it's a very reliable one." She opens to a specific page and slips her reading glasses back on her nose.

The four of us move closer as Cressida begins to read.

"A time approaches when evil will grow to such heights, our kind will face extinction. One will arise with the ability to set captives free. She alone will see evil's mark and her gifting will be complete in its power. She will be our victory."

My scalp tingles. *Her. She.*

"Or she will be our downfall."

"Wait—*what?*" *Our downfall?* Cap failed to mention that part.

Cressida holds up her finger, turns a page, and continues reading. "How shall we know the time is at hand? Hear these words. Listen carefully. When the cessation of war offers the illusion of peace, when strife divides from within and darkness gathers without, when death ushers forth in secret, the death knell will sound. The time is at hand. This prophecy was foretold by the prophet Jabed in the upper room. I, Caius, son of Decimus, was there among the witnesses."

She closes the journal.

"When death ushers forth in secret," Jillian says. "It's happening. At Shady Wood and other rehab facilities. Link confirmed it."

Cressida's eyes glitter. "Tomorrow night, a ceasefire between Egypt and Sudan will be signed, ushering in an unprecedented time of peace."

"The cessation of war. Strife from within." Jillian's voice sounds breathless. "The prophecy is coming true, isn't it?"

Cressida nods. "It seems like it."

Link looks over her shoulder and peers at the open page of the notebook. "What does it mean—*the death knell will sound?*"

"A death knell was an ancient custom where a church bell was rung to announce death," Cressida says. "I think, here, the term's being used metaphorically. The original word is alluding to something loud and unmistakable. Something that tells us we've reached the end. Something we can't miss."

"Like a grand finale."

"Exactly like that."

I shake my head, still hung up on the first bit. "I don't understand what it means about the choice being hers. Why would the One choose to be our downfall?"

"I'm not entirely sure. Prophecies are difficult to understand without hindsight and by then, they've already come to fruition. That's why a lot of people choose not to read too much into them. But I think it might have something to do with this." Cressida opens the journal again and thumbs to a page near the back. "*Victory must come through sacrifice.* The original word Caius used for sacrifice is the same one he uses later, but in this instance, the word was translated to *offering.*"

She turns to the last page and adjusts her glasses. "How will we know this One? A beacon will come before. A sign will be given. The beacon will shine light on the One who is our hope. Evil will rise up to destroy her. If an *offering* is made, she will give hope for freedom."

My ears start to ring.

"A beacon?" Jillian says. "What's that?"

"Again, I'm not certain. But if I was a betting woman, I'd say that the beacon will be a person. This person will be given some sort of sign. And the sign will point to the One."

The ringing grows louder. My grandmother kidnapped me as a baby. She said I had the power to save her. She called me "the key".

"Why is *offering* and *sacrifice* used interchangeably if it means the same thing?" Luka asks, an unmistakable note of tension simmering beneath his voice.

"The original word means both. The most accurate translation would be a sacrificial offering. But it's more than that." Cressida brings the journal down to her side. "In every other context the word is used, it refers to an ultimate act of sacrifice. One of greatest price."

The room begins to spin.

"You mean *her life?*"

My stomach turns to stone. If I've learned anything from my failed mission to rescue my grandmother, it is this: my greatest sacrifice would not be my life. It would be Luka's.

CHAPTER TWENTY-TWO

CONFESSIONS

Luka excuses himself from the library and doesn't return. I look all over the house and finally find him in the basement weight room, running on a treadmill, his sweat-soaked shirt clinging to his muscles, his brow fixed in a hard line.

I approach hesitantly, running my fingers along the bar of a bench press. As soon as he sees me, he pushes a button on the machine several times—a sharp *beep-beep-beep* until the belt on the treadmill slows to a stop. He lifts his shirt to wipe the sweat from his forehead.

His abs are more than a little distracting. "You know, you *could* run outside. The grounds are big enough. It'd probably be a lot nicer than getting nowhere in a cold basement."

He turns away from me to grab a drink.

I bite my lip. "You disappeared."

"I didn't feel like sticking around."

"Are you okay?"

He huffs, like the question is ridiculous. "I'm your Keeper, but for some reason, I can't protect you. And now there's this prophecy that says you have to sacrifice your life, which is really familiar to some dreams I've had."

"First of all, we don't know the sacrifice is going to be a person's life. And second of all, I'm not at all convinced I'm the

One." I say it for him, because I hate seeing Luka in pain. But I also say it for me, because I don't want the prophecy to be true anymore than he does. His current inability to do what Gabe did is the only reason I'm not freaking out. "There's another Fighter out there, Luka. One who took out twenty enemy soldiers at once."

"Does that Fighter have a grandmother who called her 'the key'? Because that sounds an awful lot like a beacon to me."

"She wasn't in her right mind when she called me that."

He shakes his head, like I'm in denial.

I take his hand and give it a squeeze, an attempt to get him to look at me. He's getting too good at locking his pain away. "Please talk to me."

It works. He looks. And his eyes are filled with more pain than they were last night, when the leech was sucking his life away. "What do you want me to say?"

"Something. Anything. Just please don't shut me out."

"Some things you're better off not knowing about."

"Like what—your nightmares?"

He shakes his head.

"Luka, please."

"The pain was excruciating." His words hover like a ghost—disembodied—haunting the space between us. "Is that what you want to know?"

Everything inside of me goes very still.

"It was like every one of my nerve endings was being lit on fire. Only it wasn't heat. It was ice. So cold it burned. I wanted to die a thousand times, but I knew that I couldn't." His eyes are so dark, they're hardly green anymore. "Do you know why?"

I try to form a response, but my throat is too dry. All I can do is shake my head.

"Every time I thought about dying, I pictured you. With-out a Keeper. Unprotected. And the pain of that was a hundred times worse than anything else."

A deep ache carves a hole inside my chest. I hate what Scarface put him through. Hate, hate, hate it.

"Relief wouldn't come in death. It would only come by being with you, so I could keep you safe. Make sure you were protected. If I could do that, then I'd be able to breathe again. And now here I am, right here with you, and it's like I'm being tortured back in that chamber all over again." He moves to walk past me, like he's done. Like he's going to leave.

I grab his hand tighter. "Luka."

He stops. "They captured me, and tortured me, and now I'm useless."

"You are not useless."

"I can't protect you."

"You protect me all the time!" The anger I feel toward Scarface, toward the prophecy, toward Claire and Clive—it floods to the surface, gathering together and rolling off of me in great, giant waves. I move my hand to his face and force him to look at me. "You protect me by being here."

"Tess."

"I love you." It's the first time I've said the words out loud. Not even Luka has said them, but I'm too angry to be self-conscious. Too angry to feel shy or awkward. "I love you, Luka. Not because you're my Keeper, but because you're *you*. So please *be* you. Don't check out on me." My anger morphs into embarrassing tears. I hate that I have to swipe at my cheeks.

Luka's eyes soften. He pulls me into a hug. He smells like sweat and salt and soap. I wait for him to tell me he loves me too. I wait for him to promise that everything will be okay as long as the two of us are together. I wait in vain.

"I will find a way to protect you again. I promise."

Fear wraps its icy fingers around my heart. He doesn't get it. I don't want Luka to get his gifting back. That's the last thing I want.

After dinner, we filter into the great room with the Rivards to watch the evening news. Two anchors discuss the latest updates on the ceasefire—a constant buzz in the media these days. Why shouldn't it be? When the news has been so abysmal for such a long time—when the world held it's breath, on the cusp of WWIII—the sudden, positive shift is more than newsworthy, if not a little suspicious.

When the cessation of war brings the illusion of peace ...

Victory must come through sacrifice ...

I glance at Luka, sitting in an armchair, staring intently at the screen. With my stomach in knots, I slip out of the room and wander down the hall. I find a large alcove window inside a sitting room, curl my arms around my knees, rest my head against the cool glass, close my eyes, and try my hardest to push the echo of that prophecy away while the last of the daylight melts into dusk.

My thoughts turn to the Fighter. The one Cap wants me to forget. Why, though? Wouldn't finding this person be way more beneficial than reading through old journals about confusing prophecies that don't really tell us anything about how to stop the genocide? For all we know, this Fighter could be the One. The strength of my gifting is the only thing that makes Cap and Luka think it's me. And the whole beacon thing. But my grandmother was out of her mind when she called me the key. I don't think we should be so quick to draw conclusions, especially when this Fighter's gifting is obviously stronger than mine. Somewhere in the middle of my obsessing, someone joins me in the window. I crack open my eye.

Link sits across from me, twisting his Rubik's Cube. "You're the One, aren't you?"

I open my other eye. "What makes you say that?"

"Luka's reaction may have tipped me off a little." He smiles, but the mischievous sparkle in his eye is decidedly subdued. "Something tells me he wouldn't be so bent out of shape over the prophecy if it wasn't about you."

I pull the sleeves of my hoodie over my hands. "He thinks it's about me."

"And Cap?"

"Yeah. Him, too."

His voice deepens. "*Tess Eckhart, setting captives free.* It's a catchy tagline."

I huff, spreading a small patch of fog across the window-pane. My dad's in prison. He's being held captive because of me. That's the opposite of setting anyone free.

Link taps his foot against mine. "Out with it, Xena."

"Out with what?"

"All the thoughts racing through that mind of yours."

I can't. The words are stuck.

He hands me his Rubik's Cube. "Take it."

"Why?"

"Because fiddling with something helps keep the anxiety away."

"I suck at that thing."

"All the more reason to practice."

With a sigh, I take his impossible puzzle and begin twisting it around. Even though I have no idea how to twist it correctly, Link's right. Having something to do with my hands loosens the muscles across my chest. And as I fiddle, the words unstick and tumble out—all of them. Link doesn't interrupt. He sits across from me in the windowsill and listens attentively.

"You heard the prophecy. The One is either going to be our victory or our downfall. If my track record has anything to say about it, then our outlook isn't good." I shake my head. "What if I can't make the right decision? What if I mess up?"

"You won't."

He has entirely too much confidence in me.

"I want you to picture happiness."

"Huh?"

"Happiness. You know what that is, right?"

"Yes, I know what that is. I just don't understand why you want me to picture it."

"Because I believe in the power of visualization." He nudges me with his foot again. "Now humor me."

I take a deep breath and let the air escape out my nostrils.

"Picture a scene, any scene. Whatever you want your life to look like when this is all over. Something that represents happiness."

I take another deep breath. Force my shoulders to relax. Continue my Rubik's cube twisting. And the scene comes. I don't have to paint it. It's already painted for me.

"What do you see?"

A whisper of a smile tugs at my lips. "A cake."

"Cake makes me happy, too."

"There are eighteen candles on it. My mom and dad and brother are there. So is Luka. And my best friend Leela."

Everyone safe and sound. The thought warms me straight through. "So are Jillian and Cap." This time, I do the foot nudging. "And you."

"If there's cake, you can count on it."

My whisper of a smile materializes into something stronger.

"See, *visualizing*. Never underestimate its power. Whenever you start to feel panicked or confused, close your eyes and picture that scene. It'll give you something to look forward to when all of this craziness is over."

"Do you think it'll ever be over?"

"Sure, I do. Craziness never lasts forever." He leans forward and taps the cube I've been twisting in my hands. "You're capable of a lot more than you give yourself credit for, Xena."

I look down in my lap. Somehow, I've turned all six faces into solid color.

CHAPTER TWENTY-THREE

FOUND

I go to sleep thinking about the Fighter. Despite Cap's orders, I can't help myself. Somewhere out there is a person powerful enough to accomplish what I could only do after Gabe gave me his life. My curiosity has turned into full-blown obsession. I wish there was a way to find out if the Fighter is a man or a woman. If this Fighter is a she, then maybe, just maybe, the prophecy is about her …

Light flashes all around me. Like bolts of lightning illuminating the night. Only the flashes don't come from the clouds. They come from a woman. All I can see is her back as she fights a hoard of white-eyed men with the stealth and strength and grace of a tigress. Whenever her fist or elbow or foot connects with the enemy, the darkness explodes into light.

I watch in awe and scratch the inside of my wrist, an unnecessary action. I'm sleeping. And I found the Fighter. I found her without even trying. She battles in the midst of a clearing—at least thirty of them—surrounded by the redwoods of Northern California. I skirt around the scene, blending in with the trees, eager to make out her face. But as soon as I'm close, she does a roundhouse kick, whipping her long, white ponytail around as she does.

She doesn't stop until all the darkness is gone. Then she stands in the center of the clearing, her posture proud, her shoulders broad, her muscles tense and alert, as if poised to attack the first sign of danger.

I crouch in the shadows, amazed by what I just witnessed, when a voice breaks through the aftermath. So familiar. So cold that a shiver spider-crawls down my spine. Scarface is here. Hunting this Fighter like he hunts me.

"Impressive work," he says. "Your fighting is much improved."

The woman and Scarface circle each other like boxers in a ring. When she circles around enough, her face finally comes into view. And my eyes go wide with shock. Impossibly, insanely wide.

The Fighter is my grandmother.

There's no mistaking it.

She's alive. Elaine Eckhart is alive.

"Grandma!" The two syllables burst from my mouth, unplanned. Impulsive.

She spins toward the noise.

So does he, his eyes widening with delight.

My muscles coil. Maybe together, we can take him out once and for all. I step out of the shadow, into the clearing beside my grandmother. My living, breathing, impossibly strong grandmother. His attention slides to her, then me, and as if realizing his disadvantage, he disappears like vapor.

"Teresa?" Her head is cocked, as though she's not sure it's me. But her eyes—my father's eyes—they glow like the morning sun.

My mind whirls, desperate to catch up. To make sense of what I just walked into. My grandmother is supposed to be dead. Her room was empty at Shady Wood. "How is this possible? How are you alive?"

"I escaped before they could kill me."

"How?"

"That doesn't matter right now. What matters is that you found me. I knew if I made enough noise, you would." She looks over her shoulder, her muscles still tense, like Scarface might reappear at any time. There are leather straps tied around each of her wrists. "We don't have much time. Tell me where you are and I'll come to you."

"I'm in New Orleans." I give her the address. "Will you be able to get here safely?"

She nods. "I'm not too far away. Stay where you are. I'll come. And I'll explain everything."

I barge into Luka's room in the dead of night. "She's alive!"

He jerks up in bed. "Who's alive?"

"My grandmother. She's alive. I saw her."

A moonbeam streams through his window, casting his face in light. He pushes his hand through his hair, disoriented from the abrupt wakeup call. "You're gonna have to back up. What do you mean your grandmother is alive?"

"I found her. Tonight." My heart soars as I walk across his bedroom floor with bare feet. "She's the Fighter, Luka. They're the same person. She didn't die in Shady Wood. She escaped and now she's coming here."

He presses his palms against his eyes.

"Our mission wasn't a complete failure. We helped her get out." We got her off that medicine just in time. "She was strong. I've never seen anyone so strong."

"I don't understand how you found her."

"I went to bed thinking about the Fighter. When I woke

up, I was in a clearing and she was there, fighting. Scarface was there, too."

His face turns as pale as the moonlight.

I press my lips together, wishing I wouldn't have tossed out the name so carelessly. The man tortured Luka to the brink of death. I'm pretty sure he tortures Luka still every time he sleeps. I want to reassure him. This discovery? It changes everything. "I-I think he was afraid. When he saw us together, I think that made him very afraid."

He looks at me, processing. And eventually, it shows up in his eyes. The same something that has planted itself in my heart. A seed of hope.

CHAPTER TWENTY-FOUR

THE LIST

W e spend the next day in the library going cross-eyed, studying the journals with Cressida, hoping to find something useful. Some sort of clue or tangible weapon we could use against the enemy. Something more than a vague reference to a sacrificial offering.

My leg jiggles as I sit in a chair on the dais, paging through one of the journals. I can't stop it. It jiggled all through breakfast, lunch, and dinner. It jiggles still, as evening gives way to night. The more time that passes without my grandmother arriving, the faster it goes. How long will it take her to get here? What if something happens to her? Or what if last night wasn't even real? I regret, more than anything, not doing the penny trick Link taught me. I'm growing increasingly paranoid that last night was a giant construction. If I'd conjured up a penny, I could at least lay that particular worry to rest.

I shut the journal. The only sound comes from pages turning. Luka sits near the entrance studying the Keeper journals Cressida collected for him earlier this morning, his elbow on the table, his fingers fisted in his hair. Link and Jillian sit cross-legged on the floor, flipping through a stack of prophetic journals they pulled off the shelf. Cressida sits at her desk, copying words.

Ditching my notebook, I sit on the rung of a ladder nearby

Link and Jillian and clasp my hands between my knees. "Find anything?"

"Oh, you know. Super cheerful stuff. Like this gem." Link flips a couple pages. "*We will be gathered like sheep to the slaughter.* Has a nice ring to it, don't you think?"

My jiggling leg completely loses control. It bounces like a jackhammer, so fast that Jillian arches her eyebrows at me. I stand abruptly, snag the journal Cressida read to us yesterday and begin pacing in front of the fireplace. I don't want to read the prophecy, but it's turned into a gruesome car crash. The kind you want to look away from, but can't. I end up reading it over and over again until I've committed each line to memory.

"What's this?" Link directs his question to Cressida, who's hunched over her desk, and reads something from the journal in his lap. "*The king, the eye, the censor, the idol, the physician?*"

She sets her pencil down and stretches. "You found the List."

"A list of what?" Jillian asks.

"That's always been a mystery. We don't have any idea what it means." With a smile, Cressida abandons her work and joins Link and Jillian on the floor. "It was originally written in Aramaic. I don't know why my grandfather didn't translate this top word here. It means Key."

The word snags my attention. Luka's, too. I'm pretty sure we're thinking the same thing—my grandmother called me the key.

"What's this symbol above it?" Link asks.

"Another mystery. My grandfather and I researched it extensively, but we couldn't find it anywhere."

Curiosity pulls me closer. I look over Link's shoulder and recognize it immediately. It doesn't look as ominous on paper as it does in person, but the sharp, angular design is identical. "I've seen that before."

Cressida's head jerks up. "You have?"

"Yeah. Several times."

"Where?"

"The other side tried marking it on my brother." I don't say the name—Scarface. But I do look at Luka. He stares at me from across the room. "I also saw it on the inside of a girl's wrist. She was in my Honors English class at my old school. And again on a kid's neck."

Cressida takes the journal from Link—not rudely, but excitedly—and examines the symbol as though seeing it for the first time. "The other side, as in evil?"

I nod.

"You're positive it was *this* symbol?" She points to the page.

But I don't have to look. After what almost happened to Pete, I couldn't forget that symbol if I tried. "I'm one hundred percent positive."

She holds out her hand, her eyes flicking toward the journal in mine—the one I've been studying for the past hour. "Can I see that?"

I hand it over.

She flips through the pages, biting the tip of her tongue as she searches. Finally, she marks a spot with her finger and reads. "One will arise with the ability to set captives free. *She alone will see evil's mark.*"

My heart begins to race.

"That's why we couldn't find it anywhere. This symbol is evil's mark. And only one person can see that." Cressida looks up at me, her eyes filled with the same intrigue that used to fill Dr. Roth's whenever I told him about one of my dreams.

"Which means you're the One."

There's this long moment of charged, awkward silence as Jillian and Cressida gape. My cheeks turn hot. I stand there like an idiot, wanting to erase Cressida's words.

Finally, Link speaks up. "So that takes some of the mystery out of the list, then. We know it's a key to something, and it has to do with evil. Otherwise the symbol wouldn't be there."

"Right!" Cressida's bright-eyed attention turns back to the list.

I could kiss Link for the diversion.

"*The king, the eye, the censor, the idol, the physician,*" she mutters.

Luka deserts his spot on the table. "Maybe it's a hit list. Key people evil has to kill in order to carry out their plan."

"The eye and the idol could be items, though," Link says.

Jillian perks. "Or maybe, it's like us. The Gifting has Fighters, Keepers, Cloaks, Shields, and Linkers. Maybe the enemy has something like that, too."

My thoughts shoot to Scarface. Where would he fit in that hierarchy?

"That could work," Luka says. "The *king* would be the one in charge. The *eye* could be the one who keeps a watch over everything."

"Like the Eye of Sauron?" I give Link's knee a playful kick, then catch Luka watching the exchange.

My cheeks go a little warm.

Jillian sits up on her knees. "Maybe the censor picks through all the information the eye sees and reports it to the king."

"What about the idol?" I ask.

Cressida rubs her earlobe. "That would be something people worship."

"Nobody worships anything anymore." Science has made sure of that.

"We all worship something," Cressida says.

There's a moment of silence as all of us think over the possibilities.

I scratch my wrist. "What about the *physician*? Why would evil care about healing anything?"

"Physicians don't just heal." Jillian looks around our small circle. "They also medicate."

"Like the people at Shady Wood," Link mumbles.

My heart rate picks up speed again. It feels like we're on the brink of something.

Luka bites his thumbnail and peers at the list. "It could have something to do with the fetal modification clinics. They call it 'healing' the women. Treating abnormalities."

"There's been extensive testing done on the fetuses," Cressida says. "According to my mother, ninety-five percent of the time, no abnormalities are found."

My eyes go round. I don't know why I'm shocked. Luka and I suspected as much, considering he never would have been born if his mother had listened to the doctors. "Why doesn't the public know about this?"

Cressida shrugs. "It must not be newsworthy."

"That's outrageous! That's—that's—"

"Excuse me, Ms. Rivard?"

I turn around.

Geoffrey stands in the entryway with his hands clasped behind his back. "There is a woman downstairs. She says her name is Elaine Eckhart."

CHAPTER TWENTY-FIVE

DISPARITIES

I hurry ahead of Geoffrey, ignoring the faint bite in my ankle, and come to a halt in the foyer. My grandmother stands inside the doorway, her appearance shocking.

The woman I met last night was a warrior—strong and sure and formidable. This woman, however, is like a skittish dog—a shrunken, weaker version of her dream-self, with white hair that hangs limp and thin past her shoulders, sallow skin, and hands that fidget nervously. The disparity is alarming. So much so that the hope I've been harboring—that she can teach me, that she can strengthen me, that together we can take on the other side—takes a nasty hit. But then I remember Cap and myself. I'm small. Cap's crippled. Yet we are both powerful Fighters.

I take a tentative step forward, afraid any sudden movement might scare her away. It's her eyes that have me closing the rest of the distance. They don't shine like they did in my dream, but they are still her eyes. *His* eyes. My father's eyes.

A hot clog of emotion rises in my throat.

It's her. She's here. And she's alive.

I wrap her small, frail body in a tight embrace.

Her hand flutters to my back and gives me a few uncertain pats.

After fifteen years in solitude, I can't imagine she's used to affection. I let her go. Up close, her face is a maze of deep wrinkles, but beneath the age and hardship, is the woman who raised my father. "I'm glad you're here."

She grasps my arms, as though to steady herself, tears welling in her eyes. I recognize the emotion—profound relief. She's glad to be here, too.

"Geoffrey," Cressida says. "Why don't you get our new guest some hot tea?"

I lead my grandmother to the dining room. All of us sit around the table—Link, Jillian, Luka, me, Cressida. Thankfully, Vivian and Marcus are out. The crowd's big enough as it is.

Geoffrey enters with a steaming cup of tea and sets it in front of my grandmother. Ribbons of steam curl up around her face. She takes a sip, her hands shaking so badly some of the drink sloshes over the sides. The same leather straps that were wrapped around her wrists last night are wrapped around them now.

I want to be sensitive. I really do. But here she is—this woman I've been dying to talk to ever since I found out she was alive—the first time, back in Thornsdale. If I don't let some of these questions out, I might explode. "How did you escape?"

The cup rattles against the saucer as she sets it down. "I didn't have any medicine in my system. When they loaded me into the back of a semi, I was conscious. The truck was full, but I was the only person awake."

My gut turns to rot.

"We drove for a long, long time. When we finally stopped, we were in a remote, wooded area. Men dressed in scrubs began to unload us. They laid us in a long ditch and then they began the injections."

The rot in my gut rises. "Injections of what?"

"I don't know. I crawled into the bushes before they reached me. Once they finished ..." My grandmother closes her eyes, as though she's trying to press the memory away, her hands trembling so badly they shake the table.

I place mine over hers, hoping to still them. Hoping to still her.

"They sprayed them with butane and lit them on fire." Her words are dead. Hollow.

Jillian gasps.

Cressida's fingers flutter to her mouth.

Nobody speaks.

Not for a long, long time.

My nausea turns to anger. White-hot, vitriolic anger that burns like acid. At the government, for allowing this to happen. At the public, for ignoring it. At my parents, for condemning an innocent woman to a place like Shady Wood. At myself, for letting her stay as long as she did.

I clasp her hands tighter. "You've been fighting."

She nods absentmindedly. "When you've seen what I have seen, when you've lived what I have lived, there is little choice."

Exhaustion wins. My grandmother takes a hot bath. Vivian gives her a sedative to help her sleep, and she retires to a bedroom not too far from my own. The next morning, I wake up early and go looking for her.

Her room is empty. She's not in the dining room or the great room or the library. I find Geoffrey in the butler's pantry. He says he saw her walking outside. So I rush out a back door, into a courtyard, and spot her sitting on a bench at the edge of the woods. As I approach, she doesn't seem to hear me. She doesn't seem to notice when I sit beside her, either.

She sits with her eyes closed, her face soaked in shadow, the sun at our backs while birds chirp all around.

"How'd you sleep?" I ask.

"All right."

The birds chirp some more. The sun creeps higher behind us. I still have so many questions, but she looks so fragile, it's hard to know how to ask them.

"I like the outdoors," she finally says.

"Me too."

"Being indoors makes me feel claustrophobic."

I can imagine why. She was locked inside a white box of a room with no windows for fifteen years. Even a house as large as the Rivards would feel confining. I glance at the leather straps around her wrists. "What are those?"

She rubs them. "Some things are hard to get used to."

Like wrists that are free. Unbound. The thought makes me sad. And angry.

"They also remind me."

"Of what?"

"That I never want to end up there again."

My anger grows. So does an overwhelming sense of protectiveness. I will do everything within my power to make sure that never happens. "Can I ask you a question?"

"Sure."

"The man with the scars. Is he after you?"

Her face contorts. "The two of us have a long history."

A memory brushes against my thoughts, like an invisible strand of hair tickling my skin. The first time I found my grandmother in a dream and I discovered the truth—that she wasn't dead—Scarface was there. That's when I first met him.

He'd been dressed in a white coat like a doctor. He said my grandmother was no longer his patient.

"I gave him one of his scars."

My head jerks back. "*What?*"

"We fought. I won. And for one glorious week, I thought he was gone forever. I tasted freedom." She twists her fingers in her lap; it doesn't stop the shaking. "But then he returned with a vengeance, and he had his scar. A constant reminder that while I could hurt him, I could never be rid of him."

Her words are like battery acid on my tongue. I take my grandmother's shaking hand and squeeze it between mine. I picture him last night—the look on his scarred face when he saw us standing side by side. He was frightened. I'm sure of it. "Maybe together, we can."

Her chin trembles. Moisture gathers in her eyes. With her cold hand sandwiched between mine, she drops her chin and weeps. I can't tell if her tears are hopeful or hopeless.

That night, the sound of Luka's screaming tears me from sleep, my heart revving from calm to spastic in half a second flat. I kick off my covers and sprint across my room when the screaming stops. The sudden silence echoes down the hallway. I stay frozen in place for a few pulse-pounding seconds, then tiptoe toward his bedroom.

Luka sits up in bed, his chest heaving.

Vivian is already there, looking every bit as put-together in her pajamas in the dead of night as she does during the day.

"I'm okay, Tess," Luka says. He hasn't looked at me, and yet he notices me standing in his doorway like a ghost. "You can go back to bed."

Last time he asked me to leave, I listened. I left him with Cap. I let him push me away. I'm not going to do that again. I place my hand on the doorframe, as if holding on will give me the courage to stay.

Vivian hands him a glass of water. "How long have the nightmares been happening?"

Luka takes a drink. "A few days."

"Did something happen to bring them on?" she asks.

He doesn't answer.

So I do it for him. "He was held prisoner by the other side."

Luka's jaw tightens, but I press on. "They tortured him."

Vivian frowns. "It sounds like you are suffering from a form of PTSD. I spoke with Elaine today about the same thing. If you like, there's medicine I can give you that will help—"

"No." His answer escapes before Vivian can finish her suggestion.

I understand why. The medicine I took masked my gifting. Luka wants nothing more than to find his.

"It's for anxiety," Vivian says. "There's no shame in taking it."

"I'll be fine."

But it's obvious he won't. I think about the tumor on his soul. Is this one of the repercussions? Did Vivian tell Luka what Samson said? Because I sure didn't. "Is there anything else he can do that would help?"

"Finding an activity that will occupy his mind without requiring much thought usually offers a measure of relief. I suggested knitting to Elaine. It can be anything that keeps his hands busy."

"Like a Rubik's Cube." I mumble the words more to myself than anyone else.

"Yes," Vivian says. "Exactly like that."

I picture Link, fiddling with the cube. He does it while watching TV. He does it while sitting in front of a computer. His hands are always twisting, twisting, twisting. Is that what his Rubik's Cube is to him? A way to keep the bad memories away? And if so, what bad memories does he have?

Vivian asks if Luka needs anything else. He says he's fine, and she leaves.

Her sudden absence has me tugging on my shirtsleeves.

Luka has yet to look at me.

"I guess she doesn't care about purpling," I say lamely.

"You should go back to sleep."

His words are hollow. Empty. They have me coming closer instead of going away, until I'm taking a tentative seat on the edge of his mattress.

"Tess." His face is hard. "You're not staying."

"I'm not leaving you alone."

"And I'm not going to wake up screaming in your ear."

"I don't care if you do." I bring my shaky legs onto the mattress and slide beneath the covers, careful to stay on my side of the bed. It's a big one, so there's plenty of space between us. I lie down and rest my head on the pillow beside his, my heart crashing inside my chest. Because what if he kicks me out? What if he refuses to let me stay?

He remains sitting, watching me while that muscle in his jaw *tick-tick-ticks*, as if he's grinding his molars. Finally, he lays back and stares up at the ceiling. I'm not sure how long we stay like that, awake in the silence. I only know that it's long enough for my heart to settle and my eyes to grow heavy.

When Luka speaks, his voice is low and intimate. "I wish we could leave everything behind. Go somewhere safe."

I turn on my side and tuck my hands beneath the pillow. "Where would we go?"

He turns his head to look at me. "Somewhere we could stay forever."

"Like our beach?"

Luka smiles.

It's the best thing I've seen in a long, long time. And even though the thought is like heaven—leaving everything behind to be with him—I know it's impossible. My grandmother is right. When you've seen what I've seen, when you know what I know, you have no choice but to fight. As much as I want to hide, as much as I want to pretend that my father is right and evil doesn't exist, I can't. Not anymore.

CHAPTER TWENTY-SIX

THE SYMBOL

The next evening, we gather around the big screen in the great room to watch history unfold. Our president is about to address the nation in a speech predicted to garner more viewers than the last three super bowls combined. Egypt and Sudan have officially signed the ceasefire. For the first time in a long, long time, our soldiers are coming home. All of them.

I imagine Pete and my mom and Leela watching in Thornsdale. My dad watching from prison. Cap and everyone else from the hub watching in Newport, with Non most likely muttering at the television. I imagine everybody across the country—across the *world*—celebrating peace while men dressed in scrubs toss catatonic patients into ditches and set them on fire. This peace is nothing more than a giant ploy, a huge distraction, a massive red herring. Darkness is a tricky, tricky thing. Especially when it masks itself in light.

Beside me, my grandmother knits. The two large needles scrape and click in a rhythmic, soothing cadence that seems to still her shaking. Across the room, Link's Rubik's Cube is MIA. He sits with one arm draped over the back of the couch, tapping the leather with his index finger, the notebook with the list open in his lap. He's been studying it all day, as if searching for the missing piece that might make the puzzle come together.

Jillian sits beside him, her eyes glued to the television. Earlier today, I gave her back the gun I'd been hiding at the bottom of my bag. With the Rivards' permission, she brought Luka, Link, and I outside for a little target practice. My grandmother joined us, but her shaking hands kept her from participating. She watched as Jillian patiently taught us how to load, unload, and shoot. Luka, of course, picked it up the fastest. Link eventually caught on. I couldn't hit a target to save my life. But at least I know where the safety button is now. Jillian kept the gun and said we could practice some more tomorrow.

On the television, the camera pans along Pennsylvania Avenue, all the way to Capitol Hill, where celebrators squish together to hear from our president. Flanked by two bodyguards, Cormack walks to the podium, waving proudly as the spectators cheer. She waits for the crowd to quiet, then begins her speech.

Roughly halfway through, during a dramatic pause, one of the bodyguards sneezes. It's a loud, attention-getting sneeze that has his face turning red.

Without missing a beat, Cormack says, "Gesundheit," and laughter ripples through the crowd. Smiling, Cormack brushes her hair over her shoulder, and as she does, I see something that has everything inside of me going very still. A small, black symbol. Unmistakably etched on Cormack's neck.

I stand and move closer to the television.

Cormack's hair falls back into place, hiding the mark from view.

"Can someone rewind?"

Nobody responds.

I turn around. The Rivards, Link, Jillian, Luka, my grandmother. All of them stare at me. "Please rewind it!"

Marcus points the remote at the television. The feed backs up.

"There!" I tap the screen. "Stop!"

Marcus pushes pause.

The picture on the screen freezes in place.

A flood of adrenaline courses through my veins. My heart races. My mouth goes dry. The president of the United States has the mark on her neck. As plain as day. I press my finger against the spot on the screen. "It's right there."

Jillian scrunches up her nose, like she's trying to see what I'm seeing. "What is?"

I snatch the notebook in Link's lap and point to the symbol at the top of the page. "*This.*"

All of us stare at one another. It's like we're standing on the precipice of a giant discovery. The missing puzzle piece.

I hold up the journal. "I think we just found our king."

The notebook sits on the table near the library entrance, opened to the list. I pace back and forth, wearing a path in the stone from the empty fireplace to Luka, sitting in one of the chairs. He rests his elbow on the table, fingers threaded through his hair, his only movement coming from the pen in his hand, which he uses to trace the same five words on a sheet of paper. Over and over and over again.

King. Eye. Censor. Idol. Physician.

Cressida and Jillian sit across from him, studying each word. Link leans against the wall behind them, one ankle crossed over the other while he spins his Rubik's cube.

"It can't be a coincidence." I pivot on my heel and pace

back toward the stairs. "Cormack's mark has to be related to the list, doesn't it?"

Cressida rubs her chin. "It definitely seems that way."

"How do you even get the symbol?" Jillian asks. "Has Cormack been hijacked or something?"

Hijacked. When the enemy enters a person, it locks that person up inside a dream world and takes over their body and mind. Link taught me about it during training. I think about the people who've had the mark in the past. Wren, who barked at Mrs. Meecher in our Honors English class. Was she hijacked by the other side? What about the kid at the mall, who tried shooting innocent Christmas shoppers on Black Friday? Or Pete. Is that what Scarface had been about to do? If Luka and I hadn't saved him, would my brother have been hijacked?

"All we really know," Link says, "is that Cormack's being *used* by evil. Otherwise she wouldn't have the mark."

Porcelain rattles behind me. My grandmother walks into the room carrying a tray of tea. I'm surprised Geoffrey handed it off to her. He seems to take his butler duties very seriously. She sets the tray on Cressida's empty desk and begins pouring some for everyone. More tea ends up in the saucers than the cups, but she seems pleased to have something to do, so I leave her to it.

"We know what the list is about then," Jillian says. "Key people evil is using to carry out their plans. It's all tied up with the prophecy."

My grandmother sets a cup in front of Luka and Cressida, then returns to the tray for another and offers it to me.

I take it, but I don't drink. I'm too overstimulated to put anything inside my stomach right now. "Which means that if we can figure out who each person is, then we could stop the other side from carrying those plans out. We'd have a way to fight back." We found exactly what Cap wanted us to find.

"We know who the king is," Link says.

"How do we know Cormack isn't the idol?" Luka traces the C on *censor* for the third time, then untangles his hand from his hair and curls his finger around the handle of his teacup. "Everybody worships her."

Jillian nods. "He's right. Everybody does."

Cressida copies the list onto the first page of a new notebook in neat manuscript and jots Cormack's name twice. Once beside *king*. Again beside *idol*. She ends both with a question mark. "What about the *eye*?"

I resume my pacing. Eye. Spy. Cameras. Like the one we hid from at the rest stop outside of Greeley. I think about Dr. Roth and his filing system, and all these journals surrounding us. Not a single word has been entered into a computer. Doing so would be dangerous. "What if the *eye* has something to do with government surveillance?"

Link twists a row of red on his cube. "Like the NSA?"

"The NSA. CIA. *FBI*." The thrill of excitement that comes on the cusp of discovery builds inside of me. "Think about it for a second. Six of the ten Most Wanted in America are part of The Gifting. What if the eye's the director of the FBI?"

I look at Luka. He's chewing on his thumbnail.

"Actually," Jillian says, "the director of the FBI isn't the final authority on the Most Wanted list anymore. After what happened to Newport, the Department of Security and Defense was formed. The FBI, the CIA, the NSA, even immigration and border control came under its authority. According to my dad, a few months after the bombings, it came out that each agency had important information, and if they'd been sharing that information with each other, Newport never would have happened."

"Who's the head of Security and Defense?" I ask.

Cressida pulls out her phone and Google searches, the tip of her tongue sticking out in that way it does when she's focusing. A few seconds later, she scrawls the name *Secretary Young* with another question mark beside the *eye*. "Any ideas for the *censor?*"

Luka sets his teacup on the table. "The media's censored like crazy."

I glance at my grandmother. She sits at Cressida's desk, rubbing the straps around her wrists. The public has no clue what's happening to people like her in rehab facilities. They also have no clue that ninety-five percent of the pregnancy screenings are inaccurate; that perfectly healthy babies are being killed. They don't know because the news doesn't cover it.

Jillian is practically wiggling in her seat. "The Chief of Press."

Cressida does some more Googling, then writes down *Chief Fredrick* beside *censor* with another question mark.

I stare at the list, an incongruity niggling its way into my thoughts. "The Gifting live all over the world."

The prophecy was made in Rome, for crying out loud. Thousands of years before the United States was even on the map. The people on this list might be able to eradicate The Gifting in our country, but the prophecy talked about extinction. Complete annihilation.

Link pushes off the wall and leans over the back of Jillian's chair. "Every person on our list is an American leader."

Exactly. Which means we have to be missing something.

"What is that?" The question comes from my grandmother. She's pointing to my waist.

The red light on my dream phone has come on. "Cap."

"Who's Cap?" she asks.

"He's the one who sent us on this mission." I pull the dream phone off my belt loop. "Link made this so we could communicate."

"How does it work?"

I show her.

My grandmother is tickled, like a little kid amazed over a card trick.

"There are two inputs," I say. "We can both go if you want to see the dream dojo."

"I'd love that."

I hit the button, turning the light from red to green.

Luka stands from his chair, his face going pale. Like he's going to faint, or get sick all over the floor.

My brow furrows. "Are you okay?"

He cups his hand over his forehead. "Yeah. Just tired."

"Are you sure?"

"I'm fine. I promise. I just need some sleep. It's been hard to come by lately." He gives me a weak smile and wraps me in a hug. "Tell Cap I say hello. You two have a lot to catch up on."

Luka is right.

When we arrive, Cap is waiting. And my grandmother's hands are as steady as a rock.

Our mission is complete. We found exactly what we needed to find to fight the enemy. Cap wants us to get to Newport as soon as possible. Marcus Rivard called Hezekiah and arranged for him to drive the four of us north tomorrow.

It's time for Link and I to check in with Agent Bledsoe.

This time, there are no dancing teenagers. No stage. No hip-hop music. We find Agent Bledsoe sitting at an empty bus stop with a briefcase by his foot, staring at his watch, which ticks backward instead of forward.

Link clears his throat.

Bledsoe looks up. He doesn't stand quickly or fumble inside his pocket for his phone. His arms go slack. His face lengthens. His eyes widen. And there, mixed with the shock, is a glimmer of relief. Like he's been hoping we might appear. "You're back." He takes in his surroundings. There's nothing but the empty street and the bench he sits on and the bus stop sign growing up from the curb. "This is a dream, isn't it?"

Link nods. "Did you do what we asked? Did you look into things?"

"Yes."

"And do you agree that something isn't right?"

He scratches his crooked nose. He looks unsure. Noncommittal. "I want to believe you. But how can I? This is a dream."

"That doesn't mean it's not real." As soon as I speak, an odd tingling sensation circles my wrists. I rub the spot and the tingling stops. I shake out my hands.

Link grabs Bledsoe's shoulders and gives them a rattle. "We're not criminals. We're not dangerous. We are innocent. You are being lied to."

The doubt on Bledsoe's face remains.

And an idea comes. "If we gave you proof that this is real, would you believe us then?"

"I think so."

"Then we'll leave you a note in a secure location. Tomor-

row night, we'll visit you and tell you where to find it."
Something sharp bites at the skin on my neck. I slap at the
spot. "Ouch!"

Link lets go of Bledsoe's shoulders. "What happened?"

I pull my hand away and look at my fingers, expecting a
dead mosquito or a horsefly. There's nothing. "I-I'm not sure."

Link turns back to Bledsoe. "If we can get you a note, will
that be enough proof?"

The agent nods, and the bite returns, sharper this time.

I slap at my skin again. "Ow!"

Concern dances across Link's face. But before I can hear
whatever he's going to say, I wake up in bed with the barrel of
a gun pressed against my neck.

CHAPTER TWENTY-SEVEN

GAGGED AND BOUND

My heart slams into my throat. My head rears back against the pillow. My brain scrambles to process what's happening.

There's a gun against my neck. And the person holding it isn't Jillian. It's my grandmother. She looms over me, moonlight shining in through the window, bathing her face in a glow of white.

"What are you doing?" I try to scratch the inside of my wrist, but I can't scratch anything. My hands are bound, pressed tightly together by a cord of rope.

She presses the barrel deeper into my flesh.

My heart races. This has to be a dream. I woke up and yet I'm still sleeping. My attention slides toward the door, desperate for something—anything—to make sense. What I see turns my racing heart to ice.

Luka, gagged and tied to a chair, his head lolling forward.

A scream claws its way up my chest, but my grandmother jabs the gun harder and lifts her finger to her lips.

"What did you do to him?" I choke.

"Slipped a heavy sedative into his tea."

My mind spins, but nothing makes sense. My grandmother must be having some sort of episode. A symptom of PTSD. She's not right in the head. She's not thinking clearly. And she has a gun.

"If you don't cooperate, I will kill him."

"W-why? Why are you doing this?" My eyes water. I can't breathe. My attention keeps zipping from the gun at my neck … to Luka … to the door. She has a gun and my bedroom door is closed. Most likely locked. *Please someone wake up.* Surely, Link will know something weird is going on. I cried out in pain when we were in the middle of our business with Bledsoe, and then I disappeared.

Please Link. Please, please, please wake up!

My grandmother pulls the gun away from my throat. She walks to the door and presses her ear to the wood, as though listening for any rumblings outside.

Should I scream? I'm terrified she'll press that gun against Luka's temple and pull the trigger if I do. I twist my wrists, trying to loosen the rope. It cuts and burns against my skin, which means I am very, very much awake.

She points the gun at a second chair. "Sit here."

When I hesitate, she shoves the barrel against the back of Luka's skull.

I stand quickly, my knees like Jell-O. As soon as I drop into the chair, she moves behind me and uses more rope to tie my ankles to the chair legs. "I wouldn't do this if I didn't have to. I wouldn't do this if there was another choice."

The room begins to spin. I squeeze my eyes shut and take deep breaths. There has to be a way out of this. There has to be. I consider overpowering her—because she's weak—but I can't see her or the gun and Luka is one finger pull away from death.

"The night you were born, I had a vision. A visitor came and told me how important you would be. And I knew. I knew you were the key."

"The key to *what?*"

"He will never stop. He will torment me forever. For eternity. After I gave him that scar, he promised me there would be no escaping him. Not even death will keep him away." Her hands shake as she pulls the rope tighter. "Then I had the vision. And I knew if I could hand you over to him, he would leave me alone. I would finally have peace. I would finally be free."

Hope for freedom.

The words of the prophecy come with astounding clarity. I am hope and my grandmother will offer me for her freedom. She didn't try to kidnap me as a baby to protect me. She tried to kidnap me so she could hand me over. "But you were fighting. The night I found you, you were fighting them."

"It was a construction."

"There were rumors. About a powerful Fighter."

"He spread them. He made sure they would get to you. We knew it was only a matter of time until you found me." She finishes binding my ankles and comes around to look at me, her eyes flooding with sorrow. It's the same sorrow I saw before I wrapped my arm around her shoulder while she wept. "This is the only way. I don't have any choice."

"There is always a choice."

"You don't understand what I've been through. You don't understand what I've done." The shaking in her hands grows worse—great seismic waves. "It's too late now. I can't take it back. It's too late."

I look at the gun in her hands.

Jillian's gun.

The little warmth that remains in my face trickles away.

Dread fills every cell of my body. Every atom. "How did you get that gun?"

"It doesn't matter. This will all be over soon. He promised it would be over."

"Who?" The word explodes from my mouth. So loud my grandmother jabs the weapon between my eyes, the madness in her own full throttle. But I keep going. Let her shoot me. "Scarface? Is that who you're going to trust?"

"Shut up!" She cocks the trigger.

I don't care. I look straight into her madness and dare her to shoot. But she doesn't. I can see in her eyes that she won't pull that trigger. Not on me.

Behind her, Luka stirs.

Wake up, Luka, please. Wake up!

Slowly, he lifts his head. His eyes flutter open, take in what's happening, and flood with panic. He's bound, and a madwoman has a gun pressed against my forehead.

"Why don't you just get it over with?" I ask.

At my words, Luka jerks wildly against his restraints.

My grandmother spins around.

He glares up at her, his nostrils flaring, his chest heaving.

I twist my hands furiously, desperate to loosen the rope.

"I'm not going to kill her," she says. "I don't want to kill anybody. There's no need for you to die. Not if Teresa gives me her cooperation." She turns back to me.

I stop moving.

Luka starts, working silently and frantically to free himself.

"Here's what we're going to do." She walks to my nightstand and picks up one of the ear buds next to the dream phone. "You and I will use these to put us to sleep. If you do not meet me right away, I will startle awake and shoot Luka in the head."

My muscles seize. Every single one.

"Scarface will be waiting for us. You will hand yourself over willingly. I will startle myself awake and leave. You have my word that no harm will come to Luka, or any more of your friends."

Any more.

"Do you understand?"

My thoughts spin into chaos. If I try to revolt, if I try to take my grandmother out, there's no way I will be able to get to her before she startles herself awake and follows through on her promise. I could startle myself awake, too, but I'm tied to this chair. And Luka can do nothing. He can't even shout for help.

She digs the gun against Luka's temple. "Do. You. Understand?"

Wincing, he stares at me, begging me with his eyes not to agree. I've never seen him look more desperate.

But I nod—quick and fast—because what else can I do?

And then it happens.

A knock on the door—a glorious, wonderful knock!

"Xena?" Another knock. "You okay in there?"

My grandmother puts her finger to her lips. Her eyes wide. Her face deranged. She digs the gun harder into Luka's temple. "Tell him you are fine," she hisses.

"I—I'm fine, Link." But my voice trembles. I can't help it. All I can see, all I can think about, is that gun and my grandmother's shaking hands and her finger curled around the trigger and how in less than a millisecond, Luka could be gone.

"Why did you leave the dream?" Link asks.

My grandmother's trigger finger twitches.

"I—I don't know! I just woke up. I promise I'm fine!"

There's a pause, and then like a nightmare, the door handle turns. "Why's your door locked?"

She keeps the gun pointed at Luka and creeps toward the door.

My panic grows.

Link is unarmed and unsuspecting on the other side. I twist my wrists harder, faster, my heart galloping inside my chest. Frantic. Desperate. Crazed.

She unlocks the door and ducks into shadow beside Luka.

I yank and pull and jerk against the rope until one hand wiggles free.

The handle turns.

The door opens.

Link stands on the other side, his eyes widening.

No, no, no!

My grandmother raises the gun, but Luka kicks her. Somehow, he managed to free his legs. She lurches. The gun clatters to the floor and slides forward. I dive toward it, taking the chair with me.

My hands find cold metal. I clamp onto it, rise up to my knees.

My grandmother claws around on the floor, pulling herself up to standing. She stops when she sees the gun in my hand. Her mouth opens, but I don't give her a chance to form words. I point the gun and pull the trigger.

The blast is deafening.

My eardrums ring—a high-pitched, monotone scream.

My grandmother clutches her chest and looks down. When she takes her hands away, red stains her palms. A circle of deep crimson spreads across the front of her shirt. She looks up at me with my father's eyes. And then she collapses to her knees and slumps over on the floor.

Her eyes—*his eyes*—go glossy and dark.

My hands turn into my grandmother's. They won't stop shaking. The more I try to make them stop, the worse it gets.

The ringing grows louder. It has turned into a lament that drowns out all other sound. I cannot hear Vivian or Marcus or Cressida or Geoffrey as they run into the room asking questions. I cannot hear Luka, as he gently pries my fingers from the metal, unties my ankles from the chair, and whispers soundless words into my ear.

All I can hear is the gunshot.

Her body crumpling.

My ears ringing.

The shaking in my hands ripples into my arms. It moves all the way through my body until my teeth chatter so violently, I'm barely able to get the name out. "*Jillian.*"

Everyone stops and looks around, taking note of her absence. The keeper of the gun is the only one missing from the scene.

Luka sets the weapon carefully on the ground. "Can somebody check on her?"

Vivian leaves. Her husband follows.

Luka holds me, as if his strong arms might be able to still the shaking. As if his warmth might be able to chase away the coldness spreading through me like the dark crimson circle that spread on my grandmother's chest. But it doesn't matter how tight he holds on. Luka can't undo what happened.

She betrayed me and I killed her.

My own flesh and blood.

My father's mother.

From the very beginning, I was nothing more to her than a ticket to freedom. When she tried kidnapping me as a baby. When Luka and I found her in Shady Wood and she called me "the key." When I almost lost him to save her. I was only ever a means to an end. I was nothing more to her than a peace offering, a bargaining chip. And yet, I invited her here. I didn't even think to question it. I handed her our address.

And now …

Vivian returns. She stands in the doorway, her face an odd color, as though a familiar photograph has gone from glossy to matte. "I'm sorry. Your friend Jillian is dead."

Everything goes numb.

Link slides onto the seat where Luka was tied.

I move to the woman on the floor and remove the leather straps from her wrists. The symbol is there, etched on her skin underneath.

Chapter Twenty-Eight

Aftermath

I pore over the journals, turning each page with manic fingers. I should have known. I should have seen. If I would have been paying attention, I could have prevented it. Instead, I let relief blind me. I'd been so desperate to lock arms with another powerful Fighter, to have a piece of my family back, to redeem the mess-of-a-mission that was Shady Wood, that I failed to see what was right in front of my face.

Someone touches my hip.

I jump.

It's Luka. He takes a step back and holds up his hands, reminding me of the way I treated *her*—my grandmother. Like any sudden movement would chase her away.

His attention flicks to the notebook in my hand. "What are you doing?"

I open the journal wide, hold it in the air, and recite the words from memory. "A beacon will come before ... Evil will rise up to destroy her. If an offering is made, *she will give hope for freedom.*"

Jillian, dead.

The gun, vibrating between my palms.

A circle of blood, spreading like a bull's eye.

The mark on her wrist.

"The prophecy was talking about the *beacon*, not *the One.*

Evil rose up to destroy *my grandmother.* I was the offering. Hope for freedom. How did we not see it?"

And yet I know exactly how.

I was too busy ignoring the prophecy to embrace the prophecy. I didn't want that kind of pressure. I didn't want to make Luka worry anymore than he already was. I didn't want to believe. And because of that, Jillian was stabbed to death. My grandmother wasn't too deranged to realize that a gunshot would have woken up the whole house. She'd stolen a knife from the kitchen. I close my eyes, wishing I could shut my brain off. Wishing I could erase the images.

Clive, dropping his cloak.

The mark on my grandmother's wrist.

Gabe, dead.

Jillian, dead.

"Both of them were betrayers. I brought us on a mission to rescue the bad guys."

He touches my arm, but I pull away. I don't want to be touched.

I grab another journal and continue my search. For what, I'm not sure. It's a desperate scramble. A clawing for information. Maybe if I learn enough, I can prevent more deaths. Protect the people I love instead of endangering them. Maybe if I read enough, I can escape the black thundercloud of thoughts swirling overhead, threatening to unleash.

My grandmother, dead.

The mark on her wrist.

"How do you even get the symbol? Has Cormack been hijacked or something?"

The cloud breaks open and the terrible, horrible thing I've been trying to avoid pours out like acidic rain. I lifted the gun and I pulled the trigger and I took her life. "What if she was hijacked? What if she was hijacked and I killed her? What if she was innocent?"

"She wasn't."

"You don't know that."

"Listen to me. What happened was not your fault."

"Yes, it was." I'm the one who insisted we break her out of Shady Wood, never mind what Cap thought about it. I'm the one who went looking for the Fighter, despite Cap's orders to leave it alone. I'm the one who invited her here. It was all me. *Just* me. *Only* me.

"Tess ..."

"I can't trust anyone." Myself, included. Myself, most of all. I'm always wrong. I trust the wrong people. I accuse the wrong people. "It's like I have no idea which way is up. Nothing feels safe anymore."

Luka grabs my hand firmly and spins me around. He places my palm against his chest and covers my hand with his. "I'm up, Tess. I'm safe. I will help you get through this."

There's a faint bruise on his temple. A reminder that I could have easily lost him, too. Images of *what-could-have-been* grind what's left of my sanity to pulp. I remove my hand from his heartbeat, but Luka holds my chin so that I can't look away. My turmoil seems to strengthen him. Bring him back to life. It's like he only wants me when he's able to put me back together again. The dark turn of my thoughts has me squeezing my eyes shut. Retreating.

"Tess, look at me. I'm not going to let you drown."

"You can't save me. You can't even help me."

My words wound. I can see the pain flicker in his eyes, even as he hurries to cover it. Maybe if I inflict enough, he'll go away and the next person dead won't be him. Maybe I should do what I should have done forever ago, what I promised myself I would do the day I eavesdropped on his parents telling him to stay away from me. But the thought steals what's left of my breath. "Please, Luka, just leave me alone."

"Tess ..."

"I just—I need some space." I pull his hand away and turn around, back toward the journals.

There's a pause.

My heart beats into the silence as I wait for him to decide. A piece of it breaks at the sound of his receding footsteps. I'm all alone in the library, with nothing to keep me company but dark thoughts and a growing obsession. I have no idea how much time passes, how many journals I frantically skim before someone joins me.

When I look, it's not Luka. It's Link.

He sits with his feet propped up on the table, twisting his Rubik's Cube. "You know Williams is worried when he sends *me* to check on you."

I sink into Cressida's desk chair and cradle my head in my hands.

"He told me that you think your grandmother was hijacked."

"She could've been."

"She wasn't."

I look up. Link says it so matter-of-factly.

He sets his feet on the ground. "Your grandmother went through a whole lot of trouble to turn you over to this guy—Scarface. Why is that?"

"She thought he'd leave her alone if she handed me over."

"Exactly."

My exhausted brain ties into knots. Link's going to have to spell this one out for me.

"Hijackers don't act out of self-preservation. Or desperation. If she was being hijacked, she wouldn't have bothered turning you in for her freedom. Her freedom wouldn't have mattered. She would have waited for the opportune moment and killed you on the spot."

I let his words sink in. They make sense. A lot of sense. And yet, they don't bring the relief I long for. Jillian is still dead. And my grandmother was a betrayer. I resume my head-cradling and stare at the floor. My throat feels raw—like I've been screaming for hours, only I've hardly spoken all day. "I'm sorry."

"For what?"

I give him a wry look.

He sets his cube on the table. He's being strong for me, but I don't miss the pinched look in his eyes. He and Jillian were good friends. "Come on, Xena. You have nothing to apologize for. If Jilly-Bean were here right now, she'd say the same thing."

Tears prick my eyes.

"Jillian is dead because of your grandmother. Not because of you."

"But I—"

"Invited her. So what? We all let her stay. Don't play the blame game. Nothing good comes of it. Trust me, I speak from experience." He crosses the stone floor and leans against Cressida's desk, releases a long sigh and scrubs his face. "My father wasn't a very nice guy. He used to hit me. A lot."

His confession comes like a glass of ice water to the face.

"I never knew what would set him off, you know? There

didn't seem to be any rhyme or reason. He could be in a perfectly fine mood one second, laughing even. I'd say something innocent, and the next second, *wham*." He smacks his fist against his palm. "I'd be flat on the floor, my ears ringing."

I picture a ginger-haired little boy, beaten and bruised, and bile burns a path up my esophagus.

"I spent years and years trying to figure out what I was doing wrong. Trying to figure out what I could change so he'd stop hitting me. It took a solid twelve months of being free from him, away from that dysfunction, before I realized I didn't do anything to make him hit me. It was his fault; not mine. Just like Jillian's death was your grandmother's fault; not yours."

A tear tumbles down my cheek.

"I know what it's like to be betrayed by someone who's supposed to love you. I know what it's like when nothing feels safe. I know what it's like when trust feels impossible. But I also know that if we give into those feelings, if we start doubting every move we make or let ourselves live in isolation, then Xena ..." Link looks deep into my eyes. They're as serious and as certain as I've ever seen them. "The enemy has already won. We might as well surrender right now."

CHAPTER TWENTY-NINE

BURIAL

B eyond the patch of woods, the Rivard family property has a small burial plot. This is where we lay Jillian to rest. All of us gather around her grave to say goodbye.

The muggy air twists strands of hair around my face as Link gives an impromptu eulogy. He speaks like he's talking to her—his friend, Jilly-Bean. And as he does, vignettes play through my memory like moving images on a film reel. The agile way she hopped over the sofa and smiled at me that first night in the hub. The quickness with which she volunteered to go with me to New Orleans. The way she handled the gun in the alley after we escaped Agent Bledsoe. How quickly she forgave me after I accused her of betrayal. The smile we shared when she said that someday, she'd have a lifetime worth of crazy stories to share with her family.

Only now, she won't be able to share them. Death is such an odd thing, the way it happens in the middle of life. Yesterday, Jillian was here, all excited over our recent discovery regarding the list. And today … she's not. Today, she's with her father, wherever that is.

When Link finishes, we take turns dumping a shovelful of dirt into her grave. The hole becomes a small mound, one I stand by long after everyone else has gone, alone with the humidity and the bugs.

A mosquito stings my shin.

I slap at the spot, and notice another mound. Off in a lonely corner, as fresh as Jillian's. I told the Rivards to dump my grandmother's body in the river. Or burn it like the patients at Shady Wood, but they insisted on burying it. Murderer and murdered, laid to rest less than fifty yards apart. Without any thought or intention, I creep closer until I'm sitting in the dewy grass with my grandmother's leather straps clutched in my fist. They've been in my pocket ever since I pulled them off her. She couldn't see the mark. Only I could see that. Scarface must have warned her and so she covered it with these. I wrap one around my ankle and toss the other on the mound.

As dusk begins to settle, somebody sits beside me.

It's Cressida.

"She doesn't deserve to be buried here," I say.

"She was a human being."

"Not a good one."

"She wasn't an all-bad one, either."

Laughter escapes in a huff through my nose, leaving a bitter aftertaste in my mouth. "She killed Jillian. She was willing to kill Link and Luka in order to hand me over to Scarface. All for her *freedom*."

"She also raised your father. And spent the majority of her life tormented by evil and locked up against her will." Cressida plucks a blade of grass and twirls it between her fingers. "Your grandmother wasn't the enemy, Tess. She was *used* by the enemy. It's something we should never forget."

Someone approaches behind us.

I twist around.

It's Luka. We haven't spoken since I told him to leave me

alone in the library.

Cressida pats my knee, and with her words echoing in my ear, she pushes up to standing and leaves the two of us alone. Luka sits beside me, careful to keep his distance. It's only a few inches, but it might as well be the Grand Canyon.

"I spoke with Cap. He wants us to leave with Hezekiah as soon as possible."

"Does his car have enough room for all of my baggage?"

Luka doesn't answer. It was a rhetorical question, anyway. Instead, he gently takes my forearm in his hand, frowns at the angry red welts on my wrist, then nods at the leather strap around my ankle. "Why are you wearing that?"

"As a reminder."

"Of what?"

"Of who I never want to be." When I first found out about my grandmother—that she suffered from psychosis, I was terrified I would turn into her. A crazy person locked up in Shady Wood. Then Dr. Roth told me and Luka who we were—members of The Gifting. We weren't crazy at all, and that terror melted away. Now it returns. I'm afraid of turning into her all over again—a woman who let fear win. Someone willing to sacrifice lives in order to get what she wanted.

"You're nothing like her," he says.

I'm not so sure. "Sometimes I wish our roles were reversed."

He looks at me with those eyes. I could get lost in them a thousand times over, all in a single day. "What do you mean?"

"I wish I was your Keeper. I wish the only thing I had to consider was you. *Your* safety. *Your* happiness. *Your* life." I reach into his lap, slide my fingers down his palm, and thread them with his.

He grabs on tight, like my touch is his life raft. "But you're not."

I shake my head. No, I'm not. It's time to stop hiding from the things that cause him pain. It's time to stop ignoring what's right in front of my face. "As much as I want to think about you and only you, I can't. I don't have that luxury."

"I know." He pulls me into a kiss, so soft and gentle it makes me shiver. "I promise not to hold you back."

He says it bravely.

Confidently.

Like the words don't kill him.

CHAPTER THIRTY

NEW HOME, FAMILIAR FACES

Cressida gives us a new notebook that contains each of the prophecies we've been studying, along with the list. I guess she's been working on it ever since we arrived. We thank the Rivards for their hospitality, and under the cover of night, we slip into Hezekiah's sedan and drive away from New Orleans, one person fewer than when we came.

I sit in between Link and Luka in the back seat. Link sleeps against the window. Luka stays awake, looking out of his window, his knee touching mine while he messes with the attachments on his Swiss Army Knife, pulling each one out and snapping it back into place, over and over again. His own version of Link's Rubik's Cube.

At two in the morning, we stop in a small West Virginian town for gas. We drive through a sparse downtown, consisting of a bar, a pharmacy, an antique shop, a Hardee's, and a dilapidated park with a chipped bell-shaped statue. I jot a note to Agent Bledsoe and duct tape it to the inside of the bell. Luka has finally fallen asleep, so I don't have to explain. I haven't told him that Link and I've been doing a little dream hopping at night.

When I'm finished, I climb back into the car and stick the ear bud in my ear—the one that puts me to sleep. Bledsoe's dream is hazy, disjointed. But stable enough for me to find him and tell him what I need to say.

We'll see if it works.

The closer we get to Newport, the sparser civilization becomes, until eventually, we're the only car on the interstate. Dark clouds swirl overhead. A warning to stay away. To stop and turn around before it's too late. Hezekiah pulls off the interstate and stops in front of a tollbooth with a heavy-duty metal traffic gate barring cars from going any further.

I can see why.

A giant bridge looms ahead, a monstrosity climbing up out of Narragansett Bay, with crumbling towers and broken suspender cables. It looks on the verge of collapse.

"Are we driving on that?" Link asks.

A very legit question.

After twenty-three hours in a car with only two paranoid pit stops, I'm as eager as anyone to reach our destination and stretch my legs. I'm just not sure I want to risk plummeting to our deaths in order to do so.

Luka nudges my knee with his, his eyes pointed up and to the left. I follow his line of vision to a security camera. It swivels, then stops with its lens pointed directly at us. A man wearing sunglasses and a navy blue windbreaker steps out from the tollbooth, and for one panicked moment, I'm positive we've been tricked. Hezekiah isn't trustworthy either. He's led us straight to Agent Bledsoe.

But the man's nose is straight.

I release a stream of shaky breath. My heart, however, is still racing over that security camera. Our faces are being plastered on every news station across the country. We may

TH E G ATH E R I N G

almost have Bledsoe on our side, but he's just one person in the entire FBI. Society knows us as armed and dangerous criminals with a quarter-of-a-million-dollar bounty on our heads, because that's what the media has fed the public, and the public eats what the media feeds it. And here we are, sitting complacently in the back seat of a sedan, letting this man and this camera see us.

"What's going on?" Luka mutters.

"It's all right," Hezekiah says. "He's on our side."

His words offer little comfort. I wish I could trust that Hezekiah is who he says he is. Thanks to Claire and Clive and my grandmother, trust is hard to come by. Their betrayal has tinted everything in a shade of suspicion.

The man gives Hezekiah's window a rap with his knuckle.

Hezekiah rolls it down.

"I'm sorry," the man says. "You're gonna have to turn around."

"We're here to see Felix."

The man loops his thumbs through his belt loops. I can practically see his eyes behind the sunglasses, zooming in and focusing on each of us just like the camera overhead. After a beat, he returns to the booth. There's a clattering. A clanking. And the metal gate lifts.

Felix must be the magic word.

I lean forward. "I'm assuming that guy knows about The Gifting?"

"He's part of The Gifting."

"Really?" I twist around, trying to see him again, but he's out of sight.

And we're driving onto the bridge of death. There are parts of the bridge that have been blown off completely, so only one lane remains with no guardrails. Hezekiah veers around a hole. Not a pothole. A literal hole.

I grip the edge of my seat and force myself to look at the ceiling as the wind blows and our tires bump over loose chunks of gravel. The bridge is already long, and since Hezekiah has to go extra slow to avoid the whole plummeting-to-our-death ordeal, the trip across the bay drags into agonizing eternity.

When we arrive, raindrops spit at the windshield. Newport—or what's left of it, anyway—is all rubble and ash and charred buildings that stand at half-mast. We've entered a war zone while the rest of the world celebrates peace.

"I visited the city a few times before the attack." Hezekiah turns on his wipers. "Had a cousin in the navy."

"Was he here when it happened?"

He nods grimly, and I take note of the past tense. *Had* a cousin.

"Do you think they'll ever rebuild it?" Link asks.

"Not as long as the meters keep showing radioactivity."

My unease quadruples. Radioactivity? "Are we going to grow an extra arm or something?"

"Tests aren't hard to fudge." Hezekiah's gaze meets mine in the rear view mirror. "There are more people on our side than you realize. Felix is very well connected."

Felix. That name again. I'm assuming he's the captain of our new home. Makes me wonder how our own Cap feels about his demotion to mate.

The spitting rain turns into a downpour. We drive without speaking as the wipers squeak against the windshield and rain pounds the roof of the car and the clouds press lower overhead, spider webs of lightning crackling across their darkened underbellies. I think we've reached the naval base now, but it's hard to tell.

Finally, Hezekiah stops. "Welcome to your new home."

I look out the rain-smeared window at a building that was probably large once upon a time. Now, however, only the first floor remains and that looks about as stable as the bridge we just crossed.

"Push the button at the front doors." He shakes each of our hands, tells us it was a pleasure—that we're welcome in his tavern anytime—and that's that. We climb out into the rain and Hezekiah drives away.

The three of us run toward the front doors, out of the cold and the wet. A buzzing sound draws my attention upward. Another camera swivels in our direction, like it can detect movement. I shift behind Luka, who presses the button.

A computer automated voice crackles from an intercom. "State your identity."

"Luka Williams, Teresa Eckhart, and …" Luka looks at Link, apparently stumped. Link isn't his real name. It's a name he goes by because that's his gifting.

"Andrew Wyatt," Link says.

There's a loud click, like a lock being released. Luka grabs the handle and pulls the door open. We step inside to nothing. No sign of life. Just rain leaking in through the large holes in the ceiling and lightning flashing through broken bits of wall.

Not too far ahead is a doorway with a staircase sign above it. We walk through and begin our descent, my anticipation building. It's like we're in the belly of Detroit again, walking toward the red door, falling deeper into Alice's crazy rabbit hole. There's another door at the bottom, and a second security camera. We state our names, wait for the click, and step inside a small, sparse room.

This time, there is life.

A girl. Maybe my age, a little older. And a man, terribly thin. If not for the girl's healthy proportions, I'd probably worry about the food situation down here. He smiles at us while standing by a door across from the one we just walked through. She sits behind a sort of welcome desk looking mostly bored, chewing a wad of gum. Her gaze lingers longest on Luka.

"Welcome to headquarters." She picks up a walkie-talkie and presses a button on the side. "The new recruits are here. Do you copy?"

There's a brief pause, then a blast of static. "Copy that. Begin the new recruit procedure. I'll meet them as soon as I can."

"10-4." The girl lets go of the button. "Ralph'll show you around. When you're done, you'll have your interview and get your ID badges. Felix'll introduce himself whenever he's free. Dinner's over, but if you're hungry, I'm sure the cooks'll let you grab something to eat."

"What about Cap?" I ask. Surely, he's waiting for us.

"*Who?*"

"Josiah Aaronson."

"Is that the guy in the wheelchair?"

I have no idea why this annoys me. "Yes."

"He's probably with Felix." She turns her attention to the skinny man standing across from us, her expression softening, like she's talking to a small child. "Ralph, you want to take our new guests on a tour?"

Ralph bobs his head eagerly.

She skims a printed list in front of her and removes two keys from a lock box in one of the desk drawers. "Rooms 14 and 35. Make sure to come back and get your tokens when you're done."

Ralph takes the keys with an enthusiastic thank you and holds his badge up to the door. It unlocks and he waves us through. We step into a room—at least three times the size of the common room in the hub—with a large screen television, air hockey, a pool table, an old pinball machine, and several bookcases spanning the length of one wall. The room is filled with three times the amount of people, too. Sitting on couches watching TV. Chatting in small groups. Reading by themselves. I spot a girl with dirty-blond dreads and a nose ring flipping pages off in a corner. Ellen.

The familiarity of it lifts my spirits.

I raise my hand to wave at her when a small body catapults itself into Luka's arms.

"You're here!" Rosie squeezes his waist, hugs Link and then me. It feels like a lifetime since I saw her, and yet it's only been a week and a half. She says hello to Ralph, who says hello back. "You won't believe this place. It's huge. Way bigger than the hub."

I glance around, doing a rudimentary headcount. "How many people live down here?"

"A lot. And I'm not the youngest, either. They put me on babysitting duty while the parents are in meetings." She points to a small group of kids playing with action figures on the floor. The biggest looks around five or six. The smallest, a dark-haired little boy who can't be any older than two. "Where's Jillian?"

The question whacks me in the chest. Did Cap really not tell her? I turn to Luka and Link, unsure what to say. Link looks every bit as uncomfortable as me.

Luka cuffs Rosie under the chin. "Why don't we catch up tomorrow at breakfast? We have to finish this tour with Ralph."

Her big dark eyes fill with concern. Rosie's no fool. But before she can press for answers, the dark-headed boy shrieks and hits one of his playmates. She turns to us with an exaggerated eye roll and leaves us with Ralph.

He flattens his thinning hair with his palm and begins the tour, sharing facts about our new home with buoyancy in every syllable, like this place is the most interesting place on the planet. "This used to be a naval hospital. It was built all the way back in 1909. A long time ago, there were rumors that it was haunted by the ghosts of soldiers who passed away within the walls."

Link and I exchange a look.

Ralph keeps plugging along. "When it was shut down in the early 1990s, they left behind a lot of the rehab equipment, which comes in handy."

It doesn't take long to get my bearings.

Headquarters is much bigger than the hub, but the layout isn't nearly as confusing. There are three sections.

The main one has a gymnasium in the center with cement floors and a smattering of exercise equipment. Off to the side, in a walled-off corner, a smaller area contains mats and punching bags, similar to the one in the hub. There's the common room on one side of the gym and a cafeteria (which Ralph calls the mess hall) on the other, the welcome center in front, and a sort of general store (with snack food and toiletries, playing cards, magazines, and other odds and ends) behind.

Then there's the west wing and the east wing. The west consists of two parallel hallways, one of which Ralph leads us down. It's mostly classrooms and offices, with an infirmary at the end. The second hallway is closed off by a door marked *authorized access only.*

"What's down there?" I ask, interrupting Ralph's enthusiastic history lesson.

He shrugs. "They don't let me in."

I want to linger, ask more questions. I want to know what's behind the closed door, but Ralph leads us toward the east wing, which he calls the barracks.

"There's laundry at the end of the hall. Bathrooms and showers, too." Ralph unlocks a door marked 14. There are two single beds inside, a dresser, and a desk. "You boys will bunk in here."

"We're sharing a room?" Luka asks.

"Everybody shares. Unless you're Felix. He has his own." Ralph smiles, oblivious to the tension in the air.

Luka and Link—roommates? That ought to be interesting.

Ralph waits for them to set their bags inside and waves us further down the hall, stopping in front of door thirty-five. "You, Little Miss, are staying in here with Joanna."

I drop my bag on the floor, wishing I were rooming with Jillian. As soon as I step back out into the hallway and close my new door, another one opens.

A girl steps outside holding a towel. The familiarity of her hair, the slant of her shoulders, turns my breathing shallow.

I blink once. Twice. Three times.

But what I see doesn't change.

She sees us standing there in the hallway and stops, her pale cheeks flushing pink.

Ralph raises his hand and gives Claire a friendly salute.

CHAPTER THIRTY-ONE

SURPRISE, SURPRISE

I scratch the inside of my wrist. Claire can't actually be here. I must have fallen asleep in the backseat of Hezekiah's car and this, right here, is a dream. But my skin burns and she's still there, a beautiful frozen statue four doors down, her back straight, her posture regal, her attention sliding from me, to Link, to Luka.

My ears start to ring.

Clamminess spreads across my palms and under my arms. I see them. Men with white eyes, binding Luka. Dragging him away. Swirls of black mist lacerating his soul as he arches up in agony. And Gabe, dead on the chair.

The ringing in my ears turns to screaming. I lunge. I lunge at her like I did in the hallway of the hub, when Luka wouldn't wake up. But this time, Luka *is* awake. He grabs me around the waist to hold me back.

"Tess." The sharp, familiar voice cuts through the screaming in my ears.

Cap rolls toward us from the end of the hallway.

"What is she doing here?" My question escapes on a ragged breath.

"She lives here."

I shake my head. This has to be a sick joke.

"Thanks for giving them the tour, Ralph," Cap says. "I'll

take it from here."

Ralph doesn't have to be asked twice. He gives me a strange look—like *I'm* the dangerous one—and quickly scoots away.

When I turn around, Claire is gone. She must have slipped back inside her room. The monster she awoke inside my chest, however, remains. "She can't stay here."

"It's not up to you," Cap says.

"Then I can't stay here."

"Where else are you going to go?"

The monster turns into a fire-breathing dragon, scorching everything in its path. My heart. My lungs. I can't stop the memory from coming. It unfolds in slow motion—so vivid and real it's like I'm there again. Waking up with a gun pressed against my neck. Fearing for Luka's life. Then Link's life. Rope cutting into my skin. Cold metal in my hands. The blast. The kick. My grandmother, sinking to her knees, clutching a circle of blossoming red. She was supposed to help me. Instead, she turned me into a murderer. She was a wolf in sheep's clothing. Just like Claire. "She's a traitor."

"Felix conducted her interview himself. He believes she's remorseful."

"Then Felix is an idiot."

"Oh, I don't know about that." A man walks toward us— the epitome of poise—and stops behind Cap's chair. His hair is dark and slicked back. His face, thin. His clothes, carefully pressed—nothing at all like the faded rags we wore in the hub. Felix, I assume. He doesn't look like a captain of a ship. He looks like a mob boss. "I've gotten us this far."

He offers his hand. "You must be Teresa. Cap's told me all about you."

I look down at his manicured fingernails, a sour taste

spreading across my tongue. "Funny. He hasn't told me anything about you."

His dark eyes twinkle, like my comment amuses him. He turns to the two boys behind me. "You must be Luka and … Link, is it?"

Unlike me, they both shake his offered hand. Nobody mentions Jillian. It's like she never even existed. It sets my teeth on edge as Felix leads us back into the west wing, inside a room with a conference table. "Josiah tells me you've acquainted yourselves with the Rivard family journals. They have quite the extensive collection."

I don't say anything. Neither do Luka or Link.

"When you're finished catching up, each of you will have your admittance interview. They're conducted in here."

The three of us swap looks.

"Nothing to worry about. Standard procedure for all new recruits."

"Is it standard procedure to accommodate traitors?"

"It's standard procedure to accept anyone willing to fight. Claire is willing."

"Claire is a liar."

Felix chuckles. "You didn't tell me she was such a spitfire, Josiah."

Cap doesn't look nearly as amused. "It's a character trait that seems to grow stronger with time." He rolls up to the table. "Sit down, Tess."

I do. Reluctantly.

Felix remains by the door. "Once your interviews are finished, you're welcome to grab a bite to eat in the mess hall. We'll get better acquainted tomorrow." He gives the doorframe a couple taps. "I'm very eager to hear what you discovered on your mission."

As soon as he's gone, I turn on Cap. "You should have told us about Claire."

"Would you have come if I did?"

"How do you know I won't just leave now that I know?"

"Because you are smarter than your emotions. At least you're supposed to be." He massages the bridge of his nose, like he's fresh out of patience. "And you have bigger things to worry about than a petty feud."

"She nearly got Luka killed!" I look at Luka, expecting agreement. Expecting his outrage to match mine. If anybody has the right to be livid, it's him. Claire's the reason he lost his abilities as my Keeper. She's the reason he wakes up screaming in the night. But he looks largely unruffled. He doesn't even look surprised. "Did you know about this?"

He nods, that muscle tick-tick-ticking in his jaw.

"For how long?"

"Since you passed out on the train."

"And you didn't think to tell me?"

"I had other things on my mind."

"I can't believe this." I set my elbows on the table and run my fingers through my hair.

"There's something else you should know," Cap says.

Judging by his tone, it's not going to be something I like.

"Clive is here, too."

"*What?*" I stand so quickly, my chair topples back.

"Sit down." Cap slaps the table, his voice sharp and commanding. "Good leaders are not hotheads. It's time for you to get a handle on your reactions."

I swallow the heat billowing in my throat.

Luka straightens my chair.

I force myself to sit down.

Cap fills his cheeks with air and releases it in a slow, steady stream. "I had Sticks and Non bring him because he's too valuable an asset to lose. Clive gave them his full cooperation."

I keep my lips pressed together. I never took Cap for a fool. Until now.

"Everyone deserves a second chance, Tess."

"No, they don't." That is something I can never believe. Because if I do, then I would have to believe the same for my grandmother. But I didn't give her a second chance. I pulled the trigger without hesitating. I didn't aim for her arm or her leg. I shot to kill, and for the first time, I hit my target.

If Jillian wasn't already dead, she would have been proud.

A flinty-haired lady named Glenda with a tight bun, bifocals, and a sneezing problem conducts our interviews one-by-one, then leads us across the hall where we have our pictures and fingerprints taken. Apparently, we can pick up our new ID badges tomorrow. When we're done, we eat sandwiches in the large, empty mess hall—me, Link, and Luka. Turns out, Jillian was way more of a buffer than I realized. Tension has taken her place. It pulls up a seat and joins us at the table—an unwelcome fourth party.

"So …" Link crumples a napkin in his fist. "What's the update on the Bledsoe situation?"

My sandwich freezes by my lips.

Luka looks from Link to me. "What Bledsoe situation?"

I set the sandwich down. Judging by Link's expression, he had no idea I'd been keeping our nighttime rendezvousing a secret. "I've been … we've been visiting him."

"What do you mean?"

"Link and I've been hopping into Agent Bledsoe's dreams."

The hurt that flickers across Luka's face undoes me.

"It was my idea," Link says. "I thought it would be good to get someone like him on our side."

Luka's attention remains on me.

"It's not like she was in any danger or anything."

I shoot Link a look. He's not helping.

"How long have you been visiting his dreams?" Luka asks.

"Since our first night at the Rivards."

He nods a slow, singular nod.

Basically, I've had plenty of opportunities to fill him in.

Link coughs. He gives me an apologetic shrug, then picks up his tray. "I, uh, think I'll go get ready for bed."

I wish he'd take the tension with him. But that stays behind. It sits between me and Luka, as if enjoying the show. I pull the crust off my sandwich, what little appetite I had long gone.

"Can I tell you how maddening it is, hearing things secondhand from Link?" The softness in his voice pierces me way more than his anger ever could.

I can feel myself turning inward, shrinking in my seat. "I'm sorry."

"Why didn't you tell me?"

"It wasn't a big deal."

"Visiting an FBI agent in his sleep so you could turn him into a Believer?"

I twist my lips to the side, unsure what to say.

"Did you think I'd try to stop you?"

"No, I just … you had the leech that first night and then you were dealing with the whole not-being-able-to-protect-me thing and I don't know, I guess I didn't want you to worry anymore than you already were."

"You're not my Keeper, remember? It's not your job to protect me."

"I know."

"Then don't. Don't try to protect me. Tess, you have to stop leaving me out of things." Luka rubs the back of his neck. "I know you and Link have this thing—"

I shake my head. "We don't have a thing."

He gives me this look, like he knows better than I do.

"We don't. And it goes both ways, you know. You never told me about Claire."

"You're right. I'm just as guilty. It's something both of us can work on." Luka finds my hand under the table. "No more secrets, okay?"

"No more secrets." But even as I say it, there's a faint whisper in the back of my mind. *Transurgence.* I can't bring myself to ask him about it. It's like speaking the word out loud will make it real. It's like speaking the word out loud will make it possible.

He traces his finger up and down each of mine, his touch so light it makes my skin tingle. "I hate that I can't be here for you as your Keeper right now, but that doesn't mean I can't be here for you as your boyfriend."

I arch one of my eyebrows. "Boyfriend?"

"Only if you want."

Oh, I definitely want. It just sounds odd, considering the circumstances. Luka's so much more than a boyfriend. "It doesn't sound so bad."

"Okay, then." He smiles at me—that stomach-swooping, I-could-forget-my-own-name smile. "What's the *update* on the

Bledsoe situation?"

His imitation of Link is so spot-on, I can't help but smile, too.

After everything that's happened, it feels really, really good.

Turns out, my roommate is the gum-chewing girl who greeted us at the welcome center. She's no more enthusiastic during our second meeting than she was during the first. I walk inside my new room with my hair wrapped in a towel, a small bag of toiletries in hand, feeling lighter than when I arrived, while she sits on her bed, flipping through a magazine. I unravel the towel and begin combing out my hair in front of the mirror above our dresser, reliving my time with Luka.

"My name's Joanna, by the way." She doesn't look up when she says it. She speaks straight to her magazine.

"Oh. Um ... hi." She already knows my name, so what else is there to say?

Joanna flips another page. "Sorry about Ralph. His tours can get a little long-winded."

I picture the skinny man with the bounce in his step and the odd lilt in his speech. I can't seem to place him. Surely he's not a Fighter. Definitely not a Keeper. He's odd enough, like Anna. Maybe he's a Cloak. "What is he?"

"You mean what's his gifting?"

"Yeah."

"He doesn't have one." She turns another page. "Ralph's a Sleeper."

I stop mid-detangle. "What's a Sleeper?"

"Someone who shows all the right signs, but turns out to be just ... crazy. Felix has him on medicine, so he's pretty harmless."

"He, um, showed us a locked door."

"The private wing?"

"Yeah." I stare at Joanna's reflection in the mirror. She has yet to look up from her magazine. "Do you know what's back there?"

She shakes her head. "I don't have authorized access."

I resume my hair-brushing, my curiosity mounting.

"Those boys you showed up with are really hot."

I yank the comb through a stubborn knot and blink at the top of Joanna's head.

"Especially the one with the hair and the eyes—Luka? My friends can't stop talking about him."

How? We came late. When did her friends even see him? I put my comb inside my toiletry bag, give it a zip, and set it inside the top drawer of my nightstand.

"Do you know if either of them have girlfriends?"

Heat creeps into my cheeks as I fold down the comforter. "I'm sort of ... Luka's."

I slide in between the sheets, eager to exit this particular conversation. Joanna, however, has finally looked up from her magazine. She stares at me through the glow of her bedside lamp, one eyebrow quirked. "Sort of?"

"Not sort of. I'm his girlfriend."

"The other guy's single then?"

"Yeah. I guess so."

"Excellent. There's a serious shortage of cute, single guys down here." And with that, Joanna resumes her page turning.

I wrinkle my nose, feeling unduly annoyed.

CHAPTER THIRTY-TWO

BEHIND THE DOOR

B reakfast the next morning is a somber affair. Rosie's no longer in the dark about Jillian. Cap must have filled her in. Ellen, Declan, Bass, Jose, Danielle, and Ashley, too. They sit with me, Link, and Luka, asking questions I don't want to answer while all of us poke at our eggs. I'm itching to escape. The shock. The cloying grief. The prying eyes. Joanna's right. All the girls are staring at Luka. I don't blame them. The sexy brood he has going on only increases his appeal.

If the dark circles under his eyes have anything to say, he didn't sleep much better than I did. It came for me in fits and spurts, with my grandmother and Jillian haunting the edge of each dream. I'm so relieved when Cap approaches halfway through the meal that I almost forget I'm upset with him.

"Felix wants to speak with the three of you," he says.

I stand fast and leave my tray for Rosie. Luka, Link, and I follow Cap into the west wing, back into the interview room. Felix sits at the head of the table, cleaning his teeth with a toothpick.

"Here you are, bright eyed and bushy-tailed." He motions for us to sit, picks up three sheets of paper and taps them against the table into a neat pile. They're our intake forms. "It looks like we have ourselves a Linker, a Keeper. And then there's Teresa. A breed all her own."

"She's not a dog," Luka says.

Felix chuckles. The sound is every bit as condescending as it was last night. "Of course not. She's a Linker *and* a Fighter. It must be an exceptionally useful combination."

"And what about you?" I ask.

"Me? I'm just a Fighter." His response reminds me of Jillian's when we first met. *Just a Shield.* And yet she proved incredibly useful. Without her, the four of us never would have made it past that first day in Fort Wayne. We'd all be in prison cells or straitjackets.

And maybe Jillian would still be alive.

"Josiah tells me you made some important discoveries while you were with the Rivards. I'm impressed. I tried studying the collection once, but I didn't have the patience for it. Prophecies are very wooly things." Felix turns the toothpick over in his fingers. "Apparently, you found some sort of list. I'd love to see it."

I narrow my eyes. I want to trust him. Cap obviously does, otherwise we wouldn't be here. But then, Cap thinks Claire and Clive deserve a second chance. I think about Link's words—that without trust, the enemy has already won. But how am I supposed to extend any when I've been so badly burned? My grandmother's betrayal has turned my ability to trust into a tightly clenched fist, one I don't know how to open anymore. "What is it that you're doing down here, exactly?"

Felix smiles, like my question pleases him. "Perhaps it would be best if I showed you."

When Felix stops in front of the door leading to the private wing, my suspicion morphs into full-blown curiosity. He holds his badge up to a key lock. The light turns green. There's a low buzzing, a click, and just like that, we're standing on the other side.

The hallway is darker than the rest of headquarters. Damper, too. It feels a lot less like a military base and a lot more like a basement. A lot more like the hub.

Felix motions to his left, inside a small room with several metal filing cabinets. "This is where Glenda files the intake forms, along with detailed notes of completed missions."

"What kind of missions?" Link asks.

"Recruitment, mostly. Over here is the command center." Felix walks inside a room across the hall.

It's much bigger. And there are people. They wear headsets and work on computers, glancing occasionally at a series of television monitors up above, similar to the kind you'd find in a security room. Each of the screens shows something different. A view of the mess hall, where slow eaters finish their eggs. The gym, where people lift weights and run on treadmills. The empty hallway in the barracks, a flurry of activity in the west wing, Joanna at her desk in the welcome center. There's the door outside the hospital, where Luka, Link, and I stood after we climbed out of Hezekiah's car and dashed through the rain. The tollbooth, too, with the metal gate and the decimated bridge.

These monitors, I understand. The people in the command center are keeping an eye on things. Making sure nothing out of the ordinary is happening. But there are several monitors I can't figure out. Two of them show a city. Only instead of houses, there are rows and rows of tents and heaps and heaps of trash.

"What is that?" I ask, pointing.

"Newport's own refugee community."

Link and Luka move closer to get a better look. So do I, because that—right there on the screen—is nothing like the refugee communities I've seen televised on the news. Those always look clean, with small, cute houses and well-kept lawns. Never skinny, barefooted children dressed in rags, digging through piles of garbage. It looks like a picture from a third world country.

"That's here, in this city?" Link asks.

Felix nods.

I scratch the inside of my wrist. "How can there be a refugee community in Newport if the government says there's radioactivity in Newport?"

"Because this community is one of many not on record."

"And the few that are on record are carefully staged," Cap adds.

I peer at the two screens. It doesn't make sense. Why isn't the media all over this? Why pretend all is well when it's obviously not? And why would anybody choose to stay when this is how they're forced to live?

"What's that?" Luka points to a screen off to the left.

The familiar-looking hallway sends a shiver down the back of my legs.

"Shady Wood Rehabilitation Center. Josiah says you know it well." Felix slides his hands into his pressed pockets. "We're trying to hack into Detroit's Rehabilitation Center, but it's proving a bit more difficult."

"That's brilliant," Link mutters.

"Since they're two of the largest, most secure rehab facilities in the nation, we think it wise to keep tabs on the situation. Not surprisingly, we've noticed a disturbing pattern."

Link turns around. "Databases disappearing."

"Yes." A young woman with a heart-shaped face, black-framed glasses, and thick blond hair pulled up in a high ponytail rolls her chair away from a nearby computer.

"Meet Veronica," Felix says.

She stands and shakes our hands—mine, Luka's, Link's. "*Ronie.*"

"Veronica heads up business here in the command center. She's also one of the most talented hackers I've ever had the pleasure of knowing." Felix smiles. "I wonder, Andrew, if she will give you a run for your money."

Link's eyes light up. He flashes his dimples at Ronie, and a ping twinges in my chest.

"Not only are the databases disappearing," Ronie continues, "they reconfigure themselves shortly after, with all new names. We believe patients are being funneled from smaller rehab facilities around the country to these two, where they are being systematically disposed of."

A shudder ripples through my arms. I picture rows upon rows of the living dead. Holding rooms before they're tossed into ditches and lit on fire. Can this really be happening?

"Are you getting patients out?" Luka asks.

"We try to reach them before they are admitted," Ronie says.

"How?"

"We hack into government medical records and pinpoint anyone with markers."

Link rubs his chin. "Well that's a lot simpler."

"And also risky." Ronie pushes her glasses up her nose. "When we reach out to them that early, it can backfire. We have to keep our identities, our location, hidden. Many of the people we're trying to inform end up seeing our cryptic messages as proof that they are, in fact, crazy. Some end up checking themselves into rehab facilities faster, especially now with Cormack's new mental health initiative."

"That's how you ended up with Ralph," I say.

Luka turns around, away from the screens he's been studying so intently. "Our tour guide?"

"Joanna said he's not part of The Gifting."

"Joanna would be correct," Felix says. "Ralph is a Sleeper. We have a few down here."

"And you let them stay?"

"Where else would they go, Teresa? A rehab facility? Don't you think the other side will kill them as readily as they're killing us? When it comes to murder, our enemy isn't picky." Felix brushes at something on the lapel of his blazer, his attention lifting to Ronie. "How's the new project coming along?"

"Slowly."

"What's the new project?" Link asks.

"Veronica is trying to reproduce the dream simulator you created for Josiah."

Ronie looks from Cap to Link, one corner of her mouth quirking. "Maybe you can help me figure out what I'm doing wrong."

"Lead the way," Link says.

She does. We leave the command center behind and follow Ronie and Felix past a few doors into a darkened room. Ronie flips the switch. Except for two computers and a bunch of crisscrossing wires, the room is empty.

She boots up one of the computers, tapping the same key on the keyboard several times. "I've recreated the electrodes that stimulate sleep in the brain. I've also created a dream space. But I can't figure out how to send someone into it."

Link joins her at the monitor. They talk their own language—rapid-fire dialog that might as well be computer coding for all I understand. The more they talk, the more the shadow lifts from Link's face. It's a shadow I didn't even notice until now. He looks younger. Carefree. So much like the Link I knew at the hub.

Felix tucks his fist under his chin, his elbow resting on his opposite arm, an amused expression on his face. "Shall we leave you two alone?"

"It won't take long to get this up and running," Link says. "If Ronie doesn't mind, I can stay back and help."

"I don't mind," she says.

"Join us in the investigation room when you're done." And with that, Felix leaves.

Luka sets his hand on the small of my back and ushers me away from Link and Ronie and their mutual fascination with the crisscrossing wires, into a large room at the end of the hallway. Two people sit inside. I recognize them immediately, as they're right below us on America's Most Wanted list. The woman—number eight—sits at a desk off in the corner beside a metal filing cabinet. She has the same pixie haircut and astute eyes as her mug shot. The man—number nine—sits at a large table in the center of the room. He has the same round face.

Felix introduces them as Lexi and Connal.

"Welcome to headquarters." Connal stands and shakes our hands. He has crooked teeth, and surprisingly, a thick Irish accent. "Where's yer third?"

"Andrew's with Veronica, working on the dream simulator."

"He goes by *Link*." Andrew sounds way too weird. Serious-ly, what's up with Felix and his inability to call people by their preferred names? I nod at Connal. "I thought you had to be American to be on America's Most Wanted."

"Lucky us, they made an exception fer Lex and me." His friendly eyes twinkle at Lexi. Hers don't twinkle back. It doesn't seem to ruffle him too much. "We've heard a great deal about ye. A trio as scarce as hen's teeth, you are."

"Hen's teeth?"

Lexi rolls her eyes, then stands and shakes our hands, too. "You're rare, is what he means. Connal often forgets he's not in Ireland anymore." Her accent is every bit as thick as Connal's, but it's not Irish. It's British.

Interesting.

"What is that?" Luka points toward a large white board on wheels. A light bulb hangs from the ceiling and dangles in front of it, giving the board a spotlighted effect. There are sketches of faces taped onto it. The drawings don't look quite … human.

"The FBI has their wanted list," Felix says. "We have ours."

I step closer, goose bumps rising on my skin. "Who are they?"

"Enemy leaders with a high level of authority. Connal and Lexi are keeping tabs on them."

Adrenaline courses through my veins. I picture Scarface, tormenting my grandmother. Tormenting Luka. Tormenting my brother and my mom. He's been hunting me, hurting the people I love. Maybe it's time I turn the tables and hunt him. "I have someone I'd like to add."

Felix folds his hands behind his back. "When we're finished here I'll have you speak with the sketch artist. We can get a rendering. See if anybody else knows him."

"What's that board?" Luka nods toward another, off in the shadow. Instead of sketchings, this one has actual photographs.

"Believers in positions of influence. The more we have on our side, the better. Josiah tells me you've been working on an FBI agent. Michael Bledsoe, is it?"

I nod. "I can check in on him tonight."

"Excellent." Felix strolls toward a new board. One that is blank. He picks up a dry erase marker and hands it to me. "Now let's examine that list, shall we?"

CHAPTER THIRTY-THREE

A BIG DIFFERENCE

Link and Ronie join us halfway through our brainstorming. Ronie pulls up recent photographs and video of Secretary Young and Chief Fredrick. I pore over them until I find what I'm looking for. The mark—it's on the secretary's wrist and the chief's neck. Ronie prints pictures of both and we stick them on the white board beside a picture of President Cormack. We're still not sure whether she's the *king* or the *idol*.

As far as the *physician*, we start with the directors of our nation's two largest mental rehab facilities—Shady Wood and Detroit. As I study a large stack of printed photographs—my eyes slowly crossing—Luka sets a drink on the table next to my elbow. It's a small bottle of chocolate milk.

He shoots me a wink. "Thought you could use a pick-me-up."

"Where'd you get it?"

"Saw it in the general store. I convinced the lady working there to give me a freebie."

I rub my thumb over the cap, feeling touched. The last time I had chocolate milk was that night in Motel California. "Thank you."

He leans over, his lips close to my ear. "See? This place isn't so bad."

I can't help myself. His words make me smile. This *place*

houses Claire and Clive. If I had to choose between no traitors and chocolate milk, I'd choose no traitors. Since Felix isn't giving me a say in the matter, I guess chocolate milk is a nice consolation. I twist off the lid and take a long drink. It carries me through three more stacks of pictures. I'm not able to find the mark on either director, but that could be due to the fact that we haven't found anything that gives me a good enough look.

We continue our theorizing, my niggling thought from the Rivard library growing in size. This can't all be centered in the United States. We have to be missing something. We toss around ideas, but nothing sticks. Connal's growling stomach finally convinces us to call it quits. We aren't going to solve the riddle today. At least not before lunch.

According to Felix, it's time to head to the mess hall. I ask Cap to bring me to the sketch artist first. Luka comes along.

"Is this accurate?" the woman asks, holding up the rendering.

I study the two scars running the length of his cheeks—one put there by my grandmother, the other by Luka. The drawing isn't perfect, but it's accurate enough to tighten my chest. Accurate enough to put murder in Luka's eyes. "It's really close."

"Do you know of anybody else down here who's interacted with him? The more feedback I get, the better the picture."

I turn to Cap. "I want to speak with Clive."

Luka and I follow Cap into the barracks. "He's been taking his meals in his room."

"Why?"

"Self-imposed isolation. The only time he leaves is to see the counselor."

"The counselor?"

"It was one of Felix's stipulations. Before they could live here, Clive and Claire had to agree to see Dr. Sheng. He's a Shield, but he's also a qualified therapist."

I don't care how qualified Dr. Sheng is. He can't undo what Clive did.

Cap stops in front of a closed door. Clive's, I assume. I don't wait for Cap to knock. I open the door, stride through the darkened room, and smack the drawing on the mattress.

Clive sits upright. I don't know why the sight of him doesn't cause the same visceral reaction in me as seeing Claire. Maybe it's because beneath my anger, I understand his motive. He just wanted his family back. Claire, on the other hand, acted out of pure selfishness. Exactly like my grandmother.

He picks up the sketch. "What's this?"

"It's your friend. Don't you recognize him?"

He shoves it away. "He's no friend of mine."

"That's funny. He was a couple weeks ago."

"He was never my friend."

I peer down at him. His hair—cut to army regulation only two weeks ago—is disheveled, and gray whiskers cover his once clean-shaven face. How in the world can Cap trust him so easily after what he did? "Two weeks ago, you were willing to hand us over to cut a deal. What changed?"

He doesn't answer.

"At least tell me what you said to get everyone to believe you."

"I told the truth."

"Which is what—exactly?"

"If I could take it back, I would."

I roll my eyes. "Or your plan backfired and now you're trying to save your skin."

"I don't care about my skin. I've never cared about my skin. All I care about is my family. They mean more to me than anything."

"Which is why you sold us out."

"It's also why I'll never do it again. It didn't take long after I dropped my cloak to realize something."

"What did you realize?"

"If the other side wins, it won't matter who we're with. This world won't be worth living in." He slouches against his headboard. "If you want a reason to believe me, there it is. I'm on your team because more than anything, I want to give my family a world worth living in again."

The sound of conversation and clinking silverware circles the cafeteria. Luka isn't with me. On the way from Clive's room, we ran into the man of the hour—headquarters' own certified therapist. Cap must have already told Dr. Sheng about Luka, because when Cap introduced us, Dr. Sheng asked Luka if he wanted to speak in his office. I thought Luka would decline. Instead, he gave me a kiss and went with a determined set in his shoulders, like counseling might get him his gifting back.

Discomfort squirms in my gut as I file into line. A few tables away, Claire eats with some girls, chatting like she belongs. She looks up and her icy blues meet mine for a brief moment before flitting away.

Everybody deserves a second chance …

Cap's words scratch like wool. Cap's words have me picturing the look on my grandmother's face as she clutched her chest. I shake it away and grab a plate of hamburger and fries, trying to make sense of the luxury. There's no grocery store for miles, and even if there was, it would take a constant stream of Runners to supply enough food for this many people. "Where does all this come from?"

"Felix is very well connected." Cap wheels forward with his tray in his lap, scanning the busy room like he's looking for someone in particular. Straight ahead, Lexi lifts her hand to wave. Cap jerks his head for me to follow. She's sitting alone, her food untouched, like she's waiting for someone to join her.

"Fancy a sit?" she asks when we arrive.

I slide onto the bench, expecting Cap to join us. Instead, he tells me to enjoy the meal and rolls off to sit with Sticks and Non, leaving Lexi and me by ourselves. My brow furrows. Why do I feel like I've just been set up on some sort of blind date?

"Cap thought we might eat lunch together. Have a bit of a chinwag."

"A what?"

"A talk. A catch up. Whatever you call it here." She twists the cap off her bottled water and takes a drink. "He thought you might have some questions for me."

My furrow deepens. If I had questions, why would they be for Lexi?

"We have something in common, you and I."

"You mean the Most Wanted list?"

"Well, yeah. But not that. I'm going on about having a Keeper."

My mouth drops open. *A Keeper?* I stare—buggy-eyed—at the pixie-haired woman sitting across from me. Lexi has a Keeper? "Who?"

She gives me a look, like I'm being dumb on purpose. "Connal."

I can actually feel my eyes going buggier. Connal is Lexi's Keeper? I twist around, searching for the round-faced Irishman. I spot him across the room, eating with some guys I don't know, and find myself rewinding the morning, replaying every single one of Lexi and Connal's interactions through the filter of this new discovery. This is the first time I've met a whole pair before. No tortured Keeper with a dead *anima*, like Gabe. These two are fully intact. And yet ... nothing clicks. Not even with hindsight. In fact, as I do my replaying, all I see is a distance between them that doesn't line up with what I know about Fighters and their Keepers.

"I heard about what happened to Luka."

I twist back around, blinking several times. "What?"

"You're off with the fairies, aren't you? I said, Cap told me about what happened to Luka. That he lost his gifting."

The words irritate me. It's not Lexi's business. So why is Cap telling her anything? I peel open a ketchup packet and squirt it onto my plate.

"Connal would go absolutely barking if that were him."

Yeah, well. *Barking* Luka is better than no Luka.

Lexi takes a bite of her burger, chews, and swallows it down. "How'd the two of you end up together?"

"I, uh, had an *episode*." Complete freak-out and hospitalization is a little more accurate, but there's no reason to go into details. "My family moved across the country to get me some help and Luka was my next-door neighbor."

"A mystery how that happens, isn't it? The way life forces us together?" She doesn't sound mystified, though. If I had to assign an emotion, I'd say she sounded ... aggravated.

I swirl a French fry into my ketchup. "What about you and Connal?"

"I couldn't find a job after college. Employers didn't seem to care that I graduated Summa Cum Laude from Edinburgh. Funny enough, I won a raffle incentive to come here. It was like winning Willy Wonka's golden ticket. I thought for sure there'd be more opportunity. Connal and I went through the immigration screening process together."

I pull the onion off my hamburger.

"He told me he had dreams about me. I thought he was a tosser. It sounded like a really lame pick up line, until I realized he saw the same things I saw. Not long after, the pair of us were accused of crimes we didn't commit and forced into hiding. And now here we are, stuck together down here."

Stuck. Forced.

If I didn't know any better, I'd say Lexi isn't a fan of her Keeper. I take a bite of my burger and glance again at Connal. This time, he catches my eye. His attention shifts to Lexi, then he shoots me a friendly wink and returns to the conversation at his table. He seems like a nice-enough guy. "Do you not like him or something?"

"Who?"

"Connal."

"I like him just fine. Why?"

"I don't know. I get the impression you're annoyed with him."

Lexi rolls her eyes. "That's because he fancies himself in love with me."

The furrow between my brow returns. "Is that a bad thing?"

"It isn't real."

"I'm not following."

Lexi wipes her hands on a napkin and crumples it into a ball. "He didn't choose me. It's not love if it's not a choice, is it?"

Something tells me she's not actually asking. I set my partially-eaten burger down. I'm too busy digesting her words to deal with actual food. They awaken old insecurities. Insecurities Luka laid to rest that night in the hub, when Cap agreed with my plan to rescue my grandmother and Clive, and Luka flipped out. I barged into his room, all false bravado, ready to give him a piece of my mind. Instead, he gave me a piece of his heart.

Anima, Tess. Breath of life. It's not your safety I care about. It's your being.

"You're his *anima*, though. It means breath of life."

"That's just it. I depend on my breath to live. I need it. But that's not love. The two are quite different, don't you think?"

CHAPTER THIRTY-FOUR

PARTIES AND COUGARS
AND SNIPERS, OH MY

Joanna smacks a wad of gum while penciling her eyelids. Another luxury the hub never had—makeup. Or gum. The general store has both, and you can buy whatever you'd like with the appropriate amount of tokens—the currency down here beneath the decimated city of Newport.

I've learned a lot my first full day at Headquarters.

There are 140 residents now and according to Joanna, that number grows by the week. Anyone underage attends classes like we did in the hub, except here, underage is sixteen or younger. Everyone older works. And there's plenty of it to do. Felix has a pretty elaborate system set up to maintain life, complete with various offshore bank accounts and a whole web of contacts that keep us stocked in supplies and information. Jobs include accounting, analyzing, recruiting, security, sourcing, procurement, health care, teaching, training, janitorial, food prep. And those are only the ones I can remember.

Basically, everybody has a job to do. There are no freeloaders; not even the Sleepers.

But it's not all work, either. Felix is a big believer in morale. Hence, Joanna's penciling.

"You really don't want to come?" she asks, finishing her right eye. "Next movie night won't be for a month."

"I'm pretty tired." My mother's voice echoes in my head. *You should have fun*, she'd say. *Go make some friends.* But I don't want to make friends. I'm not here to make friends. And even if I were, everything feels too transient for friendship. Like the whole world could flip on a dime.

"I overheard your friend Link inviting Ronie."

I look up from the book I've been trying to read.

Joanna drops the eyeliner into her makeup bag and pulls out a tube of lipstick. "Figures one of the cute new guys would go for an older woman."

"I doubt Link is *going* for anybody. He's just friendly."

"Well, they looked awfully *friendly* in the common room a little bit ago, if you know what I mean."

For some reason, my cheeks turn warm. I flip a page, trying not to imagine whatever Joanna's implying. It doesn't work. A picture of Link and Ronie sitting together on the floor, cuddled up in front of the big screen, has that same silly twinge I felt in the private wing returning.

"Is Luka going?" Joanna feigns casualty. I'm not fooled.

All day, girls have been ogling him. While we worked out in the gym, while he played a game of air hockey with Rosie, while we ate in the mess hall for dinner. Luka ignored them as he told me about his session with Dr. Sheng. I listened, unable to shake off the things Lexi told me during lunch. They've latched on like a leech and there's no Samson in sight.

It's not love if it's not a choice, is it?

"Yoo-hoo. Earth to Tess."

My eyelids flutter.

"Did Luka mention if he's coming?"

"I don't know." As Lexi would say, I've been away with the fairies all day. Maybe he did tell me, and I nodded absently without really hearing.

"Well then, don't wait up." Joanna slides the lid onto her tube of lipstick and kisses the air. "A group of us always head to the common room after to shoot some pool. If you want to come, that's where we'll be. If you don't, have fun *sleeping.*"

Being lame, she means. I don't care. I have work to do.

As soon as she's gone, I flip another page of *The Golden Compass*. It's a book my dad read to me and Pete when we were little. I'm not sure why I snagged it off the bookshelf. All it does is tie my throat into a giant knot of sentimentality. A few pages more and I set it on my nightstand. It's only 8:35. I'm nowhere close to tired. But I slip into my pajamas, slide between the sheets, and close my eyes, forcing thoughts of Link and Ronie, Lexi and Connal, Luka and his female fan club out. I mean, really. I told Joanna that he's my boyfriend. So why is she asking if he's going to be at the party, like they might hook up or something?

I push out a breath. Felix gave me specific directions to relay to Agent Bledsoe. He's to make his way to Newport. He will tell the security guard that Felix sent him. He will wait at the south end of the refugee community, near a statue of a soldier and a tank. I run over the directions again and again, my mind fixed on Bledsoe's crooked nose.

But I'm still not asleep at ten. There's laughter out in the hall at eleven. Joanna's bed is still empty at midnight. With a loud groan, I stick my head under my pillow and beg sleep to come.

When it finally does, he's already waiting for me.

"I got your letter," he says.

"And?"

"I have no idea how any of this is possible, but I believe you."

"Will you help us?"

"I became an FBI Agent to protect the innocent. You're innocent. Tell me what I can do."

"How soon can you get to Newport, Rhode Island?"

"*Newport?* Is that where you are?"

"It doesn't matter where I am. How soon can you get there?"

He hesitates, the mistrust in his eyes mirroring my own. I don't blame him. Newport isn't exactly a place anybody visits these days. "I should be able to get there by three."

"Tell the guard at the bridge that Felix sent you. Then make your way to the refugee community."

"Refugee community? In *Newport?*"

"It's on the south end of the old naval base. Look for the statue of a soldier and a tank and wait there for further instruction. Make sure you're not followed and don't even think of bringing anybody along. We'll know if you do and you'll never see or hear from us again."

Bledsoe shakes his head—not in refusal, but in disbelief. "This is crazy."

The truth, I'm learning, often is.

I wake up in a cold sweat, unsure where I am or how I got here. It takes a few shaky breaths before clarity comes, but even then, the heaviness draped across my shoulders remains. I fumble around in the dark to get dressed while Joanna's snores drown out my noise. It's almost seven, but of course, there's no light down here. After two weeks of sun, losing it again chaffs. How long will I have to wait to see it again this time?

I escape into the lit hallway, which is a ghost town. I brush my teeth and rinse my face, then make a beeline for Luka and Link's room. I want to update them both on the situation. When I knock, there's no answer. Luka isn't an exceptionally hard sleeper and he's not one for sleeping in. It's five after seven now. I'm sure he's awake, unless he joined the fun last night and stayed out with Joanna. I knock again, wait a few seconds, then twist the handle.

The door creaks open.

Light from the hallway spills inside the darkened room, paving a path of fluorescent yellow on a mess of comforter and sheets twisted around Link. Luka's bed is empty, the comforter casually tossed over his pillow, glasses resting on a book on his nightstand.

"Link," I hiss.

Nothing.

"Link," I say, louder.

He turns over on his side, arm flung over his face.

A tornado could rip apart what remains of the old hospital above and he'd probably sleep right through it.

I walk to his bedside and pull out his pillow. "Link!"

He bolts upright, his hair sticking up in every crazy direction. "Who did it?"

I bite back a smile.

Link rubs his eyes, then glances from Luka's empty bed to the pillow I'm holding in my hand. "Xena? What's going on?"

"Agent Bledsoe's on his way. I met him last night. He believes us." Or at least he says he does. I toss the pillow back. "I'm going to find Felix and Cap and let them know."

"Hold on. I'll coming." He swings his legs around to put his feet on the floor, his chest completely bare.

I avert my gaze. "Do you know where Luka is?"

"No idea. I didn't hear him get up."

"Of course you didn't."

Link shoots me his lopsided grin and pulls on a pair of socks. Thankfully, he's already wearing sweatpants. "You can turn on the light if you want. Now that you've ripped me so mercilessly from slumber."

I flip the switch.

He squints against the onslaught of artificial brightness. "Sorry, by the way. For getting you in trouble with Williams the other night. I didn't know you hadn't told him about our plans."

"You didn't get me *in trouble* with him."

"No? He seemed pretty tense about the whole thing. But then again, Williams always seems kind of tense."

"Around you, maybe."

"Why is that, do you think?"

I snag a T-shirt off his floor and throw it at him. "Will you get dressed?"

Chuckling, Link pulls the shirt over his head. "So where were you last night? I kept waiting for you to show up for the movie. Ten tokens if you can guess what it was."

"Star Trek."

"How'd you know?"

I raise my eyebrows. "They seriously showed Star Trek?"

"*Star Trek into Darkness.* You missed out on complete and utter epicness."

Somehow, I have a hard time picturing Joanna getting all pretty for Spock.

"Guess who's a Trekkie?"

"Ralph the Sleeper?"

Link laughs. "Ronie."

Of course she is. "What's up with you computer nerds and those movies?"

"First of all, we prefer the term technogeek. And second of all, they aren't movies. They're a way of life."

I roll my eyes. "Isn't Ronie a little old for you?"

"A little old for me? Why Xena, what are you insinuating?" Judging by his smile, he knows exactly what I'm insinuating.

A slow burn works its way into my cheeks.

Link reaches past me to grab a bottle of Listerine off the dresser and leans close to my ear. "She's twenty-three. I'm nineteen. I don't think that makes her a cougar." His attention dips to my lips. "And it's not like anybody else is interested."

The burn in my cheeks intensifies. I scratch my ear and take a quick step back, bumping into the dresser as I do. "There's Joanna."

"Joanna?"

"My roommate. She thinks you're hot."

Link laughs and walks out into the hallway.

I take a deep breath and follow him. I don't get very far.

Claire is standing by the doorway, looking every inch the eavesdropper as she holds out Link's Rubik's Cube. "You left this in the common room last night."

Disgust blisters inside my mouth. Claire was at the party?

"Thanks," Link says, taking it.

Her attention slides to me. "If you're looking for Luka, I saw him go into the private wing."

"What are you, stalking him now?"

"Just trying to help."

"You've helped enough, thanks."

"Xena ..."

I don't stick around to listen to Link's reproof. If you don't have anything nice to say, and all that jazz. Or in my case, if you want to karate chop someone in the neck. I quicken my stride, desperate to get as far and as fast away from her as possible.

Link catches up with me outside the door of the private wing, a bottle of Listerine and his Rubik's Cube in hand. He let's out a low whistle.

"What?" I stick my badge up to the lock (Glenda got me a new one with authorized access yesterday).

"Remind me to never get on your bad side."

"Don't try to kill me and you won't."

We find Luka in the training room, hooked up to the new dream simulator with Connal. Link's new BFF is there, too, the glow from the computer monitor reflecting off the lenses of her glasses. When she sees Link, her cheeks turn pink—a reaction that has me making more insinuations—and then she quirks her eyebrow at his Listerine. "That's one way to fight plaque."

He glances down at the bottle in his hand, as if just noticing it.

I look at Luka, lying on the floor attached to wires. Even unconscious, frustration furrows his brow. Poor Connal will probably be stuck in there until Luka has his powers back.

"How's it working?" Link asks.

"They just went in. So far, everything seems to be going smoothly."

I leave the new lovebirds to their conversation and continue down the hall into the investigation room. As I suspected, Felix is already there, sitting at the table with Cap and Lexi. The three of them are hunched over something, but I can't tell what.

"I met with Agent Bledsoe last night."

Felix looks up. "And?"

"He'll be at the refugee community at three o'clock this afternoon."

He nods approvingly.

My attention drifts to the white board we created yesterday, the one with the list. "So what happens now?"

"I'll have Isabelle meet him at three."

"Who's Isabelle?"

"One of our residents." Felix stands, buttoning the single button of his suit coat with one hand. "We found her living in the refugee community, which means she's familiar with the people and its layout. She also happens to be quite skilled at losing a tail, should the skill necessitate itself."

My nerves start to stir. What if Agent Bledsoe is as good of a liar as Claire and Clive and my grandmother? What if I'm about to send another innocent person to their death? "How do we know it's not a setup?"

"We'll send Joe, just in case."

"Who's Joe?"

"The security guard at the bridge. He's a former Navy SEAL officer and a very talented sniper. He'll keep an eye on the situation should Isabelle require any assistance."

CHAPTER THIRTY-FIVE

LIKE SHEEP

I stand in the command center between Cap and Connal, staring at the two monitors above that show the refugee community. Felix holds a walkie-talkie as he strolls up and down the aisle of computers, each manned by someone wearing a headset. Non happens to be one of them, off in the far corner, focusing intently on her screen. Link peers over Ronie's shoulder as she sits at a computer of her own, typing on the keyboard until a third monitor blinks to life.

"Got it," she says.

The feed comes from Joe the Sniper's eyepiece. Ronie rigged a tiny camera up so we could see what he sees. Right now, that's nothing but his boots and moving patches of sparse grass. I can't watch for too long without getting dizzy, so I focus on the screen to the left.

Three barefooted children play King of the Hill on a heap of trash. A stream of dirty water and who-knows-what-else runs beneath clotheslines bowing low with the weight of ragged laundry. I still can't believe this exists here—in the United States. Not just one, but several. "I don't understand why people keep coming here if this is what they're coming to."

"They don't know any better," Lexi says. "The refugee and immigrant communities I saw advertised in Great Britain—and I'd wager, everywhere else in the world—are the same staged advertisements on the news here. Everybody wants to come to America, because America promises hope. By the time we arrive and catch on, it's too late to go back."

That niggling sensation returns. Something's not adding up. Our country was a hot mess until recently. The turnaround in unemployment rates and street violence happened so fast it still has most people's heads spinning. Lexi and Connal and Newport's refugee community have been around long before the change. So why would they think America could offer any hope?

A flash of sunlight fills the screen of the third monitor, momentarily blinding us as Joe peers into the sky. The camera jostles downward. Blades of grass and weeds poke up from the bottom of the screen, as though he's lying on the ground.

The walkie-talkie crackles to life.

"Found a secure location. Have Isabelle in my sight. Over."

Sure enough, the monitor from Joe's eyepiece comes into focus, and off in the distance stands Isabelle—a large, hefty woman with dark skin and a head wrap made out of brightly-patterned fabric. According to Felix, she came from the refugee community she's standing outside of now. Supposedly, several people in Headquarters have.

Felix pushes a button. "Copy that."

Movement in the periphery of my vision grabs my attention. Luka walks inside the room, the tension around his eyes not as intense as it was after his training session with Connal. Afterward, he met with Dr. Sheng again. Either the session helped, or he's getting better at hiding his frustration.

Luka stops beside Connal and nods at the monitors. "Any trace of Bledsoe?"

"Not yet," Cap says.

I look at the clock on the wall. Ten to three.

A monitor showing newsfeed from a local station cuts to commercial. B-Trix fills the screen, her pearly white smile undoubtedly dazzling millions of viewers as she starts talking about an amazing new breakthrough in pregnancy screenings.

"Not only is this new screening less invasive," she says, "it's five times as accurate, virtually eliminating the risk of false negatives."

"What a load of bollocks," Connal mutters under his breath.

I couldn't agree more. Is B-Trix even aware of what she's saying? What she's supporting? Those screenings are nothing more than a ploy to eradicate The Gifting.

Pregnant women aren't the only ones being screened.

The thought comes out of nowhere, bringing about the shape of an epiphany that has my heartbeat picking up speed. I step closer to the three screens, my eyes darting back and forth, taking in all the people. Immigrants and refugees crammed together.

From all over the world.

It doesn't make sense. Why invite these people in when up until very recently, we were struggling to take care of our own citizens? Why continue to invite them in when we're still trying to get our feet under us as a country? It's a question Jillian had in the hub. A question I've had before, too. One that's never made sense. A disconnect in President Cormack's manifesto. The singular odd duck that doesn't fit with the rest of her philosophy—*we're only as strong as our weakest links.* My mother made a flippant comment once—that we were only letting in the strongest and the smartest. That's what the screenings were for. But the people I see now, foraging for food, don't look strong at all.

"Hey Connal, when you went through your immigration screening process, did you undergo a body scan?"

"Sure. Is there a reason yer asking?"

Goose bumps march across my skin. *"We are gathered like sheep to the slaughter."*

"What are ye going on about?" Connal says.

"Our president. *Our* chief of press. *Our* secretary of security and defense." The missing puzzle piece falls into place with astounding clarity. I point at the screens. "This is why."

Everybody stares. Even Non from across the room.

"We're being herded. The United States is like a giant pen." I stare from Isabelle, waiting by the statue, to B-Trix, flashing her smile. I see it, right there on her neck. "And I think I just found our *idol.*"

The investigation room hums with palpable energy. All of us—me, Luka, Link, Ronie, Lexi, Connal, Felix, and Cap—have come alive with my latest discovery. Our uncertainty, our sense of something missing, has turned into confidence.

Felix erases the board and rewrites everything we know in bold strokes.

King – President Cormack, neck

Eye – Secretary Young, wrist

Censor – Chief Fredrick, neck

Idol – B-Trix, neck

Physician – Director of Shady Wood/Detroit Rehab Facility?

Luka stops biting his thumbnail. "Why the neck and the wrist?"

It's a question I'm mulling over, too. Surely there's a reason for the different locations.

I prop my foot on the seat of my chair and twist my grandmother's leather strap around my ankle, thinking about the other times I've seen the mark. It was on my grandmother's wrist. Barking-Wren's, too. It was on the neck of the teenager who tried opening fire on innocent shoppers in the mall on Black Friday. My brother Pete almost had it on his forearm, which is close enough to the wrist. There doesn't seem to be any rhyme or reason. No pattern. At least none that I can see.

At quarter past five, Felix's walkie-talkie crackles to life.

"Isabelle arrived." It's Joanna's voice. "Do you copy?"

"Copy that. Please have her bring our new guest to the conference room."

"Ten-four."

Felix lets go of the button on his walkie-talkie. "Shall we, Teresa?"

I blink, looking around—at Cap, Lexi, Connal—waiting for Felix to invite them, too. But he doesn't. "Just me?"

"You are the one who got him here, aren't you?"

"Me and Link."

"That's nice, but we don't want to overwhelm the man. We also don't want to keep him waiting. Ronie, do you have the pictures?"

"I put them in an envelope in the conference room."

"Very good." With that, Felix straightens his suit coat and leads the way out of the investigation room.

When we arrive, they're already inside. Agent Bledsoe is blindfolded. According to Felix, Isabelle's been driving him around all this time to ensure our location remains secure. Felix shuts the door and pulls out a chair for me. The legs scratch against the cement floor. Bledsoe turns his ear toward the sound, as if trying to make sense of his surroundings as Felix unclasps the button of his coat and sits at the head of the table. "You may remove his blindfold, Isabelle."

She does.

Bledsoe squints against the fluorescent lighting.

This entire thing has to be incredibly disorienting. Visited in dreams by two alleged criminals, traveling to a decimated city that's supposed to be off limits, discovering a refugee community straight out of a third world country, then being blindfolded for over two hours while riding in the back seat of a car. As one who knows what it's like to take a tumble down Alice's rabbit hole, I feel bad for the guy.

"Where am I?" he asks.

"I'm afraid we can't tell you that." Felix picks up a white envelope off the table—the one Ronie must have been talking about. He pulls out a thin stack of photographs and slides them over to our new guest. "What we can tell you, is that everything you've been led to believe is false."

Bledsoe looks from Felix to Isabelle to me, all wariness and uncertainty, then picks up the photographs and thumbs through them. The further he gets, the chalkier his face becomes. "What are these?"

"We're not the bad guys, Agent Bledsoe."

He sets the stack of pictures aside, like if he looks at them any longer, he'll be sick. As soon as I glance at them, I understand why. I have no idea how Ronie got ahold of them—but there, in glossy finish, are pictures of the horror my grandmother described. Bodies—so many bodies—lying on top of each other inside man-made ditches.

The sight of it turns my bones cold.

"I don't understand," Bledsoe says.

"Courtesy of your employer—the United States government. They're killing off patients in mental rehabilitation centers across the country."

"Why?"

"To get rid of us." Felix folds his hands on the table, and tells Agent Bledsoe everything. It's interesting, hearing him explain The Gifting, our purpose, the reason we're being targeted. I'm not sure why, but it doesn't sound as crazy coming from him. "The enemy has infiltrated our government. It's time we do the same. Which means we need more Believers like you, people on the inside who know what's really happening, and who are willing to help us fight. That's where you come in."

Even though the suspicion in Bledsoe's eyes has morphed into equal parts determination and outrage, he shakes his head. "Nobody will believe this. The second I open my mouth, I'll be admitted into a rehab facility myself."

"Exactly. Which is why I don't want you to try to convince anyone. We're asking you to feed us information about your cohorts. Bios. Pictures." Felix's dark eyes flash to mine. And I find myself smiling. Because it's brilliant. With pictures and bios, I can convince them just like I convinced our newest Believer.

CHAPTER THIRTY-SIX

HOUSE OF CARDS

While everyone else heads to the mess hall for dinner, a group of us in Headquarters gather in the investigation room around the table—me, Luka, Link, Cap, Lexi, Connal, Ronie, Joe the Sniper, and surprisingly, Glenda the interview lady, who brought in a plate of donuts left over from this morning, an assortment of random mugs, and a large thermos of coffee.

A naked light bulb hanging from the ceiling illuminates the board of influential Believers. Felix scrawls a new name at the bottom of the list—Agent Michael Bledsoe.

Shaking his head, Connal pulls a glazed donut in half. "That's a fret. You, snaggin' an FBI agent on yer first recruit."

"I can't believe you snagged anyone, period." Ronie pours a cup of coffee into a mug that says Keep Calm and Surfs Up. It reminds me of all the times I watched Luka surf while I sat on my back deck, journaling my descent into insanity. It feels like a thousand lifetimes ago.

Ronie mixes in some creamer. "When it comes to recruitment, we're only successful about one out of every ten attempts. Your method is a lot more effective."

"What's your method?" Joe asks me.

"I visited him in his sleep."

His eyebrows shoot upward. "You're a dream hopper?"

"So is Link." And it's not the first time I've recruited someone. I essentially did the same thing with Leela, only instead of leaving her a note like I did with Bledsoe, I called her on the phone. The memory of shouting *jelly donut* into the receiver makes me smile. That's all it took for her to believe. A ridiculous code word.

"It's also a lot less risky," Ronie says, bringing the mug beneath her chin. "Every time we send a message, we risk someone tracing that message back to our location. With your method, that step is eliminated from the process. By the time we contact anyone, they're already Believers."

Felix crosses his ankle over his knee and leans back in his seat. "I think it's safe to say that we're in need of some numbers. Agent Bledsoe has agreed to procure a list of coworkers. People we can start recruiting."

"By *we*, you mean Tess." The statement belongs to Luka.

"And your roommate." Felix inclines his head toward Link. "The two seem to make a good team."

"Of course we do." Link flashes me the kind of smile that says he's ready for an adventure. The kind of smile Luka can't stand.

I glance at him. He doesn't look amused. Or comforted. He looks exactly what Link called him earlier—*tense*. I can tell he wants to say more, but he keeps whatever thoughts he's having to himself.

Next to him, Cap runs his hand over his short, bristly hair. "I'm not sure it's wise to rest the entire recruitment process on the shoulders of two people."

"Three, actually." Glenda sneezes and her bifocals slide down her nose. She grabs a Kleenex. "One of our teachers is a dream-hopper. His name's Kwahu."

"Are you kidding?" Link says. "Three's plenty. Especially when we don't have to be the ones who do the actual convincing. All Tess and I and Kwahu have to do is bring someone to the dreamer and let them do the work."

I can't help myself. Link's excitement is contagious. After everything the enemy has stolen, I'm ready to take action. To fight back. To choose victory. So Luka can surf again. So I can see Leela in more than just dreams. So my dad can be free and my mom and Pete, safe. "We can organize a team. Infiltrate on every level. Police force. Border control. Government officials. The staff at rehab facilities and fetal modification clinics."

"*The media*," Ronie adds.

The room grows quiet. We look around at one another, the potential we have at our fingertips slowly sinking in. The media shapes everything. Our thoughts. Our opinions. Our outlook. Infiltrating it would be like infiltrating the mind of the public. We'd be unstoppable.

"Everything's filtered from the top down, though," Link says. "And we already know whose side the Chief of Press is on. Xena and I could convert a hundred people who work in the media and the chances of anything reaching the airwaves are slim to none. It would take an entire uprising."

Felix turns a toothpick over in his fingers. "I don't think we need a takeover as much as we need access."

"But unless there's a takeover, I can't see us getting access."

"From Josiah's account, I'm talking to the most skilled hacker in the country. Sitting right beside the other." Felix's dark eyes glitter as he looks from Link to Ronie. "Surely between the two of you, we can find access into some media streams."

Ronie sits up straighter, color rising in her cheeks. "We can form another team."

"The hackers and the evangelists." Connal licks glazed sugar from his thumb. "Has a nice ring to it."

Felix continues his toothpick twirling. "We don't need long broadcasts. I'm envisioning smaller-scale raids. Surprise attacks. Hit-and-run tactics. A little bit here and there to stir up doubt. Cause questions."

"Like guerilla warfare." Link's grin has become uncontainable. "Only in cyberspace."

"And if they *trace* it back to our location?" Luka asks the question, his sarcasm obvious. They must not be too concerned about that particular danger.

"This is wartime, Mr. Williams. Calculated risk comes with the territory. And since there isn't another way to get this particular job done, we do what's necessary." Felix flicks his toothpick into the trash and strolls to another board. *The* board. The one we worked on earlier after my revelation. "Now what shall we do about this?"

A hush falls across the room.

Everyone stares at the list. *The key.*

It's like the linchpin. If we can find a way to remove it, then the enemy's plans will come tumbling down like a house of cards.

Never in a million years did I think I'd be involved in a serious conversation about assassinating the president. But there it is— one more thing to add to the list of things I never thought I'd do. It's getting impressively long. Breaking into a high-security mental facility. Running away from home. Making out with the hottest boy in school. Becoming America's Most Wanted criminal. Killing my grandmother.

I shake that last thought away and the anxiety that comes with it. It's a new day down here in Headquarters and despite another fitful night of sleep, I'm not tired. I'm ramped up. Glad the night is over and determined to tackle the morning. I grab a bagel from the mess hall, head to the private wing, and slip inside the small room where the records are kept.

At the end of last night's meeting, we decided that assassination was off the table. According to Joe the Sniper—retired Navy SEAL officer—it would be virtually impossible to take out the president. And as Cap reminded us, Cormack might not even be a willing participant. For all we know, she's been hijacked. Unlike our enemy, we aren't going to kill innocent civilians. So we decided to organize a third team. A special ops team. A team that consists of the most highly skilled individuals in Headquarters. Our mission? Figure out who, if anyone on the list has been hijacked and set them free.

When it comes to organizing such a team, looking through the intake forms seems like a logical first step. At the end of the meeting, Glenda gave me permission to do a little researching and reorganizing. Right now, she's busy interviewing a newbie who arrived late last night. Currently, the files are organized according to admittance date. I get to work pulling them out and organizing them into eight piles.

Of the 140, three are Sleepers; six are kids who aren't part of The Gifting, but children of parents who are part of The Gifting; fifteen are Cloaks; thirty-one are Fighters; eighty are Shields; two are Linkers; two are Keepers; and then there's me—the oddity. A Linker and a Fighter in one. I've finished off my bagel and sorted the last form into a pile when someone knocks on the opened door.

It's Link. At eight-fifteen in the morning.

"I didn't think you functioned at this hour."

"I figured sleeping is lame when there's a war to win." He joins me on the floor and rubs his eyes. "Plus, your boy Luka isn't the easiest roommate when it comes to sleep."

I frown. "Did he have another nightmare?"

Link gives me a sad smile. A comforting smile. A half-smile. "Want some help?"

I toss him a pen and explain what I'm doing, a fresh bout of determination stretching its way through my muscles. On the front of each manila file, we write the person's gifting, along with territory size and any special skills. Like computer hacking for Link. Pickpocketing for Bass. If Jillian were alive, we'd write gun-handling. Turns out, the information we have is sparse. Apparently, asking about territory and skill sets isn't part of Glenda's admittance interview.

I click the end of my pen. "We'll have to re-interview everyone."

"We should ask about connections, too." Link scrawls *Fighter* on the top of a folder labeled *Benton, Emmett* and skims the intake form inside. "Joe's a former Navy SEAL. I'm sure he knows other Navy SEALs. He can't be the only one with helpful connections."

"That's a good idea."

"I have them every now and then." Link sets Emmett's file aside and grabs the next one off the stack. "Hey, look. It's your favorite person."

Bedicelle, Claire.

My scowl is immediate.

Link laughs.

I don't understand how he can. "You know what she did.

You saw. And yet you joke."

"You've heard the saying, right? If you don't laugh, you'll cry. Well, Xena. I'd rather laugh." He pokes me in the ribs.

I jump.

His expression turns playful. "Ticklish much?"

I bite back a smile, because this is serious stuff. Claire is scum. "Don't you dare."

"But dares are so much fun." He wags his eyebrows.

And somehow, I'm trying to squirm free while Link tickles my sides. Our laughter fills the small room. It feels good, laughing like this. Like a release. It feels—

"Are we interrupting something?"

Link stops.

I scramble into sitting.

Ronie stands in the doorway. So does Luka.

My cheeks explode with heat. I yank my shirt down and grab a file, unable to make eye contact with anyone. Not Ronie. Not Link. Definitely not Luka.

Link clears his throat. "What's up?"

"I was going to add some extra security blocks to our data drives. I was wondering if you wanted to help, but it looks like you're already busy."

"No, I can help." Link stands.

And then he leaves with Ronie.

I feign intent interest in the file I'm holding while Luka leans against the doorframe. I'm being a coward. I should look up and smile. Say hello. It's not like Luka caught me in the midst of a crime. It's not like Link and I were kissing or anything. The thought doesn't help much with the fire-in-my-cheeks situation.

"What are you doing?" His voice comes out gentle. One

hundred percent non-accusatory.

It breaks me a little. Here he is, in complete angst over his inability to protect me. And here I am, flirting with Link. Seriously, why was I just flirting with Link? If the tables were turned, if I was the one who caught Luka wrestling around on the floor with some girl that wasn't me, I'd be sick to my stomach.

I explain the new filing system.

"Can I help?" he asks.

"Of course."

Luka joins me on the floor, not as close as Link. And yet, his presence is stronger. It fills the room. The air crackles. My skin tingles. What I can't figure out is whether it's a Luka and Tess thing, or a Keeper and *anima* thing. And if it's the latter, how in the world does Lexi resist it?

It's not love if it's not a choice, is it?

I shove her sentiment aside as Luka picks up one of the smaller piles. It only has two files—his and Connal's. He stares at them intently. I wish I knew what he was thinking.

"Were you training with Connal again?" I ask.

He nods.

"Any progress?"

"It's not really helping. He trains a lot differently than Gabe."

I grab another file, an excuse to hide my relief. I don't want Luka to see it. I read through the intake form and write *Shield* on the front. Territory, *unknown*. Special Skills, *unknown*. When I look up, Luka studies a different file with a deep furrow etched between his brow. I can't tell if it's the result of a question, a concern, or an idea.

The file belongs to Claire.

CHAPTER THIRTY-SEVEN

COMPLETE

Luka and I spend the rest of that morning and part of the afternoon labeling each file. When we're finished, Felix calls for an all-headquarters meeting. One hundred forty residents sit inside the gymnasium while Felix lays out the plan of action. We will form into units, each with a different job, all with the same objective—victory.

Ronie and Link gather those who are computer savvy—most of whom already work in the command center—and begin nightly training classes. We put Kwahu—a sixty-seven year old Cherokee Indian—in charge of the Evangelists. By far, our biggest team. He keeps a running list of people we're trying to convert, then assigns them to someone at Headquarters whose job is to do the converting. No special skill set is required. All that's needed is the truth, and the ability to communicate it quickly and confidently. Any potential Believer inside Kwahu's territory falls to him. Any outside, falls to Link. And any outside Link's territory falls to me.

Once the person we're trying to convert is on the verge, we reach out to someone in our growing network of Believers. They take care of the rest by making a simple, yet convincing phone call. The name of the game is *inform, convince, and invite.*

It works.

Our success rate hovers around ninety-five percent.

Our army grows.

The trickle of people arriving at Headquarters turns into a steady stream.

I work side-by-side with Cap and Felix, organizing and overseeing while Glenda and a couple others she's taken under her wing (Ellen happens to be one) conduct extensive interviews with every single resident. There's no down time. Not when I'm awake, and certainly not when I'm asleep. I prefer it this way. It gives me less time to miss Leela and my family. Less time to stew over Claire and Clive. Less time to worry about the future. Or dwell on things that happened in the past.

Turns out, the past is persistent. No matter how busy I keep myself, it finds a way to slither in between the cracks.

I jerk awake in bed, sucking in a sharp, loud breath and slapping at the point of pressure against my neck. My heart pounds into the silence. Fast, hard, insistent knocks, like whatever's inside demands to be let out. I touch my throat. There's no gun. It was just a dream.

"Are you okay over there?" Joanna asks, her voice thick with sleep.

"Y-yeah. I'm fine."

I hear her roll over and a few seconds later, her snoring resumes. My body's not so willing to settle. I sink back in bed and wait for my heart rate to return to normal. It doesn't seem to know how. Sleep refuses to come. And even if it did, I'm not sure I want it to keep me company, especially with my work for the night already finished. I untangle my legs from the sheets, swap my sweaty shirt for freshly-laundered clothes, and sneak out of my room.

The hallway is dark and quiet. I don't know where I'm

going. I only know that I need a distraction. I end up in the common room, standing in front of the bookshelves, scanning the spines under the yellow glow of a nearby lamp. They have a diverse collection. I pull several out and read snatches of text, but not even Charles Dickens or Harper Lee can calm my nerves.

"Tess?"

I suck in another sharp breath and spin around.

Luka stands several feet behind me.

I set my hand against my chest. "You just gave me a heart attack."

"Sorry."

We've barely seen each other over the past couple weeks. I've been so busy with war tactics and he's been ... what? Meeting with Dr. Sheng? Training with Connal? Battling his inner demons? I don't really know. Seeing him now, with his hair all disheveled, makes me realize how much I've missed him.

"What are you doing in here?" he asks.

I could ask him the same thing. Instead, I hold up a collection of poems by Jack Kerouac. "Some middle of the night reading?" My voice is as shaky as my hands.

Luka cocks his head and studies me through the dim lighting. We promised each other no secrets.

"I had a bad dream." I slip Kerouac between Mark Twain and Stoker.

"A bad dream, huh? I wonder what that's like."

I turn around.

His eyes are filled with compassion. Of course they are. Luka gets it. If anybody understands, it's him.

"What do you do when you have them?" I ask.

"Lately?"

"Sure."

He takes my hand and we walk into the gymnasium where Luka flips the light switch. Brightness floods the large space, illuminating the basketball hoops and weight machines.

"Dr. Sheng says exercise is one of the best ways to fight anxiety." He squeezes my hand and gives me this sideways smile, so subtle it's almost not there. "I've been exercising a lot these days."

"In the middle of the night?"

"It's better than listening to Link snore."

"Snore, huh?"

"Really, really loudly." His smile grows as he leads the way around the corner, into the mat room, and holds onto one of the punching bags. "Hitting things usually helps, too."

It feels silly at first—punching the bag while Luka holds it steady against his shoulder. But he's right. The activity chases some of the anxiety away. "So what else does Dr. Sheng say?"

"He's a big proponent of talking."

"Therapists usually are." I give the bag a quick one-two jab, remembering the feel of the gun pressed against my neck. Usually, the weapon is pointed at my grandmother and I'm the one holding it. The deafening blast as I pull the trigger always wakes me up. I punch harder, until beads of sweat form along my hairline.

"I know you've been busy," Luka says. "At night especially. But if you ever need a safe place—somewhere to visit between your nighttime evangelizing—you know where to find me."

I throw a right hook. "Our beach?"

"It might help keep the bad dreams away."

I stop and wipe my forehead with the back of my arm.

"You still go there?"

His green eyes capture mine. "Always."

I stand with my arms crossed at my chest, watching Anna's cloak expand. It nearly covers the entire dojo (which Link has substantially enlarged for the purposes of today) before any thin spots appear. I'm impressed. Not just with her cloak, but her physical appearance. She has color in her cheeks and they aren't so hollow anymore either. The transformation gives me hope. Evidence that worn-out things can become strong again.

All day, Ronie has sent Cloaks into the dream simulator as we search for the final member of our special ops team. Right now, it consists of me, Felix, Cap, Lexi, Connal, Link (in case we need an extra Linker), and surprisingly, Glenda, who can throw an impressive shield.

As soon as Anna's gone, I turn to Felix and Cap. "I think we have our Cloak."

Felix folds his hands behind his back. "We have one more for consideration."

I'm about to ask who when that one more arrives. I turn incredulous eyes on Felix. "Are you joking?"

"You should see what he's capable of."

"I know exactly what he's capable of. Unless Cap is suffering from memory loss, so does he."

Cap, however, leaves me and my objection hanging.

"In case you *are* suffering from memory loss, let me remind you. The last time we brought him on an important mission, he *dropped* his cloak. If not for Gabe sacrificing his life, none of us would have made it out of there alive." I glare at Clive, standing at attention in the center of the room, seemingly unaffected by the fact that we're discussing him like he's not there. "He *dropped* his cloak, Felix. And now you want to consider him for the special ops team?"

"I believe he'll be a valuable asset."

I shake my head, disbelief and outrage wrestling for attention.

"I think," Felix says, "that Teresa is in need of some convincing, Mr. DeVant."

I roll my eyes. Anna's cloak is perfectly adequate. Unless Clive is able to cloak the whole of North America, I don't see how he could possibly be an asset to our—.

My thoughts freeze midstream.

Clive's cloak, while starting off as every other one I've seen today, slowly morphs into something strange. The umbrella of light turns into odd wisps that darken at the edges and creep closer to my feet.

I step back, but not fast enough. One of the wisps wraps around my ankle and curls up my leg. It's hot. I try shaking it off, but my leg won't budge. This cloak—*this thing*—anchors me in place. "What the—?"

The wisp wraps around my waist. Panic swells. White-hot, scalding panic. I try jerking free, but it's no use. I can't move at all. My panic builds. It paralyzes my lungs. Fills my chest. Shoots down my arms, into my fingertips, so intense I can't keep it inside. So intense, I do the same thing I did when Gabe transurged. I throw out the mounting energy like a freaking hot potato.

A burst of light shoots from my fingers.

Clive's cloak falls away. Disappears.

I take a couple quick steps back, my chest heaving. "Never do that to me again, understand?"

But Clive doesn't answer. He's staring at me like I'm the one who just did something weird. So are Felix and Cap.

"What?" I snap.

"You just threw a shield. Fighters don't throw shields. Neither do Linkers." Felix tilts his head, studying me intently. "Have you ever done that before?"

I look down at my fingers, as if they might explain themselves. No. I've never had to do it before. Except ... Did Gabe somehow leave some of his life behind? Was it lurking in some corner of my body, waiting to escape? "Yes."

Cap shakes his head. "What happened with Gabe is not the same thing as throwing a shield. What you threw was a shield."

"Let's see if she can do it again." Felix nods at Clive.

Before I can object, he does the thing I told him to never do. His cloak wraps around my leg. My panic builds. And I chase his cloak away. Felix has Clive do it again and again. Five times over. Each time ends the same way. A shield of light shooting from my fingers.

Felix chuckles. "Not only a Fighter and a Linker, but a Shield, too. Teresa Eckhart continues to amaze us."

I stand there, dumbfounded and replete while Felix welcomes Clive to the team.

A Fighter. A Linker. And a Shield, which falls under the category of Guardian. I'm all three. Pieces of the prophecy keep coming true. My grandmother as the beacon, trading hope for freedom. Being led like sheep to the slaughter, the United States acting as a giant pen. Seeing the mark of evil. And now this.

A gifting complete in its power.
She will be our victory ... or she will be our downfall.
Victory will come through sacrifice.

My mouth goes dry. I remind myself that Luka can't do transurgence. Luka can't even throw a shield. A fact that I know is killing him, even though he didn't say a word about it last night. I want to startle myself into consciousness, remove the probes from my temples, and go find him. Tell him about this latest development. Surely it will comfort him. I mean, I can shield myself. The thought makes me smile.

I can shield myself.

"Teresa?"

I blink rapidly.

Felix and Cap are staring again.

"Sorry—what was that?"

"It's time to figure out if anyone is being hijacked," Felix says.

"Oh." I shrug dumbly. "I don't know how to do that."

"Link does," Cap says. "I think it's time for the two of you to do some dream searching."

CHAPTER THIRTY-EIGHT

BLIND

Tonight is game night. At first, I thought it was a little weird that Felix would continue something like game night when we're in the middle of a war. But he's all about morale and it does sound kind of fun. As soon as I'm done with Felix and Cap, I go searching for Luka to see if he wants to go.

The problem is, I can't find him. He's not in his room, Dr. Sheng's office, the common room, the mess hall, or the general store. I head to the entrance of the gym. Inside, four guys play a game of two-on-two basketball. A girl runs on one of the treadmills. A few people lift weights. Luka is nowhere. But over the sound of the squeaking shoes and the bouncing ball and the clanking iron, I can hear the unmistakable *thud-thud* of punching. That has to be him. Since Cap, Felix, and I have been using the dream simulator all day, he's probably sparring with Connal.

I round the corner and stop dead.

I'm right. Luka is inside the mat area, his T-shirt plastered against his body as he wallops the same punching bag I accosted last night. But he's not with Connal. His partner holds the bag steady, her lithe muscular figure every bit as perfect as it's always been.

"You've got to be kidding."

Luka stops.

Claire turns around.

I absolutely can't believe what I'm seeing.

He pulls off his gloves and wipes his forearm along his sweat-soaked brow, locks of dark hair sticking to his skin. "Hey."

Hey? Hey! The annoying ringing starts up in my ears again. There are no words. I'm speechless. Utterly, profoundly speechless. And I cannot—*will not*—look at Claire. Just imagining the smug expression on her face is enough to make me want to vomit. I mean, seriously. I might really vomit. I take a step back. Then I turn around and walk away as quickly as possible, as if distance will erase what I saw.

I'm halfway down the hallway in the barracks when Luka grabs my arm. "Tess."

I jerk free. "What *was* that?"

"Nothing. She's helping me train."

"She's helping you train?"

"She was there when I first learned everything."

"So what?"

"So she saw how Gabe trained me. She knows what worked. And she wants to help."

"Help?" I let loose a gargled laugh. "Luka, she's the reason Gabe died. She's the reason you lost your gifting to begin with!"

"Don't you think I know that!"

A girl skirts around us, her attention fixed on the floor.

I shake my head. "I can't believe you didn't tell me. What happened to no secrets?"

"I wasn't keeping it a secret. We've barely had time to talk."

"We had time to talk last night."

"You were struggling. That wasn't the time to bring it up."

"I thought we were going to stop trying to protect each other."

"No, you were going to stop protecting me. I'm *your* Keeper, remember? Even if I can't do anything about it." Luka pushes his fingers through his hair, then runs his hands down his face. "Come on, Tess. I have to sit here, every day, doing nothing, while you and Link hop all around America playing army together."

"We're not playing."

"Are you sure? Because Link sure treats it like a game."

"No, he doesn't."

Luka takes a deep breath. "I haven't complained about watching you two—joined at the hip. I'm trying to give you space. Let you do what you need to do. But you see me working with Claire and you flip out."

"Because it's Claire! Link's never turned on us. He's on our side. If not for him, we never would have gotten you away from Scarface."

"Right. My bad. Link's a saint."

"You know, Luka. You sound kind of jealous."

"That's because I am jealous! You light up every time he's around. You're not being honest about your feelings for him. And here I am, about as useful as Ralph. I can't protect you. I can't do anything. What makes it worse? You seem happy about it."

"I'm not happy about it." But even as I say the words, warmth spreads into my cheeks, giving me away. "And you have absolutely nothing to be jealous about. Sure, I have feelings for Link. *Friendly* feelings. Link and I are friends."

He looks skeptical.

"Besides, he likes Ronie. But even if he didn't, it wouldn't matter. I don't choose him. I choose you." As soon as I say it, Lexi's sentiment roars to the surface. There's only so many times I can stuff it down before it refuses to be stuffed any longer. "Which makes me a fool, because you can't choose me."

"What are you talking about?"

"I've fallen in love with someone who doesn't love me back."

Luka narrows his eyes. "Care to tell me how you reached that conclusion?"

"For one, you've never said it."

"I love you."

I toss the flippant remark aside. "It's not love if it's not a choice."

He takes a step closer. "Am I talking to Tess right now, or am I talking to Lexi?"

My cheeks turn hot.

"You don't think Connal's told me what Lexi has to say about the whole Keeper thing? You don't think he thinks it's as ridiculous as I do?" Luka takes another step, so close now I have to tip my chin up to look at him. "He used more colorful language than that, but you get the idea."

"It's true, though. You didn't choose to have this crazy, overwhelming urge to protect me. You didn't choose to have dreams about me before we met. None of that was a choice." Take those two things away and I'm willing to bet a whole lot of money that Luka Williams never would have given me a second glance.

"You're right. Those weren't choices." He tucks a strand of

hair behind my ear. "And they definitely played a role in my attraction."

"See?" The word escapes on a rasp. His admission rips my heart in two.

"Can I ask you a question?"

I cross my arms in front of my middle. A small barrier between us.

He traces his thumb along my jaw. "Are you attracted to me?"

I close my eyes. If his touch wasn't so achingly good, I'd laugh. It's a laughable question. I've yet to meet a girl who's not attracted to him.

He runs his knuckle down the length of my arm and curls his hand around my hip. "Did you choose that attraction?"

I look up at him.

"We don't choose who we're attracted to. But we do get to choose who we love. That is always a choice. And I choose to love you, Tess, whether you believe it's real or not." He pulls me to him and covers my lips with his.

Both of his hands cup my face.

My arms remain crossed in front of me. Not because I want the space any more, but because I'm too caught up in Luka's kiss to undo them.

If I'd known earlier that making up with Luka would be so euphorically good, I might have picked a fight sooner. I hit the ping-pong ball long. Luka snags it out of the air with one hand and grins. "You're getting better."

"Liar."

His grin widens. "You almost hit the table this time."

"You're actually really, really bad at this," Rosie says.

"Brutal honesty. I can appreciate that."

Luka chuckles and holds up his paddle. "Ready?"

"I'm ready."

He serves over the net—a lob ball that is way beneath him. I know because I watched him play a game with Declan. Of course Luka would be good at something as obscure as ping-pong. I watch the ball in—like Rosie's loudly coaching me to do—and return it successfully. A volley ensues. Five whole back-and-forths before Rosie's excitement gets in my head and I hit the ball into the net.

"That's game!" Rosie says. "I'm playing the winner."

I gladly hand over the paddle.

Luka shoots me a wink. "I can give you a personal lesson later, if you want."

My lips turn into the shape of a happy crescent moon. Personal lessons with Luka sound quite fun.

Turns out, Rosie's a lot better than me, but not as good as Declan. I watch, transfixed by the effortless way Luka moves, even when he's purposefully losing, until Rosie hits one long and he chases after it.

The common room is packed. I spot Link at a poker table, a pen dangling from his lips like a cigar, a ridiculous visor on his head as he deals cards to Ronie, Jose, and Bass. There are drinks and snacks and a smattering of board games laid out on the floor. With the music and the chatter and the flirting and the playing, it's hard to believe Link and I are on the cusp of an incredibly important mission. It's hard to believe that tonight could be the beginning of the end.

Luka serves. Rosie misses. The ball bounces off the corner of the table, lands near my feet, and rolls to a stop in front of a woman playing chess with a boy. They share the same almond hair-color and the same large ears, which stick out from their heads. The boy picks up the ball and hands it to me, then plunks his elbows on his knees, props his chin on his fists, and furrows his brow at the board.

The game reminds me of Jillian.

The woman offers me a friendly smile. "I'm trying to teach my son how to play. Unfortunately, I'm not that great."

I toss the ball to Rosie. "I'm sure I'm worse."

The boy perks. "Maybe I can play you next, then."

I laugh. "Smart kid."

"He's very much like his father, who happens to be the chess expert in the family. But it's game night and I made a promise, so here we are." The woman sticks out her hand. "My name's Felicia. This is Henry. He just turned eight last week."

I shake her hand. "My name's Tess."

"It's an honor to officially meet you."

An honor?

Henry moves his knight two spaces forward and one space left, right into the path of his mother's queen.

She pretends not to see it. "It hasn't been easy, being here. We had to separate from my husband and Henry's little sister after he started showing signs of The Gifting. The two of us came here, underground. We haven't seen them for two years."

"I'm sorry."

"Ever since we left them, I've dreamed about the day we can be together again. I didn't start believing it until you arrived."

I shift awkwardly, unsure what to say. This woman stares at me like I'm … hope. Like I have the power to put her family back together again. But what if I'm no better than all the king's horses and all the king's men?

Felicia wishes me a good evening. I wish her and her son one back and return to the ping-pong table, where Luka has one eye on the game and one eye on me. Rosie hits a zinger that grazes the corner. Luka stops the ball with his paddle so it doesn't get away. "Everything okay?"

"Yeah. It's fine. You two want anything to drink?"

"I'm good."

"I'll take a water," Rosie says. "All these points are making me thirsty."

With a laugh, I head toward the row of coolers and pull out two bottled waters. When I straighten up, I'm standing face-to-face with the last person on the earth I want to see.

"Can we talk?" Claire asks.

"I'd rather not." I step around her.

But she steps, too. Blocking my path. "Please?"

"What could you possibly want to talk to me about?"

"I want to say that I'm sorry."

I let out a laugh. There's not a trace of humor in the sound. "For what? Trying to hand me over to the other side, or your inability to successfully manage it?"

Her pale cheeks turn pink. "Haven't you ever made a mistake?"

A mistake? Is she serious? "Is that what you told Felix? That you made a mistake?"

"It's the truth."

"What you did wasn't a mistake; it was a deliberate choice."

"Sometimes those are the worst kind of mistakes."

I shake my head. "Your remorse is an act. You're playing the part now because you have nowhere else to go. You might have Felix and Cap fooled, but not me. I saw what you did.

And I saw what happened as a result." In fact, if I let myself, I see it every time I close my eyes—Luka being bound and dragged away. Luka arching up in agony, his screams shredding my soul. It has the plastic water bottles crinkling in my grip.

"Link and Luka don't think I'm acting."

"Stay away from them both." Just hearing her say their names sets my teeth on edge. Seriously, if I don't walk away now, I might set a bad example for Henry. I take a deep breath and tell my feet to start moving.

"Why are you so threatened by me?"

The words hit their mark. I stop and turn around.

A few people close by stare, some more covertly than others.

"I'm not."

"You sure act like you are." She takes a step closer, shortening the distance I created. I guess she's no more eager than I am for people to overhear this particular conversation. "You don't have anything to worry about. Link and Luka are both yours."

"What are you talking about? Link likes Ronie." And why are we even discussing this? I'm not worried Claire's going to take Luka or Link away from me. That's not why I'm upset about her being here. I'm upset because she betrayed us. I'm upset because she tried to have me killed and Luka ended up suffering for it and how do we know she won't do the same thing if the opportunity presents itself?

"Okay, but he's totally in *love* with you."

I huff. Claire is nuts. "Link is not in love with me."

"Trust me. I see the way he looks at you. I've been on the receiving end of that look too many times not to recognize it. Link's definitely in love with you." Claire looks me up and down, like she doesn't get why. "You're blind if you don't see it, too."

Chapter Thirty-Nine

Clouds and Bars

I find Link waiting for me inside a familiar gladiatorial arena. He constructed it once before—the night I perfected the art of manipulating the physical while in the supernatural realm. The night we went around Cap's orders and ran into Scarface on a street corner in Detroit. I have no idea why the sight of him sitting there in the stands, waiting for me, should unleash a hoard of butterflies in my stomach.

It's Link.

I don't get nervous with Link.

But Claire's words are still fresh in my mind.

You're blind if you don't see it.

I'm not sure what makes the butterflies flap faster—the idea of Link being in love with me, or my reaction to the idea of Link being in love with me. It shouldn't make me pleased, that's for sure. I'm in love with Luka, which means *if* Link is in love with me—and that is a monumental *if*—I can't love him back, and loving someone who doesn't love you back is a miserable feeling. I wouldn't wish it on anyone, especially not one of my best friends.

I shake my head. This is dumb. I'm not going to let Claire get in my head, and that's exactly what she's trying to do. Like I told Luka, Link and I are friends. Period. I expel a breath and hold my hand up like a visor against the sun. Link made it extra bright. "You've used this one before, you know," I call up to him. "You're getting lazy."

He looks down at me with a smile. "Are you kidding? Do you know how much work it took constructing this bad boy the first time around? I didn't want it to go to waste, considering this is our final lesson."

"Our final lesson, huh?"

"After tonight, I'll have taught you everything I know. The student will surpass the teacher."

"I surpassed you months ago."

Link's smile grows.

The butterflies zoom around a little faster. I tell them to chill out as I climb the stairs and sit beside him. "So, Teach, how am I supposed to tell if somebody's being hijacked?"

"We hop into their dream and look for the signs."

"Like?"

"Clouds."

I quirk my eyebrow.

"When a person's been hijacked, they are stuck in a perpetual dream. Happily oblivious while the hijacker takes over their mind and body. In this dream world they mistakenly assume is reality, the sun doesn't come out."

"Ever?"

"Never. There's also bars on all of the windows."

"Wouldn't the dreamer notice something like that?"

"The enemy is smart, Xena. They make their captives so comfortable, they don't *want* to notice."

"Is that how we free them, then—we get them to notice?"

"That's the first step."

"Doesn't sound too hard."

Link shakes his head, like I'm being naive. "Right now, this is my dream. I constructed it. If I want Cap to join us ..."

All of sudden, Cap appears. Only it's not dream-Cap with strong, sturdy legs. It's wheelchair-Cap, slightly different from the one I know because this is Link's version.

"Here he is. A projection straight from my subconscious mind. When it comes to hijacking, however, the people you meet inside the dream aren't projections of the dreamer. They're projections of the hijacker, put in place to monitor activity. If any unwelcome guests appear—like us—the projections report immediately to the hijacker. And since the hijacker controls the dream ..." Link gives his wrist a bored flick, and half of the gladiatorial arena crumbles away in a deafening rumble. "The dream quickly becomes unsafe," he yells over the sound.

I wait for the debris to settle. "It's a dream though. The worst that could happen is waking up."

"Well, not exactly."

"What do you mean?"

"The hijacker is literally inside the prisoner's mind and body, which means he's also inside the dream. When we enter that dream, we're stepping inside enemy territory. We're exposing ourselves in a way that could prove incredibly dangerous, especially since hijackers are, by nature, extremely powerful." Link leans back and clasps his hands behind his head. "To free someone, we have to find the prisoner without being seen, get them alone, convince them that they've been shanghaied, and help them break free."

"When you put it that way, it sounds impossible."

"It's not easy, but it's not impossible."

I set my elbows on my knees. "How do you know all of this?"

"Experience." Link smiles. "One of my first missions at the hub was a hijacking rescue mission. I went with Gabe and Cap."

"Were you successful?"

"We were close."

Somehow I get the feeling that close doesn't mean a whole lot when it comes to this.

"Relax, Xena." Link reaches into my lap and takes my hand. "We're not rescuing anyone tonight. We're just scouting the situation to see if we can find any of the signs."

"Right." I release a deep breath and squeeze Link's hand. "Clouds and bars."

He squeezes back. "Clouds and bars."

Felix puts a red star next to the *king*, the *censor*, and the *idol* on the whiteboard. "You're sure all three have been hijacked?"

"Absolutely," Link says.

"What about Secretary Young?" Cap asks.

"We couldn't get to him," I say. I tried several times, and each time, nothing happened. It was a giant déjà vu, only this time I wasn't trying to dream-hop to my grandmother in Shady Wood or Luka in that dank chamber. My failed hopping abilities then had turned me frantic. I thought it meant we were too late and they were dead. But really, I'd been too distraught to get to Luka, and my grandmother ... she wasn't sleeping.

I turn to Link, who's looking back at me with a knowing twinkle in his eye, as though he's waiting for me to realize something he already knows.

"Secretary Young hasn't been hijacked." I look at Felix. "I

couldn't get to him because he was awake. If he were being hijacked, he couldn't be awake. He'd be stuck in a perpetual dream."

Lexi, who's been peering extra hard at the board while mindlessly flicking her thumbnail stands and joins Felix. She picks up a black marker and draws a confident line from each of Felix's red stars to the same word written three different times—*neck*. The location of the mark.

As soon as she does, Connal grins—wide and proud. "That's my girl."

Lexi, of course, ignores him. "It can't be a coincidence."

She's right. It can't. Cormack, B-Trix, and Fredrick are all hijacked and all three of them have the mark on their neck. Young isn't hijacked, and he's the only one with the mark on his wrist. My grandmother also had the mark on her wrist, confirming Link's theory—had she really been hijacked, she wouldn't have acted out of self-preservation.

Felix caps his marker and taps it against his palm. "It certainly makes figuring out whether someone's been hijacked or not much easier."

Glenda wipes her nose with a crumpled ball of tissue. "What about the *physician*?"

The question bothers me. Mainly because we still have no idea who it is. I couldn't find any mark on Shady Wood's director or the director of Detroit's Rehab Facility. And that's having pored over every picture and video Ronie and Link could find. We've since moved on to smaller rehab facility directors, along with directors of the larger fetal modification clinics, but we're not having any luck with those either.

"I'm sure he or she will surface eventually," Felix says. "Until then, we have three people we need to set free. You said

Cormack had the most guards?"

"Xena and I are lucky we weren't spotted."

"Then let's begin with these two, shall we?" Felix points to the *idol* and the *censor*.

And the planning begins.

We split our special ops team in half, which means we need one more Cloak. Cap agrees to speak with Anna. I'd rather have her than Clive, but there's no way I'm sending Clive with Link. Especially since he can't defend himself. So it's settled. Me, Cap, Glenda, and Clive will go after B-Trix. Link, Felix, Connal, Lexi, and Anna will go after Chief Fredrick. Tonight. Everyone agrees there's no reason to wait.

"How are things progressing with the media?" Felix asks.

"Slow," Ronie says. "The channels we're trying to hack into are much more encrypted than we anticipated."

Connal leans back in his chair. "If tonight doesn't go arseways, we'll have the Chief of Press on our side, won't we? I'd wager he'd be able to help us with a little public awareness."

"We'd also have B-Trix on our side," Lexi adds. "She's highly influential."

The group is excited. Confident.

I'm mostly nauseous. The last big mission I went on was a big giant failure. And I've never done this before—freeing someone who's been hijacked. Cap has, but according to Link, they weren't entirely successful, whatever that means. It doesn't instill any confidence, that's for sure. Especially since whoever they tried to rescue wasn't one of five key players in evil's master plan. Their not-entirely-successful rescue mission couldn't have been as high stakes as the ones we're about to embark on tonight.

"What about Secretary Young?" Luka asks. It's the first

time he's spoken since our meeting began.

Felix glances at the board of Believers, which has grown substantially over the past two weeks. Among others, we've gathered two more FBI agents, a CIA agent, and—thanks to Joe—two former Navy SEALs. "I think we can ask Joe to gather up a team and take care of it."

I shift uncomfortably. "Take care of it—as in kill him?"

Felix raises one of his dark eyebrows at me. "He made his choice. Secretary Young allied himself with the enemy and he did so willingly."

I can't help thinking about Pete. If Luka and I hadn't gotten to him when we did, he'd have that same mark on his wrist. Would Felix be so quick to take my brother out, too? I'm not sure Pete was so much a willing participant as he was a blind and foolish one—in way over his head. How do we know Secretary Young isn't the same?

Felix picks up his walkie-talkie and asks Joanna to page Joe and send him inside. "Good work, everyone. Why don't you go enjoy some lunch?"

The investigation room clears out.

I stay in my seat.

So does Luka.

He stares at the board, biting his thumbnail. I'd ask what he's thinking, but I can make a pretty good guess. I bring my foot onto the edge of my chair and wrap my arms around my knee. "Can I ask you something?"

His green eyes turn to mine.

"You don't want me to go."

"Not exactly."

"Then why aren't you trying to talk me out of it?" He definitely hasn't had a problem trying in the past. Why isn't he now?

"Would you listen if I tried?"

"Probably not."

He shoots me a sideways look, one corner of his mouth quirked. "I have this battle going on right now. There's the guy who's your Keeper. And there's the guy who's in love with you."

In love.

He said the words yesterday. Hearing him say them again is more intoxicating the second time around. "I didn't know those were two separate guys."

"They're very, very different."

"Sounds like Multiple Personality Disorder. Dr. Sheng might have medicine for that."

Luka smiles. It's short-lived, ousted by this deep, dark brood that belongs on a magazine cover.

"So what are they battling about?"

"The Keeper wants to find a way to stop you from going. The guy who's in love knows that this is what you were meant to do." He scratches the back of his head. "As someone who can't do what he was meant to do, I would never wish that on you."

I swallow. "Which side is winning?"

He grabs the underside of my chair and pulls me closer, the legs scrapping loudly against the floor. "The guy who's in love with you. But can the Keeper please say something?"

"Of course."

He brushes my hair over my shoulder and presses the softest of kisses against my cheek. "If you're in danger, promise that you'll startle awake."

With his lips traveling to my earlobe in that way they do, I would promise him anything.

Chapter Forty

GESUNDHEIT

Clive's cloak is strong and warm. It hides Glenda, Cap, and me easily. Even so, I don't feel safe. Because I don't trust Clive. And yet, I'm giving him my trust anyway.

It's an unnerving thing.

So are the iron bars covering the windows of the room we stand inside. B-Trix has three stateside homes—one in L.A., one in Miami, and another in upstate New York. Judging by the cloudy ocean view outside the barred windows, we're in the dream-world version of her L.A. home. And judging by the furniture and plants, we've landed in some sort of sitting room.

Voices filter inside from somewhere nearby. It sounds like the television.

Cap waves us ahead and we creep out into the hallway. A woman dressed in a maid's uniform walks toward us, her beady eyes moving left and right—another sign that B-Trix has been hijacked. Projections don't move independently of the dreamer. Not in a real dream. It's also a reminder that we've entered a hostile environment. We aren't welcome here.

I hold my breath, press my back against the wall, and stare hard at Clive as the lady walks past. His cloak remains.

We tiptoe toward the sound of voices and come out into a large, open living room. B-Trix lounges on a leather sofa, her bare feet propped up on the arm rest, a pan of mostly eaten brownies on the coffee table while she and a girl watch a popular zombie show. Without all the makeup, without the flashy outfit, without all the lights and glitz that are as much a part of her celebrity persona as her music, she's nearly unrecognizable.

"You really aren't going on tour this fall?" the girl asks.

"My manager wants me to rest my vocal chords. Since sales on my last record are so bloody brilliant, he's not too worried about it."

"You finally get a break."

B-Trix snags the last brownie from the pan and breaks off a bite. "And enjoying every second."

The girl laughs. "That's your fourth brownie!"

B-Trix wiggles her toes. "No tour, no dieting, and my trousers fit just fine. It's a dream come true, really."

Cap and I exchange a look. She has no idea.

Glenda taps me on the shoulder and points. Across the room, a man stands against the wall, his large hands clasped in front of him, his legs splayed shoulder-width apart. B-Trix is no doubt used to bodyguards. How convenient for the hijacker.

The four of us engage in a silent conversation beneath the safety of Clive's cloak. Basically, how in the world are we going to get B-Trix alone? Not only is she with this girl, but we have the burly bodyguard to contend with. We stand there in the entryway for who knows how long, my mind spinning in useless circles. Just as panic sets in—because seriously, we could be here for a long, long time—B-Trix hops up from the sofa.

The bodyguard shifts. "Do you need something?"

"I'm going to scrounge up some nosh."

"I can have someone get it for you."

"Don't worry about it. I need to stretch my legs." She walks out of the room, right past us. The bodyguard follows. The lack of privacy would drive me nuts.

B-Trix, however, doesn't seem fazed.

We follow a safe distance behind as she enters a pristine kitchen with marble countertops and begins searching the cupboards, humming one of her songs while Cap pantomimes a plan.

He will go into the adjoining dining room under the protection of Clive's expanding cloak. Once there, he'll cause a diversion. Hopefully, Mr. Bodyguard will go check it out and I'll make fast work of convincing B-Trix that she's being held prisoner inside her own mind. It's amazing how much can be communicated without speaking. It's also amazing how easily plans can go awry.

Just as Cap takes his fifth step away, Glenda's nose twitches. The sneeze comes so fast, she doesn't have time to cover it. The sound escapes in a high-pitched squeak, her face registers horror, and she disappears.

The bodyguard's attention shoots in our direction.

Clive's cloak remains steady.

My heart jumps into overdrive. *Glenda and her allergies!*

She must have sneezed in real life, which jolted her awake, and now she's left us here, in this dream, holding our breaths. None of us move. We have turned into a terrified tableau. I stand in place, paralyzed by fear while B-Trix—who must not have heard the sneeze—rummages for snacks.

Slowly, agonizingly, the bodyguard peels his attention away.

I release a silent, shaky breath.

Cap finishes the step he began to take before allergens

attacked Glenda's nose.

And the ground shakes. It rises up, pitching me backward into the wall. Cap stumbles. B-Trix shrieks and clutches the counter. The floor shakes again, so violently it knocks Clive off balance. His cloak falters, and for a split second we're visible. He recovers, but it doesn't matter. The damage has been done. The bodyguard has already seen us.

He stares in our direction, unconcerned by the earthquake, an enigmatic gleam in his eye as another, identical bodyguard appears. B-Trix is so busy clutching the counter and screaming, she doesn't notice our new guest. Or the two others that arrive after him.

The edges of Clive's cloak turn into the strange mist that circled my ankle when he tried out for our special ops team. Only this time, it wraps around the bodyguards and immobilizes them. But three more show up, and the ground shakes so hard it's almost impossible to stay vertical. The hijacker knows we're here. He's trying to kick us out. I should do what Luka asked. I should startle myself awake, but Cap and Clive are fighting, and B-Trix stands not more than two feet away.

I grab her shoulders and spin her around.

Her panicked eyes are wide with terror. "Who are you? What's happening?"

"This is a dream!" I rattle her shoulders harder than the rattling ground, desperate for the truth to sink down deep in the crevices of her brain. "You are being held—"

The temperature in the room plunges to ice.

An entire cupboard rips from the wall and hurls itself against B-Trix. She flies back, crumples to the ground, and lays in a motionless heap beside a man who looks nothing like the bodyguards. The hijacker is here. He flicks his wrist and another cupboard tears off the wall and slams into Clive. He lifts his arms and black mist rises up around us like the iron bars on the windows.

"Startle!" Cap yells.

I try, but it doesn't work. I don't wake up. Neither does Cap. We're every bit as trapped as B-Trix.

The bodyguards surround Cap.

The hijacker sets his sights on me, prowling closer like a hungry lion. He stretches his arm in my direction and a blast of invisible ice slams me against the wall. I hit the ground with a loud *oomph*, momentarily breathless. The black mist creeps toward my foot and winds itself around my shin. It's so cold, I scream. It's so cold, I can't move. I'm paralyzed. The same feeling that overtook me when Clive attacked me with his cloak builds now.

Panic.

White-hot panic. It scorches my insides and shoots through my limbs, so intense I act on instinct. I throw out my hands and hurl a shield at the hijacker. It slams into him. Only it doesn't disappear like most shields do. It expands, growing in brightness. As soon as it touches the bodyguards attacking Cap, they disappear.

"No!" the hijacker yells.

More show up in their place, but my growing shield consumes them, too, and the hijacker's yell turns into an enraged scream.

I fall to my knees and shake B-Trix's shoulder. She needs to wake up. I need to explain. But the ceiling begins to break apart. Everything bursts into light. And I wake up in bed, drenched in sweat.

Chapter Forty-One

ARSEWAYS

Luka hops a checker on the board.

It's Sunday.

Like the hub, the routine is lax on Sundays. There are no classes, and only work that's absolutely necessary to maintain life in Headquarters. Rosie finagled Luka into playing a second game of checkers, but he's not paying much attention. Like me, he keeps staring at the news on the television, as if the anchors on CNN might offer up some answers.

Nobody has any idea what happened last night. Not Cap. Not Felix. Not Link. Definitely not me. We don't know what happened to the hijacker. We don't know what in the world I did to make the dream collapse. We don't even know if B-Trix is free. It wouldn't be difficult to find out. We have the dream simulator. I could hook myself up, try hopping, and if it doesn't work, well, at least we know that much. But nobody will let me return.

They'll be waiting for you, Cap said.

It'd be highly dangerous, Felix agreed.

I scratch my ear and glance toward the west wing door. Link and Ronie are working on getting in touch with Chief Fredrick. Apparently, they didn't run into any problems. No sneezes or dreamquakes. With a little patience, they were able to get Fredrick alone, Link worked his magic, and Lexi and

Connal fought off the hijacker so Fredrick could escape.

"Your move," Rosie says.

Luka scoots a checker forward.

One of the CNN anchors says a name that has me sitting up straighter.

B-Trix.

The television screen pans to a press release, where the pale-looking popstar sits behind a table on a podium, cameras flashing as reporters shout questions.

"The truth is," B-Trix says, fidgeting uncomfortably. "I've been suffering from lapses in memory. It's a frightening ordeal to go through. After speaking with my team, I've decided to check myself into a private rehab facility. I adore my fans and I'm terribly sorry to cancel my tour, but right now the most important thing is that I get well."

The camera cuts back to the two news anchors, who applaud her decision. They talk about how refreshing it is to see such a high-profile celebrity publicly admit her struggles. To set an example and take advantage of the services our country has in place.

"There's no shame in that," one of the anchors says.

I feel sick.

"I guess we have our answer," Luka mutters. "She's no longer being hijacked."

And yet, it feels the opposite of victorious. We freed her, but it made no difference. She's handing herself over to the enemy by checking herself into a rehab facility. How many of B-Trix's fans will follow in her footsteps? How many will end up dead in a ditch?

"Unfortunately," the news anchor continues, "this comes on the heels of some very upsetting news. Our own Chief of

Press, Henry Fredrick, was found dead in his home earlier this morning."

I stand from my seat, my breath turning shallow.

"Authorities have said that the injuries appear to be self-inflicted, but aren't releasing anymore information at this time ..."

I look at Luka. "I thought they said they got to him."

"They did."

"Then why would he commit suicide?" But even as I ask the question, a part of me already knows the answer. What happened to Chief Fredrick is the same thing that happened to Dr. Roth. It wasn't suicide; it was murder. We set him free and the enemy killed him for it.

How long before B-Trix ends up the same way?

The soles of my shoes eat up the tread. My lungs burn. Sweat drips down my face and between my shoulder blades. Yet I increase the speed like I might be able to outrun my frustration. There's no word from Joe, who left last night on his mission to remove Secretary Young. Chief Fredrick is dead, accused of a suicide he didn't commit. And B-Trix will most likely be gone before nightfall.

How will the media spin it? Another suicide? I can hear the news anchor now. *If only she'd checked into a rehab facility sooner, she might not have become so desperate.*

I'm tired of innocent people dying. I'm tired of every single mission going south. I hate that there's nothing we can do to protect B-Trix until she falls asleep. I run harder. I don't stop until I reach five miles, and then I hit the weights. Claire is lifting too. An ever-present thorn in my side. I stay far away from her and push my muscles until they feel like overstretched rubber bands. Halfway into my fourth set of bench presses, Luka strides inside the gymnasium. Claire attempts to intercept him with a sultry hello, but he walks right past her without returning the greeting. I'd feel a little victorious about it if his face wasn't so alarmingly pale.

I wipe my forehead with a small, white towel and stand. "What's wrong?"

His attention slides to the bench, then back to me. "Maybe you should sit down."

I follow his suggestion, my pulse going fluttery. "What is it?"

He sits beside me with dark shadows beneath his eyes and rubs the back of his neck.

"Luka, you're freaking me out."

"California's State Penitentiary is under quarantine."

"What?"

"There was a report on the news that a virus is killing off prisoners."

The news hits me like a sucker punch to the gut. A virus? Killing off prisoners?

"Link and Ronie are trying to find out how many have died." Luka takes my hand. "It doesn't sound good."

"Do they know if—?" Fear clamps tightly around my voice box. I can't say it. I can't even think it. I left him there. He was innocent and I did nothing. I relegated my father to a box marked *later* because I didn't know how to help him. And now he might be ...

The room starts to spin.

My lungs contract, sucking and expelling the air like a fish out of water, but I swear there's not a drop of oxygen to be found.

Luka squeezes my hand tighter. "He could be fine. We don't know yet."

I stand. Too fast. Everything tilts, like I'm back in B-Trix's dream. Luka grabs my elbow, but I shake him off and force my rubbery legs to move. I have to find out. I have to know. If my dad is—if he's ...

I squeeze the thought away and force my legs into a speed walk, out of the gym, through the main section, until I'm in front of the door to the private wing, shoving my badge up against the access scanner. I fling the door open and run straight into Link.

His arms wrap around my waist, steadying me.

"Whoa," he whispers in my ear. "It's all right. I was just coming to find you. Your dad's still alive. He's listed as healthy in their system."

CHAPTER FORTY-TWO

DEAR DADDY

The choice between saving B-Trix and saving my father is a no-brainer. One's a linchpin in evil's master plan. The other is the man whose shoulders I rode on as a little girl. Felix and Cap work every possible angle, reaching out to any Believer with a measure of authority who might be able to get my dad out of there. Until then, I need to get to him. I need to see with my own eyes that his heart is still beating. I need to explain that we're working on a rescue plan.

I fall asleep thinking about him, dredging up my earliest memories and working my way forward. I recall every single Saturday together in his office, when I was Tess the Freak with no friends to hang out with on the weekends. The sound of his voice in the morning as he read the paper out loud to me and Pete. His steadiness. His certainty. His love and support. His unwavering belief that logic always wins.

Has that changed, these last four months behind bars? Does he still cling to logic now, when his life has become so illogical? Convicted of a felony he didn't commit. His family split apart. His daughter on the run—America's most wanted fugitive.

I don't know who my dad will be when I find him. I just know that I have to find him. So I continue to pore through the memories until I wake up inside his dream. It's soaked in an anxiety I know all too well. Dark and frightening, with shadows looming. The kind of dream where you're running— away from something, toward something. Only you can't get away and you can't get ahead. Despite his frantic motion, my dad is stuck in place.

I grab his shoulder.

He whirls around, his eyes going wide. "Teresa?"

Before I can even nod, he wraps me in a bear hug, pressing short, relieved kisses against the side of my forehead. Over and over again.

Tears sting my eyes. How can a man so obsessed with logic love so well—so deeply—when love isn't logical?

He grabs my shoulders. "What are you doing here?"

"This is a dream, Dad. You're dreaming right now."

The skin between his eyebrows puckers.

I start explaining. In an onslaught of words with no pause in between. I tell him everything that has happened. I tell him everything that I am. Everything the world is. Hoping with every ounce of hope that he will believe. And when I'm finished, I wrap him in a hug. "I'm so glad you're alive."

"Of course I'm alive. Why wouldn't I be alive?"

"They're saying half the prisoners are dead."

"Tess, what are you talking about? Who's saying?"

"The news. The virus. The whole prison is on quarantine."

"That's ridiculous. Nobody's dying here."

Now I'm the one with the furrowed brow. Nobody's dying? Is my dad right, or is he unaware? Are they hiding the deaths to keep the prisoners calm? "Listen. I don't know what's going on, I just know that you're not safe. You don't belong here. We're going to get you out. We have connections. People on the inside. You have to remember this dream, and you have to cooperate."

My dad kneads his temples. "This is a dream."

"But it's real. I'm real. Everything I just told you is real."

His eyes go cloudy with doubt.

Desperation expands inside me like a balloon about to burst. And a sensation like tugging grows behind my bellybutton. It's a sensation I know well. A doorway is opening, and with it, an idea. My dad needs to be on guard, but he can't guard himself against something he doesn't believe. And he won't believe without evidence. Well, if it's proof he needs, then that is exactly what I will give him.

"When you wake up, you'll know the truth. I'll prove that I was really here." I give his hand a squeeze, then back away. I move toward the tugging, until it's so strong I can barely keep my feet in place. I'm standing on the threshold. "Promise me that you'll stay safe."

The clouds of doubt swirl with confusion. "I promise."

I give him a small wave, and then I step through the doorway. Straight into his prison cell. My dad sleeps on a cot in a cold, damp room with nothing but a thin blanket to cover him. He's so much thinner, so much paler than I remember.

Except for a couple books, the cell is empty. There's nothing at all that I could use to scratch a message against the wall. The books will have to do. As I stare at my father, I let all the memories well into one single overwhelming emotion—*love*. It builds. It consumes. And then I get to work, ripping out pages, crumpling them into balls, and arranging them on the floor in a clear, concise message.

Tess was here.

"How sweet."

The sound of that voice makes my blood curdle. I remain

crouched on the floor, one final page crumpled in my hand.

"A message for dear Daddy."

Slowly, I turn around and stare up into a face marked with two scars.

He folds his hands behind his back and strolls to the foot of my father's bed.

My teeth clench.

"I like to think of myself as a patient person, Little Rabbit. But then your grandmother failed to bring you to me, and I will admit, I was more than a little frustrated." A glint of evil flashes in his ordinary, forgettable eyes. "You're making me look bad. I don't like to look bad."

Hearing his voice, seeing him standing there so close to my father, knowing what he did to Luka, what he did to a weak woman like my grandmother—it has every cell in my body, every atom, quivering with hatred.

"I was certain you'd come after your father eventually. You do like to play the hero. But then you didn't and I decided to take matters into my own hands." He traces one of his fingers along the mattress, inches from my father's foot. "I think it's time for dear daddy to fall ill."

"Leave him alone."

"And then once he's gone, I'll make sure to destroy everyone else you care about. Mommy. Petey. What's the name of the girl you're so fond of? Ah yes, Leela."

I lunge toward him, but a wall of black mist rises up between us.

"Such a temper." He clucks his tongue and sits at the head of my dad's bed. "Of course, you could always turn yourself over, and I won't touch a single hair on their heads." He presses his finger against my father's forehead.

Dad's entire body shudders.

"Don't touch him!"

"That, Little Rabbit, is up to you."

White-eyed men appear. They surround me on all sides, closing in. I look at my dad, lying there in a prison cell. I look at Scarface, the liar. Handing myself over will not ensure their safety. Of that, I'm sure. Before anyone can grab me, I startle myself awake.

CHAPTER FORTY-THREE

FRANTIC

As soon as my eyes open, I hurl myself out of bed and start waking people up—Link and Luka, Felix, Cap, Connal and Lexi, Ronie, and Glenda. Anybody who might be able to help me. Felix has a table of coffee and donuts and muffins set up in the command center as Link and Ronie rig up a secure phone line.

We contact a Believer in our network—a filthy rich, bigwig director who owns his own private jet and lives five hours south of Thornsdale.

"Where should he take them?" Felix asks.

I scramble about, trying to think of a safe place. A secure place. But my mind is all frantic energy. I haven't been able to sit still since waking up. I pace from the donut table to the wall with the monitors showing the refugee community and Shady Wood's hallway—back and forth, back and forth. All motion, but getting nowhere. Just like my father's dream.

"New Orleans."

I stop and look at Luka, who answered the question, and remember the guardians standing outside the gate—impossibly, brilliantly bright with blinding swords. "He's right. The Rivards will take them in."

All that's left to do is call Leela and my mother.

It's nine fifteen in the morning in Newport. Six fifteen in

Thornsdale. Leela answers the phone on the fifth ring with a groggy hello.

The sound brings a giant wave of relief. "Leela?"

Nothing.

"Leela, are you there?"

"Tess?" I picture her sitting up in bed, batting hair from her eyes.

I clutch the receiver to my ear, so thankful she's alive and well. "Yes, it's me."

"Oh my gosh, Tess! Are you okay? Your face is on the news every single night. So is Luka's. You're the most wanted criminals in America."

"I know. Listen, Leela. You're in danger."

Now there's a conversation stopper.

"I don't have time to explain. I just need you to trust me and do exactly what I say. My mom and Pete are in danger, too. I need the three of you to pack up and drive to San Francisco." I give her the address, and then the name.

"Wait. You mean the *director?*"

"He'll be waiting for you. As soon as you get to his house, he's going to fly the three of you somewhere safe."

"In his *private jet?*"

"Yes."

Leela doesn't respond.

"You still there?"

"Just pinching myself to make sure this isn't a dream."

"I know this is crazy. It's absolutely insane. But I need you to be careful. Don't trust anyone. Don't talk to anyone. Just get to San Francisco with my mom and Pete as quickly as you can, all right?"

"What about my family?"

I bite my lip and look at Felix. He and Link are both wearing headsets that patch them into the phone call, listening in for anything strange. Monitoring for bugs or wires. Felix lifts his shoulder, as if to say it's my call.

My gut screams no. Don't trust. I don't care about Leela's family. I care about Leela. But she loves her parents as much as I love my parents. I can't ask her to leave them behind. I rake my teeth over my bottom lip and go against my gut. "If you think you can trust them. If you think they'll cooperate, then you can bring them, too. Just be really, really careful."

Leela agrees.

We say goodbye. And before I can let myself worry over my decision, I call my mother. I haven't seen her since the night I disobeyed Cap's orders, jumped through a doorway, and found her being tortured by Scarface. The last time I heard her voice, she was screaming in agony. My heart twists as the phone rings once, twice, three times, and then ...

"Hello?"

I wait a beat, unable to speak past the onslaught of emotion knotting in my throat. I want, more than anything, to crawl through the phone line, straight into my mother's lap. I want to feel her fingers stroking my hair, her voice promising me that everything will be okay. That Scarface won't be able to follow through on his threat. If he does—if anything happens to my family ... I let the train of thought drop away, unable to finish it.

"Hello?" she says again.

I swallow the knot down. "Mom, it's me."

There's a sharp intake of breath. An agonizingly long, silent pause. And then sobbing in my ear. I can see her sitting there. Maybe in our kitchen, dressed in her robe, getting breakfast ready for Pete, if she still does that sort of thing with me gone and Dad locked in prison. I want to ask how she's doing. I want to ask how Pete's doing. But there's no time.

"I need you to listen very carefully."

As she sniffs into the receiver, I tell her as quickly and succinctly as possible what she needs to do. "Do you understand?"

"I can't believe it's you. I can't believe you're okay."

"I'm okay. At least I will be once I know that you're okay."

"Your father. What about your father? There's this virus. They're saying it's spreading fast. Killing inmates. They won't let me talk to him. They won't let any visitors in. I don't even know if he's alive."

"He's alive. We're working on getting him out. You get to safety, okay?"

"When will I see you again?"

I close my eyes, picturing eighteen candles on a cake. "As soon as possible, I promise."

The rest of the day passes in a frantic blur.

I'd be worried about my mom and Pete and Leela if I wasn't so busy working on my father's escape. We all grab a computer in the command center and search for connections. Ronie's the one who finds it. A prison guard with a sister in our network. When she shouts out the discovery, I almost hug her.

Felix calls the woman and explains.

She agrees to contact her brother—the prison guard—and convince him to break my dad out.

It's dangerous and crazy and about a million other things. Felix asks her what she knows about this virus. He's fixated on the fact that my father's inside the prison and he didn't know about it. Felix wants to know what's going on.

Me?

All I want is my family, alive and safe. Where evil can't touch them.

Cap kicks me out of the command center. He says my pacing is driving everyone insane. He promises to alert me the second he receives word, but it won't be for awhile, so I should go do something to occupy my mind. I spend the afternoon training in the dream simulator with Lexi, and when she's done, I head to the gym.

Dr. Sheng says exercising is good for anxiety. Maybe if I work out for the next five weeks straight, I'll figure out a way to manage mine. It seems crazy to me that people are going about their regular routine. Classes. Work. War tactics. I can't join any of it. I'm all manic energy, sprinting on a treadmill. Only it isn't helping.

My anxiety grows.

I ditch the running and try stretching, but that doesn't help either. The what-ifs spin faster and faster, matching the acceleration of my heart. No matter how hard I try, I can't stop them. I clutch my chest with one hand, my breaths coming in short, quick spurts, and grab onto a nearby machine to keep myself upright. I try to inhale, but I can't do it. I can't catch my breath. I can't breathe. I think I'm seriously having a heart attack. After everything—after all of this—I'm going to die in the basement of a haunted hospital in Newport, Rhode Island.

"Tess."

It's Luka. His firm, commanding voice.

Only it's too late. I'm about to go down.

He comes up behind me. "Breathe."

"I-I can't."

He places his hand over my stomach, his fingers spreading wide. "Exhale first. Push the air out."

I do as he says.

"Now breathe with me." He takes a calm, slow breath in, his lips right next to my ear. His fingers tighten across my abdomen. "Hold it here."

He waits a few seconds, then exhales.

I exhale, too.

"Close your eyes," he whispers.

My eyelids flutter shut.

All that exists is Luka's strong, steady presence behind me.

"Picture our beach. Breathe with the waves." His hand slides to my hip. He uses his other to gently remove mine from the weight machine and places it over my bellybutton. "You're okay. I'm right here. Slow inhale in. Hold. Slow exhale out."

I breathe with the waves. I breathe with Luka, relaxing against him as my heartbeat settles and the pain in my chest recedes.

He's given me my breath back.

I wrap a towel around my body and peek out of the bathroom into the empty hallway. Everybody's eating dinner in the mess hall. I hurry toward my room, the cool basement air prickling my damp skin. As soon as I step inside, Luka is there. He sits on my bed, his elbows on his knees, his hands clasped, his head bent so all I see is his messy hair.

I stop in the doorway. "What is it?"

He looks up and stands. "They're safe. Your mom just called from the Rivards."

My relief is so profound, I have to steady myself against the doorframe. "What about my dad?"

"No word yet." His attention dips to the towel and my bare legs.

I curl my toes and clasp the towel tighter, heat pooling in my cheeks. "I, uh, thought everyone was at dinner. Otherwise I would have gotten dressed in the bathroom." I definitely wouldn't be traipsing around in a towel had I known I'd run into Luka. That's something Claire would do. Not me, even if I had the body for it.

My embarrassment seems to amuse him. "I thought we could go check in with Cap together. See if he's heard anything."

"I should probably get dressed first."

He lets loose an exaggerated sigh and heads toward the hall. "If you insist."

I grab his hand as he passes by in the doorway. "Luka?"

He stops.

"Thanks for earlier."

"Of course."

"It helped a lot."

"Tess." He looks down at me—his body close, but not quite touching mine—and tucks a strand of wet hair behind my ear. "If the only way I can help you is by helping you breathe, then that's exactly what I'll do."

"It was so much more than that."

He gives me a sad half-smile, then leaves me to my privacy.

I change quickly. Shakily. A combination of leftover flutters from Luka and concern for my dad. Two-thirds of my family is safe. I won't be able to relax until I know the final third is too. I finger-comb my hair and hurry out into the hallway.

Luka stands outside. Cap's with him. Their somber expressions have me stutter-stepping to a halt. "Did you hear something?"

Cap sets his hands on his wheels. "I'm sorry. By the time our prison guard got to him, it was too late."

My head begins to shake.

Luka steps forward and pulls me into a hug—his body warm and strong.

Mine is cold and lifeless.

"They're saying he died of the same virus that's killing the other inmates." Cap keeps talking. His voice turns into an indistinct mumble, as though he's talking from the bottom of a deep, deep well. Or maybe it's me who's at the bottom. I stand there, my arms dangling like dead weights by my sides. It's a lie. My father didn't die from a virus anymore than Chief Fredrick committed suicide. My father was murdered.

It's time for me to go after his murderer.

CHAPTER FORTY-FOUR

OVERCOME

My heart has turned to ice. It's frozen over with hatred. All of it points at one singular target—the man with the scars. The man who won't stop until he's destroyed everything and everyone I love. He nearly ruined Luka. He almost enticed Pete into darkness. Because of him, my grandmother turned traitor and Jillian is dead. And now, so is my father. It's a truth I can't process. It's a truth I don't want to let sink in. I'd rather focus on hate.

As Joanna snores, I lay in bed, focusing every ounce of mental energy on the source of my hatred. The enemy can worm its way inside a person's soul and take over. A Linker can hop inside dreams, which is essentially the same as hopping inside a person's mind. Scarface isn't a person, but he most definitely has a mind. Is it possible for me to hop inside of it?

The people I love won't be safe until I destroy him once and for all. He's been waiting for me. Hunting me down. He wants me to come. That's exactly what I will do. I fall asleep with the image of his marred face pasted to the underside of my eyelids, the memory of his cultured voice crooning *Little Rabbit* in my ear.

When I wake, darkness surrounds me. A heavy, oppressive darkness—like I'm sitting at the bottom of the ocean, crushed beneath the weight of all that water. It takes strength and concentrated effort to expand my lungs. I squint into the cold, heavy blackness, but my eyes won't adjust.

The sound of laughter rises up out of the darkness. Malevolent, bone-tingling laughter that bounces off the walls, as though coming from every direction. As quickly as it comes, it stops. The echoes fade away. There's a loud *scritching*—like a match against cement. A small flame dances to life and casts shadows along the face I fell asleep hating. His expression is triumphant. Deranged. Gleeful. Like my presence thrills him.

"Little Rabbit, here at last. And a few hours too late. If only you'd come sooner, your father wouldn't be so decidedly ..." His mouth twists with pleasure. "Dead."

A volcano of rage erupts in my soul. I want to lunge at him. I want to gouge out his eyes. But the invisible weight bearing down on my shoulders is so heavy, I can't move. Not even a finger. What's happening? Why am I paralyzed?

"After all this time, after all the trouble you've caused me, I finally get the pleasure of ending you." He comes closer.

I try to jerk away, but my muscles are frozen.

"Poor Luka will be so crushed."

I try to move again, but it's impossible.

Panic beats like a drum in my chest. This is all wrong. This isn't what was supposed to happen. I can't fight him when I can't move. I try to startle. To abort the mission. But I can't do that either. It's like B-Trix's dream all over again, with the black wall of mist locking me inside. Only this time, I'm not in B-Trix's dream. I've entered Scarface's mind. I found a way inside without considering if there would be a way out.

"I can see him now, sitting by your side as you waste away, wondering what could have been had he not been so weak and powerless to protect you. Oh, I will have fun whispering those reminders in his ears. So, so much fun."

Leave him alone!

But I can't say the words. I can't even breathe, and this time, Luka's not here to help me.

"Your father got your sweet message, by the way. You should have seen his face when he realized that everything he believed was a lie. Then the hope. Oh, the hope. He really thought you'd come. He really thought he had a chance. It was a delight to watch the life drain from his eyes."

Fury strikes like lightning, scalding me from the inside out. A giant, electrical jolt that fissures the ice encapsulating my frozen, stone-of-a-heart.

"Had I known killing dear daddy would be the thing to get you here, I'd have done it much, much sooner." He strokes my cheek with the tip of his finger.

His icy touch sears my skin. Pain. Indescribable pain. Unlike any pain I've ever felt. The kind of pain that has a scream clawing up my throat and my insides writhing in agony. And yet I remain as still as stone.

"Don't worry, Little Rabbit. I'll make sure the rest of your family joins you soon. Leela, too. Luka can live. I'll enjoy watching his misery." With a widening grin, the man I hate wraps his hands around my neck and squeezes.

My eyes bulge. My body convulses. I gasp for air that doesn't come. I can't let him kill anybody else that I love. I can't let my father's death be in vain. Heat seeps into my bloodstream. It courses through my veins. Gathering and swirling. The tighter his fingers close around my neck, the more sinister his evil smile, the more the heat builds. Until it's hotter than the agonizing cold. Until I can't hold it anymore. With every ounce of strength in my possession, I force my palms up and release it.

Ribbons of light escape into the darkness.

Scarface lets go of my neck, his pleasure giving way to alarm. He takes a step back, but the light snatches him. It wraps around his body like the black mist wrapped around Luka's. He tries to tear the light away, but he can't overcome it.

His demented eyes go wide. With shock. With disbelief. With fear.

I keep my palm up, releasing more as my head splits in two. The light seeps into Scarface's nostrils and his ears and his mouth. His body begins to fissure. Shafts of blinding white shoot from the cracks, breaking him apart from the inside out. He screams—one long, piercing note before he shatters into nothing and the world goes black.

When I open my eyes, I'm laying on the ground in a white room. A magnificent creature stands in front of me, so dazzlingly beautiful I can't look away. This being is brighter, more stunning than the guardians outside the Rivard home. Only instead of wanting to fall to my face in fear, I want to move closer and touch. I try, but my muscles are so weak, I can't even lift my head.

The being smiles down at me with a face like the sun.

"My family." Scarface will kill them. He'll hunt them. After what I did, he won't stop until each person is dead. "Please. Will you protect them?"

"You have no reason to worry." The voice. It's unlike anything I've ever heard. Serene. Hypnotic. Alluring. "Your family is safe, dear one. You eliminated the threat."

"Eliminated?"

"It was extraordinary work. You should be very proud of yourself."

I try to remember. The unbearable heaviness. The dark. The pain. And then the light. It came from me and it destroyed *him*. I did what I set out to do. But his destruction doesn't change the fact that my father is dead. He has been eliminated, too. A heavy ache builds in my throat. I don't want to feel it.

"My dad." I choke over the word, my eyes filling with tears.

"Shhh. You don't have to think about that now." The being strokes my hair and shushes me like a parent comforting a frightened child. "Rest, dear one. You deserve to rest."

Exhaustion drags at my eyelids. I'm so, so tired. I let them close. The sharp talons of grief digging into my heart release their grip. And I slip away. When I wake up, the being is still there. Humming a soothing lullaby.

"How long have I been sleeping?"

"Shhh, not long. Rest. It's important that you regain your strength."

I am lulled back to sleep—over and over again—but my strength does not return. I remain listless. Numb. Floating in a cloud of nothing. No pain. No fear. No sadness or anger. No motivation. No pressure to save the world. Just this angel and its lullaby and its reassuring touch. After all that I've been through, it feels good. It feels safe. So I stay. Why should I go? What is waiting for me out there but more loss and pain and hardship and a frightening, unknowable future?

Then I remember Luka and something deep down in my soul beckons me to wake.

Chapter Forty-Five

The Death Knell

"Any improvement?"

"None."

There's the sound of somebody sighing. "You should come get something to eat."

"I'm not hungry."

That voice is familiar. It pulls me to consciousness even though I'm not sure I want to be conscious. My head throbs. My stomach lurches. My tongue is impossibly thick, like every last drop of moisture has evaporated and will never, ever return.

I crack open one of my eyes.

The room I lie in is dimly lit and deathly still. Like a tomb. I open my other eye, trying to make sense of my surroundings. This isn't my bedroom. It's … the west wing infirmary. Was I injured? Judging by the way I feel, I wouldn't be surprised if I was hit by a truck. I try remembering what got me here, but all is fog and haze and jumbled memory.

I turn my head—a movement that makes me nauseous.

The blurry form of Cap sits in his wheelchair near the doorway, his mouth fixed in a grim line. I follow the direction of his stare, past a short, pudgy nurse named Penny and see Luka sitting in the corner. He sits with his elbows on his knees, fingers threaded through his hair, staring at the floor. An ace bandage wraps around his right hand. Was he injured, too?

"You need your strength," Cap says.

"For what?" His posture is so defeated—so utterly despairing—that I try to reach out and comfort him. But the effort is torturous and a groan slides past my lips.

Luka's head jerks up. His hair is a mess, his jaw covered in scruff, his eyes bloodshot beyond all reason. When he sees me, they widen in disbelief, like I'm the last person he expected to find in this bed. "Tess?"

I want to ask what's wrong. Why is he here like this? Why am I here like this? What's going on? But my throat is too dry for anything more substantial than another groan.

The nurse comes to my side, shushing me like ... like that angel. There was an angel and a white room and a hypnotic lullaby.

Penny places her hand behind my head and brings a cup to my lips. "Here, drink this."

I do. The cool liquid is heaven. I drain the cup and ask for more. Luka jumps out of his chair. He takes the cup from Penny, quickly fills it, and sits on my bed, cradling the back of my head like Penny did, only his hand is bigger, stronger. It's also trembling.

Cap mutters something under his breath and wheels away. Out of the room.

Penny stands behind Luka, a sheen of moisture building in her eyes. I don't understand why. I don't understand what's happening. Why do I feel like I'm suffering from the world's biggest hangover? Why does Luka look like he's suffering from one, too?

I drain the cup, ignore the pounding in my skull and attempt to shove clarity into place. There was the angel and the soothing lullaby and before that ... Scarface. I went to bed last night thinking about him and it worked. I found him and somehow, I destroyed him. He's gone. He can't hurt the people I love anymore.

Luka returns with a fresh cup and this look on his face. This crazy, intense look. I can't tell if he's going to kiss me or yell at me. Instead, he helps me sit up and hydrate my Sahara-Desert-of-a-mouth. Cap returns with Felix and Link, who looks every bit as wrecked as Luka, only his hand isn't wrapped in a bandage. He stops in the doorway, like he can't believe what he's seeing.

Penny scoots Luka aside. "I need to check her vitals."

"What's going on?" Despite all the water I just drank, my voice is gravelly. "How did I get here?"

Penny presses the stethoscope against my chest. "You were moved here three days ago."

"Three days ago?" Surely I heard wrong. "That's impossible."

Felix shakes a toothpick from a small container in his pocket. "Apparently not."

Penny moves the stethoscope to my back and asks me to take a deep breath. "We weren't sure you would make it through the night, but your heartbeat sounds nice and strong now."

Link steps further inside my room. "Where'd you go, Xena?"

"What do you mean?"

"I kept trying to find you, but I couldn't. We thought ..."

I look from one to the other—Luka and Link. Dark hair, ginger hair—sticking every which way. Green eyes, amber eyes—haunted and tortured. Faces covered in scruff. Cheeks hollow. They thought I was gone. They thought I was gone like I once thought Luka was gone.

"How have I been out for three days?"

"Not *out*, Tess," Luka says. "*Gone.*"

"What were you thinking?" Cap's voice explodes inside the small room, so sudden and loud I clasp my head against the pain piercing my skull. "Were you on a suicide mission?"

"No."

"Then why in the world would you go after the enemy *on your own, without* backup?"

"To protect what's left of my family!" My anger matches his. If only it didn't cause so much physical pain to maintain it. I sink back against the pillows. "He would have killed them just like he killed my father, and everyone else I care about. Somebody had to stop him."

"So you decided to stop him by yourself?"

"I didn't even know if it would work."

"It sure as hell almost didn't."

"I think it's best for the patient," Penny says calmly, "if everyone would avoid yelling."

Cap paws his face. When his hand drops away, he has dark circles beneath his eyes, too.

The room oozes with tension.

Guilt twists my stomach. I picture them—the last three days—sitting by my bedside, imagining the worst. Waiting for me to waste away like Gabe's sister. Thinking that the One who was supposed to save them was as good as dead. I'm sorry I put them through that, but I'm not sorry for what I did. I remember the shafts of light breaking Scarface apart from the inside out. I didn't just fight him off. I abolished him altogether. And doing so knocked me unconscious for three days.

I clear my throat and ask nobody in particular, "How's my

mom?"

Everyone exchanges a strange look.

My guilt turns to alarm. "Is she okay?"

"She's fine. So's your brother and your friend." Link takes another step closer, the torture in his eyes ebbing away. Luka isn't so quick to recover.

"Then what is it?"

"A lot's happened the past three days, Xena."

"Is somebody going to fill me in?"

"Secretary Young is dead," Cap says.

"When?"

"Yesterday. Heart failure. The coroner will most likely uncover poison."

"And B-Trix?"

"Also dead."

I fist the thin comforter covering my legs. "Let me guess. Suicide?"

Cap shakes his head. "The virus."

"*The virus?* What virus?" He can't mean the one that put the California State Penitentiary on quarantine. B-Trix checked herself into a rehab facility on the east coast.

Felix removes the toothpick from between his teeth. "The same one that supposedly killed your father." His blunt words make me wince. "Three days ago, the government declared our country in a state of emergency. The virus is airborne. It's highly contagious. And it's lethal. Apparently, it has the potential to wipe out the entire population."

I scratch the inside of my wrist and gape as Felix continues.

"The country's on lockdown. A zero-tolerance policy has been enforced. Police have permission to shoot looters on site. They're saying desperate times call for desperate measures."

I shake my head, unable to believe what I'm hearing.

"Perhaps you would like to see it for yourself."

My legs are so weak, Luka has to partly carry me to the command center.

Link enters the room ahead of us and has a chair waiting. "Ronie was able to patch into several city-wide security systems so we have eyes on the situation." He wheels the chair closer. "I have to warn you, Xena. It's not pretty."

I sink into the seat, cupping my clammy hand over my clammier forehead. I take a few steadying breaths, then look up at the monitors. I recognize the cities. New York. Chicago. Detroit. What I don't recognize is the chaos. Each one has morphed into an apocalyptic Hollywood film set, with military men dressed in hazmat suits, shooting at looters setting fire to buildings and throwing rocks at windows.

This can't be the United States. It's like I went to sleep, battled my worst demon, and woke up in an alternate universe. One where anarchy reigns.

On another monitor, a somber-faced President Cormack sits in the oval office with someone I don't recognize. An egg-headed man wearing an outfit like a pilot's uniform, with glasses and a part down the middle of his hair.

Ronie rises from her spot behind one of the computers and stands beside me. "It's good to see you awake."

I'd say it's good to be awake, but I'm not so sure. I give her a faint nod and keep my attention on the man.

He intermittently looks from the screen to his notes as he speaks to viewers. "Authorized personnel are working around the clock in every county across the nation. If you need food or water or medicine, call the hotline number for your county and it will be delivered as soon as possible. Anybody found outside their home will be arrested. Anybody resisting arrest will be shot on sight."

I glance at the two monitors that show the refugee community in Newport. Rows and rows of tents. What are they supposed to do? How can an airborne virus be contained in places like that? Felix's words come back to me on an echo.

Desperate times call for desperate measures.

What sort of desperate measures will the government go to when it comes to the nation's refugees?

"Effective today, trained health care professionals will travel door-to-door to test each individual in the home. If any one member of the household is infected, every person inside that home will go into immediate quarantine. We cannot stress enough how imperative it is that you remain calm and give us your complete cooperation. Please wait patiently until a professional arrives to administer the screening."

Screening.

My breath comes quicker. I stand on shaky legs and move closer, staring at the man on the screen. He sits with his hands folded neatly on the desk in front of him. "Who is he?"

"The Surgeon General," Cap says.

President Cormack takes over—espousing her usual crap. Something about uniting together for the greater good. I don't pay attention. I'm too busy staring at the Surgeon General. At the very end of the broadcast, he straightens his notes and I find what I'm looking for—the mark. On the inside of his wrist.

I found the *physician.*

And the death knell is sounding.

CHAPTER FORTY-SIX

AN UNEXPECTED TWIST

With the nation in chaos, all forms of communication have been disrupted. Even our expert hackers—Link and Ronie—have a difficult time getting through to anyone to verify what I already know. This virus is the final blow—the death knell mentioned in the prophecy. The symbol on the Surgeon General's wrist is the only verification I need.

Cap drops a plate of food in front of me on the table in the investigation room. "Eat."

I'm not hungry, but I obey orders. If I'm right—and I know that I am—then I will need my strength. Halfway through the bagel, Ronie enters the room with a ream of paper in hand. "We received confirmation that at least two refugee communities have been wiped out."

It's happening. The Gifting has been herded into the United States and now they're being exterminated. I think about those little barefooted kids playing on top of trash heaps and nausea balls my stomach into a tight fist.

Felix taps the eraser of his pencil against the tabletop. "And the screening? Do we know what it entails?"

"We're still working on that."

I force the last of my meal down and push the plate away. "There's no virus." I'd bet my life on it, along with every other life in this room. Considering Link and Luka are among them,

I'm obviously more than sure. "The screening is the same one used on pregnant women. The same one used on immigrants and refugees. This virus is a ploy. A convenient way to identify everyone who's part of The Gifting."

Glenda wipes her nose with a tissue. "Wouldn't the public realize nobody's dying? Wouldn't doctors?"

"How can they when everything is shut down?" Luka says.

"Exactly." My knee begins to bounce. Cap was right. The food has helped me focus. "The media has everyone holed up inside their homes, convinced they'll either contract a deadly virus or be shot on sight if they go outside. All they know is what the media's feeding them and we know who's controlling the media."

"What are we to do then?" Lexi asks.

Everyone looks to Felix, our leader. But Felix sits there, his fingers steepled beneath his chin, and defers to me. I don't shrink away. I sit up straighter. For my dad. "We'll need Joe to take care of the Surgeon General."

Felix picks up the walkie-talkie and tells Joanna to pass along the message.

I stand and move to the board. The *eye*. The *censor*. The *idol*. All three have been eliminated. The *physician* will soon follow. All that remains is the *king*. I turn around and face the group. "It's time to go after Cormack."

Felix nods at me over his fingers, his dark eyes glittering with approval.

"We have to free her successfully. She needs to come out of this alive, with full understanding of what's been happening. Otherwise nothing will change. Not the rehab facilities. Not the pregnancy screenings. Not the refugee communities. If Cormack dies or checks herself in to a rehab facility due to lapses in memory, this genocide will continue until every last member of The Gifting is dead." And if that happens, evil will have free reign. The world as we know it will end. "We need her on our side so she can uncover what's happening, and then put a stop to it once and for all."

The planning begins.

We've done this twice before, neither time successfully. With B-Trix, my weird shield broke the dream apart and chased the hijacker away before we had a chance to explain anything. Sure, we freed her, but it didn't do any good. She had no idea what was happening, and she ended up dead. I tap the dry erase marker against my palm. "What went wrong with Chief Fredrick?"

"We didn't follow through."

Everybody looks at Connal, who sits at the table, fiddling with a switch knife.

"Think about it. Fredrick was one of the key players, wasn't he? Of course they'd be prepared. He was probably being guarded. They killed him off as soon as he woke up, before he could say a bloody word to anyone. It's not enough to free Cormack. We need guards of our own. Someone who can get her to safety."

Lexi raises a skeptical brow. "Oh, is that it?"

"We have a secret service bodyguard on our side," Cap says. "He's ready to help."

I shake my head, because it's not enough. If our botched mission at Shady Wood is proof of anything, it's that the enemy has numbers on their side. Those white-eyed soldiers came out of nowhere when we were attempting to free my grandmother and Clive, and at the time, neither were actually on our team. How many more will be there, surrounding

Cormack—the *king*? "The enemy has to know we're going after the list. Cormack is going to be heavily guarded."

Felix drums his fingers together. "What are you suggesting?"

The room grows quiet, but the answer is obvious. At least to me.

"We bring our own army." I look at Link, feeling more and more alive by the second. "While our team is freeing Cormack, you can find the doorway. Once you find it, you can link up two people at a time and bring them through. As soon as they're out of the dream, you sever the link and grab two more. When we've done our job with Cormack, we can pass through before the dream collapses. We'll have numbers on our side. If the enemy is there, we'll be able to fight."

"I can grab Anna first," Link says, his excitement matching mine. "She'll be able to keep everyone hidden."

"We can go tonight."

"Hold on a second." Cap raises his arm like a traffic cop. "You just woke up from a three-day coma. Don't you think you ought to give yourself time to recuperate?"

"You heard the Surgeon General. The screening has already started. Two refugee communities have been wiped out." Urgency presses me forward, but Cap eyes me in a way that brings me back to the hub. I was foolhardy once before, rushing into plans without considering all the ramifications. It nearly lost me Luka.

This time, though, we know who we're rescuing. And we know what we're up against. I understand Cap's concern. Up until that bagel, I could barely walk on my own. Now, however, enough adrenaline courses through my veins, I'm pretty sure I could take on Felix, Cap, and Lexi at once. "Let's go spar in the dream simulator. If you're still concerned about my strength, then we'll wait. But I don't think you will be."

Link catches my eye with a lopsided grin.

Cap, however, still looks unconvinced.

"Let's not forget," Felix says, "that our fearless leader will have the protection of our newest team member."

The announcement comes like a hiccup. "Newest team member?"

Felix inclines his head toward the boy sitting beside me. The one with the messy hair and three day's worth of scruff and a mysterious ace bandage wrapped around his right hand. The one who's supposed to be safe, because he's not going on any missions. My heartbeat goes slightly erratic. Why would he be on the team? There's absolutely no reason for him to come. "I don't understand."

It happens incredibly fast.

One second, Connal is leaning back in his seat. The next, he flicks open the blade of his knife and whips it directly at my face. I don't have time to react, but it doesn't matter. I don't need to. There's a flash of light—so bright everyone in the room covers their eyes. The knife clatters to the table, thwarted from its trajectory.

I stare at Luka. His green eyes are glued to mine, blazing brighter than the blast of heat that lit the room. The blast of heat that came from him. He threw a shield like it required no effort at all.

CHAPTER FORTY-SEVEN

A CHOICE

The room has gone quiet.

Luka studies me with his head slightly cocked. It's the same way he studied me my first day at Thornsdale, when I was the new girl. Like he's trying to read my thoughts. I'm glad he can't. He wouldn't like them. My body goes from hot to cold, feverish to clammy—back and forth, like a broken thermostat. "When?"

"Three days ago."

I stare back at him. Three days ago, I destroyed Scarface.

"I woke up and it was back. All of it. I didn't understand why until you wouldn't wake up."

Cap rubs his jaw. "We could make a pretty good guess at what happened."

"How?"

"Vivian Rivard told you that Samson found a tumor on Luka's soul."

All the feverish heat in my body pools in my face. I never told Luka that bit of information. I did, however, relay it to Cap via our handy dandy dream phone. I guess I've been keeping more secrets than I realize.

Cap continues. "When you destroyed the individual that left the tumor, you destroyed the tumor as well. It's what bound Luka's gifting as your Keeper."

The bagel in my stomach churns. I clamp my lips together to keep it down. I destroyed Scarface to protect the people I love. To keep them safe. Somehow, the opposite has happened. Luka has his powers back, which means …

"You're looking kind of chalky, Xena," Link says.

I swallow the saliva accumulating in my mouth. "Just trying to catch up."

"Why don't we catch up in the dojo? If we're going on the mission tonight, I want to make sure you're up for it." Cap reverses his wheelchair from the table.

I want to tell him never mind. I take it back. I'm not ready to go tonight. I'm not ready to go ever. But I can't find my voice. So I follow him with a growing sense of dread.

As soon as we're inside, I pour out my mounting anxiety on my two opponents—Lexi and Cap. Connal and Luka stand on opposite sides, watching intently. I pay no attention to the two-person audience. I drum up every ounce of strength in my possession, because maybe if I can drum up enough, the thing barreling toward me—the thing threatening to paralyze me—won't be a thing at all. Maybe I can be stronger than the prophecy.

Cap jabs.

I flip backward, out of reach, then spin around, the heel of my foot hitting Lexi's jaw with such force, she drops to the floor.

Connal steps forward. "Easy."

Lexi glares at him, then wipes her cheek and clambers to her feet.

She and Cap circle me like the thoughts in my head. A hidden genocide. Unprecedented peace. The beacon, giving hope for freedom. The Gifting, being led like sheep to the slaughter. The One with the ability to see evil's mark. The sound of the death knell. All of them, prophecies. All of them, fulfilled.

Victory must come through sacrifice.

The thing barreling toward me comes closer.

Transurgence.

Kataphagon.

Luka as dead as Gabe.

I dodge a high kick from Cap, spin in a quick circle and swipe his legs so fiercely he falls flat on his back with a loud *oomph*. Lexi throws a punch, but I catch her arm, twist her around, flip her over my body. Her eyes widen as I cock my fist back.

A burst of light erupts in the dojo and hurtles toward me.

Another blast follows the first—bigger and brighter—from the opposite side of the room. The two collide in an explosion of heat.

Lexi tears off her gloves. "Stop being a wanker, Connal. We're just sparring."

"Yer sparring, sure. She's trying to murder ye."

My lungs heave.

Cap sits up and sets his elbows on his knees, sweat pouring down his face. "I think it's safe to say your strength is fine."

I look at Luka, who threw the second shield to stop Connal's from hitting me, and I pull my gloves off, too. I can't keep it inside any longer. I have to know. "What did you and Gabe do during your training?"

His brow puckers. "Why?"

"I want to know what he taught you."

"You know what he taught me. How to throw a shield. How to cloak you. How to stop you from dreaming."

"You've already told me about those things."

"What do you want to know, then?"

"The things he taught you that you haven't told me about."

Luka avoids my eyes.

"You know what Gabe did, don't you?"

He doesn't answer.

But of course he does. If he didn't know, he would have asked me about it. He would have obsessed over it. Neither of us said a word to each other about how Gabe died. I close the gap between us and force him to look at me. "Luka?"

His eyes fasten on mine, only they're no longer tortured. They are determined and confident.

It absolutely terrifies me. "Promise me you will never do that."

"I don't need to. Look at you, Tess. You're stronger than ever. You defeated one of our biggest enemies on your own. With no help. You didn't just fight him. You *destroyed* him. I'm pretty sure nobody's done that before."

"That's not a promise."

He stares down at me, his eyes filled with sympathy, but he doesn't give me what I want.

"You'll die."

"And you'll live."

The heat billowing in my chest grows hotter. I turn away, fear and desperation clawing and scraping at my soul, frantically scrambling for a solution. A way out. I don't want to do this anymore. I've changed my mind. We need to abort the mission. We need—

"Are you two going on about transurgence?" Lexi asks. "Because if you are, you have a choice too, you know."

"Lex." Connal says her name in a low growl.

She tosses him an eye roll. "Oh, sod it, Connal. There should always be a choice."

I've seen him upset with her before, on multiple occasions. Connal is generally an easy-going guy, but his *anima* gets under his skin in a big way. Her rejections frustrate him. Her stubbornness drives him crazy. But the look he's wearing right now is different. His nostrils are flared. His legs planted wide.

I turn to Lexi. "What do you mean?"

"Just because he chooses to transurge doesn't mean you have to accept the sacrifice."

"What?" Luka's monosyllabic question escapes like a yelp more than a word.

Connal swears. "Dry up, Lex."

"You dry up. She deserves to know. It's a choice for both parties involved." Her eyes flash at her Keeper. "You can *choose* to give me your life and I can *choose* to reject it."

"Just like I can choose to give you my love and you can choose to reject that?"

"It's not love."

Connal swears again, his round face going crimson. I'm pretty sure it's not from embarrassment.

"Will he live?" I ask.

The two quarrelers stop their bickering.

"If I reject it, does he live?"

Lexi ignores Connal's death stare and raises her chin. "Yes."

"That's grand," Connal says, "and then we'll all be in the grave. A Keeper doesn't do transurgence fer nothing. We do it only when it's absolutely necessary."

CHAPTER FORTY-EIGHT

THE WHOLE THING

I stride through Headquarters, desperate to get away from Luka's and Cap's and Connal's objections. I need space. I need quiet. I need to think. I barge inside my room to Joanna tweezing her eyebrows in front of our mirror. Luka follows me inside and grabs my arm—to get me to stop, to get me to listen.

I pull away, not wanting to do either.

Joanna's tweezers freeze. She gapes like a fish. "You're awake."

"Unfortunately."

She looks from me to Luka. Tension rolls off his body in waves. I'm sure she's trying to figure out why the pair of us seem so furious about my wakeful state. "I'll, uh, just give you two some privacy." She drops her tweezers inside her bag and slips out of the room.

Luka turns on me. "You can't reject it. That isn't an option."

"According to Lexi, it *is* an option."

"Not one you would take."

"Why not?"

"You have bigger things than my life to consider. You're not my Keeper. You said so yourself. It's not a luxury you have."

"I said that when you weren't at risk of dying." When transurgence was off the table. When protecting him meant sparing his feelings, not his life. Darkness swirls inside of me, gathering like storm clouds. "I already lost my dad, Luka. I can't lose you, too."

"What about your mom? And Pete? You think either of them can lose *you*?"

"What about *your* parents?"

"I already told you. I stopped considering their feelings as soon as they tried having you locked up in mental rehab facility."

"They're still your parents. Your mom risked everything to give you life. You should value it more."

Luka releases a frustrated growl and rakes his hands through his hair. "This is stupid. We're fighting over something that might not even happen."

"You read the prophecy—victory requires sacrifice."

"We don't know what that means."

"You used to think it meant my death." When we came upon the prophecy at the Rivard's, Luka was wrecked. Tortured. Just now in the dream simulator? He wasn't tortured at all. He looked confident. In control. The kind of look a card player has when he's holding the highest trump. That is, until Lexi shared her latest bit of info. Turns out, I'm holding the final trump, but it doesn't feel victorious. No matter how I play my cards, I'll end up losing.

"You want to know the dream I had the night my gifting returned?"

I don't answer. It's hard to talk past the growing tightness in my throat.

"The same dream I've had a thousand times. Only this

time, it was different. This time, I could finally get to you. We were unstoppable, Tess."

If he's hoping to instill some confidence, it doesn't work. No offense to Luka, but the prophecy has more credibility than his dreams.

"I've had the same dream the last three nights. I thought it was a cruel joke—all of it. Finally being able to protect you when you weren't there to protect. Victory in my dreams when I'd already lost everything. But it wasn't a cruel joke." He shifts closer. "You're here. And you are incredibly, amazingly strong. You'll make the right choice if the time comes."

"You're wrong. I'm not strong. I'm weak."

"You have *weaknesses*. We all do. But we don't have to let those weaknesses define us. We don't have to let them stop us from doing what we were born to do."

"You were born to live."

"I was born to protect you. To keep you alive so you can do what *you* were born to do." His eyes are fastened on mine. "And you're doing it. You're leading the army. The dream I've had since I was a kid is coming true."

His confidence undoes me. I don't want him to believe in me. I want him to forbid me from going on this mission like he forbade me from going to Shady Wood. Only this time, I'll listen. Because this time, I know something I didn't then. Losing my life isn't the worst thing that can happen. Not by a long shot.

"Listen, we have a powerful team. We have a solid plan. And contrary to what you might be thinking, I don't *want* to die. I'm not looking for the opportunity." He brushes a strand of hair away from my eye. "I want more time with you. I want all of it. The whole thing. The happy ending. You and me, together, sharing a lifetime of memories and moments. I'm not looking for an excuse to give my life away. I want to keep it, and live it with you."

They are amazing words. Perfect words. At the moment, they also feel like impossible words. It's that impossibility that makes me ache. I take his hand between mine and run my fingers over the bandage around his knuckles. "What happened?"

"I punched a wall."

My attention jumps to his face.

"It wasn't my finest moment." He rubs his thumb along my jaw.

I close my eyes and lean into his touch. His skin is the perfect combination of rough and warm.

"I will do everything in my power to keep us both alive. I promise you that. But if something happens, and there's no other choice," he cups the side of my face, "you will be okay without me. I know you will."

I shake my head fiercely, but Luka doesn't let me start my objection. He curls his fingers into my hair and covers my lips with his. I kiss him back. I kiss him like he can save me from the dark cloud swirling inside. I kiss him with all the urgency I feel.

And he responds. After three days of thinking I was as good as dead, he drinks me in like he's a parched man and I'm a glass of cold water. I wrap my arms around his neck. He lifts me onto the dresser, his scruff scratching against my skin. And somewhere beneath the loud pounding of our hearts comes the sound of a knock.

"Hey Xena, you in—?"

Luka steps away, his chest rising and falling.

I sit on the dresser, my lips puffy and bruised.

Link stands in the doorway, his face as red as a beet. He scratches the back of his head and looks away. "Uh, Felix wants everybody in the gym in thirty minutes."

I run shaky fingers through my tussled hair. "W-why?"

"Joe called. The Surgeon General's been taken care of."

"That was quick," Luka says.

"One of his team members was in the right place at the right time. Cap told Felix that tonight is a go. He's going to tell everyone the plan."

The pit in my stomach opens wider. It's like I woke up on a train barreling down a track that's ruined up ahead. It's going a thousand miles a minute and there's no hope of jumping off.

CHAPTER FORTY-NINE
HE'S NOT THE ONLY ONE

Most people linger after Felix finishes laying out the plans and answering questions. They talk in small pockets around the basketball court. So many bodies inside the basement gymnasium make the usually cool space warm and sticky. Nerves and excitement and fear charge the air. I wind around the groups and keep my eyes down, avoiding the stares and the way people look at me—like I'm some dazzling angel of hope—feeling increasingly claustrophobic.

As I near the exit, a tiny voice catches my attention.

"I don't want you to go." Henry stands with his arms wrapped tightly around Felicia, who combs her fingers gently through his hair—a gesture that has me missing my own mother terribly.

"It'll be okay," Felicia murmurs. "This will be over soon. And when it is, we'll be with your dad and your sister again."

Henry hugs her waist tighter. "But what if something happens to you?"

Felicia unwraps his arms from her waist and bends down so she can look him in the eyes. Hers are thick with moisture. "What happens in the stories I read to you at night? Who wins?"

"The good guys."

"Remember that, Henry. The good guys always win."

The air grows stuffier. I skirt around them and make my exit. As soon as I'm out in the corridor, I take a deep breath. I want to be alone. But where can I go? Joanna will be in our room soon, and I'm sure she'll want to rehash everything Felix discussed during the meeting. I find myself wishing for the greenhouse in the hub, which goes to show how much has changed. Plants in a warehouse basement? I used to long for the redwoods in Northern California. Only those are impossibly far away.

Except ...

An idea comes. I'm surprised I didn't think of it sooner. I make a beeline for the private wing, slip past the bustling command center, and enter the room Ronie set up for the dream simulator. I flip the lights. I've never worked it before, but I've seen Link and Ronie do it plenty of times. How hard can it be? I turn on the machine. The screen lights up with a bunch of scrolling numbers that make zero sense.

Muttering, I untangle the probes, trying to figure out which ones are which.

"What are you doing?"

I spin around.

Link leans against the doorframe.

"I want to be outside, and since I can't, I'm doing the next best thing." I unwind two of the probes and plug one of them in.

"Here." Link nudges me aside, unplugs the probe, takes the other from my hand, and hooks it to the machine. He attaches the end to my temple. I lie down on the cold floor while he sets everything up.

When I open my eyes, I'm standing in the middle of a forest much like the one outside my home in Thornsdale.

Towering trees surround me. Sunlight dapples through the branches, casting flecks of gold along the mossy ground. I inhale the rich, woodsy air deep into my lungs and begin walking—faster and faster. But it doesn't matter. My thoughts follow me.

She will be our victory. Or she will be our downfall.

I can't escape it. Not even here, in this world I can control. I lift my arms. Several trees rise up from the ground and grow into the sky like Jack's beanstalk. I wave my arms left and the earth crumbles away, creating a sharp cliff that drops into the sea. I point my hands at the sky and the darkness inside of me gathers overhead, obscuring the sun, swirling like ominous storm clouds. The wind stirs and strengthens, whirling in a circle until it roars like a freight train and bends large trees like they're nothing more than saplings.

"Well, this is interesting!"

I turn sharply.

Link stands a few yards away, shielding his face against the wind and debris.

I drop my arms to my sides. The world goes still and silent. I sink onto the wet, mossy ground and wrap my arms around my shins, wishing I could go to sleep—a dream within a dream. Maybe then I could escape whatever lies ahead.

Link sits beside me. He plucks a clover from the ground and twirls it between his thumb and pointer finger. "You know, you could construct a fourth leaf on this bad boy and have yourself some good luck."

"That would be cheating."

Link flicks the clover into the air. "Luka came by looking for you, saw you laying on the floor. He was worried you went to go do something crazy. I set him straight."

"Thanks."

"He told me about the whole transurgence thing."

I hug my shins tighter. "You two are confiding in each other now?"

"Oh, you know us. We're best buddies." Link gives me a playful nudge with his shoulder. "He's under the impression that I have some influence over you. That you might actually listen to me if I offered up my two cents. And here I thought Williams knew you well."

I try smiling, but the gesture falls flat.

"C'mon, Xena. Talk to me."

"About what?"

"About the crazy storm I just walked into."

I set my chin on my knee. "I'm afraid."

"Of losing Luka?"

"Of becoming my grandmother."

He shakes his head. "That's not going to happen."

"You sound so sure." The same blood that ran through her veins runs through mine. Does the same darkness, too?

"Your grandmother was looking out for herself. You're looking out for someone you love. That's not the same thing." Link makes me sound a whole lot less selfish than I feel.

"All right. I'm going to give you my two pennies' worth. Feel free to take it or leave it." His shoulders lift and fall with a big breath. "I know you love Luka, and nobody can touch that. But don't forget the scene you pictured in your head, the one that represents happiness. He's not the only one there."

"I know." My throat goes hot and tight. That's why none of this is easy.

Link takes my hand. "Here's the deal, Xena. For three days, we all thought you were gone. And for three days, everyone was lost. The world stopped making sense. This planet's a lot better with you in it. So for the betterment of the world, can you please try your hardest to stick around?"

I stare at Link's hand holding mine, a slow burn rising in my cheeks. "You're not … You aren't … in love with me, are you? Claire thinks you are, but I think Claire's an idiot, so—"

"Maybe."

I look up, the fire in my cheeks spreading down my neck. "Maybe she's an idiot?"

He shakes his head.

I bite my lip, unsure what to say. In my most honest parts, I know Luka's right. Link's more than just a friend. We *do* have this thing. With him sitting next to me, it's impossible to deny. There's chemistry. And attraction. I'm attracted to Link. Of course I am. He's good-looking and funny and about a hundred other amazing qualities. If Luka wasn't in the picture, I'm positive I'd have a massive crush. I'd probably doodle his name on my notebooks, write about him in my journal, daydream about kissing him. My attention wanders to his lips and the heat in my face grows hotter. It's a silly thing to imagine, because Luka *is* in the picture.

"Don't worry. I'm not waiting for you to reciprocate. What you have with Williams? It's not something I can compete with." His tone is light. The tightness around his eyes, however, tells a different story.

I hate that I'm hurting him.

"Would you please stop looking at me like that?"

"Like what?"

"Like I'm a puppy you just kicked. It's a crush. To be honest, you're kind of hard not to have a crush on."

I laugh. Because no, I'm not.

"What? You have this whole fierce-adorable combination going on. It's a little bit irresistible." He gives me another shoulder nudge. "I promise I'll get over it, all right? Now will you do me a favor?"

"Anything."

"Don't disregard what I said because of my feelings for you."

"Okay."

"Okay." With a nod, he sets his hands behind him. "A little sound would be nice."

I lift my attention to the trees and just like that, a chorus of birdsong bursts through the silence. The birds fly in impressive circles around us, an impromptu choreographed air show.

Link leans back against his arms. "All we need is some popcorn."

A bowl appears in my lap. I hand it to him with a smile, rest my head against his shoulder, and enjoy the show.

CHAPTER FIFTY

WE MEET AGAIN

M y plan? Grab Luka last. Maybe my linking abilities will fail like they did when we tried rescuing Gabe and he'll have to stay behind. I definitely feel distraught enough.

I grab Felix, Lexi, Connal, Link, Clive, and then Cap, who gives me this look, like he knows exactly what I'm doing. It doesn't matter. My hope is a no-go. Instead of feeling squished and exhausted, I feel strong, like I could grab ten more and keep going. Even my own gifting refuses to cooperate with my selfish desires.

With no more excuses at my disposal, I close my eyes and think of Luka. I feel the connection before he shows up. It's this hot, pulsing thing, so strong it will not be severed. The eight of us hold hands—Link to my left, Luka on my right. Before we went to sleep, we created a separate board for Cormack in the investigation room and wrote down everything we could find. Widowed at the young age of thirty-two, long before she ran for office. No kids. An older sister with three. An avid golfer who's no good at golf—a running joke in the media. A senator for the state of Maryland for twelve years before she considered running for presidency.

I run the random facts through my mind now. The ground beneath my feet gives way. My stomach drops. And when I open my eyes, the eight of us stand on the edge of a wood, covered beneath Clive's cloak, the sky overhead a dull gray.

This is it. We're really here.

Link squeezes my shoulder. "I'm off."

I give him a hug and hold on tight.

"Remember what I said," he whispers. Then he lets go and slinks off into the shadows, in the direction of a faint tugging behind my bellybutton.

There's a lush, green fairway in front of us. Up ahead, the sound of laughter. A party of four gathers on the tee box, Cormack among them. In real life, the president of the United States would be surrounded by bodyguards. Not here. She's golfing on an empty course with what appears to be three friends. But they aren't really friends at all. They're projections. The hijacker's eyes and ears. If any of them see us or suspect our presence, things will get dangerous fast.

I watch as Cormack takes a few practice swings, then drives the ball straight and far, right down the middle of the fairway. Her fake friends break into applause.

"We have to figure out how to get her alone," I mutter.

But how?

We wait through two more agonizing holes before my suspicions are confirmed. Not one of her balls strays from her target. And she's not aiming for the woods. Each shot lands in the center of the fairway, far away from us. The gentleman she rides with in the cart never leaves her side either. We're going to have to take a risk.

On the third tee off, on a hole where the fairway is slightly obscured by a hill, Lexi sprints toward Cormack's ball under Clive's expanding cloak. She grabs it and sprints back.

When she hands the ball to me, my insides stretch. It's a familiar feeling, one that happens anytime I link someone. Link must have found the doorway. He must be pulling people through and since I'm linked to him, I can feel it. My breathing grows shallow. This is really happening. There's no turning back.

Cormack and her projection buddies crest the hill on two golf carts. We duck further into the woods, listening as they search for the ball. My insides stretch again. Link's getting more people through. He's doing it fast.

A twig snaps not too far away.

"Just when I thought I got rid of that slice," Cormack calls, her voice drawing nearer.

"I don't think you were that far off, dear," someone calls back.

"Let me just look in the brush over here."

Cap moves left, circling around her. And then, when she's close enough, he creeps up behind Cormack and clamps his hand tightly around her mouth.

Her nostrils flare. She tries to scream, but Cap traps the noise in his palm and drags her deeper into the woods, out of earshot. Her attention zips from me to Luka to Lexi to Connal, her eyes growing wider. She can't recognize us from the Most Wanted list, not when she hasn't been living in the real world. Unless, of course, the hijacker transferred that bit of information into her dream in case any of us decided to show up. Judging by the look of sheer terror on her face, that's exactly what the hijacker did. And here we are. Four of us.

Cormack's chest heaves. Her legs flail.

"Please." I hold up my hands and step closer. "We're not the dangerous ones. The people you're golfing with are. We're not going to hurt you. We're here to protect you."

The gray sky darkens.

My heart thuds faster. We don't have much time, and this conversation is about to get really bizarre. "This, right now, is a dream. You've been locked up in here for months while the country you're supposed to be leading falls to pieces."

Cormack's flailing loses its edge.

"I want you to think really hard. When's the last time you went to work? You're the president of the United States, but I'm willing to bet you've been spending your days improving your golf game. Which is strangely flawless, don't you think?"

She goes still, a subtle crease forming between her eyebrows.

I hold up her ball. "We had to grab this off the middle of the fairway." My attention shifts upward, toward the sky, which continues to darken, as if the dream is alive. As if the dream *knows*. "When's the last time you saw the sun? Or windows without bars? Think about it. Why would a clubhouse on a course this nice need bars on the windows?"

"Sweetie?" The voice belongs to the same man who called to her earlier. "Did you find your ball?"

At the sound of his voice, Cormack begins flailing again. Cap tightens his grip over her mouth and around her waist.

I glance in the direction of the golf course. "Is that your husband?"

She nods wildly.

"Your husband is dead. He died of an aggressive form of testicular cancer sixteen years ago. It's not possible for him to be golfing with you right now."

The faintest pulse of clarity flickers in her eyes.

"We're here to help you. We can't do that unless you let us."

"Sweetheart?" Her fake husband's voice draws nearer.

"Where did you wander off to?"

The wind stirs, rustling the tree branches.

Cormack has gone very, very still. Slowly, Cap removes his hand. She stares at me, her chest rising and falling quickly. "If my husband is dead, then who is that?"

"Nobody you can trust."

There's another shout from the man. "Abigail, answer me now, please!"

We try retreating further into the woods, but the brush grows taller, denser. Forming an impenetrable barrier of snarls and thorns.

"What's happening?" Cormack asks.

"It knows we're here." I set my hands on her shoulders and squeeze until she looks me directly in the eye. "We don't have much time. Listen carefully. Your body has been hijacked. You're being held prisoner inside a dream." I give her a rattle, like Link did when he awakened my grandmother and Clive from their drug-induced stupors.

Surprisingly, she doesn't object.

"We are here to set you free. Your country needs you more than ever." I give her another rattle. "When you wake up, trust nobody but Adam. He's one of your bodyguards and he's on our side."

The clouds press lower. The wind strengthens, making the trees groan and sway.

All three golfers call the president's name now.

"Adam will get you to safety. He will explain everything." I shake her again, gathering her attention. "Trust nobody but Adam. Do you understand?"

"I-I think so."

It's not good enough. I rattle her as hard as I can, the wind whipping our hair about our faces. It howls so loudly, I have to yell. "Only Adam!"

"Only Adam," she repeats.

The ground begins to vibrate. Luka grabs my hand. I grab Cormack's. The thickening trees push us out into the open, but Clive's cloak holds steady. Dark mist swirls with the clouds, forming a funnel that stretches toward the ground. The hijacker is trying to kick us out.

Luka grabs the trunk of a tree, his arm locked around my waist. With superhuman strength, he pulls me closer so I can grab on, too. I hold on for everything I'm worth. If I let go, I'll wake up in my bed, Cormack will remain here, and our chance will be lost. If we don't do this now, the *king* will be so heavily guarded there will be no hope of another rescue.

Clive grapples to hold onto a nearby tree, but it rips up by the roots and hurtles toward us. Clive and his cloak disappear. He vanishes into thin air. Cormack screams. Luka throws a shield that deflects the tree like it's nothing bigger than a twig. He curls his hand into a fist and pounds the grass. A blast of light ripples through the ground and shoots up into the tornado, blowing it apart in an explosion of darkness and light.

The wind stops.

The dream goes still.

Cap, Lexi, Connal, Felix, Luka, and I stand out in the open, exposed. Cormack stands with us, her eyes round with shock. My muscles coil, preparing for attack. At any moment, the hijacker will appear. I'm sure of it. My heart pounds out the seconds. It thuds in my ears like a gigantic, amplified countdown—ten, nine, eight, seven, six ...

Felix turns, surveying the course. Lexi stands up a little straighter. Connal's attention darts back and forth.

My heart reaches *two* and a light appears. It grows out of nothing, taking shape until it's as beautiful and stunning as I remember. It's the being that sang to me after I destroyed Scarface. The same one that stroked my hair and lulled me to rest. It smiles at me approvingly. Proudly. "Well done. Your work is finished."

What?

I look around, my body filling with hope. Is it really? Am I done fighting?

"You have won. Victory is yours."

Lexi looks as transfixed as I am, but Luka's hand tightens around mine. "Tess."

The being grows brighter, bigger. More magnificent. So beautiful I ache to touch. I want to step closer, but Luka won't let me.

"Tess," he says again. His voice is far away, even though he stands right beside me. "We have to go. We have to move."

I close my eyes. I don't want to listen. I don't want his words to be true. I want this war to be over. I want this angel to be right. I'm so tired. And afraid. But something tugs at my bellybutton. The doorway.

That's right. We have to destroy the hijacker and pass through the doorway.

As if sensing my thoughts, the ground turns into a thick mucus that swallows my feet. Panic coils as tightly as my muscles. The same panic I felt when I met with Scarface. The same panic I felt when Clive's cloak wrapped around my legs. I let the sensation build in my hands until it's impossible to hold and then I throw it out. A shield that sets captives free. A shield that chases the darkness away. Only this time, it chases away the beautiful angel in front of me.

The mucus binding my feet lets go.

I grab Cormack's shoulders. "Remember what we said! Trust nobody but Adam!"

The sky begins to crumble.

I take off running, yelling for the others to follow. The ground quakes violently, pitching us up and down. It splinters open and swallows Felix whole. I sprint faster, urging everyone on toward Link, who stands at the doorway with Felicia and Bass. The dream is about to collapse. The doorway will shut. I scream for everyone to *go, go go*! *Get through*! I throw one final shield. It rips open what's left of the dark sky and just before it all shatters into light, I grab Luka's hand and we dive.

CHAPTER FIFTY-ONE

THE PROPHECY FULFILLED

The air crackles and pops, emitting heat like a furnace. Flames crawl up the drapes, inhaling the room's oxygen, exhaling plumes of thick, black smoke that eddy and churn toward the ceiling, obscuring visibility.

Cormack screams in bed.

A door crashes open. Two secret service agents run inside, coughing and sputtering, covering their noses and mouths with the crooks of their elbows as the flames grow, feeding off the fresh bout of oxygen.

"Adam!" Cormack shrieks. "Where's Adam?"

The taller one makes his way toward Cormack's bed. "I'm here!"

There's a glint of metal as the agent in the doorway pulls his gun. Adam doesn't see. He's too busy getting to the president, who shouts his name, paralyzed in her bed. The agent lifts the weapon and aims it at Cormack.

No.

She will not be killed. Not now, when we're so close. If any mission has to succeed, it's this one. I run and dive at the man with the gun, my emotions so heightened I barely have to expend effort to focus them.

We tumble to the ground.

The gun fires.

Adam spins around, sees the secret service agent sprawled on the ground, and without hesitating, he shoots. The crack of the gun makes my heart seize. Cormack screams louder. I scramble off the ground. The man's glossy eyes stare at nothing. There's a bullet wound in the center of his forehead, a wedding ring on his finger, and the mark on his neck. He was hijacked. Innocent. And now he's dead.

Adam scoops Cormack into his arms and carries her toward the door. Luka and I run ahead of them, ready to clear a path and fight away the enemy, except there's nothing but black smoke and fire. It curls up the walls as Adam hurries toward the exit, his face twisted with determination as he steps over bodies. All of them secret service agents. All of them dead or grievously injured. All of them with the same mark on their necks. Adam keeps going. He doesn't see us. He can't see us. But we are there, prepared to fight.

A chandelier crashes to the ground, throwing glass shards everywhere. Adam hugs Cormack tighter to his chest. A flaming beam slams to the floor behind me, but in front of Adam. He dodges it and hurries through the foyer, out into the night, away from the inferno that has become the president's home in Camp David.

All of us pour onto the grounds, away from the popping and hissing and crackling. Luka stands beside me. Link, Cap, Connal, Lexi, Glenda, Sticks, Non, Claire, Rosie, Ellen are here. Others, too. Link pulled at least fifty through. Smoke billows into the star-spotted sky. Sirens sound in the distance.

Cormack collapses on all fours, her body wracked with coughs, her nightgown covered in soot. She's out, but she's not safe. Not yet. An army of white-eyed men form a wall up ahead, blocking Cormack's escape. And in front of them all—

the angel of light from the dream we just left. From the dream I had after destroying Scarface. It's impossibly large and bright and beautiful.

Felicia bursts through the door, pulling Bass out with her. She skids to a stop on my left, her expression as fierce as Adam's.

It happens so fast, I don't have time to react.

The angel throws out one of its gargantuan arms. A ball of black flame hurtles toward me. Luka throws a shield. The black flame ricochets off the side and hits Felicia square in the chest. She makes a sound like she's been sucker-punched in the gut and clutches the spot. Tentacles of black slowly spread down her arms, up her neck. Her blackening face freezes in wide-eyed shock and she crumples in the grass.

I watch in horror, my mouth completely dry, waiting for her to disappear like Clive and Felix so she can wake up in her bed and comfort Henry. But she doesn't disappear. The attack didn't happen in Cormack's dream. We already crossed through the doorway. Her unmoving form remains in the grass, as still as death.

The angel laughs a spine-tingling, mirthless laugh that sucks every drop of heat from the air. The creature grows, morphing into a sinister something I've seen before—the horned beast I doodled on my folder back when I lived in Jude. Its mesmerizing beauty is replaced by a vile ugliness unlike anything I've ever seen.

"Do you think you can beat *me*, Teresa Eckhart?" The beast holds up its hands and spins another ball of black flame between them. "Don't be a fool. Forfeit now, and I'll spare the ones you love before they end up as dead as your father. As dead as your mother. As dead as your brother."

No. It can't be true. They can't be dead. This monster is lying. It's a liar like Scarface. "My mom and Pete are alive."

It lets loose another bone-chilling laugh and twirls the flame faster. "For how much longer? I'll give you to the count of three to decide. One ... two ..."

My ears pop. The air seems to shrink, pressing in around my skull.

"Three." The beast throws the ball of fire. Only it doesn't zoom at me; it zooms at Link. I watch in horrific slow motion as his warm, amber eyes widen like Felicia's.

A scream tears up my throat.

Light hurtles toward the black, but it doesn't come from me. It comes from Luka, who's protecting me. Always. Forever. By saving Link. His shield collides with the black fire right before it hits its mark and explodes, blasting Link off his feet, onto the ground where he lies beside Felicia.

The beast commands its troops to charge.

I let out a savage cry and with fire raging in my heart, I sprint headlong into battle, Luka right beside me, the others following behind. We collide in a mass of chaos. I twist and turn and spin—throwing knees and elbows, feet and fists— taking out ten, fifteen, twenty at a time, determined to get to the beast. To kill it like I killed Scarface.

I race ahead of Luka, who throws his shield again and again—so powerful, it blasts the white-eyed men apart. Even so, there are too many. We are impossibly outnumbered. They keep coming at me, closing in until I'm completely swarmed. I want them to bind me so I can throw my shield. So I can chase this darkness away. But they don't. It's like they know what I'm capable of and how to avoid it.

Luka sprints toward me, but they come at him, too. No

matter how many shields he throws, he can't get to me. We're losing. It's hopeless. All around, our side is brought down and bound—Jose, Rosie, Ellen, Bass, Sticks, Non, Claire, Connal—who thrashes in a desperate attempt to escape—and Lexi, who's doing everything she can to get to him.

The beast stirs up more fire and lightning and a fierce wind. Adam and Cormack lay flat on the ground, his body covering hers from flying debris.

"Tess!" Luka's eyes find mine, and this look crosses his face. It's the same look Gabe wore before he died, when it was Luka we were fighting for.

Don't, I want to scream. *Don't give me your life!*

The enemy brings Lexi down.

Cap, too.

Luka lifts his arms.

"No!" The word scrapes its way out, ragged and raw.

But it's too late. A blinding flash of light illuminates everything and hurtles toward me.

Some people say a person's life flashes before their eyes moments before death. I don't know if I'm going to die, but snippets come. A reel of images that play in fast forward. It's not just my life. And it's not just things that have already happened. It's a mixture of the past and the future. Felicia, dead in the grass. Henry, growing up without a mother. My father, murdered in a lonely prison cell just when he finally believed. Luka on my first day of school. Link and me, watching the birds and eating popcorn. My mother's tight, trembling embrace when she found out Pete was going to live. Luka, carrying me out of the Edward Brooks Facility. Leela sitting on my bed, painting her toenails. Clive, saying he wants to give his children a world worth living in. Entire refugee communities, wiped out. Mass graves. Innocent lives. Gabe dead. Jillian murdered. The gun between my hands. My grandmother crumpling to the ground. And Luka's life, hurtling toward me.

I brace myself. I don't have to accept it. It's my choice. This is what I know. I can save Luka. I can keep him alive. He doesn't have to die. I don't have to lose him.

Fear only has power when you let it make your choices.

This I know, too. My grandmother's blood might run through my veins, but that doesn't mean I have to make her choices. With Luka's eyes fastened on mine—filled with confidence and victory and all the love that's left in the world—I open my arms wide and with a strength that doesn't belong to me, I accept his sacrifice.

I absorb it.

I take it in.

Luka's life fills everything. Every atom. Every corner, every crevice of my soul, even the dark parts. It's a thousand times more intense than Gabe's. So hot and powerful I have to throw it out immediately. I heave it from my hands and it rushes forth in a sonic boom, consuming all traces of evil in its path, and it doesn't stop. It keeps coming.

My heart shatters into a million pieces as I fight. For my mom and my brother and Leela and Link and Cap. For my father and Jillian and Felicia and Gabe and Dr. Roth and all the innocent people who've been murdered in secret. I fight for the dead and I fight for the living. I fight for Luka. I will be everything he believes me to be. Brave and strong, a warrior who chooses light over dark, good over evil, no matter the cost. Even when it's impossible. Even when what waits on the other side might kill me.

I heave out what's left of his transurgence. It chases down the horned beast and splits it wide open. A shaft of light rises up out of its chest, into the clouds, stopping the wind. Stopping the lightning. There's an atrocious, ear-splitting sound—like the screams of a million people writhing in agony. The beast shatters into jagged pieces, like my heart. They fly apart and fade away. And then it ends and all the darkness is gone.

Flashing lights and sirens surround the property.

Adam lifts President Cormack to her feet and rushes her to safety.

I take several staggering steps toward Luka and drop to my knees by his still form.

We won.

Victory is ours.

And my Keeper is dead.

CHAPTER FIFTY-TWO

TO DIE IS TO LIVE

Firefighters pour out of firetrucks and start dousing the flames with large hoses, unaware that a battle just ended. Unaware that people are scattered about the grounds, shell-shocked over the sudden end. At first, everyone stands in a confused daze, looking around for something else to happen. When nothing does, they fall into relieved celebration. Lexi scrambles to her feet and throws herself into Connal's arms. Sticks kisses his wife. Declan and Jose thump each other on the back. Ellen rubs the top of Rosie's head, then draws her into a hug. Two women I don't recognize approach Felicia's lifeless form.

I stay where I am, on my knees. Unable to move. Unable to breathe.

Cap bends over Luka on one knee with his head bowed, like one honoring a fallen soldier.

A tear tumbles down my cheek, carving a wet path through the grime and the grit. I scratch the inside of my wrist. It's numb. I can't feel it. But this isn't a dream. This is all very real. Luka Williams—the boy who changed my life forever—is gone. There will be no rescue mission. No last-ditch effort to get him back. His life is over. He gave it all away.

Mori est Vivire.

To die is to live.

But he's not living. Not anymore.

A hole rips open inside my chest. I cup my hand over my mouth, trapping the sob inside. Link kneels beside me. He's alive. He's okay. Because Luka saved him. Luka saved us all. Link wraps his arm around my shoulders. I turn my head and cry myself ragged into his chest. His grip tightens as if he can hold me together. But it's too late. I've already broken apart.

He's dead. Luka's dead. He's never going to wake up. Or graduate from high school or go to college. He'll never tease Rosie or get to know my mother. He'll never surf again, or teach me how. I won't feel his warm hand holding mine. No more crooked smile. No more kisses that set my skin on fire. No more hand against my stomach, lips next to my ear—giving me my breath when anxiety has its way.

People gather around us, their whispered questions—*What happened? How did we win?*—fall into a hushed reverence, punctuated by the shouting of firefighters. It's not until the first rays of sunlight crest the horizon that people begin to disappear. They will wake up in their beds in the decimated city of Newport, Rhode Island. They will toast to victory. They will probably toast to Luka.

Cap squeezes my shoulder. "We should go."

I shake my head, because I can't. I can't leave this place, not when I can still feel Luka's life. It's like a phantom limb, one I cling to for all I'm worth.

"Come on," he says.

"No." I don't want to rejoin my body. Not now. Maybe not ever. I'm pretty sure my body can't handle this amount of pain.

Cap releases a long sigh, gives my shoulder another squeeze, then disappears. It's only Link now. He stays with me while the firefighters snuff out the last of the flames. He sits with me in the grass and holds my hand while I stare numbly at Luka's still form. He wanted a lifetime of moments and memories together, but we won't get them. All I can do is run the ones we did have over and over in my mind while the hole in my chest widens. Leaving a chasm where my heart should be.

Link shifts beside me.

I blink several times and sit up straighter.

Luka fades away.

I reach out to grab him. It's too soon. I need more time. But he dissolves into nothing, and so, too, does the phantom limb. He takes all traces of his life with him. I'm left with nothing to stare at but the grass.

"Come on, Xena," Link says.

I'll never be ready, but there's nothing for me here. All that remains is a charred house and smoky haze. Luka is no more. Nothing I can do will bring him back. There's no reason to stay on this battlefield. Not when the war is over.

CHAPTER FIFTY-THREE

CLOSURE

A rtificial light squeezes through the crack beneath my door. So does the sound of excited conversation. People out in the hallway—speculating, hoping, celebrating. That this is it. That the war is over. Joanna's bed is unmade and empty. The fluorescent green numbers on the clock read 6:26.

My stomach rolls. A lump of pain expands in the back of my throat. All the world's gravity parks on top of my chest. My heart, however, remains numb. Or maybe it's gone. Maybe I'll live the rest of my life without one.

The door opens, letting in a flood of brightness. Cap wheels inside wearing a pair of sweats over his emaciated legs. It's how I feel. Emaciated. Mind, body, and soul. He flips on the light switch. "Come with me."

I curl onto my side and stare at the wall. I did what I was supposed to do. I played my part. I'm done now. I have nothing left. I don't have to go anywhere. I want to sleep. Escape to a dream like the people who are hijacked, only I will go voluntarily. I will construct a world where Luka is alive and I'll stay forever.

Cap wheels closer. "You're gonna want to see this."

I'm positive there's nothing I want to see, but I also don't have any energy to argue. So I force myself to sit up, every muscle in my body sore and stiff. Slowly, I stick my arms inside a zip-up hoodie by my bed and shuffle after Cap, each step an exhausting effort, like I'm trying to push through Jell-O instead of air.

The hallway is all movement and chatter.

"It's breaking news on every station," Cap says. "They're calling it an internal terrorist attack."

I stare at the back of his head as I shuffle behind him. Does he really think I care?

"Felix, Ronie, and Link are working on getting word from Adam. We want to make sure Cormack is safe."

He stops in front of room fourteen.

The pain in the back of my throat throbs. This is what Cap wants me to see? It feels cruel. Uncaring. Cap is neither. I shake my head and walk away, faster than when I came. If I see Luka, the pain in my throat will turn into pain in my heart and I need that to stay numb.

"You should go inside."

I stop, tears welling in my eyes. "You think that'll make me feel better? Give me some sort of closure or something?" I swipe at my cheek—nausea morphing into anger. Red hot anger. I whirl around. "I don't want to see him—"

My heart stops.

My breathing, too.

Luka.

He's standing beside Cap. He—he's standing. He—he's alive.

"I told you to stay in bed," Cap mutters.

"I told you she wouldn't come in if I did." Luka looks at me. His green eyes are actually looking at me.

I can't move. I'm afraid to move. I'm positive if I do, what I'm seeing will go away. So I stand there, my knees shaking like twin earthquakes, terrified to hope, the numb wall surrounding my heart fissuring apart. I'm already dreaming. Constructing. I never woke up. Because this can't be possible. Luka transurged. I felt his life more powerfully than I felt Gabe's. And I threw it out as surely as I threw Gabe's. With trembling fingers, I touch the inside of my wrist. It's not numb.

It's not numb.

He cocks his head, his mouth turning up in that crooked grin. The one I never thought I'd see again. "Do you really not want to see me?"

I release a shallow breath. I take one step. Then two and three. Until I'm running, flinging myself into his arms. I bury my face in the crook of his neck and it's there—unmistakably there. A pulse that throbs against my cheek. Our hearts crash in unison—one crazy, hopeful heartbeat.

"As soon as I woke up," Cap says, "I went to check on him. Scared me half to death when he opened his eyes."

"How?"

"I don't know." Luka's voice rumbles in his chest, his breath warm against my ear. "I did it. I didn't see any other way. I transurged, but my life never left me. I felt it the whole time. I felt *you* the whole time. It was like we were tethered by an invisible wire. It was like we were—"

"Linked."

We turn and look at Cap.

"You asked me once if a Keeper has ever survived transurgence and my answer was no. Every instance of transurgence has resulted in the Keeper's death. But every instance of transurgence has always been between a Keeper and Fighter."

My eyes widen. "I'm a Linker, too."

"And you were linked to Luka. When he transurged, his

life flowed through the link to you, but it never fully left him."

"But what about Gabe?" Luka asks.

"Tess wasn't linked to Gabe. Link was."

Cap's right. I was too distraught at the time. Link brought Gabe over. Not me. A hot tear tumbles down my cheek. Followed by another. And another.

Luka cups my face in his hands and wipes the wetness away with the pads of his thumbs. "I'm alive, Tess."

He's alive.

He's alive!

My chest collapses, releasing a sound that is half-laugh, half-cry. Luka pulls me in for a kiss. One that has me curling my fingers into his messy hair. And Cap—the man against any sort of purpling—chuckles softly and wheels away.

CHAPTER FIFTY-FOUR

BEYOND EXPLANATION

The next several days are busy ones. A frenzy of corroborating information and tying up lose ends. Basically ensuring that our victory remains a victory. The news runs 24-7. Not just down in Headquarters, but everywhere. It's hard to tear ourselves away, so much is being announced and recapped and updated.

Currently, all of us are gathered in the common room to watch a much-anticipated interview between Loraine Masters—the most well-known broadcast journalist in America—and President Abigail Cormack, live from the Oval Office. It's the first time the nation will see her after all the craziness that ensued on the second of June. But it's not the first time I've seen her.

Over the past three days, I've visited her twice. Debriefing. Questioning. Verifying. Turns out, her last clear memory before being freed went all the way back to her senator days, which means she was hijacked for a long, long time. Understandably, she's shaken. Full-out paranoid, actually, which is a good thing. It'll keep her vigilant. On guard. Combine that with Felix working his connections and getting her four new personal bodyguards (two Shields and two Fighters) and we're feeling pretty confident that the leader of our country will remain safe and secure.

Luka and I sit on one of the couches, holding hands as Cormack explains what happened. We've barely let go since our reunion in the hallway. I'm not sure we ever will. I still can't stop scratching my wrist. We're alive. We're together. And thanks to Cormack, we're free. Turns out, we aren't deranged or dangerous. This was another bit of breaking news—one more piece of an elaborate ruse organized by a group of unnamed terrorists. Link, Connal, Lexi, Sticks, and Non have been acquitted, too.

"Our government was infiltrated on every level," Cormack says.

This is how the truth is being spun. Substitute evil for terrorists, and it's all pretty accurate. Except for the Surgeon General's innocence. The public believes these terrorists assassinated him once he realized the virus was a hoax.

"So there was never a virus?" Masters asks.

Cormack shakes her head. "They breeched our country's most secure networks and plugged in false information, which was spread via media channels, who then, of course, reported what we thought was fact."

A modern day Orson Welles' *War of the Worlds*. On steroids.

"Why do you think they did it?" Loraine asks. "What were they trying to accomplish?"

"Exactly what their name implies. To stir up as much fear and chaos as possible."

"For what purpose, though?"

"To distract us. We believe they've been planning a takeover for a long time. It was systematic and widespread, and tragically, they took a lot of lives."

Cormack and Masters go on to discuss the disturbing information coming out of the woodwork—massive inaccuracies surrounding pregnancy screenings, the gross mistreatment of patients in mental rehabilitation facilities, the disturbing conditions in refugee communities—and the measures being taken to ensure these wrongs are made right, that such colossal injustices never happen again.

"Our country has a lot of healing to do," Cormack says.

She's right. All of us do.

I glance at Henry, playing chess with Connal on the floor. Connal shows him how to move the horse. He and Lexi have taken the kid under their wing until he can be reunited with his father and sister, both of whom are alive and on their way to Newport. I'm not sure I'll ever be able to erase the sound of Henry sobbing into the phone as his dad spoke words of comfort into his ear. I'm not sure I'll ever be able to erase the look on Link's face when he phoned Jillian's mother to tell her where her daughter had been laid to rest.

"There's a question everyone keeps asking. I'd be remiss not to ask it tonight." Loraine crosses her slim leg over the other and folds her hands over her knee. "How did you survive? How were you able to escape? Every secret service agent at your home in Camp David was in on the terrorist plot except for one." Adam, who's being lauded a hero. And rightfully so. Our mission would have failed without his fast thinking and exceptional aim. "It doesn't seem possible."

"It wasn't. Logically speaking, I should be dead."

"So how do you explain it, then?"

"I can't." Cormack takes a deep breath and tucks her hair behind her ear. There's no trace of the mark anywhere on her neck. "If I've realized anything over the past few days, it's this. Some things are simply beyond the realm of explanation."

CHAPTER FIFTY-FIVE

GOODBYE

E veryone is packing up. Saying their goodbyes. There's no reason to stay. We're no longer in danger. As more and more people leave—returning to what's left of their former lives—Headquarters grows increasingly quiet.

It's odd, watching the rooms empty. It reminds me of the summer camp I went to in junior high (another one of Mom's attempts to find me some friends). The final day, all the girls were crying and hugging and promising to keep in touch while I stood off to the side, brimming with relief that it was finally time to go home. Only now, as Luka and I eat our last meal in the mess hall with Link, Rosie, and Declan, there are two goodbyes I'm dreading.

Declan folds up his empty carton of milk. "When are you two leaving?"

"One-thirty." I glance at the large clock on the wall, nerves swimming around inside my stomach like hyperactive tadpoles. In two hours, Luka and I will go above ground. We'll cross that freaky bridge. We'll board a plane. And we'll fly home—to Thornsdale, where I will see my mom and Pete and Leela.

Link glances at me across the table.

I take a sudden interest in swirling a glob of ketchup around my plate with a French fry. If it's a goodbye he's looking for, I'm not ready. We still have two hours.

"What about you, Link?" Rosie asks over a mouthful of food. "Have you decided where you're gonna go yet?"

"I'm thinking Denver."

I look up from my ketchup-swirling. Last I heard, he was still undecided. I invited him to California, but he laughed it off like I was joking. I wasn't, but I don't blame him. If I were in love with a boy who was in love with another girl, I sure wouldn't follow him and that girl across the country to start a new life. Link is so much more than a third wheel. Still, though, the selfish part of me wishes he would've said yes. I guess there's still bits of my grandmother in me after all.

Rosie holds what's left of her sandwich beneath her chin. "What's in Denver?"

"Mountains. And a lead on a pretty cool job opportunity for a hacker like myself."

"And a really hot girl named Ronie," Declan adds with a smirk.

"*Oooo.* Link and Ronie sitting in a tree ..."

Link throws a French fry at Rosie while I battle a bout of jealousy. It's a stupid reaction, one I need to ditch pronto. I can't have them both—Luka *and* Link. And even if I could, Link deserves to be someone's first choice. That's what he is with Ronie. She's crazy about him. I should be ecstatic that he's going with her to Denver.

"What about you small fry?" Link asks. "Where are you off to?"

Her face brightens. "I'm going back to Detroit."

Detroit? I can't imagine anyone wanting to go back there. It's cold, for one. And a hot mess, for two. "Why?"

"Cap and his wife are gonna take in me and Bass." She practically bounces in her seat when she says it. "Cap says his wife's a really good cook. And I finally get to go to school. A *real* one."

My heart lifts. It's funny what war can do—tearing families apart, then putting them together again, often in the most unlikely of ways. "That sounds amazing."

"Don't give her the wrong impression. It's not going to be all sunshine and roses." The gruff voice belongs to Cap, who's rolled up behind me. His weathered face and stoic expression fool nobody. Underneath that rough exterior is a man who cares deeply. I can't think of a better father for Rosie and Bass than him. He nods at me. "Can I have a word?"

I scratch my wrist. This is one of the goodbyes I've been dreading, but there's no more avoiding it now. With a hard lump in my throat, I slide my tray to Rosie and follow Cap out of the mess hall.

"If you're not careful, Rosie might eat you out of a house," I say, stuffing my hands into my pockets as we reach the hallway.

Cap chuckles, then pivots his chair around, his demeanor turning serious. "I wanted to tell you something before you left."

I scuff my shoe against the floor, waiting for him to say what he's going to say. You'd think I'd know better. This is Cap. He won't speak a word until I've given him some eye contact. When I look, his silver eyes are fierce. And if I'm not mistaken, a little dewy.

"You're a remarkable soldier, kid."

I blink several times, but this stinging in my eye is a stubborn thing.

"You fought the good fight, all the way 'til the end. Even when it was impossible. You made me proud. And there's nobody else I'd rather have on my side."

I look down at my shoes.

"Even if you do drive me crazy half the time."

I laugh. And sniff.

"You know you'll always have family in Detroit."

I bob my head, mostly to keep my emotion in check, and then I bend over and give him a hug. I think it surprises us both. "Thank you," I whisper into his ear, his whiskers scratching against my cheek. "For everything."

Cap pats my back a couple times, wishes me safe travels, and one of my two goodbyes is over. On my way to the barracks, I spot Claire standing in front of the general store, a small duffel bag strapped around her shoulder as she hugs Ashley and Danielle. She was there in the end. So was Clive. They risked their lives to fight.

She catches my eye over Danielle's shoulder and pauses.

I lift my hand—a simple, resigned wave. A peace offering. One she returns. While I will never ever be her fan or her friend, I suppose Cap is right. Maybe one horrible choice doesn't have to define us forever. Maybe it's the choice we make next that matters more.

When I reach my room, Joanna is inside zipping one of her bags shut.

I stare at my bed. Everybody's been stripping their rooms, putting sheets and comforters and towels and other random things into a makeshift supply room. I pull the fitted sheet off my mattress and begin folding it into a tidy square. It's a trick my mother taught me—how to neatly fold a fitted sheet. Something I could write on the front of my file. A useful skill. One I hope to be using a lot more than my others. "What do you think will happen to this place?"

Joanna wipes at her red-rimmed eyes and shrugs. Of all the people sad about going, she's been a particular mess. Head-quarters has been her home for over two years. Whereas I have nothing to pack, she has three suitcases' worth. Whereas I have only one more goodbye I'm dreading, she's already had to say several.

"I really am excited to see my brother again." It's like she's trying to convince herself more than me. "I'll get to meet my niece for the first time."

"That'll be great."

She nods a little too fast, then leaves the room, muttering something about forgetting a shirt on Cassie's bed.

I set the sheet on the bare mattress, smoothing my hand over the edge when a knock sounds on the door. It's Link. But I'm not ready. Just the sight of him makes my throat all hot and itchy.

"So ..." He snaps his fingers and claps his palm over his fist. "Are you ready to talk to me?"

"I'm always ready to talk to you."

"You're a lousy liar."

I guess some things never change.

He steps inside the room. "You've been avoiding me like the plague. The question is, why? Did I do something wrong?"

I shake my head, tears building in my eyes. They've been coming all too quickly these days. "I don't want to say goodbye."

"*Goodbye?* You're planning on getting rid of me that easily, huh?"

"I'll be in California. You'll be in Denver."

"You act like Denver's on Mars."

After living down the hall from him over the past several

months, it sure feels that way.

"The two aren't that far away, you know. There's also this invention called a phone. Not to mention," he dips his chin and wags his eyebrows, "a little thing called dream hopping."

This makes me smile. And completely lifts my spirit. Right. I forgot about that.

"And I believe you have a birthday coming up. You think after all that visualizing, I'm gonna leave you high and dry?"

I go to him by the door and wrap my arms around his neck. "I don't know what I would have done without you these past few months." It doesn't seem possible that it's all the longer we've known each other. I feel like Link's been a part of my life forever. I guess that's the way it is with some people. Two souls primed for friendship. One that isn't forged by time, but this mysterious, immediate connection. You meet them and you just … fit. "I wish I could give you something more than a lame, slobbery hug."

"Are you kidding? Xena, you gave me my happy ending. You're here, on planet Earth. All is right with the world."

He's too good. Too generous. And while seeing him with Ronie still produces that ridiculous twinge of jealousy, I hope the two fall madly in love and get married and have little computer whiz kids and all the happiness the world has to offer. Because that's what Link deserves. The whole stinking package.

I rest my head against his chest, relishing the sound of his strong heartbeat against my ear, and for one terrifying second, I see it all over again. The black flame that killed Felicia hurtling toward Link. Deflected at the very last second. "You have no idea how happy I am that you're here on planet Earth, too."

"It was a close call, wasn't it?"

I shudder. "Way too close."

"I owe Williams one. I guess there are worse guys to be indebted to."

The two will never be friends, but over the past few days, there seems to be a growing respect between them. "I love you, you know."

"Oh, don't worry. I know." I can hear the grin in his voice. His lips brush the crown of my head. "I'll see you when you're legal. I'm really looking forward to that cake."

CHAPTER FIFTY-SIX

REMINDERS

"We're right by carousel six!" Leela talks in exclamation points.

I called her as soon as Luka and I arrived at our gate. She made me promise I would.

"We just got to baggage claim," I say, holding the phone with clammy hands. My jaw chatters, only I'm not cold. No matter how many times I tell myself it's just my mom and Pete and Leela, my body doesn't listen. The entire thing is ramped up on nerves and adrenaline.

I'm so eager to see them, I barely pay attention to the double takes Luka and I keep getting from travelers and airport security. We may have been acquitted, but that doesn't erase the fact that our faces were plastered on the world news every night for the past two months.

"Do you see us yet?"

I lean right to see past a heavyset man in a Hawaiian shirt, then left as we walk by carousel four. "Not yet. Do you see us?"

"Oh my gosh! It's you! I see you! Tess, I can't believe I see you!"

I swivel around until finally, I see her too. My best friend—Leela McNeil—hops on her tiptoes, clutching a phone to her ear with one hand and waving like a crazy person with the other. Pete stands beside her—taller and ganglier than I remember. And next to him stands my mother.

A hot ball of emotion inflates inside my chest.

I never thought I'd see her again. Now, here she is, her hands clasped beneath her chin as she searches the crowd with frantic eyes. Leela points and as soon as Mom sees me, she cups her hand over her mouth. We stare at each other across the span of distance. For a moment. For an eternity. Then she breaks into a run, pushing past weary travelers until she has me wrapped up so tight, so strong, I swear I can feel both of their arms—hers and my dad's.

She peels me away and takes my face between her hands just long enough to look at me—to rove me over with her mother's eye—then crushes me against her again. After several shared breaths, she finally lets go and hugs Luka. "I asked you to keep her safe and you did. You kept my baby safe."

His eyes lock with mine over my mother's shoulder. "She's not so bad at taking care of herself."

I shake my head. We both know the truth. I wouldn't have survived without him. But he wouldn't have survived without me. The truth is, we kept each other safe.

Leela has apparently given me and my mom as much of a moment as she can. With a squeal, she runs over and squeezes my neck, smelling like sugar cookies and everything else that's good and comforting and familiar. I squeeze her back. And then my brother, Pete. Mom folds all of us in one giant hug—this new family of mine.

It's not the same one that I left. We are forever altered. I guess that's what time does. It changes things. Sometimes subtly, sometimes profoundly. After everything, I'm finally home. But that doesn't mean I get to go back. Life doesn't work that way. The only route is forward. And so we travel it, taking the things we've learned and the people we've lost along with us.

Mom lets go and shuffles a bit to the side. A man and woman stand behind her, not nearly as put together as I've seen them in the past. It's Luka's parents—his father, as impressive as ever, his mother, somehow diminished. I have no idea how they're here. Luka never called them, despite my promptings. He turns eighteen next week. According to him, he doesn't need parents. I look at my mom who looks back at me, her hands fidgeting in that way they do whenever she's uncertain about something.

Luka's mother approaches him hesitantly. She touches his cheek, then wraps him in a hug. Luka doesn't hug her like he hugged my mom, but he does place his hand on the small of her back. When her shoulders quit shaking, she wipes her eyes and surprisingly, turns to me. "I'm very sorry. For everything."

"It's okay. I understand." Everything his parents did was to protect Luka. I get it way more than they probably realize. Fear makes people do crazy things. The proof is wrapped around my ankle. I'm not sure I'll ever take the strap off. Some reminders need to remain indefinitely.

Mom slides her arm around my waist as Luka's mother hugs him again. His father—who's in no hurry to offer up apologies—rubs her back stiffly. And yet, I know they'll be okay. We all will. The pain and the loss and the hurt is real. I don't think it ever really goes away in this lifetime. But maybe it's not meant to. Maybe the pain's another reminder. Not as visible as the one on my ankle, but there just the same. To hold onto all the pieces of good and light in our lives as tightly as we can.

CHAPTER FIFTY-SEVEN

BIRTHDAY WISHES

Eighteen candles flicker on the cake, illuminating a portion of our kitchen. A pocket of warmth expands inside the room. One that has nothing to do with the people or the cake in front of me. The feeling doesn't originate inside of me at all. It radiates from beyond the border of the light's reach, pulsing in the dark. Something shimmers beside our refrigerator and for the briefest of moments—before that beautiful shimmering thing disappears—I feel terrified and brave all at once.

I blink and it's gone. The only thing hovering near our refrigerator is empty air. The temperature returns to normal. Pete smiles and shakes dark hair from even darker eyes—one of many guests at my crowded birthday party. Mom clasps her hands beneath her chin and nods encouragingly. "Go on, Tess. Make a wish."

It's amazing how much can change with one extra candle on a cake. I look around at my ragtag group of guests, six of whom used to be on America's Most Wanted list. Connal and Lexi. Sticks and Non. Link and Ronie. Luka and his parents. Cap and Dot, along with Rosie and Bass. Cressida Rivard. And my best friend, Leela, who stands between Pete and her kid sister, Kiara. They've come from all over—Detroit, New Orleans, Denver, Dublin (Connal decided to move back and Lexi went with him), and Augusta.

The room is full, and yet empty, too. I wish Jillian were here. She and Leela would have hit it off. And I miss my dad every single day. But I've learned a few things this past year. One of which is this: just because I can't see something doesn't mean it's not there. And besides, I get a glimpse of my father every single time I look into Pete's eyes.

"What'll it be, Xena?" Link asks.

"Better make it a good one," Luka adds, his words tickling my ear.

I stare at the candles, unsure. What does one wish for after the year I've had, with the weight of the world no longer wrapped around my shoulders? With the people I love mostly safe? I rub my chin and suddenly, I know. Tomorrow, Luka's taking me out in the ocean. He's going to teach me how to surf. So I fill my lungs with oxygen and wish for something silly. Something ordinary. Something normal.

Please don't let me make a fool out of myself.

I blow toward the candles as hard as I can. The room goes dark.

Acknowledgments

It's interesting how a story comes to be.

This project was never something I intended to publish. It was something I started for myself because I needed to find the fun in writing again. I had no idea how exponentially I would find it. This series stoked my creativity in a way like nothing else has. Tess, Luka, and Link made me fall in love with my first love all over again and for that, they will always hold a special place in my heart.

It's hard to believe that the final installment is done. It's hard to believe this project has come to a close. The magical thing about books, though? They're never truly over. As long as readers keep reading them and sharing them, Tess's story doesn't end. And that, my friends, is pretty awesome.

Immense gratitude and special thanks go out to these people ...

My brother. Dude, those emails. We must have sent a hundred back and forth. Talk about synergy. You were every bit as passionate as I was about this project. So many of the ideas began with you. I love the way your mind works. I love that I get to call you my big bro. I love how convinced you are that these are going to become movies (ha ha ha). But seriously, if on the insane, *miniscule* possibility Tess ever sees the big screen, you can have your percentage. You more than earned it.

Amy Haddock. The guru of young adult lit. I'll never forget sitting at that Mexican restaurant, telling you about this crazy (very off-genre) idea I had. I'll also never forget your fun response. Our brainstorming session spurred me onward and influenced the entire series. Thank you a million times over for your input, your cyc, your encouragement, and your friendship. I think you're pretty fabulous.

Melissa Gilroy. Girl. You know. You know how much you mean to me. You know how amazingly helpful you've been throughout these books. I love that you get just as giddy over Tess and Luka as I do. I love how willing (and eager) you were to help me work through several of the plot points. But most of all, I just love you. I seriously couldn't ask for a better friend.

My husband. The guy who enables me to write with his unending support. The guy who read each of these books before anybody else. The guy who doesn't mind his wife peeking over his shoulder, constantly asking, "What part are you on?" Your belief in me means the world.

My family, for the gift of time. Thank you for all the hours you take my kids so I can sit at the computer and do what I love to do. With a special shout out to my dad, who read these books as soon as I finished writing them and kept telling me to hurry up and get the next one finished so he could read it already. I love you more.

My early readers, who offered that much-needed feedback—Janice Boekhoff, Jessica Patch, Erin DeVore, Stephanie Vass, and Carrie Pendergrass. Y'all rock.

A special thanks to Lauren and Nicole Gardner for being my first legit young adult readers. Your enthusiastic response gave me the confidence I needed to move forward. And of course, to your amazing mom—literary agent extraordinaire— Rachelle Gardner. Thanks for being in my corner!

Lora Doncea, for your talented editing eye. I'm so thankful providence led me your way when I was in need of a good copy editor.

Sarah Hansen with Okay Creations, for your artistic talent. I mean, really. The covers you created for each one of these stories is absolutely perfect.

Paul Salvette with BB eBooks, for your crazy quick formatting skills and your unending patience with my sporadic emails. Rest assured, should anybody need formatting, I'm sending them your way!

Heather Sunseri, my Obi Wan. Seriously friend, I hope you know how grateful I am.

Every reader who has shared Tess's story, written a review, or sent me an encouraging message. You all bring gigantic smiles to my face.

And last but never ever least—my Lord and Savior, Jesus Christ. You created me with the incessant need to tell stories. To write words. Any measure of talent is all from you.

About the Author

K.E. Ganshert was born and raised in the exciting state of Iowa, where she currently resides with her family. She likes to write things and consume large quantities of coffee and chocolate while she writes all the things. She's won some awards. For the writing, not the consuming. Although the latter would be fun. You can learn more about K.E. Ganshert and these things she writes at her website at www. katieganshert.com. You can also follow her on Twitter, where she goes by @KatieGanshert.

Want to stay up to date on new releases, book deals, and *The Gifting Series*? Visit K.E. Ganshert's website (www.katie ganshert.com) and subscribe to her mailing list.

CPSIA information can be obtained
at www.ICGtesting.com
Printed in the USA
LVOW08s1740160217
524502LV00004B/847/P